# The Seven O'Clock Club

# The Seven O'Clock Club

## AMELIA IRELAND

Black&White

First published in the UK in 2025 by Black & White Publishing
An imprint of Bonnier Books UK
5th Floor, HYLO, 103–105 Bunhill Row,
London, EC1Y 8LZ
Owned by Bonnier Books, Sveavägen 56, Stockholm, Sweden

Hardback: 978-1-78530-705-8
Trade Paperback: 978-1-78530-704-1
eBook: 978-1-78530-703-4
Audiobook: 978-1-78530-701-0

All rights reserved. No part of this publication may be reproduced, stored in a retrieval system, or transmitted in any form or by any means, without the prior permission in writing of the publisher, nor be otherwise circulated in any form of binding or cover other than that in which it is published and without a similar condition including this condition being imposed on the subsequent purchaser.

A CIP catalogue record for this book is available from the British Library.

Cover design by Bonnier Books Art Dept
Typeset by IDSUK (Data Connection) Ltd
Printed and bound in Great Britain by Clays Ltd, Elcograf S.p.A

1 3 5 7 9 10 8 6 4 2

Text copyright © Amelia Ireland, 2025

The right of Amelia Ireland to be identified as the author of this work has been asserted in accordance with the Copyright, Designs and Patents Act 1988.

Every reasonable effort has been made to trace copyright-holders of material reproduced in this book. If any have been inadvertently overlooked, the publisher would be glad to hear from them.

www.bonnierbooks.co.uk

*Dedicated to my mum and dad – my star in the sky and my rock here on earth. I have you both to thank for everything and I love you very much.*

"There is no such thing as an orderly journey when it comes to navigating the grief process and, as more studies are undertaken on the subject, opinion has become divided as to the precise number of stages that the journey encompasses. Recent theories have evolved away from the traditional five stages, towards seven and perhaps more."

(Metcalfe, 2024)

# PROLOGUE
# SHOCK

# Witness transcript: Genevieve Dempsey

There comes a time in every person's life when you have to take a gamble. Sometimes that gamble pays off. Sometimes it doesn't. But having never been much of a risk-taker myself, agreeing to what I did that day was, without a doubt, the hardest thing I have ever done.

I still have nightmares about what happened. For weeks afterwards, I thought I'd lost everything. My job, my credibility, the respect I'd built up with you. I know, I know, we aren't supposed to focus on *feelings* in these investigations, but you can't ignore how you feel when a decision you make results in those kinds of consequences.

Why did I say yes? I'm sure you asked me that at the very start. I did it because I cared. Maybe you find that unacceptable, coming from someone who is supposed to remain impartial. But over the course of those few weeks, Victoria, Mischa, Freya, Callum – they'd become more than just patients. Or subjects. Or whatever it is we're supposed to call them nowadays. They'd become my friends. Worthy of my respect and my admiration. And worthy of putting my job on the line for. Even though it didn't work out the way any of us wanted it to.

Yes, I do miss them actually. Very much. Oh, stop it! I can see the look on your face. But they were my first trial subjects. I like to think they were unique. With the other groups I've had since, I've been fine, haven't I? I've kept a professional distance. You know I have. I like to think I never make the same mistake twice.

Yes, I was pleased with how the experiment went overall. To start to see the process implemented with new groups already is great. And to be Project Leader – I can't tell you how much that means to me. And I just wanted to say, *on the record*, that I'm really grateful for your support, Dr Metcalfe. I know we haven't always seen eye to eye. But given what happened, I have to say I was surprised you didn't try to scrap the whole thing. Or at least take me off Phase Two. I'll always be grateful for what you wrote in that report. I don't think I'd be here now if you hadn't.

Oh, did she? That's nice. I agree, Victoria is a formidable woman.

Is that everything then? I feel I've been answering your questions for months. It's good to finally draw a line under it all.

Do I wish I could see them again? Of course. But it's enough that I know where they are. And more important than that, that none of them need me anymore.

# PART ONE
# DENIAL

# Chapter 1

# Freya

It's a funny thing, time. It only really matters when you have a life to lead. I checked my phone: 7 p.m. on Tuesday 6 September. A time and date of zero importance aside from the fact it was the first time in six months I had managed to leave the house.

Given it was such a momentous occasion, the room in which I now found myself couldn't have been less inviting. Everything about it, from the nondescript ivory walls to the mismatched chairs we were perched on, exuded an obvious, albeit unintentional, sense of neglect. No, neglect was too strong a word. Rather a lack of attention by someone who had more important things to worry about than interior design. How anyone lived day to day in a space like this was beyond me.

The woman who had let me in and whose flat it was – Genevieve – smiled at me. The other two avoided all eye contact.

I observed them both as subtly as I could. The one sitting across from me, who Genevieve had introduced as Victoria, looked like she had stepped out of *Hello!* magazine. Perfect nails, enormous engagement ring. Stupidly shiny hair. Roughly two decades older than me, but with way better skin. The other woman – Mischa, I think Genevieve said she was called – was far less intimidating, and couldn't have been older than nineteen. A girl, really. The human equivalent of a baby mouse – small, innocent and fully aware that, at any moment, there was every chance she might get swallowed. There was something about that I found oddly reassuring: she looked how I felt.

I gave her my best attempt at a smile, something that Genevieve appeared to take as a signal to begin.

'Thank you all very much for coming. We're still waiting for one more, but we should probably make a start. Would anyone like a drink before we kick off?'

We all looked at each other, then shook our heads. It seemed I wasn't the only one who wanted this to be over with as quickly as possible.

'No? Okay then.'

Genevieve pulled her dress delicately over her knees, smoothing out the creases in the olive-green chiffon with the tips of her fingers before moving both hands upwards to tuck a shock of curly auburn hair behind her ears. She seemed young for a psychologist. Mid-twenties maybe? Pretty, but in a nerdy kind of way.

I felt for her then. It couldn't have been easy, bringing together a bunch of people with nothing more than a brief email and an even shorter telephone conversation to go on. But then again, it was her choice, wasn't it? To bring us here, I mean.

I hoped to God she knew what she was doing. The last thing I needed was to end up in an even worse mental state than I was already in.

*I want you to open yourself up to something a bit different.* Those were the precise words she'd said to me on the phone a week ago.

*It's based on a theory I've been working on. A different approach to group therapy.*

*Ha ha, don't worry, it's nothing illegal!*

Oh God. Why the hell had I said yes? How had she convinced me to come? Now I was here, in her flat, I couldn't think of anywhere I less wanted to be. At some point she was going to ask me to open up about what had happened. In front of other people. Even the idea of it made me feel physically sick.

I tried to think about something else, but it was too late; my ears had already blocked up. Oh please, no, not here. I felt the panic as it started to build, a small ball of it swelling inside my stomach like a fast-growing tumour. The room began to swim and ice-cold sweat pooled and soaked into my jumper, sticking to me like an unwelcome second skin. My eyelids felt sticky – I squeezed them shut in a desperate attempt to clear my vision. I was going to pass out. I gripped the arms of the chair and willed myself back into the moment, taking several long, deep breaths as quietly as I could, just as the doctor had told me to do. I concentrated on the sound of my heart as it hurled itself against my ribcage like a convict desperate to escape. Please, brain, don't do this to me now. Calm down, Freya, calm down. Just. Calm. Down.

And then it all went black.

# Chapter 2

# Mischa

OMG. I knew she was a goner as soon as I looked at her. Her face went all grey and then she started breathing weirdly, like she didn't have enough air.

I was ready to catch her the second she tipped out of her chair. Managed to skid forwards onto the floor and get hold of her by the shoulders, just before she face-planted into the – gross – brown carpet.

'Oh my, is she okay?' said a voice behind me.

I looked down at the woman's head on my lap. Freya. Same name as a girl in my old class. She was totally out of it.

'I'm not sure. I think she's fainted.'

Did those words really come out my mouth? What a stupid thing to say. It was *so* obvious she'd fainted. I moved a bit of blonde hair away from her eyes and touched her forehead, wiping off the sweat with my thumb before drying it on my skirt. Poor thing, she must have been panicking like anything to go like that.

The head on my lap made a noise.

'Let me get her a sugary drink,' said the same voice as before, which I realised had to belong to Genevieve. 'I have a bottle of Coca-Cola somewhere. That might help.'

I realised the other woman – Elizabeth? Victoria? – hadn't said a word. She was staring at the two of us on the floor, looking like she wanted to disappear. She reminded me of the people on trains who pretend they aren't there when a homeless person gets on and starts asking for money. I watched as she reached down towards her handbag, then seemed to change her mind. Instead, she leant back in her chair and crossed her legs. She looked rich. Posh. I could tell because her bag was made from real leather and had a proper gold chain.

'I think I'm going to be sick.'

Uh-oh. I stopped staring at the bag and looked around the room in a panic.

'Can you grab me that?' I shouted, gesturing towards a wastepaper basket under the desk. That got the posh woman moving. She uncrossed her legs, jumped out of her chair and ran past me to get it.

From somewhere behind me I heard a loud smack.

'Bugger.'

I turned around. The woman was standing bin in hand, rubbing her shoulder. A whole load of paper and pens lay in a mess around her feet. She stared at the pile helplessly. Completely frozen to the spot.

'Can you give me the bin please,' I said. Loudly. Like she was a bit special. But it snapped her out of it and she did as she was told before immediately bending down to pick everything up off the floor.

I turned my attention back to Freya, who was now on all fours, her head hanging over the bin. As I scraped as much of her hair as I could into a ponytail in case she really was going to be sick, it occurred to me that it had been a while since I'd had any kind of contact with another human being.

Just as I thought I was going to be stuck there all evening holding the hair of someone I had never met before, I felt her body start to relax. A few seconds later her breathing returned to normal. I let out a big sigh of relief. The bin was metal and full of holes; if she'd been sick, it would've gone everywhere.

'Thank you. I feel much better now.'

'Here, take this.' Genevieve was back. She handed Freya a glass bottle of Coke and the two of us helped her into her chair.

'I'm really sorry. It's been ages since I've passed out like that.'
'Please don't worry,' Genevieve said. 'It's absolutely fine.'
'Yes, I know, but it's still embarrassing.'

She laughed then, looking over at me for the first time. Her face was pale but she definitely had more colour than before.

'Victoria, would you like to come and sit back down?'

*Victoria. That was it. I knew it was the name of a queen.*

Victoria was leaning against the desk, arms crossed, staring past us through the open window. I realised she'd sorted the untidy mountain of papers into four perfect piles. She looked a bit taken aback by Genevieve's question, as if she'd forgotten the reason she was there, but did as she was told.

'Freya, are you sure you're okay for us to begin? There's a toilet down the corridor if you need it.'

'No, it's okay. I'm fine now. Really.'

I saw Genevieve open her mouth to say something else, but then a buzzer of some kind went off loudly behind us, making me jump. *What was that?*

Victoria sighed. Freya seemed completely oblivious.

Genevieve looked at us, clearly pleased. 'Oh good. Our final volunteer has arrived!'

And with that, she got up and hurried out of the room. *Poof!* Her floaty dress made a breeze as she ran past, knocking a few sheets of paper off the desk again.

*Don't laugh, Mischa.*

Victoria pressed her lips together, just like my old teacher Mrs Crossley used to do when she was angry, but she didn't try to pick the papers up. Instead, we all sat, bums in seats, none of us saying anything. I felt shy all of a sudden and, even though the room was warm, I shivered, like someone had opened a door to the outside.

I could hear sounds coming from down the corridor. Slowly getting louder. Two voices, definitely, but I had no idea what they were saying. As they got closer, I realised the one who wasn't Genevieve was a guy. Oh *God*.

He appeared first, walking into the lounge like he'd been there a million times before. I knew he was good-looking before I even saw his face properly. Some people just gave off that vibe.

'Alright, ladies? Apologies for being late.'

I forced myself to smile at him and nearly passed out like Freya. And who would've blamed me? I mean, how often is it you're sat waiting for a counselling session to begin and the most famous singer in the country walks in and sits down opposite you?

# Chapter 3

# Callum

Right, where the actual fuck was I? When I got the message from Skye saying she wanted me to see a cousin of some workmate who she thought might be able to *sort me out*, my first thought was great, I'll go chat about my inner-fucking-child for an hour, get given a journal and then leg it home. But I figured she'd be sending me to a swanky Shoreditch warehouse with free jellybeans and the world's most expensive mineral water, not some shitty tower block in the arse-end of nowhere. I made a mental note to call her when I got home, although I already knew full well I wouldn't; I didn't call anyone anymore.

And hang on. Who the hell were these other people?! If there was one thing I'd gotten used to in my career, it was exclusivity. If I had the clout to get the cast of a reality TV show chucked out of a VIP area, you'd have thought I wouldn't have to share intimate details about my private life with a bunch of fucking randoms. I thought about getting up and leaving, but then I remembered I was on very, very thin ice with my management at the moment and I should probably do the full hour. Besides, I had nowhere else to be. And I wouldn't be going anywhere for a while either, not until my shitshow of a label decided I was allowed out in public again.

I pulled myself out of my head to look at the other people in the room properly. Hmm. Hot, but a bit too old. Definitely could be hot if she ate a few more Krispy Kremes. Too hippy to be hot. No way man, too young – even I had limits. I smiled at them all anyway. You never knew.

Fuck me, I was shattered. Last night had been heavy. I hadn't left the apartment. Hadn't seen anyone. (Hadn't seen anyone for a while, come to that. Couldn't face it.) But that hadn't stopped me from seeing away most of a bottle of tequila. I had that haze. That thing you get when you feel like you've got a thick fug of something shitty wedged in front of your eyeballs. I was used to it now, but that didn't mean I liked it.

I realised then that the hippy was talking, and I tried my best to focus. '. . . impact of grief, and the stages that we go through in order to come to terms with it. I've selected the four of you for quite different reasons, which we will go into later.'

The hippy took a breath and started chewing on the end of her pen. I could tell she was on edge, but I couldn't be arsed to feel bad for her. Instead, I exhaled loudly and looked at my watch. With any luck she'd get the hint and wind up early.

'Now, I want you to be honest with both me and each other in these sessions. It doesn't matter what you say, or whether you agree or disagree with my views, as long as you are completely truthful about your own feelings. And I would like you to commit to come to at least four sessions, once a week, at 7 p.m. Is that okay?'

For fuck's sake – four sessions?!

She stared at each of us in turn. I nodded for the hell of it, along with all the others, though the hot older bird didn't seem impressed. I doubted she'd last two weeks. Maybe even less than me. I got a feeling the skinny blonde had said yes without realising. She had that expression about her. Away with the fairies. Drug problem, maybe, although she didn't quite look shit enough for that. Only the third one showed any interest. She was wriggling around in her chair like a puppy on speed. And she kept looking at me. That wasn't surprising – I could see why I might have caused a bit of a stir – but it made me feel tense. I tried my hardest not to look at her. The last thing I needed was some love-struck teenager following me back to the apartment and setting up camp on my doorstep. I'd only been in the place a year and I really couldn't be fucked to move again. Even if I did hate it.

'Good. In that case, I think we should start by saying a little bit about ourselves. You don't need to say why you're here, not if you don't want to. Is that alright?'

None of us said anything. I fought the urge to shut my eyes.

'Right. Shall we start with you then, Victoria?'

Victoria – the hot but old one – looked at us. There was something about her air of constant irritation that was mildly erotic. She had that horny professor look.

'Fine,' she said. 'I'm Victoria, I'm a senior partner at a law firm and I work in the City. I'm 52 and I'm here because my husband made me come.' She laughed in a way that sounded forced. I should know – I could recognise a fake fucking laugh a mile off.

'In fact, I feel a bit of a fraud. Clearly other people are here because they feel they need to be. But I don't, you see. I'm not actually grieving.'

I looked up. The other two women did too, and our eyes met for a second. We were all thinking the same thing, I could tell.

Lucky fucking bitch.

# Chapter 4

# Victoria

I was going to have serious words with Andrew the second I got back to Hampstead. This was absolutely, positively awful. I was stuck in a ghastly room, in a dreary grey tower block that appeared to be the undesired love child of a slipshod 1970s Labour government and some lax planning laws, having to open up to four people, all of whom I was 99 per cent confident I would never see again after tonight.

I tried to recall how it had come to pass that I had even agreed to cross the threshold of this woefully ill-maintained building. It had all been Andrew's idea. Unsurprisingly.

'Darling, I've seen something.'

We'd been eating breakfast at the time, flicking through different supplements of *The Sunday Times*, as was our weekly custom.

'There's a psychologist here looking for volunteers.'

'Volunteers for what?'

'She's looking for four volunteers to talk about their experiences of bereavement.'

'Sounds like a riveting topic. What else does it say?'

'Not much. Just that she's exploring alternative ways of navigating the grief process. It says she wants to work with a small group of people who have recently lost someone and that she plans to put them together based on the information you give her. There's an email address if you're interested. And three questions to answer. All rather abstract, but quite intriguing, wouldn't you say?'

'Andrew, you know there's a very good reason why people shouldn't respond to things in the back pages of newspapers. I'll wager you twenty pounds it sits squarely between an advert for a clairvoyant called Crystal and a revolutionary weight-loss pill.'

'It doesn't, actually. It's next to a feature about breast implants.'

'Ha! There you go.'

But I'd agreed to email her – in truth because I'd refused to do absolutely everything else Andrew had suggested, and I felt slightly guilty about that. But I'd reasoned there would no doubt be an astronomical number of people out there flooding this woman's hopeful little inbox, craving the opportunity to unburden themselves. There was no way she'd pick me.

You can imagine my surprise when she phoned me up two days later.

'Hello, Victoria. My name is Genevieve. You responded to the ad that I placed in *The Times*.'

At which point, what could I do? I suppose I could have backed out, but that would have disappointed my husband. And, in a bizarre way, I found I had a kind of perverse pride in the fact that she'd chosen me over possibly countless others. A small part of me felt like a competition winner, only with a really crummy prize I couldn't donate to the golf club raffle.

Anyway, regardless of underlying motive, here I was. Feeling overwhelmingly grumpy, but also, as of about ten minutes ago, somewhat awkward. A foreign and unwelcome emotion, the sensation of which I was not enjoying one little bit. Because clearly the two other women were damaged. You could see it before they'd even opened their mouths to speak – they had the same look about them as my associates did after finishing all-nighters at work. People who, not that long ago, had been full of enthusiasm and life but had, with the passage of time, been slowly and utterly eroded, leaving behind what could only be described as a carcass of a human being. God, I pitied associates nowadays. But I pitied these women more.

As for the young man, who had seemingly appeared out of nowhere and looked unnervingly familiar – although for the life of me I couldn't work out why – he was concealing it better, but you could see something wasn't quite right with him either. I was pretty adept at reading people in the job I did. Especially men. Whose huge inflated egos I had to pander to almost every single day of the bloody week.

He was certainly proficient at putting on the appearance of not giving a toss. I took a long hard look at him, earning myself a lazy wink in return. He was handsome, without a doubt. Tanned. Muscly. Unusually vibrant green eyes that made me wonder briefly if they were contact lenses. That annoying hair men seem to have nowadays – the kind that flops in the eyes as if by happenstance, but which probably takes hours in front of a mirror to achieve.

He was sitting sprawled across one of Genevieve's chairs, legs akimbo. I took in his ripped jeans, white vest and leather jacket. Against the backdrop of the androgynous décor, he looked like he was doing a shoot for *Tatler*.

But brushing aesthetics aside, beneath that carefully crafted exterior, there were tell-tale signs of a haunted human being. His eyes were beautiful, but drained. He clearly hadn't slept properly in a very long time. And he had a strange compulsive habit of scratching at the side of his head. Others might put it down to nerves, but anyone with a modicum of intelligence could see this man was not the nervous type.

Sitting there, amongst all these troubled people, was not in the least bit gratifying. Rather, it was embarrassing. And the reason for this embarrassment? The fact I wasn't one of them. Something I had told Andrew time and time again. Not that he believed me. And neither it seemed, did Genevieve. For she simply nodded and looked at me sympathetically through the thick frames of her glasses, making me feel even more exasperated.

'I'll come back to you on that point, Victoria, if I may, but first I'd like to hear from the others. Freya, would you like to go next if you feel up to it?'

The sound of her name broke her out of her reverie. She looked like a tiny sparrow, wishing the ground would swallow her up. Not surprising really. I'd have felt the same if I'd passed out that dramatically in front of a group of people I'd never met. But at least she hadn't vomited everywhere. I'm not sure I could have coped with that.

'I don't know what to say really. I'm Freya. I live at home with my husband, Joe. I'm thirty-one and I used to work in interior design.'

'Thank you, Freya,' said Genevieve. 'How about you, Mischa?'

Mischa looked up from where she had been studiously biting a nail. It took every ounce of my willpower not to slap her hand away from her mouth, as my housemistress used to do. I examined my own nails instead.

'I'm Mischa. Like you said. I was working as a full-time carer for about three years, but now I do a bit of customer service stuff for an insurance company. Not very glam. Oh, and I'm twenty.'

'That's great, Mischa, thank you. And finally – Callum?'

Callum sat up and graced the room with a well-practised smile. 'Do I need an introduction?'

Genevieve gave him a look. 'I wouldn't assume everyone here knows who you are, Callum. It would be helpful if you could tell us a bit about yourself, like everybody else.'

Callum smiled again, but I sensed a slight slip in the mask. He paused, his forehead creasing into a multitude of tiny pleats as he did so. It looked remarkably like the lower half of my old school tunic.

'Sure. My name's Callum Raven. I'm a singer song-writer. I'm 29.'

Wonderful; perhaps that meant we could all leave.

Sadly, it seemed Genevieve had other ideas.

'Thank you, everyone. Now, since this is our first session and we're still getting to know one another, I don't want you to feel you have to launch straight in. Initially I'd simply like to try and get you talking. My hope is that as you start to feel more comfortable sharing things as a group, you'll want to open up a bit more. And that's when we can start to discuss your experiences and try to work through ways to help you move on. I'd like to think that over a period of time, you'll reach a state of understanding and acceptance. But that's further down the line. As I said, I don't think it's fair to ask any of you your reasons for being here just yet. Instead, we're going to do something else.'

My word, she was boring. It was like listening to the shipping forecast on Radio 4.

'First off, I'd like you each to spend a few minutes telling the group a happy memory about your childhood.'

And with that, my heart promptly sank through the floor.

# Chapter 5

# Freya

'Does it need to be about anything specific?' I asked.

'Not really,' Genevieve said. 'But from a psychological point of view, your childhood is very important when it comes to assessing how you deal with events as an adult.'

I'd been trying to work out how I could make my excuses and leave but Genevieve had offered me a tiny lifeline. At least this was something I knew I could talk about without falling to pieces.

What to say though? I laced my fingers together as I pondered, willing my brain to kick into gear. It had been a while since I'd had to think about anything other than getting through the day, and however hard I tried nothing sprang immediately to mind. Just as I thought I was going to have to admit defeat, completely unexpectedly a memory bubbled to the surface.

'Okay, I've got something. I suppose one of my happiest memories would be of a birthday party I had when I was at primary school.'

I waited a moment to check my heart rate was still normal. Yes, so far so good. I heard my voice before I realised it was me talking. 'There was one party in particular I remember – I was quite young – maybe seven. I'd invited my whole class over. At least twenty-five people. It was something you did in those days. I'm not sure if you still do. Maybe children are more selective now. Or it's too expensive. I wouldn't know.'

I was conscious that my voice sounded painfully reedy. When had I started to talk like that?

'Go on if you can, Freya.'

I nodded.

'It was an incredible party. My parents had organised an entertainer. A clown. With a disco light and a bubble machine. I remember thinking how amazing it looked. It was back in the days when you couldn't buy things like that off Amazon. He filled the whole room with rainbows and bubbles. It was like being in a fairy tale.'

'I used to feel like that about helium balloons,' said Mischa. She looked at me and blushed. 'Sorry, I didn't mean to butt in.'

'No, that's fine, Mischa,' said Genevieve. 'These sessions are supposed to be interactive.'

When Mischa didn't say anything else, I took that as my cue to carry on. I felt light and enthusiastic, temporarily caught up in the memory.

I could picture it still, even now. The enormous buffet lunch we'd had after the clown had left: a selection of cheese and ham sandwiches oozing butter on pillow-soft white bread, the crusts cut off at my express instruction, even though Dad used to say I should eat them because they would make my hair go curly. Tupperware pots full to the brim with Twiglets, Hula Hoops and Chipsticks standing guard in front of a makeshift melon hedgehog with squares of cheese and pineapple wedged indiscriminately onto cocktail sticks to act as spikes. A slightly sideways-leaning pink blancmange rabbit, nestled in green jelly made to look like grass. And the best bit by far – the birthday cake. Mum had taken one of my dolls and layered the sponge around her from the chest down, covering it with pale blue butter icing and hundreds and thousands to make it look like she was wearing a rainbow-coloured ball dress. I could still remember how good it tasted.

'. . . then, after lunch, because the sun was shining, I opened all my presents in the garden. Someone had given me a Barbie doll dressed like a bride. She was absolutely perfect. I remember thinking I wanted to be just like her when I grew up. And at the end of the party, I handed out party bags full of treats. It was such a fantastic day, I'll never forget it.'

I was slightly out of breath from the effort of talking. It was probably the most I'd spoken in months. And for a few precious seconds I felt almost euphoric. Until that is, with a sudden jolt in my chest, I came back to the present and the oppressive heat of the room. The energy disappeared as the adrenaline faded and I felt myself fall back into the grey fog of exhaustion I'd woken up to every day for the last six months.

To make things worse, I was also consumed by a sense of complete shame. Why had I told everyone that stupid story? Why did they care what I'd done for my seventh birthday party? And why did I have to think of something that childish?

'Do I need to say anything else?'

'It's up to you,' said Genevieve. 'It sounds like a lovely memory. Was your whole childhood happy, would you say?'

I thought about it for a second. 'Yes, it was, actually. My childhood was perfect.'

'May I ask why you think that?'

'I suppose because I had two parents who loved me, who thought I was their world. Who did everything they could to make me and my sister happy. They still do.'

'Thank you, Freya, that was great.' Genevieve smiled at me, then turned to the others. 'Right, who's up next?'

I didn't voice my final thought.

*I wish I'd never grown up.*

# Chapter 6

# Mischa

I wasn't sure I could come up with anything. I couldn't remember much about being little. Being little meant being looked after.

'What sort of thing should I say?' I felt like an idiot asking the question. But I didn't want to get it wrong.

Genevieve glanced up at me from the notebook she'd been writing in while Freya was talking. Her handwriting was tiny. Way too small for me to read. She caught me looking and closed it.

'If nothing comes to mind, why don't you start by telling us a little bit about your life growing up?'

I was about to say I couldn't think of anything interesting, but then I remembered what Mr Keith used to tell us sometimes in History. 'Start with the bare facts as your foundations. And build from there.'

What were my bare facts?

'My whole life it was just me and Mum. Nani, Nana and Auntie never left Kenya, which is where my mum was born. Nana emigrated from India to Nairobi after the Second World War to work as a doctor. I did a whole project on it in junior school because my mum was so proud of him. Then Mum left Kenya to come to England with my dad when she was eighteen – but he died when Mum was pregnant with me. I don't know anything about him. But I do have a photo of him and my mum on their wedding day. Mum thinks I look like him but I could never see it.'

I stopped. *Arghh*. What else?

'You don't have to talk about your father if you don't want to.'

The comment surprised me, until I realised Genevieve must have thought I'd stopped talking because I was upset about my dad.

'Oh, no. Talking about my dad doesn't bother me. You can't miss what you've never had, can you?'

I could hear my mum's voice in my head, spurring me on like she always did. *You're doing great, Mischa. Keeping going.*

Then I remembered something. 'Oh, we went to Nairobi once to see my grandparents and my auntie!

'It must have been the summer before I went to secondary school. Mum had taken me to meet my family for the first time. I remember it was stupidly hot. The airport was full of people. And Mum shouted at some luggage guy for trying to make us give him money for taking our things when we hadn't even asked him. But I saw lions at the national park. Nana took me. Which was cool. We hired an open-top jeep thingy with a driver and we had to get up crazy early. I remember being really tired, but Nana had brought all these yummy pastries in these little metal pots and a big Thermos of chai.'

'It sounds like you had a great day.'

'I did! And afterwards we went back to the house and Mum said she wanted to take me into town to buy me something nice to wear. We got in the car and we drove to this little shopping centre. Only the traffic was *really* bad. We kept getting cut up by all these cars and mopeds, and these little yellow buses full of people.

'God, poor Mum, I'd tried on so much stuff that day. None of the clothes had looked any good. Everything was too bright or too big. But as we'd gone to leave the last shop, I'd spotted this pair of dark red leather boots with a small heel. I knew Mum would say they were too old for me but I told her I thought they were nice. And she'd rolled her eyes and said that since I hadn't seen anything else, she didn't mind getting me those.

'Me and Mum went back to my grandparents' house and I put them on the second I got through the door. Nani couldn't stop laughing because I kept walking up and down the hall. I must have done it about fifty times. I kept them for years, those boots. I might even still have them. I'm not very good at throwing stuff away.'

My voice caught in my throat and I swallowed. 'Is that okay? I don't think I've got anything else to say.'

'No, that's great, Mischa,' Genevieve said. 'Good job.'

'Thanks.' I wasn't sure why, but I felt like I was going to cry. I blinked to stop it, but I wasn't quick enough. A single teardrop landed on my lap, making a dark spot on the material of my skirt. I quickly rubbed it, hoping no one else had seen.

'Here, Mischa, take this.'

I looked up to see Freya handing me something. 'Is that a handkerchief? Nani had those.'

'I know, a bit old fashioned, isn't it? I bought them at some vegan fair in an effort to save the environment. Don't worry, I don't need it back. You can keep it.'

'Thank you.'

It was the first time anyone had given me anything in such a long time. I bit the side of my cheek, then rubbed my eyes against the material. It smelt of perfume.

'Did you have anything else you wanted to say, Mischa?' Genevieve asked.

'No, I'm good. Can we please go to someone else?'

'Of course. Well done. Shall we move on to Callum?'

We all looked over at him. I could almost hear Summer's voice in my head: *OMG he's such a 10/10.*

Then Mum joined in. *Good-looking young man, isn't he?*

Callum scratched his head. Maybe trying to decide if he could be bothered to join in. I watched as he ran his tongue slowly over his teeth. I shivered.

'Uh . . .'

He looked like he was going to say something but then changed his mind and went quiet. Was he going to leave? I really didn't want him to. But it wasn't as if I could say anything to make him stay if he did.

Then all of a sudden, he started talking. Fast as anything. He had an accent of some kind but I couldn't work out where from. I was rubbish with stuff like that. But he definitely wasn't from London.

'Me and my older brother Finn used to get up to all sorts of shit as kids. We got in trouble literally all the fucking time.'

Then silence. He coughed, then leant forward, his chin resting on the balled-up fist of one hand. He stared at the floor.

*Is that all he's going to say?*

'Is there anything in particular you feel you can talk to us about?' Genevieve asked. She sounded more cautious talking to him than she had with me and Freya, like she'd found a lost dog and wasn't sure if it was going to bite her.

Callum blew into both cheeks, then let the air slowly out. We all waited. Then he sat back up.

'Yeah okay. There was this one day, during the summer holidays, I reckon I was about twelve, me and Finn were bored senseless and decided to have a water fight in the front garden. My dad had bought us two of those Super Soaker things and man, we fucking loved them. But after we'd pretty much drowned each other, we thought it'd be a laugh to hide in the bushes and shoot at cars as they drove past. We had these two massive old trees in our front garden and they grew right next to the pavement. Meant we could hide behind them and shoot straight through the branches at people and they had no idea we were even there.

'Anyway, we saw this one car coming towards us from way up the street and knew straight away it was the money shot. It was one of those convertibles everyone wanted at the time – a Z3 or something like that. Stood out like a sore thumb because you didn't see many of those up our way. The guy driving it was pretty old but clearly thought he was the tits in that car. I remember we pumped up our Super Soakers to full pressure and just went for it. Only thing was, the guy slammed on his brakes, got out his car and started legging it towards us. Me and Finn jumped out from the trees quick as anything. I don't think we've ever run that fucking fast. Luckily the dude was pretty unfit and he had to give up halfway up the street. Fuck knows what would've happened if he'd caught us. Probably given us a good kicking.'

'It sounds like you and your brother got on,' Genevieve said.

'We did yeah, but we used to fight. A lot. Not just arguments. Proper punch-ups. But we'd soon get over it. Probably just too similar, to be fair.'

'And the rest of your family?'

He looked uncomfortable. The words that came out next sounded like he'd practised them. 'We were close. My whole extended family – grandparents, aunties, uncles, cousins, we all lived in the same place and always had. My mum and dad were those boring types who met at school, fell in love and stayed in the town. Proper pair of lovebirds they were. Finn and I thought it was gross how they used to snog all the time.'

He seemed like he was about to say something else, but then went quiet. He looked down at his hands, rubbing the top of a silver ring on his little finger.

'I'm guessing that's enough for you, yeah?'

'Yes, Callum,' said Genevieve. 'Yes, that was perfect.'

I saw her make a quick note in her book. I wondered what she'd written.

'I think that just leaves you, Victoria?'

# Chapter 7

# Callum

What the fuck had just happened? There I was, getting ready to haul myself up, go home and lose my shit at Skye, when all of a sudden, I got this memory. And it was sharp as fucking day. And it made me think, why not come out with it? Make Jennifer happy.

It was a weird feeling, reliving something even that small. Like seeing a scene from a film of my life play out in front of my eyes. And part of me felt that if I stopped talking, it would disappear. And that would be that. Only problem was, I'd nearly said too much. I looked at my watch. Couldn't be more than fifteen minutes left. I could stick it out, no sweat.

It was then I realised a bit of an argument was playing out. Brilliant – with any luck I could be out of here quicker.

'I just fail to see what the point of any of this is.'

'Victoria, I am asking you to trust me on this, if that's possible.'

'No, Genevieve, that's not possible. I don't know you from Adam. Or anyone else for that matter. Yet here we all are, having a lovely little fireside chat, when for all I know you could be absolutely potty. I have seen zero written evidence of your professional credentials. I have no idea what your ultimate agenda is. And I am completely and utterly perplexed as to what my childhood has got to do with what happened to me six months ago.'

Now, based on what I'd seen of this Victoria bird, she was not going down without a fight. And Genevieve (not Jennifer – shit, hope I hadn't called her that) was a bit of a wet fucking fish. In fact, I would have put my life savings on the lawyer pulverising the psychologist.

'I need you to listen to me, Victoria. You are here because you, at some level of your subconscious, made the decision to come. You can claim as much as you like that your husband forced your hand, that you don't want to be here, that you don't want to share anything with the group, but I can tell you for a fact that nobody, *nobody*, would be in this room against their will. And you know that better than anyone. So yes, of course, you can choose to be difficult, make life harder for everyone and disrupt the sessions. But if you're going to do that, I would much prefer it if you got up off that chair right now and left. And if you do, I wish you all the best. Or you can agree to give it a go. I don't expect you to open up immediately, or say anything about the experience that brought you here, but I do expect you to try. Now, what would you like to do?'

And with that, we all turned to look at Victoria.

Game on.

Victoria fixed Genevieve with what can only be described as a ballbreaker of a glare. But when Genevieve didn't look away, something in her deflated and she gave a small shrug. 'Fine, I'll give it a go. But I'm doing this for my husband, not for you.'

'I understand, Victoria. Whenever you're ready.'

I was glad I hadn't put that fucking bet on.

# Chapter 8

# Victoria

It was a story I hadn't told in years. And as much as it pained me to say it, it was probably the only happy childhood memory I had. Not that these people needed to know that.

I spoke as quickly as I could, conscious of the need to get the story out as concisely as possible and bring an end to this debacle of an evening.

'My father was a Jaguar pilot and Wing Commander in the RAF. He was based at Coltishall in Norfolk, which meant he wasn't home very often. And even when he was, I rather got the impression he didn't want to be there. My mother sent me to boarding school at the age of three. I'm not entirely sure why. It's not as if she had any other children to look after. She claimed to be busy with her charities and social engagements, but I can't say I saw any evidence of that growing up. Or at any time after, come to think of it.

'I remember one day, at the start of the school summer holidays, I must have been about fourteen, I was sitting waiting for my mother to collect me. She was late, obviously, and everyone else had been picked up what felt like hours earlier. She'd clearly forgotten it was a half-day and as a result the garth was deserted. This was before the days of mobile phones, so I couldn't even call her to find out where the ruddy hell she was. I sat there, waiting, in front of my boarding house, hoping that the matron wouldn't see me and make me sit inside with her.'

As I started talking, a funny thing happened. I felt myself transported back to that day. Long-forgotten memories that had lurked for years at the back of my mind resurfaced, turning a story that I had thought foggy and forgotten into something colourful and vivid. I could picture myself exactly as I had been back then – small, skinny and dishearteningly flat-chested, finishing off the last of my meagre tuck box. Resigning myself to having been well and truly abandoned. (The fact this didn't seem to bother me, as I waited there polishing off a packet of custard creams, probably spoke volumes about my expectations when it came to anything involving my mother.)

But then out of the blue, a car came roaring round the semicircular drive towards me. And winding down the window, it was my father who poked out his head. 'Hello, pumpkin. Need a lift?'

To this day, I've never forgotten that image of him. Tall, tanned, handsome and utterly dashing, with his slicked-back hair and neat moustache. He was everything a daughter could possibly have wanted in a father. At that particular moment at least. My only regret at the time, I seem to recall, was that my school friends weren't there to witness it. It would have been my one and only opportunity to impress my peers. And a laughable contrast to my usual pick-ups: the sudden apparition of an inappropriately dressed mother; a faint waft of vodka masked by a cloud of heady Chanel N°5. It still brought me out in a cold sweat even thinking about it now.

That day couldn't have been more different. He'd cheerfully grabbed my huge array of cases, sports kit, books and cello and somehow managed to shove it all into the back of his tiny sports car. Then I'd climbed into the passenger seat beside him, and I'll never forget this – he'd said, 'Fancy taking a quick flight before we head home?'

'That's seriously fucking cool,' said Callum, interrupting my story.

I smiled at him. I couldn't help myself. 'Yes, I suppose it was. I remember I was unbelievably nervous. I spent the whole journey to Upavon worrying about what it would be like. But twenty minutes later, we were airborne. Just seeing my father in front of me flying – that in itself was inspiring. And looking out over the countryside at the world shrinking beneath us, it was magical.'

'How long were you in the air for?' Callum asked.

'Not long. About twenty-five minutes perhaps?' I looked at Genevieve, trying to convey to her in no uncertain terms that was as much as I was willing to say. 'So, there you go. That's my favourite childhood memory.'

'Thank you, Victoria. Thank you very much for trying.'

I nodded. I refrained from telling the group what had happened after we landed and drove home. How we'd found my mother totally inebriated. How she'd thrown a plate at my father, presumably for being late. How he'd abruptly turned around after dumping my luggage unceremoniously in the hallway and stormed out of the house. Gone to see his mistress, Mother had said. She always said that's where he was. I had no idea whether it was true or not, but he certainly had another home to go to because he didn't come back at all that summer.

'So, Victoria, is that okay with you?'

It was only then that I realised Genevieve had been talking to me. How long for exactly? Goodness knows. I should have asked her to repeat herself. But all those years alone with my mother had taught me the importance of thinking on my feet and never, ever, getting caught not paying attention. I took a punt. 'Yes, yes that's absolutely fine.'

'Brilliant, I'm pleased. I think it's really important that we are all fully committed to session number two. I look forward to seeing you all next week at the same time.'

Oh, bloody hell.

# Chapter 9

# Freya

The house was quiet when I let myself in – Joe must have gone to bed. I never saw him in the evenings now. He was either working all hours, out with clients, at the gym, or in bed. I knew that because every excuse he'd ever given was catalogued in his scruffy handwriting on a neat little stack of Post-it notes on the kitchen table. The weirdest thing about it, though, was that his absence didn't feel unnatural. Partly that was down to my intense desperation to be alone. I'd shut him and my family out months ago and refused to let them back in. But partly I knew Joe and I had started to drift apart romantically long before this happened. Something we might have one day acknowledged had life gone according to plan. Now it was just another thing I avoided having to think about.

As I slung down my bag in the hall, I caught a brief glimpse of my face in the hallway mirror. *Urgh*. The twenty-year-old me would have been horrified. I hadn't worn make-up in months. I had shadows under my eyes and lines across my forehead. My hair was dull and oily – I couldn't remember the last time I'd washed it. And God, I was pale. Thinking about it, when was the last time I'd been out in the sun? Was I imagining it, or was every day I woke up to the same relentless mass of cloud?

Deciding I couldn't be bothered to eat, I opted instead to go straight upstairs. As I crossed the landing, I found myself glancing over at the door to the spare room. It was closed, of course. I stopped to study the door handle, longing for a different time when the prospect of opening a door in my own home didn't make my heart sink.

Should I bite the bullet and go in? What would happen if I did? I allowed my hand to touch the doorknob, my index finger instinctively seeking out a minuscule chip on the porcelain surface. Something was holding me back. That room was full of memories of a happier time, but it was also symbolic of precisely how badly my life had turned out.

Six months on, I'd thought I was beginning to come to terms with it all, but the pain, the despair, was never far from the surface. I felt the tickle of a tear as it made its way down my cheek, and I searched in my pocket for a hankie (my constant companion nowadays, it seemed) before remembering that I'd given it to Mischa. I wiped the tear away with my finger instead and went into the bathroom.

A waft of fragrant magnolia greeted me, thoroughly at odds with my mood. Once upon a time, this space had been my sanctuary. I'd even designed it like that – *a place to relax and unwind* – and was overjoyed when I managed to get it featured in an online interiors magazine. Now I felt crushed by the sheer pointlessness of it all.

In the old days, my nightly skincare routine had taken a good 30 minutes from start to finish. I remembered how I used to go over every inch of my face for any sign of a wrinkle, ready for the moment when I would need to resort to something more drastic (even though I swore to Joe I never would). Looking back, my old obsessive habits seemed stupid – especially when, nowadays, I was in and out of the bathroom in 45 seconds flat. I glanced up at my huge array of potions and lotions that I'd painstakingly collected over the years and which had once seemed as vital to my life as breathing. All neglected and covered in dust – a bit like me. The thought almost made me smile. Nothing like comparing yourself to an unused pot of moisturiser to really make you value yourself as a human being.

After a cursory brush of my teeth, I left the bathroom and went into my bedroom, the king-size bed covered with pillows, throws and cushions. I threw them onto the carpet, pulled back the thick feather duvet and climbed in. The bed felt cold and empty. I tucked the duvet in around my body as best I could, wrapped my arms around my stomach and shivered, looking out through the window at the inky night outside. I could scarcely believe there was a time when I used to enjoy the simple act of going to bed. The pleasure I would get from wriggling myself backwards like a centipede until Joe's warm body connected and wrapped itself around mine.

I tried to clear my mind but I couldn't. My brain had put me on a rollercoaster ride of memories that I would now have to see through to the bitter end. Although that wasn't necessarily such a bad thing since I wasn't sure I wanted to sleep either. Because sleeping meant having to dream, and I'd been having the same one almost every night now for as long as I could remember. It was starting to get exhausting.

I turned over onto my side to try to make myself comfortable, gripping the pillow between my arms and lacing my hands together. I closed my eyes, even though I knew the act was hopeless. Whatever I did, it would be at least a couple of hours before I fell asleep.

# Chapter 10

# Mischa

The last seven days had *flown* by. I'd no idea how. Work had been boring. But that wasn't a shocker – all I did was pick up the phone and talk to people about insurance claims. It was hardly rocket science, and lately – since, well, you know – I couldn't really remember a lot of stuff.

I did know the rest of the team hadn't spoken to me, which I still found really weird. When I'd first started the job, they were loads nicer. I even thought I might make some friends. There was one girl, Ellie, who was really sweet. She used to bring in homemade cakes and biscuits every day. She tried to get me to come to her spin class a couple of times. And then there was Anil, who fancied himself a bit for someone who wore Bart Simpson T-shirts at the age of 22. But he was cute. And smiley. He used to ask me loads of questions, which I liked. I wondered once, maybe, if he fancied me. Stupid really.

But then something changed all of a sudden and they stopped coming over.

Mum's voice in my head reminds me. *You had one of your episodes, didn't you?*

*Yes*. But that was nothing major – I'd just been upset. About what'd happened. I thought I'd handled it alright at the time. And everyone had been nice afterwards, telling me to go home early and have a rest. Ellie held my hand the whole time, telling me not to worry. That everything would be okay.

But now they didn't really talk to me anymore, so I must've made a bigger idiot of myself than I realised. For the first few days after I came back to work, I would lift my head up every time one of them walked past, thinking they would appear over the divider like they used to, to tell me about their day. Or ask if I wanted a cup of tea. But when no one did, I got too shy to speak to them. Instead I listened to their quiet chatter on the other side of the office as I got my work done and kept my head down when I left.

That meant when it got to Tuesday, I almost skipped out of work when I remembered I had something different to do that evening. Counselling session number two! I couldn't say counselling session number one had made me feel all that 'counselled' but at least I would have people to talk to.

And Callum would be there. The thought made my tummy go funny. He was *so* good-looking. I had no idea why he was coming to our sessions. He could pay to go to one of those super swanky celeb retreats. Like the ones in America they talk about all the time in *Heat* magazine, which cost thousands and thousands of dollars a day. But for some reason he was with us and, better than that, he'd said he'd come back. Even Victoria had said yes. That had been a surprise. I thought we wouldn't see her again for sure.

God, this bus was taking ages. Why was there this much traffic?

I leant my head against the window. Everything was a little bit steamy. I could barely see outside. That weird thing that happened to windows when it was rainy but warm at the same time.

I looked around the bus to see how busy it was. The top deck was almost empty. There were a few kids at the back making some noise. As usual. I didn't turn to look. Didn't want to get involved in their chat. Or their insults. White boys could be funny sometimes, especially the ones round my way.

I distracted myself from the boredom of the bus journey by thinking about the other people I would be getting to know over the next few weeks. Any chance of a friendship with Callum seemed too stupid to even dream about, so I pushed him out of my mind completely. Freya seemed lovely but I was sad that someone so sweet seemed to be struggling so much. Also passing out and having no control of your body was horrible – I knew that better than anyone. That left Victoria. She was a funny one. Super classy and sophisticated and clever. I wondered why she was there. Yeah, we'd all had things happen to us. Things that meant we weren't coping. But I could kind of feel that with Freya. And maybe Callum, too. But Victoria seemed completely normal.

*Sometimes it's the ones who seem fine on the outside who are suffering the most.*

I knew all about that also.

# PART TWO
# ANGER

# Chapter 11

# Callum

I had no fucking idea why I was going back. But here I was anyway, slumped in the back of my car, Rob pushing his way through the heavy London traffic.

'How's the family, Rob?'

No response. Christ, even my driver hated me.

I looked out through the blacked-out windows. We were heading through the West End now, the streets rammed with people who didn't seem to have a fucking clue how to cross a road. I felt completely removed from them – like I was watching everyday life play out from behind a screen. Which I guess I was. A couple of pissed girls, arms around each other, skirts only just covering their arses, fell off the kerb, right in front of the car. We slammed to a halt and they started laughing hysterically. As if the fact they'd nearly got squashed by a 4x4 was something to fucking laugh about. I took a deep breath. I needed to chill the fuck out.

The satnav told us to turn right and Rob swung the car down Manette Street, passing a bar I recognised. A little dive joint where I used to play when I first moved to London. Everything about it screamed of a happier, easier time. I smiled at the skull and crossbones over the door. Thought about the wood panels and the peeling plaster inside. The dodgy rock and punk memorabilia all over the walls. Warm beer, bottles of whisky coated in dust. Toilets that never got cleaned. Fuck, I loved that place. Even though I was at least 30 years younger than most of the clientele.

One night I'd played there, I must've been about eighteen. The room had been fucking rammed. Not because of me – some old rocker who'd had a couple of hits in the eighties had been listed to play. But I'd managed to blag a fifteen-minute set right before him by flirting with a manageress who looked like a Hell's Angel. It was the first time I'd played my own material and I'd been nervous as hell. Just a cocky young kid from up north who wanted to make rock music great again.

If I closed my eyes now, I could picture that night like it was yesterday. The crowd heaving and loud and drunk. The walls vibrating with the warmth of too many bodies. The nerves in my belly mixing with the vodka shot I'd downed to sort myself out. The sensation that came with satisfying a crowd that knew exactly what it wanted to hear and who'd throw you out the second you didn't make the grade.

Then I'd started singing and the place went quiet. Just like that. The shouting, the shoving, the scraping of chairs. It'd all stopped. I'd looked up into this sea of faces in front of me. Close enough that I could smell their sweat. Feel the energy that came off them like static. In that moment, I'd felt connected to every single fucking person in that room.

My thoughts were interrupted by Rob slamming on the brakes again. A fucking Uber driver cutting him up no doubt. Those losers didn't have a fucking clue. I rummaged in the drinks compartment, hoping there might be some booze in there to get me through the next couple of hours. Even a beer would do. But there was nothing. Just fucking mineral water. I might as well go vegan and take up yoga while I was at it.

I tried to remember why I was going back to this counselling shitshow. Oh yeah. For some reason my record label, in its infinite fucking wisdom, had decided that *in the circumstances* I would get more benefit from some cheap-arsed group therapy than proper private rehab. I knew why they were really doing it: it was their way of punishing me for what'd happened. Recalling the conversation I'd had earlier that day with Skye made me want to punch something. I knew it, I should never have shagged her. She'd been out to get me ever since. Maybe it was wrong of me to have gone back to hers and then upped and left without saying goodbye, but what did she expect? It's what I did. She'd read enough of the tabloids to know that.

The voice on the end of the phone had been flat and cold without any emotion. A world away from the exuberant crazy South African girl I used to know.

'We think it would be good for you, Callum.'

I could tell she was loving it. Bitch.

'Skye, I get this whole need for counselling thing. I really do. I know I've got to sort my shit out. But why do I have to go there? It's a fucking crap hole.'

'Callum, if we send you to Arizona, people will start asking questions, hey. Don't forget, we've already had to pay a fortune to stop them publishing what happened. This way, we can avoid any more cost, hopefully get you into a better headspace, then put you back out there again.'

'Can't you just send a shrink to my apartment?'

Skye sighed. If I collected every sigh I'd heard in recent months, I'd have enough to launch a fucking hot air balloon.

'I'm going to be upfront with you, Callum. The label is seriously fucked off with you. We were running out of patience before this even happened. I've got people left right and centre telling me to cut you loose. I was tempted to do it a couple of weeks ago, to be honest, only Dermot's cousin Genevieve asked if he knew anyone who might be a good candidate for her new programme. And he suggested you. You should feel lucky she called when she did.'

'What you're saying is I'm a fucking lab rat?'

'You can see it however you want. But at the end of the day, you've got a hell of a lot of bridges to build. You seem to think that because you've made us a lot of money, we're somehow indebted to you. I can tell you that's not how it works, darling. You fucked up, Callum. Not a little bit. A lot. What happened wasn't something we can brush under the carpet. He had a wife and two kids, for Christ's sake.'

I inhaled, not trusting myself to speak for a moment. 'You don't need to bring it up, Skye. I know.'

'And I know how bad you feel about it. I feel for you, Callum, I really do. But if we're going to get past this and move on, for the sake of your career and your sanity you need to do as you're told for once. Otherwise, let's agree to part company now.'

'Fine.'

'Fine meaning what?'

'Fine meaning I'll go.'

# Chapter 12

# Victoria

I had spent all week trying to come up with reasons why I shouldn't do this. Work would be too busy – it wasn't. Andrew would forget about it – he didn't. I would discover that Genevieve, after an in-depth Google search, was actually a serial killer on the run – she, very sadly, was not. Rather, it transpired she had a first-class BSc in Psychology from Cambridge, an MSc in Psychiatric Research from King's College London and a whole host of excellent references from her lecturers and hospital placements. Damn her to hell.

We were positioned in a circle, as appeared to now be our quaint little custom, gazing at each other like complete ignorami while Genevieve poured us each a glass of iced tea. The whole montage was deplorable. Normally, I had no issue whatsoever conducting small talk with people I barely knew. I did it every day at work. I had always assumed, rather naively I now realised, that I could talk to anyone, irrespective of where they came from. But here, I couldn't help but feel that anything and everything I said was being noted down and analysed to the nth degree, each syllable I uttered in some way symbolic of my underlying mental capacity. Or lack thereof, as the case may be. That this ridiculous experiment was actually a test of some kind that I had to somehow pass. However, for the first time in my life, I could neither prepare for it in advance nor guarantee I would make the grade.

Consequently, I said nothing, and neither did anyone else.

I allowed myself a quick glance around the room at my colleagues – I refused to think of us as patients, because to do so implied there was something genuinely wrong with me. Freya looked the same as she did last week, perhaps more drained. She might even have been wearing the same outfit. It struck me as strange that someone that thin seemed intent on wearing clothes that drowned her. Callum looked thoroughly pissed off – an expression he pulled off effortlessly, it had to be said. And Mischa. Mischa looked kind of happy. That was a start, I suppose. She caught me looking at her and smiled. It felt churlish not to smile back, so I did. She seemed even happier and, for a second, I felt good about the whole situation. Until I remembered that at some point, I was going to be required to share something.

'Right, everyone, shall we begin?'

Genevieve handed out the drinks she'd made up and sat down. She looked calmer this week, perhaps believing we'd now bought in to the process and that life would be easier for her. I had a feeling she was in for a rude awakening. Despite the abundance of qualifications she had in her armoury, I still couldn't shake the impression that she didn't really know what she was doing. But maybe that was an unfair assessment based on her age – she was at least two decades younger than me. Taking guidance from her was a bit like taking legal advice from a trainee – they could demonstrate all the intelligence and intuition in the world, but that didn't mean I would listen. But then again, my trainees were, as a rule, bloody useless.

'I wanted to say that I thought you all did a wonderful job last week,' Genevieve said. 'The fact you were able to identify happy memories from your childhood is a very important step in the process. It shows you have the capacity to feel a positive emotion, even though you may not have experienced that recently. I know some of you think that what you have been through means you can never be happy or at peace with yourself again, but I want to reassure you now that that's absolutely not the case. It's far more difficult working with people whose lives have been a constant source of unhappiness, and believe me, I have encountered many of those. They, sadly, have no reference point to look back on, no point in their lives when they are able to recall being truly at peace. For people like that, this process would take a lot longer.'

'Surely you're not saying we should be grateful?' Callum asked, voicing the same thought that had been going through my head.

'No, Callum, I am not saying you should be grateful. I am saying you should be aware that you all have the capacity to move on. But you need to have faith that you can do it.'

'I'm not sure I have faith in anything anymore,' Freya muttered.

'I know it feels like that now,' Genevieve replied. 'But you do at least know the sensation of happiness, and that is a much stronger source of power within you than you realise.'

She consulted her little book again – an item I now found almost as annoying as its owner – running her finger down the page as if mentally ticking off items on a checklist.

'For today's session, I'm going to ask you to talk about two things. What you were like as a person before the experience, and then how you've been since. How it has affected your life, what has changed since it happened, what that means to you. I don't want you to share the experience itself. But I am interested in understanding the person you were versus the person you think you've now become. It will give me an idea of what I need to do to help you get back into a better frame of mind. And finally, if things get too difficult, I want you to hold on to the memory that you shared with us last week and make it your happy place. However difficult things get throughout this process, remember that a part of you was happy once. And you can go back there again whenever you want, I promise.'

Genevieve looked around the room. 'Now, who would like to go first?'

# Chapter 13

# Mischa

When no one spoke, I decided something. I was here for a reason. I wanted to feel better. I wanted that more than anything in the world.

'I'll go,' I said.

Genevieve looked pleased. 'That's great, Mischa, thank you. Please go ahead and don't worry if you struggle with anything. Take all the time you need.'

*Take a couple of deep breaths.*

'Let me think. What was I like before?'

I stared at the brown carpet. Got thrown for a second by a little bit of black fluff. Was that a spider? *Gross.* I pushed it with the toe of my boot, expecting it to run away. It didn't.

'Mischa?'

Everyone was looking at me. I felt my neck go warm. 'Sorry. I forgot what I was doing for a second. I guess . . . I guess I just got on with life? Did what I had to do. Things could be tough. Like *really* tough. But it was what it was. I'm not sure I was happy about it exactly. But I had a job to do and I did it.'

'Did that bother you?' Genevieve asked.

*It did, didn't it?*

'No, not really. I felt like I was useful. I know most people would've hated it. Wondered why I didn't get someone to help me. But I didn't want that. And it wasn't as if I was looking after a stranger. It was my mum. And she needed me.'

I stopped talking for a second, thinking about what I wanted to say.

'I guess life was difficult, yeah, but I didn't really mind. I was alright. I had a routine. Oh, and you know what? I was good at it. I wasn't good at very much before that. I had no idea what I wanted to do when I left school. So when the chance to do anything went away, it was okay. And it wasn't hard all the time. Is that enough?'

'Yes, Mischa, that's great,' Genevieve said. 'And if you're up to it, could you move on to how you felt afterwards?'

I forced my mind back to the days immediately after. 'I felt empty. I tried to pretend it hadn't happened. A little bit. A small part of me thought it was a chance to start over. I feel terrible saying that. But it'd been a rough few years. The last twelve months especially. Does that sound awful?'

'No, Mischa, it doesn't at all,' Genevieve replied. 'It's very normal to feel that way.'

Her words made me feel better for saying it.

'Okay, good. I was worried it made me sound like a bad person. Anyway, my carer's allowance got stopped and I had to get a job. Which was easier than I thought it would be. That was a nice surprise. A local charity helped me find something. Lucky really because I'd had to leave school before I could finish my A levels. I thought finding something would be a total nightmare. Or I'd have to go on that Job Seeker allowance. But I got this job processing claims for an insurance company. Not very exciting. But it got – gets – me out the flat.'

'Can you tell us a bit more about your feelings at that time?' Genevieve asked.

'Yeah, okay. Sorry. To begin with, I was alright, I think. Sad, of course, but I liked my new job. The people seemed nice. I'm quite shy. I don't find it easy to just start conversations. Didn't really have friends at school. So being at work was nice. But then, after a while, I reckon maybe a month, I realised things weren't going as well as I'd hoped.'

I felt a lump in my throat and stopped talking.

'It's okay Mischa, take your time.'

I swallowed. 'I'm not sure what else to say.'

'Perhaps you could try to explain what happened to make you think something was starting to go wrong?'

I looked at Genevieve. She was in her chair, leaning towards me. Her big brown eyes didn't leave my face. At that moment all I wanted more than anything was for her to hug me. But I knew she wouldn't.

'Yeah, okay. For a start, the empty feeling got tons worse. I'd spent so long doing this one thing – caring for my mum – and suddenly I had nothing. And I wasn't sleeping. My doctor said broken sleep does that to you after a while. Your body forgets how to do it. But before I had a reason to be awake. Now I didn't. I'd stare at the ceiling for hours. Some nights I don't think I slept. I did get some pills though, so the sleeping got a little bit better.'

'And when I first spoke to you on the phone you mentioned an episode at work?' Genevieve said, reading from her notebook. 'Would you like to tell us a bit more about that?'

I felt my cheeks go red. I'd forgotten I'd told her.

*She's not going to judge, you know.*

I didn't really want to go into the details of that day but knew now I had no choice. I stared at the bows of my laces as I tried my best to describe what had happened.

'One day at work, I was sat talking to this guy on the phone. I thought he was a right idiot. He was making a claim on his wife's life insurance. I can't remember what she'd died from; it was something horrible. And I felt like he didn't care. I'm sure he did, thinking back. He was probably just trying to hold it together. But when I put the phone down, I lost it. At first I was crying, but then it was like this fog came down over my eyes and I started shouting. Can't remember what I said. I grabbed all this stuff from my desk – whatever I could find – and I . . . I kind of threw it against the wall. Kicked one of those dividers over between the desks. People tried to calm me down but I couldn't hear anything. Then I . . . I blacked out.'

'Can you tell us what happened after that?' Genevieve asked. 'When you came to?'

'I woke up and I was lying on the floor. Ellie – a girl I work with – she was stroking my hand. She knew a bit about me already because when the company took me on, the charity told HR, and my manager asked Ellie to keep an eye on me. You see, even before all this, I used to get angry sometimes. But I tried to bottle it up. Because I had to. Because if I didn't, God knows what would've happened.'

'And how have you been feeling since you had that episode?'

The question brought the anger back.

'Loads worse. That's what made me message you. Hearing that man on the phone, talking about his wife – it made me realise I couldn't deal with the world anymore. Because awful things happen to really good people. And we have no control over who gets ill . . . who dies . . . who lives. It's not fair and that pisses me off.'

I switched my focus from my shoes to Genevieve. 'Sorry, I didn't mean to swear.'

'I completely agree with you,' Freya said, quietly. 'That's exactly how I feel.'

'Clearly that's how we *all* feel, babe – why else would we be stuck together in this fucking room?' Callum said, looking at Freya like she was some kind of idiot. He caught Genevieve looking at him and rolled his eyes.

'Alright, I apologise for saying that. But really, what's the point? I don't see how sharing these fucking depressing stories is going to get us anywhere.'

'I didn't mean to make you feel depressed,' I said. I could feel tears burning behind my eyes. 'Maybe I shouldn't have talked as much as I did.'

I concentrated on my lap so no one would see I was about to cry.

'No, Mischa, I wasn't having a go at you,' Callum said.

I looked up. The smile he gave me made my heart thud.

'What I meant was, I don't understand how hearing stuff like this is going to help me feel better about myself. If anything, I think I feel worse.'

'Hear, hear,' Victoria said.

I could see Genevieve open her mouth to speak but another voice got in first.

Freya. She was sat up in her chair, looking annoyed. The first time I'd seen her look anything other than lost. She was staring straight at Callum.

'I may not be a psychologist, *babe*, and I still have no idea if this is going to work. But I'm willing to give it a go, even if you won't.'

She looked round at the rest of us and smiled. It made me realise then how pretty she was.

'To be honest, I'm ready to try anything right now if there's the smallest chance in hell it will help me move on. Genevieve – I'll go next if you want.'

# Chapter 14

# Freya

I hadn't meant to volunteer at all, but Callum had wound me up. Sprawled across his chair with his good looks and his fame oozing around him. What right did he have to decide what would and wouldn't work for the people in this room? Maybe if he put a tiny bit of effort in himself, he might see some results. Dick.

Callum was exactly the sort of guy I'd stayed away from when I was younger. The type who could flatter and charm his way into a girl's bed without even thinking about what that might mean for her. Who could make you feel like the only person in the world who mattered. For all of two weeks, that is, until he got bored and moved on to his next conquest.

I started talking, aware that I was looking directly at him. Daring him to argue with me. Or get up and leave. He stared straight back at me, a pair of emerald eyes boring into mine. He didn't have an issue with eye contact, I had to give him that. Something ignited inside me briefly, enough for me to pause. What was that? With some surprise, I remembered. It was how I used to be when I felt something.

'Okay, let me think. What was I like before . . . wow, that feels like a lifetime ago.'

I hesitated. What *was* I like before? I tried to picture the girl I once was. Oh yes, there she was. A distant shimmering mirage that I knew would disappear the second I tried to reach it. But her outline was clear enough.

'One thing I can tell you, I used to be cheerful, believe it or not. Every morning I'd wake up raring to start the day. I was the complete opposite of my husband, Joe, who wasn't a morning person at all. But I was always excited to get up – even when I had to go to work. I'd be out of bed the second the alarm went off. Although I had no real choice in that – if I didn't let Barney out by quarter to seven, the first thing I'd see when I went downstairs was a huge puddle of wee on the kitchen floor.'

The image of Callum and the others faded as I talked, replaced by memories of a different time. It wasn't difficult to remember: my and Joe's morning routine had been the same for years.

Dealing with Barney had been my job ('He's your dog,' Joe used to say nicely but firmly whenever I suggested we share the burden). It was his way of reminding me that my first and only impulsive act as a married couple had not been a very good one: agreeing to take on a dog who needed rehoming when we didn't really have the time or the space for him. Which meant that every morning at the crack of dawn it was me shaking biscuits into a metal bowl, then watching him run around the kitchen like a lunatic as he chased it across the tiles.

'I enjoyed the routine of it all. My morning coffee. Choosing an outfit for the day. Doing my hair. My make-up. Deciding what jewellery to wear. Going to work. Chatting to clients. Going to the gym. All of it. Yes, my life was a bit repetitive maybe. But it was repetitive in a good way. And even when I got pissed off, I wasn't that bothered by it. Normally I'd end up calling Joe to have a whinge and he'd manage to help me see the funny side. We used to laugh a lot. That's something I really miss.'

I stopped talking as the realisation hit me that that life, that *perfect life* I'd just told everyone about, was over. But at the same time, I knew it wasn't aching nostalgia that had shut me up; it was recognition that the whole time I'd been living that life, I hadn't been as happy as I'd seemed. Perhaps that's why I'd always been so relentlessly positive. Because if ever I'd stopped to question things, I might have found myself giving answers I didn't want to hear.

'Are you okay, Freya?' Genevieve asked. She looked mildly concerned. I wondered if she thought I was going to faint again.

'I'm sorry, I don't know why I told you all that stuff.'

*Because you're shallow, Freya*, a small voice piped up in my head. *All you cared about was your nice house, your cool job, your tick-box marriage and your dog.*

'Barney died, by the way,' I blurted out, suddenly desperate to say something mildly controversial. 'He was hit by a car chasing a squirrel out of the park about twelve months ago. I was devastated. Took a week off work. Ha! Who the hell takes a week off work when their dog dies?'

My voice sounded high, slightly crazed. For once, I didn't care.

'I should have realised then I wasn't cut out for normal life, with all its ups and downs and shitty challenges. I mean, if I couldn't handle the death of a dog, it was obvious I was never going to cope when . . . when I was . . .'

I couldn't do it. I covered my face with my hands.

It wasn't just that I felt sad. I mean, I did feel sad, of course. Sadness – grief, devastation, call it what you will – was a permanent feature of my life now. But because it was always there, I almost didn't notice it; it was just part of who I had become. But sitting there, head in my hands, tears streaking my cheeks, I also felt angry. Embarrassed. About my own humiliating inability to survive. I'd led this easy, comfortable, fortunate life. Compared to many people anyway. I knew that and, more importantly, I knew I should be grateful for it. But for all its benefits, and for all the superficial joy it had supposedly brought me, it had also made me weak and incapable. I'd become a creature of habit. Untainted by tragedy. A person who blithely accepted a perfectly nice life and pretended to the outside world to be insanely satisfied with it. And that made me hate myself.

I felt a warm hand on my shoulder. Instinctively I grasped hold of it, closing my eyes and resting my head against it, absorbing the warmth of another human like a sponge. It had been such a long time since I had been touched.

I hadn't spoken to anyone about my feelings in a very long time either. Not my family, not my friends – and definitely not Joe. They were too close to what had happened. Too likely to tell me it was time to move on from something I knew I wasn't ready to do.

Maybe talking to a group of strangers *would* be better. A chance to say whatever I liked without having to worry about what their reaction would be or how they would treat me afterwards.

Half-reluctantly I pulled away, realising with a jolt of surprise that the owner of the hand was Callum. I looked up into his eyes and felt a twinge of something. I wiped my eyes and nose with my hand (horrible, I know, but I'd given away my hankie) noticing that I'd covered the cuff of his jumper in tears and snot. I couldn't help it: I started giggling. He looked at me, confused for a second, but following my eyes downwards, pulled a face, then smiled. 'Cheers for that.'

'I'm sorry. I'll wash it for you if you want.'

'Don't worry about it. I'm used to girls crying over me.' He sat back down.

'Freya, I can see this is hard for you,' Genevieve said. 'Would you like to take a break?'

I thought about it. The easiest thing would be to chicken out altogether. But I'd spent such a long time keeping quiet about this and that had got me nowhere. Maybe I *could* do this. I started to speak again, sensing for the first time that I wanted to be honest.

'No, it's okay, I'd like to keep going.'

'Of course,' Genevieve replied. 'In which case, maybe you could try to tell us how you felt afterwards.'

It was probably the first time I'd allowed myself to remember: the mere act of casting my mind backwards felt unnatural after all this time; my memories like rusted wheels that refused to budge on the track. Eventually, though, they started to resurface.

'I didn't speak for five days after it happened. Not a single word. I couldn't eat either. Although I was on some kind of drip, so that didn't matter, not while I was in hospital anyway.

'In some ways it was easier – being in hospital I mean. Staring at the same four walls, day in, day out. I could pretend to be asleep when people showed up to see me. Make out I didn't exist. I didn't want to exist, I remember that much.'

'And do you remember what happened after you left the hospital?'

'I went home after a couple of weeks. I don't remember the drive. Joe must have collected me. All of a sudden I was back home, in my own bed. Only I couldn't function. Still can't, really. But at least now I can get myself washed and dressed. In those early days I couldn't even manage that.'

I paused.

'I find it interesting, Mischa, what you said earlier. When you said to start with, you felt okay and tried to get on with things. I never felt like that. And I slept all the time. Sometimes twenty hours a day. I think it was my body's way of coping. I basically shut down, mentally and physically.'

'Do you still feel like that?' Genevieve asked.

I considered the question. 'Kind of. I'd like to say things have improved, but they haven't really. I can't face the thought of doing anything normal. I don't want to see anyone, do anything. It's rare that I leave the house.' As I said it, I realised I couldn't remember the last time I *had* left the house, other than to come to these sessions. 'Getting here today was such a mission. Every time I open my front door I feel overwhelmed. Like the sky will flatten me the second I step outside.'

'In that case, you should be proud of yourself for even being here.'

'Hardly. Look at me. I'm a mess.'

'No, you're not,' Mischa said. 'You're sad, that's all. It's alright to be sad.'

'Thank you. But it's not just that. I feel ashamed of myself.'

'Why do you feel ashamed?' Genevieve asked.

I hesitated, conscious I was picking at a small hole in my leggings. I stopped and wedged my hands under my thighs instead.

'Because my whole life, I had a plan. I thought I knew exactly how things were going to turn out. Grow old with Joe, have kids, have a dog. But none of that is going to happen now. My dog's dead. I don't talk to my husband. I don't talk to my family. I don't go to work. I can't remember if I said the last time I was here, but I was signed off and I haven't been back. I just don't know how I'm ever going to move forward.'

'That's not something I want you to worry too much about right now, Freya,' Genevieve said, leaning over and taking my hand. It was soft and warm and I gripped it. 'You should be proud of what you've achieved today. I know it may not seem like it, but you've already made good progress.'

'Thank you.'

'Is there anything else you'd like to say?'

'No, no, I'm good. I feel a bit better for that, believe it or not.'

We sat quietly for a minute or so. Then Genevieve took away her hand. She turned to look at Callum and Victoria.

'Do either of you feel able to share something with us?'

I leant back, relieved that my turn was over, but also pleased I'd managed to get through it. I smiled at Callum and Victoria as positively as you can do when your face is puffy and you look a complete state. Victoria was looking at the floor and wouldn't catch my eye. She was going to be a much harder nut for Genevieve to crack, that much was obvious. But Callum returned my smile. Maybe he wasn't such a dick after all.

# Chapter 15

# Callum

I didn't have a fucking clue why I'd felt the need to comfort her. It wasn't like I fancied her – at least, I didn't think I did. But something about her story had drawn me in. I couldn't put my finger on it. It's not like I was the touching type. And I didn't normally go for blondes either.

Who fucking knew why I'd done it? All I knew was, my top was trashed and I was shattered.

Shattered, but not from lack of sleep – I could work that much out for myself. I was shattered by the constant fucking noise in my head. Or more to the point, the constant battle to shut it out. And as much as I could tell anyone who stuck their nose in that I didn't need to speak to a professional, I was fed up of trying to work things out for myself. Besides, if I didn't know why I'd felt the need to get up out of my chair and squeeze the shoulder of a girl I barely knew, what chance did I have of getting my head straight on anything else?

I wondered then if I should give this whole *opening up* thing a quick go. Test the waters with something I knew I could speak about. It wasn't like Genevieve's questions were that controversial. She'd already said we didn't need to talk about anything else today.

Sod it, I was going to do it. Not because I wanted to. But because I had fuck all else to lose.

'You know what? I didn't think I bought in to this, but I'm going to give it a try.'

The second the words came out my mouth, I regretted them. I drummed my fingers on my leg. Jesus, I was kind of nervous. Pull it together, Callum.

'Of course, that's fantastic,' Genevieve said. 'Please, go ahead whenever you're ready.'

I wasn't ready. I needed to stall for a bit more time. 'I don't suppose I could have a beer, could I? This iced tea is pretty ropey.'

Genevieve didn't bother to answer. She just shook her head and gave me a look that made it clear I was about as close to getting a beer as I was a comeback single. Never mind, it was worth a try.

'Okay fine. Here goes. My life before. On paper it was awesome. I first picked up a guitar when I was seven. Started writing songs at twelve. Gigging in London at seventeen. Four years later the right person heard me play and that was that. Had a number one album by the time I was 24. Platinum-selling artist at 25. Soundtrack for the last Bond movie at 26. I mean, Christ, no one can deny that's a stellar CV, right? I went to all the premières, sold out concerts in minutes, partied all night. Private jets, restaurant openings, celeb events, award ceremonies, five-star hotels, invites to things other people would sell their mother for. It was nuts.'

'That sounds so cool,' Mischa said. Ever the star-struck fan. 'You must have loved it.'

The comment wound me up no end, but I didn't want to put her down again. She was young, for a start, and also possibly a bit unstable. I decided to give the girl some life advice and put her straight.

'Actually, I didn't. 'Cause you know what? That kind of life isn't great after a while. You can't leave your house without some arsehole taking a photo of you. You can't go on holiday without some wanker who looks like he needs a wash and a shave following you around 24/7. You can't have an argument with your girlfriend – who, by the way, is usually some arrogant little princess your management set you up with – without the whole fucking world thinking you're a sadist. To be honest, it got me down quite quickly.'

'I'm not surprised in the slightest – I think that sounds absolutely dreadful,' Victoria said, the first time she'd spoken in ages. I felt encouraged by her comment – at least it meant someone in the room got where I was coming from.

'Yeah, it was. The Christmas before last, all I wanted to do was see my family. I'd made out to all my so-called mates that I was going to Necker. Richard was having this massive New Year thing. I knew one of them would phone up the press and tip them off. Dickheads. Got my PA to put some tweets out, make out I was on my way to Heathrow. Booked a hotel, a few restaurants in Miami. And then I went home.'

My voice caught, thinking back to that time. I coughed to clear it. 'My mum and dad never moved, you know? I bought them a massive house closer to London, but they've never used it. Said they wanted to stay near their family and friends. And that's where I went. And for two whole days it was fucking bliss. My brother was there with his wife and kid. My whole extended family, even my ninety-seven-year-old gran. Who asked me where I'd been for the last two years. Reminded her I was a musician. She told me to go out and get a proper job if I wanted to make any real money.

'And it was great. Until, that is, some knob on my parents' street called someone, made a few hundred quid, and suddenly my mum and dad's lawn was full of paps. And fans. God. The fans – they're even worse. They'll do anything to get near you. Desperate to turn fantasy into reality. I know I'm supposed to be grateful to them. As my label constantly tells me, they're the ones who made me. I do fucking know that. But does that give them the right to try and smuggle themselves into my mum's house and hide in her bathroom? Like fuck it does.'

'What did you do?' Freya asked.

'Within twenty-four hours, maybe less, my mum and dad's house went from being a haven to a prison. And I knew I had to get out. I called my PA to sort it, probably ruined her fucking Christmas. But she got me security and six hours later I was in a car, on my way back to London. I ended up going to Richard's party. Figured at least there I'd blend in with everyone else. Got off my tits as usual. Don't even remember it really—'

'Callum?' Genevieve asked, interrupting me mid-flow.

'Yeah?'

'Do you think you might be happy to share a bit more about that with us?'

'What do you mean?'

Genevieve hesitated. I could see she was trying to choose her words carefully. I decided to help her out. I knew exactly what she wanted me to talk about.

'You want me to talk to you about the drugs, don't you?'

'Only if you feel you can.'

I shrugged.

'Fine by me. That's probably about the only thing I do find it easy to talk about.'

I looked at the others. 'You probably know from the papers I've taken a lot of shit in my time. Pretty much whenever I got the opportunity, to be honest.'

I saw Victoria was staring at me like I was nuts.

'What?' I asked her, very much aware of how defensive I sounded.

'I just don't understand why anyone would feel the need to take drugs when they have that much going for them,' Victoria replied.

That old fucking chestnut. I laughed. Couldn't help myself. 'Yeah, a lot of people used to tell me that. But you want to know the truth of it? When you have everything you could want, sometimes, normal life, it gets fucking dull. And you gotta remember, everywhere you go, people are throwing stuff at you.

Take this, Callum. Have her, Callum. You deserve it, Callum. You're a fucking God, Callum. And after a while, there's only one way you can live up to all that hype: you have to take shit to make it as real in your own head as it is in everyone else's. And then once you start, you're screwed, man. Especially if you have a personality like mine. The thought of going back to being ordinary becomes impossible: you need that high all the time. Because you know the second you lose it, the low you get afterwards will be fucking unbearable.

'Anyhow, I took a lot of stuff, screwed myself up, and my life wasn't good. Hardly knew what I was doing half the time. Sometimes I'd read about myself in the paper just to see what I'd done the night before. That's how bad it got.'

I stopped talking. Fuck, I needed a drink.

'Callum?' Genevieve asked.

'Yeah?'

'You don't need a drink to do this, you know.'

How had she guessed?

'Are you fucking telepathic?'

'No, I can just see it's what you're thinking. But you don't. It's more a case of learning to open up by yourself. Without something artificial there to encourage you. And you're doing an excellent job.'

'Am I?'

'Yes. You really are.'

'Thanks. Remind me. What was the other thing you wanted us to talk about?'

'How you felt afterwards.'

I exhaled loudly.

'Do you think you can manage that?' Genevieve asked.

'Yeah, I can try.'

This was normally the point I'd do a shot or a line to free up my thoughts. I tried to recreate the sensation of it in my head, the rush of temporary certainty that everything I said was exactly what people wanted to hear. Unfortunately my imagination wasn't good enough. I would have to make do with the truth.

'You go from thinking your life is hard, to wondering why the hell you'd ever thought to complain about it. You go from living each day without a thought for what you're doing, to basically thinking about every fucking thing you do. It's relentless. Especially when your label has grounded you. Because that's meant I've had to spend a hell of a lot of time with my own head for company. And I can tell you something for fucking nothing – my head's not great for that.'

I paused. There was one more thing I wanted to say, but I wasn't sure if I could.

Fuck it, I'd come this far, why not go all in?

'One thing Mischa and Freya didn't mention was guilt. The emptiness, lack of purpose, yep, I get that. The inability to function – you try going cold turkey when you're used to snorting a few grams of coke up your nose every night. But combine that with knowing what happened was one hundred per cent your fucking fault? That's like taking a bulldozer to your soul.'

I looked down at my hands, rubbing at the calluses on my fingertips. They were already starting to go soft. I couldn't remember the last time I'd played.

'Could you expand on that?' Genevieve asked. 'That feeling of guilt, I mean?'

Jesus Christ, this woman never let up.

'Yeah, I can. You may have noticed I like to pretend to the outside world I haven't changed. I make out I'm still the cocky little fucker who shags around and makes shitloads of money from selling records that make women cry. But you wanna know how I really feel? I'm destroyed, man. I'm done. Checked out. And if I was given the choice to never wake up again, I'd grab it with both hands.'

I rubbed my eyes. For fuck's sake, dude, do not cry.

'Callum?'

I looked up, realised it was Mischa who'd spoken. She seemed genuinely worried about me. I felt bad then. For thinking she was unstable. I mean, she clearly was, but that didn't mean she wasn't a decent person. And unlike me she probably hadn't . . . no, don't go there.

'Yeah?'

'I just wanted to say I'm really, really sorry you feel like that. And also, please don't do anything stupid, will you?'

I had to smile at her question.

'Oh, you think I might top myself? Nah, don't worry, I won't do that. Not on fucking purpose anyway. I'm not saying I haven't thought about it. I've thought about it a lot. But I won't. I can't do that to my family. So, no, you don't need to worry about that.'

I closed my eyes, held back the tears until I knew they'd gone. Then I opened them and looked at the others. Fully expecting to see the usual combination of shock and disgust plastered across their faces. But what I saw staring back at me was the exact opposite. And you know what? Jesus fucking Christ, I think I might have felt a little bit better.

# Chapter 16

# Victoria

If I didn't feel bad enough before, I certainly did now. And I was more than a little unsettled by how much I was affected by these stories. Experiences of three people I had known for barely a week. Entire lives devastated by tragedies, the root cause of which I didn't even know.

But far from drawing me closer to them, these brief insights into their lives had pushed me farther away, making me feel even more of an outsider than I had at the start. Because however hard I tried, I simply couldn't identify with what they were saying – they were too brutal in their honesty; too ready to share. Had I ever been that willing, even as a child? Could I contemplate exposing that level of vulnerability? I didn't think so, and the realisation was not an appealing one. Had I ever, truly, felt anything meaningful at all?

I gave myself a mental shake. I was being silly. I knew that I could love and be loved. And I knew that I could be happy – for goodness' sake, I *was* happy. Did it therefore matter that even if I trawled the very depths of my soul, I would never be able to dredge up anything remotely close to the same degree of pain they had displayed in the last 45 minutes? Surely that was a good thing? It meant I was strong. Didn't it?

I knew then what I had to do. I had to be respectful of these poor people and tell them the truth.

'Genevieve, I know it's my turn to speak but I feel like a complete fraud. I apologise if I've led you on in any way. Yes, I experienced what some people would technically term *a bereavement*, but I promise you, I am the same person now as I was before it happened. I feel terrible saying this, especially having listened to what everyone had to say today, and I must add, I think you've all been incredibly brave. I really do. And I applaud your honesty. But I don't think I have a place here. Every one of you deserves better than me.'

Genevieve looked at me carefully, sweeping a handful of curly hair across one shoulder and twisting it into a rope with both hands. As soon as she let it go, it bounced back into its original position, as unkempt and dishevelled as before. Something about it gave me comfort: clearly, I wasn't the only aspect of her life she couldn't exert any proper control over.

I knew she was disappointed in me; that much was clear from her face. I tried not to care, but there was something about her expression – as if I were deliberating withholding the final piece of a complicated jigsaw – that made me feel unexpectedly remorseful. I swallowed and looked down at my lap, twirling my wedding ring round my finger in an effort to regain my composure. I was relieved when, after what felt like an eternity, Genevieve spoke.

'Victoria, I can see you feel very strongly about this. But do you think, maybe, you would be willing to talk about something else? Perhaps your experience has been slightly different to everyone else's, but that doesn't mean you don't deserve to be here. I think you'll find there's a benefit to this process that we can all take away. Only it could be that the path you need to follow is a slightly different one. What do you think?'

I was going to say no. I was going to get up and walk out the room without a backwards glance. But then I thought about what I had – admittedly unwittingly – become a part of. How these people, who didn't know me, had opened up in a way I never had. And I thought to myself then, what if? What if I revealed just a little bit of who I was to them? Gave them something to make them realise that I wasn't shunning this experience because I thought my life was better than theirs.

Far from it. I was shunning this experience because the person for whom I was supposed to be grieving did not deserve a second of my time. Let alone anyone else's.

'What sort of thing would you like me to talk about?' The voice that uttered the words sounded abrupt. I changed tack.

'I'm not very good at discussing my feelings. To anyone. Let alone a group of people I don't know. You might need to give me some guidance.'

'Maybe you could talk about why you think you're like that?' Genevieve asked. Her brown owl-like eyes, unnaturally amplified by the lenses of her glasses, didn't leave my face as I pondered her question. I could tell she really wanted me to do this. I was surprised, to be honest, that she seemed to care quite so much. If she was going to make a go of this profession, she would need to learn to be a great deal more impartial. I decided, however, to give the woman a break.

'Yes, okay, I can do that. I suppose I could blame it on my job, to some extent.'

'In what sense?'

'I work in a very male-orientated world. Not just law, but finance specifically. It's all about money at the end of the day, however much people try to argue otherwise. And it's also a world where, if you want to succeed, you have to take any ounce of compassion you might have, put it in a box and bury it.'

'Are you saying your job made you who you are?'

I thought about it.

'No. If I'm being completely honest with myself, it's not my job that made me that way. The job suited the person I already was.'

'Do you think you could tell us a bit more about that person, Victoria?' Genevieve asked.

Every fibre in my body wanted to tell her to bugger off. But I restrained myself.

'I grew up in a very privileged world. I say "privileged" in the financial sense. Emotionally it was . . . less so. The experience

I told you about last week, about my father taking me flying, that was the only time I can recall any sense of being happy during the whole of my childhood. The rest of it was bloody miserable.'

I paused. Did I want to go on? I didn't, but decided to anyway. It wasn't like I had any loyalty for the person I was talking about.

'My mother was an alcoholic with a very willing line of suitors. I adored my father but he was never around. And then he died on a mission when I was fifteen. I was looked after by staff who, apart from one, came and went as frequently as the seasons. But I learnt to deal with it. I developed a hard skin that grew thicker every year. I also learnt that I was fortunate. I did not experience poverty. I did not go hungry, unless you count the time my mother locked me in a cupboard on a drunken whim and forgot where she'd put the key. I went to an excellent, highly academic school, got perfect grades. Worked out how to make friends in the right places, meaning I could get ahead when I left. But most importantly, I escaped. I got a law degree from Oxford. I found a very highly paid job while I was there that paid for my master's. I met Andrew. We married and I never looked back.'

'I wish I could be like you,' Mischa said, looking at me like I was some kind of divine creation.

I couldn't help but laugh. 'I'm not sure you do, Mischa. Listening to all of you talk has made me realise that the things I thought made me strong are perhaps my failures.'

'Could you explain what you mean by that?' Genevieve asked.

Goodness, would this woman ever let a comment slide? I sighed. In for a penny, in for a pound.

'It meant that I learnt to stifle my emotions before I felt them. The good and the bad. I was brought up to believe that kindness and sympathy were weaknesses. I do feel love, by the way. I do. I love my husband very much. But I am sad to say, if he died tomorrow, I would probably cope. In fact, I know I would. Because that's how my mother made me.'

I looked around the room and smiled. The smile felt like a mask.

'There you go, that's me. An empty husk of a human. No children either, by the way. I couldn't bear the thought of bringing something that innocent into the world. Which was a shame for Andrew. I think he thought that when he married me I would change my mind. But how could I? I knew my mother had no maternal instincts whatsoever. And I was her flesh and blood. Which meant I couldn't guarantee I would love them in the way they deserved.'

The words that came out of my mouth next were uttered almost as an afterthought. 'And in that respect, to answer the second part of your question, Genevieve, it's very easy for me to tell you how I felt after my experience of bereavement. And I say this to you all with one hundred per cent conviction. I felt absolutely nothing at all.'

# Chapter 17

# Mischa

We sat for ages, not saying anything. Then Genevieve spoke.

'I firstly wanted to say thank you. I hope you all found some benefit from today. It's a long road, I know. What you have been through – and I appreciate that your experiences are completely different – means the healing process isn't quick or easy. But I want you to know that you've already begun a journey, whether you intended to or not, and you can either turn around now and go back to where you started, or you can take a risk and carry on. It may not feel like the end is in sight right now, but I want to reassure you that there is an end.'

*She has a very soothing voice, don't you think?*

'I love your positivity,' Freya said. 'I wish I could absorb some of that.'

'Remember, Freya, you've only had two sessions and already I see an improvement. In all of you, believe it or not. But I need you to make a pact with yourselves not to give up.'

Genevieve looked over at Victoria, who was doing a great job of messing about with her bag and pretending she wasn't listening. 'And Victoria, that applies equally to you.'

'Does it?'

'Yes, it does. You may think the event that brought you here has no relevance to what we're doing, but that's not true. But perhaps whatever it is you need to be rid of lies deeper beneath the surface. There is a reason you're here, I'm certain. You may not accept that, I am asking you to believe in me.'

'You really think you can help us in a few sessions?' Freya said. 'I thought therapy took years.'

'True. But I also told you when you agreed to take part that this wasn't what I would term a conventional therapeutic process.'

'Fuck. This isn't some kind of cult recruitment programme, is it?' Callum said.

Genevieve laughed. 'No, I can assure you this has absolutely *nothing* to do with religion.'

'Good. Because you were starting to give me Charles Manson vibes.'

I had no idea who Charles Manson was but laughed with the others anyway.

'Is it safe to say then that everyone is happy to come back next Tuesday at 7 p.m. for session three?' Genevieve said. 'There's quite a lot I would like us to work through, and I'm sure you all know that the subject matter is going to be harder for you next time. There's nothing I can do about that, unfortunately; we were always going to get there eventually. And I think you're ready, I really do.'

*Do you think you're ready, Mischa?*

I nodded. And one by one, the others said yes too. Even Victoria, although I wasn't sure her heart was in it. Not sure Genevieve thought so either, because Victoria was the only person she looked at the whole time she was talking. I got up from my chair and grabbed my scarf. I was going to ask Genevieve if I could use her toilet but suddenly a weird buzzing noise sounded from somewhere. Genevieve looked back and, for some reason, seemed annoyed.

'I should probably sort that. Would you mind letting yourselves out?'

I nodded, but as the others headed for the door, I decided she wouldn't mind me nipping to the loo. I turned around and ran back down the corridor, finding the toilet and peeing as quickly as I could. Hopefully I could get out without having to say goodbye again. I hated saying goodbye twice. Felt super awkward.

I had a weird feeling. Like I'd overstayed my welcome at a party. What if Genevieve was talking to another patient? I tried hard as I could to tune out what she was saying but as I walked past the door she'd gone through I realised she hadn't shut it properly.

'Yes, everything's going well so far which is good . . . No, nothing major to report – I told you last week I would check in with you if there was. I'm hoping we'll get more done during the session next week. No, of course I haven't. But there's still time. Yes, I know I need to work that part through. You don't need to worry.'

I walked as quietly as I could towards the front door and let myself out.

The others were chatting on the landing, still waiting for the ancient lift to arrive. I was just about to tell them what I'd overheard but then Callum asked a question out of nowhere and it threw me completely. Made me forget all about Genevieve, in fact.

'Don't s'pose you lot fancy coming to mine for a drink?'

# Chapter 18

# Freya

I wasn't sure this kind of thing was allowed – fraternising outside of the therapy sessions. But when was the last time I'd done anything other than sit at home, feeling lost and lonely and miserable?

'Sure, why not?' I said. 'I'd love a glass of wine after all that. Do you have any?'

This was totally unlike me. I didn't go out for drinks with people. Definitely not unplanned ones anyway. And definitely not with men like Callum.

It wasn't like I even really drank. A glass of champagne on special occasions. An Aperol spritz here and there. But certainly not drinking like my university friends used to. In fact, thinking about it, I wasn't even sure I'd ever been properly drunk. The thought of letting myself go, even for a second, had always been too daunting. Why was I so boring? In light of everything that had happened, my obsession with self-control felt stupid. The old me was starting to make the current me feel sick.

'Is that a serious fucking question? Of course I do. Anyone else?'

I saw Mischa look at Victoria. Victoria would definitely say no. And if she did, I thought Mischa probably would too.

'I could murder a G and T. Do you have any decent gin in that apartment of yours?'

'Got a fully stocked bar in the lounge – pretty sure there's some gin in there. Mischa – you coming too? Full house?'

'Alright,' she replied. 'That would be nice.'

'Perfect. Rob's downstairs with the car. We can all fit if none of you drove.'

Five minutes later, I found myself climbing into a massive black car with windows you couldn't see into. I'd never seen anything like it. It didn't even look like a car. It looked like a living room on wheels.

What would I have done if Victoria and Mischa had both said no to the invite? Would I seriously have gone back to the apartment of a guy who everyone knew had a terrible reputation when it came to almost everything? Not that he would have been interested in me in that way, dressed as I was in a saggy pair of leggings and a faded navy hoodie. But Joe would've gone mad. Or at least the old Joe would have done. I doubted the new Joe would even notice I wasn't home.

I glanced at the others as we drove through the back streets of west London. Victoria was chatting easily, something that seemed to come naturally to her now we'd left Genevieve's flat. She couldn't have looked more confident and assured, leaning forward to speak to Callum from the passenger seat, her huge diamond ring and wedding band glittering on her finger as she gestured around the car. I looked behind me at Mischa, sitting in the second row of seats by herself, her forehead pressed against the glass, staring out. She reminded me of a small child going on her first family holiday. All she was missing was a chocolate-stained face and an iPad.

The car slowed down outside a pair of black wrought-iron gates and drove into the cobbled courtyard of what looked like a converted warehouse. The driver pulled up outside the main entrance and stopped.

'Here we are. Home sweet home.' Callum jumped out his side and jogged round to open the passenger door. One by one he let us all out, offering Mischa his hand as she clambered out from the back.

We went into the building and walked past the concierge desk.

'Evening, Jonathan,' Callum said, nodding at an old guy in a suit who barely even looked up. We traipsed past him to the lift door and I watched as Callum punched in a code on a little pad directly below the call button.

'1234. I mean, what the fuck? This place is supposed to be top-level security and they can't even be arsed to come up with a decent code for the lift.'

'At least it means you can't forget it,' Victoria said.

'That, Victoria, is a very valid point.'

Seconds later we filed out onto a vast landing, entirely empty except for a framed Banksy on one wall and a single heavyset oak front door. Clearly the penthouse. Callum rummaged in his pocket, found a set of keys and let us in.

'Go ahead,' he said. 'Make yourselves at home.'

I looked around, interested to see the kind of place someone as wealthy as Callum would live in. I wasn't disappointed. Directly in front of us was a gigantic open-plan kitchen and living room – easily three times as big as the ground floor of my house. I took in the exposed brick and bare piping, the polished concrete floor; the matte metal kitchen. Although it was bang on trend and must have cost a fortune to decorate, for some reason it was not somewhere I would have pictured someone like Callum living. It was too clinical and cold; the only sign of human life being a small carton of milk on the kitchen counter.

'Man, I hate this place,' said Callum, confirming my suspicions. 'It reminds me of a prison.'

'Then why on earth do you live here?' Victoria asked. 'If you think it's that awful?'

He shrugged. 'That's a good question. I've no fucking idea. Anyway, grab a seat.'

We dutifully filed over to the living area, Mischa and I taking the soft leather sofa into which we both promptly sank, and Victoria selecting a much firmer-looking upholstered armchair on the other side. She gingerly lowered herself onto it as though she were afraid it might eat her, then discovering herself to be safe, relaxed and crossed her legs.

Callum meanwhile, had wandered back to the kitchen where we could hear him crashing about behind the vast island. He reappeared moments later holding an ice bucket and four glasses. Then he looked over at us and grinned like a schoolboy.

'Now I don't know about you,' he said. 'But I feel like getting absolutely wasted.'

# Chapter 19

# Callum

How many had I had? I'd no fucking idea. Not loads. The fact I was even trying to remember was a good sign. Needed to rein it in though, otherwise it could end up getting really fucking messy. Thank God Skye had erased my phone contacts. Used to have my dealer on speed dial and I definitely didn't want to go there.

The apartment was full of women laughing, something I hadn't heard in a long time. Mischa was telling a story about some guy who'd called her up at work, accusing her of stealing his cat. Turned out she was quite funny after a couple of drinks.

She finished her story and her glass of wine at about the same time. Then she hiccupped loudly and covered her mouth with her hand. Fuck, was she about to be sick?

'Callum?'

'Hmm?'

The fact she was slurring probably wasn't a great sign.

'I think I should probably go home now. Do you know where the nearest bus stop is?'

I got up from the sofa. 'Don't be stupid, Rob'll take you. He's on the clock til midnight.'

'Is that alright?'

''Course. He's probably bored out of his fucking mind down there.'

Mischa got up – way too fast – then lost her balance, landing smack on her arse. She looked a bit shocked for a second and then started laughing. 'Oops. Looks like I can't stand up.'

'Mischa, you know what?' I watched as Victoria glided out of her chair – did that woman ever do anything awkwardly? – and held out her hand to Mischa. 'I should probably make a move, too. Otherwise Andrew will be wondering what the devil I'm doing. We can go together. Would that be okay, Callum?'

'Yup, of course, I'll take you down now. Freya – wanna stay for one more?'

She looked uncertain. I wasn't sure why, but I suddenly felt a desperate urge to keep her in the room.

'It'd be rude not to finish the bottle,' I added before she could tell me she was leaving too. 'Rob can easily do a second trip.'

She looked down at her wine glass. It was still half full. I thanked the fact I'd remembered to top her up while Mischa was telling her story.

'Sure, why not? If Rob really won't mind.'

'Great.'

I turned to Victoria and Mischa, noticing Mischa was now swaying quite a bit. I thought about offering her some water, but then realised I really wanted her out the apartment. 'Come on then, you two, let's go.'

I waited while everyone hugged each other goodbye – why did women always feel the need to do that? – then walked Victoria and Mischa out the front door and down in the lift to where Rob was parked in the underground carpark. I ran ahead to open the car door and helped Mischa as she half climbed, half fell into the back seat. Jesus Christ, she was battered. She crashed across all three seats, then closed her eyes and hugged her feet into her chest. Brilliant, guaranteed vomit right there.

'Will she be alright?' I asked Victoria, knowing the answer was unlikely to be yes, but hoping to God Victoria didn't change her mind about taking her home.

Victoria, however, seemed completely chilled about the situation.

'I'll keep an eye on her, don't worry. Do you have anything she can be sick in?'

'Erm, check the glove compartment. There might be a carrier bag in there.'

'Thanks, Callum. And thank you also for a very pleasant evening. I've had a lovely time.'

'Me too.'

I felt a sudden flash of guilt. 'You know what – take my number. Message to let me know you both get back okay.'

Victoria smiled. 'I never knew you cared.'

'What can I say? It happens every now and then.'

Victoria handed me her phone and I added my number to her contacts. She looked at it briefly, typed something in and put it back in her bag. Then she leant in to kiss me on both cheeks, her gaze lingering in front of my face as she pulled away. Was it me, or was she trying it on? Maybe giving her my number had made her think I was interested.

Was I interested? Maybe. There was something about her that was really fucking sexy. She was definitely a woman who knew what she wanted. I liked that about her. And I'd bet a million quid she was rocket fuel in bed.

But something was holding me back. I wasn't sure what – the old Callum wouldn't have given a flying fuck by this point. He'd have given it a stab, even if it meant getting kneed in the balls. Maybe I was growing sensible in my old age? Or maybe I had something else on my mind. Who fucking knew. Didn't matter now anyway – Victoria was already in the front seat waving me goodbye.

I turned round and walked back towards the lift, shouting out to Rob as I left to make sure he dropped Mischa off first; she was already snoring.

# Chapter 20

# Freya

The first bottle of wine hadn't lasted long, and we were now working our way steadily through a second. I hadn't touched a drop of alcohol in months, and I knew I was drunk.

But I felt good. Great, in fact. I think I'd been worried that drinking would bring back too many memories. But to my relief it was having the opposite effect – it was helping to blank them out entirely.

'Tell me more about yourself, Freya.'

We'd been chatting about nothing of any substance up to that point, the conversation flowing without me really having to think. It turned out we were actually quite similar – we liked the same food (spicy), films (Quentin Tarantino) and even music (not his). But I'd lied when I told him I didn't listen to his albums. He probably knew that. Everyone under the age of 40 listened to Callum Raven's albums.

'What's left to say? I think I've told you everything already.'

'Okay, how about we start with: have you always been this uptight?'

'Callum! I am not uptight!' I tried to look offended, but failed miserably and started giggling. 'Well, maybe I am a little bit.'

'You've got a nice laugh. For an uptight person.'

I threw a cushion at him. 'For your information, being uptight restricts the vocal cords. It helps to give you a sexy laugh.'

'Maybe I should give it a go. It might help with my singing.'

'I don't think you could be uptight if you tried.'

He was staring at me intently, his head cocked to one side, waiting for me to carry on speaking. Had he moved an inch or two closer on the sofa, or was I imagining it? And should I move away? I knew I probably should, but something was stopping me. Instead, I inhaled until my lungs were full, appreciating the woody scent of his aftershave as it hit the back of my nostrils. It smelt manly. And expensive.

'I don't know. I suppose I've never been very good at letting go. I'm not really sure why. Whenever I've thought about doing something a bit wild, I've always worried about the end result. What if I do it wrong? What if I make a fool out of myself? What if I hurt myself? What if, what if, what if. Stupid stuff.'

'It's not stupid. It's called self-preservation. I could do with more of that.'

'You're welcome to have some of mine if you want.'

I took another large gulp of wine, savouring the acidic taste of it on my tongue. God, it tasted good.

'Okay,' I said. 'Your turn. Tell me why you're irresponsible.'

He sighed dramatically. 'Who told you I was irresponsible?'

'Not that I believe everything I read in the papers, but some of the photos I've seen of you are quite incriminating.'

'Are you talking about the time I jumped off that yacht?'

'Nope. I was thinking about the time you abseiled down that drainpipe.'

'Jeez, I'd forgotten about that. That's not being irresponsible. That's being a fucking prick.'

I laughed. It sounded way louder than I meant it to, and I was suddenly conscious of the silence of the room. The music we'd been playing when Victoria and Mischa were here seemed to have stopped. How long ago was that? An hour ago, maybe two?

'You really do have a great laugh. Here, have some more wine and we'll see if we can make it any throatier.'

I held out my glass and he tilted the bottle, the liquid inside pouring out too fast and spilling over the side. I was conscious of a few cold droplets splattering on my hand and running down my arm, seeping into the material of my top.

'Sorry,' he said, taking hold of my wrist and casually wiping off the excess liquid with his thumb. 'You make me nervous.'

'I doubt that. You're avoiding the question, by the way.'

'What question? Oh yeah. You distracted me. Right. Why am I irresponsible? I don't have a fucking clue. I'm the youngest of two brothers. A psychologist would tell you that means I'm an attention-seeker. I'm a Leo. An astrologer would tell you that makes me naturally reckless. But other than that kind of bullshit excuse, I don't know. I like taking risks. I like the feeling I get from it. That rush when you come close to danger, and you don't know what's about to happen. Whether you've made the right decision or not. I love that.'

'That speech gave me palpitations.'

'Did it? Sorry. Probably not a great time to suggest a ride on my Triumph then?'

'I'd say no even if you hadn't had five beers and nearly a bottle of wine.'

'Wow, you've been keeping count?'

'It's what uptight people do.'

'You need to sort that out. It's seriously off-putting.' He looked at me thoughtfully. 'In fact, can I show you something?'

I wasn't sure this was a good idea.

'Er . . . okay.'

'Follow me.'

He jumped to his feet and hauled me up alongside him, grabbing both our glasses between the fingers of his spare hand. Then, my hand still in his, he led me over to the other side of the kitchen.

'Where are we going?'

He didn't answer. He simply let go of my hand, put our drinks down on the counter, and began a brief wrestle with a large bay window in front of us. After a few failed attempts, he eventually managed to open it about a metre.

'What are you doing?'

Again he ignored the question. I watched, thoroughly confused, as he hitched a leg onto the windowsill, pulled himself up with both arms and promptly disappeared outside.

'Pass the drinks, would you?' said a voice from the dark.

I peered out of the gap. He was standing two feet lower than the window, on what appeared to be a small metal fire escape. My heart started beating loudly in my chest, the sound of it echoing in my ears.

'Are you kidding me? I'm not getting on that.'

'Trust me, baby cakes, I got this.' He bounced on the rickety iron frame and I felt my stomach turn over. 'It goes all the way from top to bottom. C'mon, join me. You'll be fine.'

I thought about it, tempted to tell him to abandon his plan and come back inside. But then, feeling a rush of confidence that could only have come from the alcohol, I grabbed the two glasses, passed them to him and climbed out.

A minute later, we were standing one storey up on the roof of his apartment building. A roof that was definitely not designed for human habitation in any way, shape or form. Apart from the fact that someone had built a small wooden den on it, complete with decking, a large battered beanbag and a heavy-duty guitar case that had seen better days.

'Are we even allowed to be here?'

I tilted my head. The sky around me felt enormous, an endless expanse of black desert in a starless sky. It was kind of depressing: I felt like I never saw stars anymore. My attention was caught by the sound of a car horn; people laughing at a distance; a bottle smashing against a kerb. More laughter. I followed the sounds towards the edge of the building, boldly placing a foot on the cold hard ridge of the roof before feeling dizzy as I realised how easy it would be to fall. The sensation made me stumble backwards, but two arms caught me and lowered me onto the beanbag.

'Wow, you're drunker than I thought.'

'No shit, Sherlock. It's your fault, you know.'

'I know. I'd like to say it was an accident, but it wasn't.'

He threw himself down next to me on the slightly damp material, our combined weight forcing our legs together. I tried to ignore how close we were and leant back, staring up at the night sky. Wishing for a single star.

'So,' I said, as casually as I could. 'Is this where you bring all the girls?'

Callum snorted. 'No. Believe it or not, you're the first.'

'I don't believe that for a second.'

He turned towards me, propping himself up on his elbow. 'No, I really haven't. Funnily enough, when I want to have sex with a girl, it's a damn sight more convenient to take her to my bedroom.'

I smiled at him, feeling strangely disappointed by the remark. 'Then why did you bring me up here?'

'Because I wanted to see your reaction.'

'Oh . . . okay. It's cool. I like it. You could do a lot more with this space though, you know.'

'Maybe you could redesign it for me.'

'Maybe I could. Why didn't you want to show it to the others?'

'No offence to either of them, but Victoria would have thrown a hissy fit. And Mischa would've probably fallen off.'

I giggled. 'Yes, I think you're probably right.'

We fell into silence, savouring what little remained of our drinks.

'Is this where you play?'

'Sometimes. Not as much anymore.'

'How come?'

'I haven't felt much like playing in a long time.'

'Because of what happened?' I felt bold asking the question. We were straying into new territory.

He sighed. 'Kind of. But not entirely.'

'What do you mean?'

He went quiet, suddenly preoccupied with a thread of cotton on the knee of his jeans.

'Let's just say my best material came from a happier place. I'm not sure I've been happy for a while.'

'Why didn't you try to get help sooner?'

He stared at his hands. 'Because I prefer to find the answers to life's questions at the bottom of a bottle of wine, evidently.'

I sloshed the last inch of liquid around my glass, staring at it as it ran up the sides and then drained slowly back down again. 'I'm starting to see the appeal.'

'Don't let me corrupt you, Freya.'

I looked across at him. Something about his manner suggested he was only half-joking. I felt the need to lighten the mood. I wasn't in the right place for dark thoughts.

'Don't worry,' I replied. 'I have better things to do with my time than be corrupted by you.'

'Really?' he said, pretending to be surprised. 'Like what?'

'Oh, you know. Sleeping. Cleaning the house. Staying true to my boring uptight nature.'

He laughed. 'I think I need to hang around with you more often.'

'Ha. I have to warn you, I'm quite dull nowadays.'

'Yes, you are.'

I responded by hitting him on the shoulder.

'But I feel like you're good for my soul.' He gestured at my glass. 'D'you want a top-up? I can go grab us another bottle.'

'No thanks. I probably shouldn't.'

I looked out over the rooftop at the twinkling lights of the city beyond, feeling the strange sensation that we were the only people alive. Then I glanced over at the guitar case, propped up against a sad-looking pot plant. It felt wrong to ask but the wine in my belly had brought back a self-assurance I'd forgotten I had.

'Would you play something for me?'

He eyed me cautiously. Then looked at the guitar. He appeared to be weighing something up in his mind. 'Would you like me to?'

'I wouldn't have asked if I didn't.'

'You know if I play for you, you'll want to have sex with me?'

I rolled my eyes. 'I think I'm willing to take that risk, Casanova.'

He sighed. 'That's what they all say.'

He stood up and went over to the guitar case, laying it down on the floor as he slowly unclipped the fastenings. He threw back the top, revealing an acoustic guitar nestled in velvet lining. He carefully took it out and then returned, sitting cross-legged on the decking in front of me. He strummed a few chords and winced. 'Shit, it's seriously out of tune. Give me a second.'

I rearranged myself in the middle of the beanbag, sweeping my legs to one side. Something about the moment was making me feel young and giddy. Like a teenager drunk for the first time. Callum finished tuning and looked up at me expectantly. 'What do you want me to play?'

My mind went blank, the haze of alcohol erasing the memory of every song I knew. Then I had a flash of inspiration. 'Play me something you haven't played for anyone else.'

He looked at me, a bit too sharply. 'Then I've only got one song. But I'm not sure I can play that.'

'Why not?'

'Because I wrote it after . . . you know.'

'Oh right. Don't worry then,' I said quickly, feeling a rush of guilt. 'Play something else. Play whatever you want.'

He stared at me, studying my face as if trying to satisfy himself about something. Then he looked back at the guitar, strummed a couple of chords and without any warning, started to sing.

*'I'd give up my life
A thousand times over
Just for a glimpse of your face.
Time would be cheated
Death's plan defeated
To grant me one stolen embrace . . .'*

I watched his fingers skimming over the strings of the instrument with the assurance of someone who no longer had to think while they played. Yet while his fingers knew exactly what to do, I felt as though his mind did not, his features forced into a look of concentration I was sure had more to do with masking the strength of feeling that lay behind it than any difficulty remembering the song.

*'. . . All I can taste is that moment
All I recall is that day
Existence so fleeting
Quickly retreating
And Heaven's so far far away . . .'*

*All I recall is that day.* His words hit me then like a tsunami. I felt a blockage form in my chest, clogging my ability to breathe. Memories I had spent all evening pushing to one side came rushing back and for a moment all I wanted was to launch myself off the edge of that roof and disappear into the abyss beyond. I forced myself to return to the song, to him, reminding myself that these were his words, his story, and not mine.

*'And I'm dying inside
From wounds I can't nurse
I'm dying inside*

*My life now a curse.
I'm dying inside
Dying inside.
Dying from you.'*

And with that, he reached the end of the song. In the silence that followed, after the wind had carried the final notes into the air, I felt as if the universe had been laid bare in front of me. I'd spent the last six months believing that no one else could understand the pain I was going through. But I was wrong. As the tears fell down my face, I drank in the essence of Callum as he crouched in front of me, his hands still frozen in place on the strings, his thoughts somewhere else entirely. At that moment, I didn't see a famous musician or a shameless flirt. I saw an ordinary guy, part-dissolved by his own suffering. He hadn't cried. He hadn't needed to. His pain had been exposed by the words of that song. A song he had sung for me.

I got up from where I was sitting, took the guitar away from him and placed it gently down on the floor beside us. Then propelled by a sudden desperation to extinguish the sadness in both of us, I took his face in my hands and I kissed him.

# Chapter 21

# Mischa

I woke up with a pounding head in a bedroom that smelt of lavender. For a minute I thought I'd died and gone to heaven. Then I had a flashback from the night before. Callum's apartment. Me telling stupid stories. Victoria saying she'd take me home. Then nothing. *Ohhhh godddddd.*

I sat up slowly, rubbing my eyes.

*It's no wonder you feel bad; you don't drink.*

I looked over at the little table by my bed. Someone had left me some water and two pills. I shoved them into my mouth and downed the contents of the glass. Then I took two deep breaths, pulled myself up and went downstairs.

At first, I couldn't see anyone. Then I looked to my left. Who the hell was that?! There was a man sitting in the lounge, eating toast and reading the paper. Oh my God – had I gone home with someone I didn't know? Where had I met him? I was sure I remembered getting in Callum's car. Yeah, it was all a bit foggy, but I had no idea how I could've met some random old guy and ended up at his house. Was it Callum's driver? It couldn't be. The house was too posh.

'Good morning, Mischa,' said the man. 'Grab yourself a seat. Victoria is in the shower.'

Thank *God*.

I sat down as slowly as I could and tried my best to smile. I must've looked like crap. I put my head in my hands and groaned.

'Golly, are you okay? You poor thing. Is there anything I can do?'

'No, I'm sorry. I'm okay. Honestly. I just need the pills to start working. I'm so sorry.'

The man smiled at me. 'Don't think anything of it, my dear. I know what it's like to have one too many. Been quite a while though, I must admit. Can't say I miss it either. Here, let me pour you a nice cup of tea. I'm Andrew, by the way. Victoria's husband.'

So, this was Andrew. I hadn't really thought about what Victoria's husband might look like. If I had, I would've probably gone for tall, tanned and sporty. The man in front of me was tall. But he also had grey hair and glasses. He looked like someone's dad, not the husband of the most glamorous woman I'd ever met.

'I'm not what you expected, am I?'

'No. I mean, yeah. I mean, I hadn't really thought about it.'

'You wouldn't be the first, you know. Every time I go to one of Victoria's work shindigs I get asked who I'm there with. No one can ever quite believe it when I say Victoria.'

*Be polite, disagree with him.*

'Actually, she's very nice about you at our sessions. She must like you.' I cringed. What a stupid thing to say.

'Is she? I'm surprised. She blames me for making her go.'

*Yes, you're right, she does.*

'She's never said that.'

I was sure he knew I was lying. I was a terrible liar. Even when I didn't have a headache.

'That's good to hear. Can I offer you some toast? It will make you feel better.'

'I don't know if I can eat anything.'

'How about a bacon sandwich? I've never known anyone, even with a stonking hangover, to turn down a bacon sandwich.'

My tummy rumbled loudly. I felt myself go red.

'That answers it then. I'll be back in a jiffy. Red or brown sauce?'

'Red please.'

'Righty-ho. Do help yourself to more tea.'

Seconds later, I heard the sound of bacon frying from across the hall. I drank my tea a sip at a time, looking into Victoria's back garden. It was so pretty. A massive lawn with a brick wall all the way round. And flowers everywhere. We couldn't be in London. No one had a garden that big in London.

Andrew came back in, putting two of the world's biggest sandwiches down in front of us. Mine smelt amazing. Thick as a brick with loads of butter and ketchup. And so much bacon. He must've used a whole packet. I picked it up in two hands and took a big bite.

'This is amazing,' I said, catching a dollop of ketchup on my finger as it escaped from the sandwich and ran down my chin.

'Thank you. Maybe you can see now why Victoria married me.'

I laughed. He was such a lovely man. I felt myself relax. 'Thank you very much for letting me sleep over. I never drink. It must've gone to my head.'

'Please don't worry about it. It's nice to have a guest to stay. I don't think Victoria's ever brought anyone home before. It seems a shame to have guest rooms that never get used.'

His comment made me feel warm and tingly. It'd been a while since someone had been this nice to me. Come to think of it, it had been a while since I'd even had a *conversation* with someone, other than in Genevieve's sessions.

We went quiet as we ate our breakfasts. When I finished, I licked my fingers to get every last bit of sauce off. I doubted I'd ever eat anything that good ever again. I noticed then that Andrew was staring at me.

'Mischa, may I ask you something?'

'Yeah, course.'

'How do you think Victoria is getting on?'

The question threw me. Part of me wanted to tell him that she'd been ever so good at the last session. Telling us stuff about her childhood that I didn't think she would've told us before in a million years. But I felt bad telling Andrew that. I thought about what Victoria would say if she were asked the same question.

'She's definitely opened up a bit. Why don't you ask her yourself?'

'I have, believe me. Several times. But you know what Victoria's like. Doesn't much like to communicate her feelings.'

He suddenly looked very tired. He pushed his hand up under his glasses to rub his eyes. 'Mischa, I don't expect you to tell me what goes on in your sessions. Clearly that's private and I'm glad, to be honest, that Victoria is even going. But if I could ask a small favour of you, I would be very appreciative.'

'Okay.'

'What happened to Victoria has affected her more than she makes out. She pretends she doesn't care, but she does. Perhaps next week, if you get the chance to reassure her, encourage her to tell you all what happened. I think it would do her the world of good.'

*Ask him what he means.*

'I'll do my best,' I said.

'Thank you, Mischa.'

A noise on the stairs brought the chat to an end. Seconds later, Victoria came into the room, looking *amazing* in a white woolly dress and knee boots. I looked down at my old jeans and wrinkly T-shirt, the front of it stained with a big blob of ketchup. I tried to cover it up so she wouldn't see.

'Andrew, I hope you didn't use up all the bread. I am in dire need of some refined carbohydrates. And a strong double macchiato.'

Andrew smiled and left the room. He came back with another massive bacon sandwich. And what looked like the world's smallest coffee. He put it down in front of Victoria and kissed her on the forehead. She grabbed his hand and kissed it back.

He looked at me and winked. 'I told you that's why she loves me.'

# Chapter 22

# Callum

I could feel a laser beam of daylight boring into my face like a hot needle. I'd forgotten to close the fucking blinds.

I sat up, scraping my hair back and opened one eye, like a rodent coming out of hibernation. Result – I felt alright. Ish. But just as I was about to climb out of bed and go for a piss, I realised someone was lying next to me. Fuck. Freya. I'd forgotten she'd stayed.

My gut reaction was to panic. There was a reason I never let girls stay over – you couldn't get rid of them. But worse than that, they were way too into that post-shag analysis shit. Obsessed with talking about what the night before had *meant*. When all you wanted them to do was help out with your morning glory and go straight home. But then I remembered: we hadn't had sex. Thank fuck. I collapsed back down onto the pillow with a thud and waited for my heart rate to go back to normal.

Seeing Freya was still asleep, I turned towards her and took a good long look at her face, in the sort of way you can only really get away with when the person you are staring at is flat out, unconscious. It felt a bit seedy, watching her like that, my head two inches from hers. But I wanted to see what she really looked like. If only for a moment, before she woke up, caught me staring and twatted me.

I'd always had this weird idea that you needed to look at someone when they were sleeping to see what sort of person they were. Sleep strips you of everything – insecurities, emotions, regrets, life. The second you close your eyes and drift off, that stuff evaporates from your face like vapour on a flaming sambuca. If you're ever unsure if you can trust someone, take a good look at them while they're sleeping.

It turned out Freya was beautiful. Not beautiful like Victoria was beautiful. She wasn't wearing a scrap of make-up for a start and her blonde hair was all over the fucking show. But when I looked at her asleep, the sadness evaporated and you could see the woman she was meant to be. A natural beauty, that's what Mum would've said. I wanted to take a picture of her. But I held off for obvious reasons – I wasn't a perv and besides, the last time I'd done that I'd ended up getting slapped. Turns out girls expect you to tell them before you take a picture of them sleeping. Especially if you post it on Instagram.

I rolled onto my back and thought about the night before. I'd been completely caught up in that song, I hadn't even seen it coming. I knew I'd been giving her the come-on all night, but to be honest that's just what I was like. I hadn't in my wildest imagination thought she would act on it. Which meant there I was, wrapped up in my own miserable little world full of grief and self-pity, feeling like my heart was about to crack open, when Freya had appeared from nowhere and straddled me.

And fuck, she was a great kisser. I wasn't really a kissing type of guy. Maybe because I'd spent the last few years permanently coked up, even wanking had felt like a chore. It was maybe the first proper kiss I'd had with a girl since I was a teenager. But it wasn't just the kiss. It was what lay behind it. Like everything Freya had been through had been locked up and forced into that moment. Hitting me like a nuclear warhead. And I knew exactly what she meant by it. Because I felt it too. The sheer shittiness of having your life ripped away from you, turned upside down by a single event that you couldn't reverse and could never fucking forget.

Without thinking I'd grabbed her round her waist and kissed her back, the taste of wine and salty tears on her tongue sparking something I didn't know I could still feel.

I vaguely remembered pushing her onto the beanbag. Pulling off her trainers and leggings. Feeling a pair of ballerina-like legs wrap themselves round my hips with a strength that surprised me. Staring at her hands as they messed about with the metal clasp on my belt, the end of it whipping me hard across the stomach as she got it free. Me launching my body forward before she had a chance to do anything else, grabbing a handful of her hair in one hand and cupping her jaw in another, absorbing the excited moan which came out of her mouth as I pressed my lips hard against hers. Kissing the entire top half of her body, then clocking the angry scar and kissing that too. Trying my fucking hardest not to pull her pants off with my mouth, even though both her body and the sounds she was making were giving me every signal she wanted me to. I don't think I'd ever wanted anyone as much in my life.

But then, completely fucking unexpectedly, something had stopped me. I still had no idea what it was. All I knew was that I didn't want to shag her on that grotty beanbag, on the freezing cold roof of my soulless penthouse apartment. She didn't deserve that. And she definitely didn't deserve me.

As quickly as I'd launched in, I'd pulled away, seeing the shock on her face as I did. 'I'm sorry, I can't do this.'

The look she'd given me had hit me like a bullet in the chest. I almost backtracked. But by then the moment was lost. She pushed herself away from me and stood up, pulling her top back over her head and retrieving her trousers from the floor. Swaying as she bent down to put them back on.

'I should probably go home. Can you show me back downstairs?'

She was formal, polite, nothing like the Freya I'd been talking to minutes earlier. It felt like a fucking lifetime had passed. I waited while she put her shoes on, seeing her hands shake as she tied the laces, then helped her off the roof and onto the fire escape. She walked carefully down without once looking back and disappeared into the kitchen.

As I climbed through the window and pulled it shut, I wondered to myself what the hell I'd just done. But I knew I didn't have a choice. The thought of letting another person into my life who I could fuck up all over again was too much.

She was sitting on the sofa, her legs hugged into her chest. She looked up at me as I came over. 'I'm sorry. I shouldn't have done that. I don't know what came over me.'

I collapsed next to her, every fibre in my body, my crotch in particular, wanting to grab her again and pick up where we'd left off. 'You don't have to apologise.' I let the silence linger for a little longer. 'I did tell you if I sang to you that you'd want to have sex with me.'

She laughed, thank God, and gave me a small nudge in the ribs.

'I'm joking.' I said. 'It's my fault. I wanted you to kiss me. I mean shit, I pulled out all my best moves to get you to do it. And I got you fucking wasted. It's me who should be apologising to you.'

'Why did you pull away then?'

'I don't know. I'm not in a good place right now, Freya. And neither are you. If we rushed into something, one of us would get hurt. And let's face it, based on my track record with women, it would probably be you.'

'Don't flatter yourself, Callum Raven.'

'I didn't mean it to sound like that.' I fumbled with the belt hook of my jeans, aware that it had been a very long time since I'd felt the need to explain myself to a woman. But for some reason I really wanted to.

'I'm just trying to say that I like you. And I feel like we actually understand each other. You're probably the first girl I've bonded with in years. Maybe ever. But as much as I wanted to rip your fucking clothes off on that dirty beanbag and do all kinds of things that I probably shouldn't say out loud, I just can't. I can't risk breaking you. I'm falling apart enough as it is.'

'You're friend-zoning me, aren't you?'

'Yes, I'm friend-zoning you.'

'Right. Okay.'

We sat in silence for a bit. I felt surprisingly comfortable around her, considering what had happened.

'I do understand, you know,' she said. 'I guess I was trying to be irresponsible for once. It clearly doesn't suit me.'

'Under normal circumstances I would have encouraged it. Especially if I liked you a bit less.'

She laughed and leant against me, her head on my shoulder. 'Callum?'

'Yeah?'

'This is going to sound like a weird question but could I stay over? I don't really want to go home.'

The sense of warmth I felt from her request threw me off guard. It occurred to me it was also the first time I'd ever said yes to a girl sleeping over in the full knowledge that sex was off the table.

'Sure. I'll sleep on the couch. You can have the bed.'

'Would it be okay if . . . if you slept next to me? I promise I won't jump on you in the night or anything. I just need a bit of physical contact with another human being.'

It felt forward asking the question but I was curious. 'Don't you share a bed with your husband?'

She hesitated a moment before replying.

'Not anymore. Not for quite a long time, actually. We've never spoken about it, but ever since I came back from hospital he's not even come into my bedroom. Or come home at all, some nights. I guess he wanted to give me space. But now it's become the norm. And I don't know how to change that. I'm not sure I want to change it either. It's . . . complicated.'

I didn't feel the need to push her further.

'Come on.'

I got up, held out my hand and showed her to my bedroom. What a fucking pigsty. Fortunately she didn't seem to notice. She got under the duvet and I climbed in behind her, automatically wrapping my arms around her body. I breathed in the smell of her hair. It smelt of coconuts.

'Did you just smell my hair?'

'Yeah, sorry.'

'That's okay.' She sighed, and I felt her body relax against me. I could tell from her breathing that she was almost asleep.

'Thank you, Callum.'

'What for?'

'For being you.'

I was pretty sure no girl had ever said that to me before.

# PART THREE
# BARGAINING

# Chapter 23

# Freya

It had been exactly a week since *the kiss*. During that time, it was basically all I'd thought about. In my defence, I didn't have much else to do. I had no job, no one to look after and a husband who may as well have not existed. He was like a shadow in my life, flitting in and out of the house like an absent relative. Sometimes I wondered if I'd made up our entire marriage.

But the bit I was only recently starting to process was the nature of our relationship before all this had happened. The fact that Joe had decided to sleep in the spare room over a year ago, blaming my insomnia and his early work starts. How we'd slowly stopped going out together, just the two of us, citing a need to save for the house. How we'd blamed the fact that we had no one to look after Barney whenever anyone asked why we'd stopped going on weekends away. But the strangest thing about it all was that neither of us seemed to notice. Or at least it never came up in conversation. Maybe because we were still friends. Or maybe because our focus for so long had been on ticking off the usual marital wish list of life goals, it was easy to overlook the fact that something in the foundation of our relationship had got lost. Or had been missing from the start.

Then, of course, we got blindsided. And while I had a habit of blaming Joe for what happened to us after that awful, awful day, especially when I was angry or tired, in truth it was entirely my fault. I'd refused to talk to him at all for weeks. Or even acknowledge he was there in the early days. It must have been really hard. I'm sure he'd wanted to care for me, share my pain, but I wouldn't let him. And when I was finally ready to face the world again, it was too late – a divide had opened up between us that I hadn't been able to bridge.

I wondered briefly if he was having an affair. He was attractive, sociable, physically fit. I remembered a couple of times I'd gone to his client events and been surprised how many people had come up to me just to tell me what a nice guy he was. He could have found someone else. And I wouldn't have blamed him. I mean, there's only a certain amount of time you can live with someone who doesn't get out of bed and who won't accept your help before deciding that you probably deserve some comforting of your own. Part of me even felt relief at the thought – a human who wasn't me making him happy. It would at least alleviate some of the guilt.

I picked up a magazine from the coffee table and began leafing through the pages in an effort to distract myself. It made me think back to the time when I'd first seen the article *The A to Z of Trauma* in which a few people, including Genevieve, had been interviewed. I'd been doing the exact same thing as I was now – looking for something, anything, to keep me entertained for the few hours of the day when I wasn't eating, sleeping or staring at the wall. I still remembered the exact words that had caught my attention.

**Millennium Magazine**: *Would you say that time really is the best healer?*
**Genevieve**: *No, not at all. Acceptance is. Which obviously takes time, yes. But if you don't accept what's happened to you, all the time in the world can go by and it won't make the slightest bit of difference.*
**Millennium Magazine**: *Surely most people who experience trauma accept what's happened to them?*
**Genevieve**: *I don't mean acceptance in the form of acknowledgement that the event happened. I mean acceptance in the sense of being ready to let go.*

***Millennium Magazine:*** *And how do you help people to reach acceptance?*
***Genevieve:*** *You have to do whatever it takes.*

I'd circled the feature with a pen and left it out on the kitchen table – a silent question to Joe to see what he thought. When I woke up the next day, he'd written two words next to it in capital letters: *EMAIL HER*. It wasn't exactly the kindest of encouragements, but at least I knew what he thought.

And now there was Callum. Callum, with his perfectly chiselled face, cat-like eyes and stupidly floppy hair. Callum with his natural tan and athletic physique and his annoyingly strong arms. I realised with a pang that what I had felt in my few hours with him were things I'd never experienced with Joe, or indeed any guy. What sort of person did that make me? A fucking groupie, clearly.

But that kiss. Christ, that kiss. Not to mention the 30-odd seconds that came after it. It may have meant nothing to him, but it meant something to me. It was obvious Callum hadn't felt the same way about it as I did. He couldn't have been sweeter when it came to letting me down, but he'd still pulled away. He'd still made it clear that it wasn't what he wanted. *I wasn't what he wanted.*

I wasn't sure if this bothered me. My life had at least been simple before. Now it felt horribly complicated.

Wherever my life was going, I knew I had to forget about Callum. He wasn't good for me. He was a drug addict for a start – he'd said that himself. He was reckless and unpredictable. Something had happened to him that had left him scarred and probably mentally unstable. I might not understand a huge amount about human psychology, but I knew enough to know that I, of all people, shouldn't be hurling myself at someone like that.

My mind wandered back, like a yo-yo, from Callum to Joe again. Could I fix my relationship with him? Maybe if I made the first move, there was a chance we could patch things up. The only problem was if that was really what I wanted, wouldn't I have done it already?

I collapsed on the sofa in defeat. I was going round in circles. I needed some proper advice.

Suddenly, I had an idea. I got up, went out into the hallway, found my bag and searched for my phone. And then I called Genevieve.

She picked up on the third ring, greeting me like a long-lost friend.

'Freya, how lovely to hear from you. How are you?'

'I kissed Callum after the last session,' I blurted out. Probably should at least have said *hello* first.

There was a long silence on the end of the line.

'Hello? Are you still there?'

'Yes, I'm still here. Would you like to tell me exactly what happened?'

And I told her. Every detail. It seemed I was getting really good at this whole sharing malarkey. When I'd finished, I felt flushed. Out of breath. Reliving it for those few minutes had made me remember details that I'd previously forgotten. How I'd woken up the next day to find him staring at me. How we'd chatted for an hour in his bedroom, lying on his bed side by side. How he'd made me breakfast (waffles with maple syrup and a strong black coffee) before calling his driver to take me home. How he'd looked at me for a second too long before kissing my cheek as I left.

And then that was it. Zero communication since.

I realised that Genevieve was talking to me.

'Freya. Look, I'll be frank with you. The fact that you all met up outside the session environment is ... unorthodox. And absolutely not something I can endorse professionally. But since it's happened, what I will say is that these types of feelings are completely normal. You've spent a long time with very few encounters with the outside world. You've shied away from physical contact. It's not surprising that the minute you start to open up again you reach out for something or someone to help you. But you have to think carefully about whether or not Callum is the right person to do that. Do you understand what I'm saying?'

'Yes, I do.'

*I didn't.* What came out of my mouth next sounded rehearsed, even by my standards. 'And I know, you're right. I think I needed to hear someone else say it. You don't need to worry anyway. Callum told me he doesn't want things to go any further.'

The tone of Genevieve's voice made me think she didn't believe me either.

'I'm sure that was hard to hear. But give it time, Freya. You're in a fragile place and the last thing you need is to get hurt. You'll make things even tougher for yourself. Are you still okay to come to the session tonight?'

'Yes. I think I'm ready for it now.'

I hung up and stared at my phone. She was right, I knew she was. In which case, why did I feel so heartbroken?

# Chapter 24

# Victoria

The atmosphere between us had changed. On the one hand it was more convivial. We greeted each other with a hug and a kiss. I insisted on two kisses, one on each cheek – if I was to be forced to engage in social niceties, I was going to do things properly.

On the other hand, the room felt strangely charged. I'd initially put it down to the fact that we were all – I assumed – going to be asked to reveal something significant today. But that wasn't the only reason. Something in our dynamic had shifted and I couldn't quite put my finger on it. The lawyer in me was suspicious and intrigued. And absolutely determined to find out what had happened.

I looked around the room, observing its occupants with a well-trained, analytical eye.

Genevieve was exactly the same: friendly, efficient, welcoming. The nerves she had exhibited during our first two sessions seemed to have dissipated – her manner was more relaxed as she moved amongst us, making sure we were settled and comfortable. Even her mane of wild curls had been temporarily tamed – forced within the confines of an orange silk headscarf. (The only thing was, alongside the billowing cream blouse and rust-coloured corduroys, she looked more like a backing singer in a country-and-western band than a professional. She really needed to revisit her wardrobe choices if she ever wanted to be taken seriously.)

Mischa, meanwhile, was also more or less the same: smiling, innocent, verging on unnecessary overexcitement. She even looked like she might have dressed up for the occasion – her usual trainers replaced by a pair of heeled ankle boots. She proceeded to use them to good effect as she kicked her legs against the side of her chair in anticipation. The only one in the room eager to get started.

That left two people: Freya and Callum. I studied them carefully. Callum caught my eye and looked away. That wouldn't have happened previously.

Freya wouldn't look at me at all.

Genevieve left the room, no doubt to go get us some overly diluted squash, and that's when it hit me.

'Oh my God, did you two have sex?'

I hadn't meant it to sound quite as blunt as it did, or anywhere near as loud. My words echoed round the room like a poorly fired missile. Mischa gazed at me, uncomprehending, her eyes widening in shock as she realised who I was directing my question at. She tittered nervously. Callum was the first to respond.

'As the only male in the room, I assume that question is at least half directed at me?'

He was trying to display his usual forthright arrogance, but for once, like a peacock that had lost all its feathers, he was failing. The shield was down and I couldn't resist the urge to pick at him. Perhaps Freya was his kryptonite.

'I suppose in today's age of sexual liberality I could be directing my question elsewhere, but actually yes, Callum, I was indeed asking you.'

'No, we didn't have sex. We just kissed.'

'Callum!' Freya looked mortified.

'What?' He glanced over at Freya, his usual unfaltering gaze wavering slightly as he looked at her. 'What's the issue?'

'It might have been nice if you'd thought to tell me you were going to declare our business to the entire room.'

'Why? It was only a quick snog. It's not like it meant anything.'

And that was when I saw it. Freya's body sagged. She definitely cared more about this than she was letting on. But she wasn't the only one trying to hide something: Callum was lying. I could see it a mile off. The only unfortunate thing about the whole situation was that Freya apparently couldn't. I decided to try and rectify the situation before Genevieve came back in the room and accused me of sabotaging the entire session. I couldn't imagine she would thank me if I managed to ruin two weeks of hard graft with a single senseless remark.

'Look, I'm sorry, both of you. I was out of line saying anything at all. Let's forget about it. You all know I spend too much time saying what I think and not enough time thinking about the consequences. It's none of my business what you get up to in your spare time.'

Freya looked grateful but still slightly crestfallen. Callum shrugged and examined his fingernails in such a way as to suggest that nothing anyone said made any difference to him anyway. The room promptly fell silent and I mentally kicked myself for having been responsible for the sudden change in atmosphere. Yes, something had been slightly amiss before, but now there was a gaping chasm and I didn't have a clue how to join it back together.

Fortunately for me, Genevieve came back into the room at that point carrying a large metal tray. She proceeded to hand out drinks, after which she placed three bowls full of crisps, nuts and olives on the small coffee table beside Mischa. If she sensed anything was amiss, she didn't show it.

Once she'd laid everything out, glancing affectionately at Mischa for immediately tucking into the crisps, she settled back down into her chair and looked around the room.

'Right, everybody. I think you know that my hope is to get you to talk a little bit about the reason you are here – that is, the trauma you've experienced – during this session. You don't have to share everything and we don't have to do it all in one go. And if it's easier I can ask some questions first to help everyone get into the right frame of mind. But before I do, is there anyone who would like to go first?'

'I will.'

No one was as surprised as I was to hear those words come out my mouth. Even Genevieve looked slightly dumbfounded. But as soon as I'd spoken, I knew that I owed it to the others. Maybe telling my story would help them tell theirs. Maybe that was the real reason I was here.

# Chapter 25

# Mischa

I'd been wondering what it'd be like to kiss Callum. I'd never kissed a boy before. How would it feel to snog a rock star? Exciting maybe. But surely kissing any guy was exciting? If you liked them.

But the big surprise of the night wasn't Callum and Freya. It was Victoria saying she'd go first. I mean, what the *hell*? I'd been worrying all week about what Andrew had asked me at their house. Couldn't work out how I was going to be able to help. Now it looked like I wouldn't have to do anything.

'That's great, Victoria, thank you,' Genevieve said. 'Did you perhaps want to start talking about events leading up to that day?'

'I can do. But I think I probably have to go back a bit further if anything is going to make sense to you all. Is it okay if I start talking and see where I get to?'

'Of course, by all means. Go ahead.'

We all looked at Victoria. She looked a bit nervous. It made me feel nervous too, even though I hadn't been asked to say anything. I guess I was just used to her being the strong one.

'Okay. Golly, this is slightly harder than I thought it would be.'

She sat up straighter in her chair, and carefully removed a hair on the sleeve of her beautiful white blouse. She then pulled down the cuff of the other sleeve, which had got caught up on the strap of her gold watch. Finally happy that there was nothing else she could possibly sort out, she spoke.

'You all know that my relationship with my mother wasn't very good. I mean, that's an understatement in itself. In fact, after I left university, I made a conscious effort not to talk to her unless I absolutely had to. Or visit the house. Obviously, there were times when it was necessary. To arrange to collect some of my things, for example. And Andrew would make me call her on her birthday and at Christmas – simply because he's such a nice man and he thought it was important I didn't lose contact with my family altogether. But other than that, I made it through many years with minimal contact. I was glad about that, because the last time I spoke to her, just before Christmas last year, we had a blazing row. She told me it was my fault she drank as much as she did, my fault she wasn't happy, my fault my father wasn't around. Saying those things sounds horrible, but in truth I was used to it. It was like water off a duck's back. That said, after that final phone conversation, I made a pact with myself never to speak to her again.'

I was trying my best to listen, but what she was saying didn't make any sense to me. She could have been talking another language. How could anyone make a decision that big so quickly? But I said nothing. It wasn't my story.

'Anyway,' Victoria carried on. 'One day, about three months later, I got a call from her, completely out of the blue. I ignored it, but she left a message, asking me to go over to the house. She said there was something she needed to speak to me about. That it was important. I didn't go. And then she called again a couple of weeks later, left another message on my voicemail. I deleted it. Then she called Andrew, and gave him some kind of sad little sob story about how it really was absolutely vital that I went to see her as soon as possible. He tried to convince me to go, but I ignored him too. Then she called my work, which pissed me off no end, because my PA came in to an important client meeting and announced to the room that there had been a family emergency and I was urgently needed at home. Safe to say, I didn't go. And then the calls stopped, and I forgot all about it.'

'I wish I could be as ruthless as that,' Freya said. 'But curiosity would have definitely gotten the better of me.'

Victoria wrinkled her nose as if she'd smelt something off. 'It most certainly didn't me. The more she called, the less I cared.'

'What happened next then?' Freya asked.

'Nothing. Until about a month later, when I got another call at work but this time from Petra, my mother's housekeeper. She told me my mother had passed away in the night. She said she'd called the doctor to get a death certificate and the funeral director to collect her body but wasn't sure what to do next. She was in a hysterical state so I said I would go over at the weekend to see what needed doing.'

Er, *what*? I felt my head snap up like it had been let out of a jack-in-the-box. How were the others taking this? I looked at them all, one at a time, but it was difficult to read their faces. Was I the only one who was shocked? Victoria was recounting her mother's death, but didn't seem remotely upset by what she was saying. Her voice hadn't changed at all.

*Not everyone feels the way you do about people, Mischa.*

'That weekend,' Victoria continued, 'I went back to my childhood home for the first time in twenty years. Not much had changed. Aside from the fact that the house was even more of a shambles. Petra had tried her best, poor dear, but she was now close to 80 and wasn't quite as compos mentis as she'd been in her youth.'

To one side, someone asked a question, but I missed it entirely. All I could hear was the sound of my heart, getting louder the longer the story went on. Victoria answered, taking a moment to reach a hand round to the back of her head to smooth down her already perfectly smooth hair. As if that were the most important thing to focus on.

'I confess, I didn't know where to start. How do you go about sorting out the affairs of a woman with whom you hadn't had more than a ten-minute conversation in two decades? Eventually I managed to find some paperwork that suggested she'd made a will and had sent it to a firm of solicitors in the City. I called them; they confirmed they were her executors and I sent them a copy of the death certificate. I had no idea whether or not my mother had left me anything, and to be completely honest with you, I didn't give a monkey's.'

'Did you turf poor old Petra out then?' Callum asked. Something about his voice made me think he wasn't quite as chilled about Victoria announcing the kiss as he'd made out at the start.

Victoria chose not to rise to it.

'No, I didn't, Callum. I asked Petra to stay on to look after the house. And I explained in no uncertain terms that, until she heard otherwise, she should not feel she had to leave. I also told her that if, by some miracle, my mother had left me the house in the will, that she could stay there as long as she needed. I was very fond of Petra. There was no way I would see her *turfed out*, as you so delicately put it, with nowhere to live. And as much as I wasn't a fan of my mother's, I don't think she would have done that to her either. I was fairly confident that the will would provide for her in some way. If it didn't, I would have worked something out.'

'No other servants to stick into early retirement?'

This time Victoria gave Callum a proper look. He smiled at her and raised an eyebrow. Like a naughty kid at school trying his best to get a detention.

'No, Callum. There were not. There were no other staff left to deal with, thank goodness. One by one they had left, and my mother had never replaced them. Which made things slightly easier. Most rooms in the house had already been shut down – the only real living space being my mother's bedroom, the drawing room and the kitchen. And Petra's annexe, of course.

'All in all, it was a quick trip and I was back home the following evening. Andrew asked lots of questions, but I told him that it really wasn't my problem – the solicitors would contact me if they needed to. And that as they say, was that.'

And with that, she stopped talking.

*Surely that's not all she's going to say?*

The words came out my mouth before I could stop them. 'I don't understand why you don't care about your mum.'

Oh God, I was crying. When had that started? Worse than that, I didn't seem able to stop.

Victoria turned to look at me, obviously surprised by what I'd said. 'Explain to me, Mischa. Explain to me why I should.'

'Because she was your mum.'

'She may have been my mother, yes, but she certainly didn't act like one.'

That made me even angrier. I felt my hands ball by my side. The hot feeling in my belly ready to explode. My body going all shaky and weird like it always did just before something happened. I knew if I didn't keep it under control, I would lose it. In front of everyone. But I *wanted* to say something. I was done with bottling things up.

'It doesn't matter. You should have been there for her. You should have called her back. What if she'd wanted to say sorry? What if all she wanted was your forgiveness? She died thinking you hated her. That's horrible. Don't you feel bad? Even a little bit?'

I knew I was shouting, but I couldn't help it.

'Yes, if you must know. I do regret it now, in light of the circumstances. But there's nothing I can do about it, is there? Hindsight is a wonderful thing. And not all of us can be as caring or as naturally forgiving as you. Remember that.'

I could tell she wanted to say something else. But then she looked at me and stopped. I saw the anger go out her face.

'But, Mischa, why on earth are you this upset?'

Why was I so upset? I didn't even have to think about it. 'Because . . . because. . .' I realised I couldn't get the words out. My chest felt heavy. Like someone had sat on it. I wiped my face with my sleeve and tried to calm myself down.

'Because I would do anything, anything on the planet, for five more minutes with my mum. I'd give away everything I owned to see her again. To hear her voice. To hold her hand. To hug her. And you gave that chance up. You gave it up without even thinking about it.'

# Chapter 26

# Callum

Looking at Mischa, seeing her cry like that, made me realise what a fucking arsehole I was. Not because of the whole kiss situation, but generally. Like, in life.

I mean, what the fuck was my problem? I'd come from a great family. Supportive, funny, basically awesome in every way. I'd been blessed with this weird ability to hear melodies in my head. Put down words on a page that made other people feel like I'd turned their souls inside out (direct quote from *Rolling Stone*). And what had I done with that? Wasted my whole fucking life.

My musical CV played out in front of my eyes like the credits at the end of a film, making me feel even shittier. Seven years old and grade three on the guitar. First song at number one within two weeks of release. Soundtrack to a fucking Diet Coke advert six months later. And what had I done with that? I'd taken that success and, let's be honest, abused it for all it was worth. I'd allowed myself to become the personification of a tortured rock star for no logical reason other than – what? Fucking boredom? A feeling that I deserved to live on a higher existential fucking plane to everyone else? Who the fuck did I think I was? A fucking bellend, that's what.

Because slouched in front of me, crying her eyes out, was a young girl who'd clearly had a pretty crappy life. Who'd had no opportunities, no social life, no luck. And what did she want, despite all that? Five fucking minutes with her mum.

I watched helplessly as Genevieve got out of her chair, knelt down in front of Mischa and took both her hands. 'Mischa?'

Mischa looked up, tangles of dark hair stuck to her cheeks. Something about her reminded me of my brother's little girl, the time she'd fallen off a swing in Mum's garden and couldn't stop crying. The memory made me feel even worse.

'Mischa, do you think you might like to talk about what happened?' Genevieve asked. 'We'd all like to listen to you.'

'I don't know,' she replied. 'I don't know if I can.'

'Mischa, listen to me for a second,' Genevieve said. 'I know sometimes it can feel easier to bottle things up inside and not tell people how you really feel. But that's not good for anyone. And I think you know that with you, when you keep things to yourself rather than talk them through, it seems to result in a very physical reaction when it gets too much. Do you understand what I'm referring to?'

'Yes. You mean when I get angry.'

'Exactly. You're very young, Mischa. You've had to deal with an awful lot in your life. It's understandable that your brain created a coping mechanism. A type of shut-down, maybe. But I think now, rather than do that, you might find it better to talk about how you feel instead. What do you think?'

Mischa sniffed loudly. I saw Freya lean over to hand her a tissue.

'No vegan hankies today, Freya?' The words were out my mouth before I could stop them.

'Piss off, Callum. I've not done any washing this week.'

'Been busy?'

She didn't reply. I found myself wanting to say more, but distracted myself by looking at Mischa, who'd had a pretty decent stab at wiping her face.

'Would you like to have a go?' Genevieve asked.

'Yes, okay. I think so.'

'If you need to take a moment before you start, take your time.'

For some reason, Mischa's eyes landed on me. I couldn't think of anything helpful to say. I gave her a quick thumbs up instead and immediately regretted it. A thumbs up? What the fuck? Not cool, dude. But it seemed to do the trick because she gave me a thumbs up back.

I glanced sideways at Freya. She was looking at Mischa, her face full of sympathy. Thank fuck. At least she hadn't caught me impersonating some knobhead children's TV presenter. I wasn't sure why I cared about what Freya thought of me. But as annoying as it was, I'd discovered that I did.

# Chapter 27

# Mischa

Everyone was looking at me.

*Are you sure you're okay to do this?*

'I'm sorry, Victoria. I didn't mean to shout at you,' I said.

Victoria reached over and touched my shoulder. 'It's okay, Mischa. Honestly. I've had far worse thrown at me in my time.'

She took her hand away and I reached up to feel the warm patch she'd left behind. It had been so long since I'd had human contact, I realised. I couldn't remember the last time I'd been hugged.

'No, it's not okay. It's not for me to be mean about your decision. But your story made me angry.'

I took a deep breath. 'You see, my mum died too. That's why I'm here.' I scrunched Freya's soggy tissue up in my hand. I was worried I was going to start crying again. 'I'm sorry. This is a bit harder than I thought it would be.'

'Mischa, don't worry about it,' Genevieve said. 'There's no rush.'

'Thank you.'

*Tell them what happened.*

'My mum had Alzheimer's.' There, I'd said it. A stupid, posh-sounding word for a whole load of pain. 'We found out she had it at 40,' I added, for some reason wanting people to know she hadn't been old. 'Which is really, really young. I had to look after her for about five years. Before she died.'

'That must have been awful, Mischa,' Freya said.

'It was. And the horrible thing about it is that people can have it for ages and not even realise they've got it. They just start doing weird stuff. It's only when things get really bad that their loved ones realise there's a problem. But by then it's too late to do anything.'

'Can you tell us a bit more about it?' Genevieve asked.

I nodded. 'I remember with my mum, there was a sudden obsession with leaflets. Leaflets through the door I mean. They started to pile up on the coffee table and they never went anywhere or got chucked out. They just stayed there. Getting covered in dust. That was another thing – Mum stopped cleaning the flat. She didn't seem to notice that everything was dirty.'

I felt bad all of a sudden. I didn't want people to think my mum was unclean. But then I remembered none of this was her fault and decided to carry on. 'Anyway, these leaflets started appearing, looking like someone'd been reading them over and over again, even though I was sure no one had. Because I knew Mum didn't read anymore. All the things she used to love doing, like reading and watching television – she'd stopped doing all that. It wasn't something I noticed to begin with. She still bought books from the charity shop down the road, like she'd always done. Almost like she wanted to trick me. But she didn't talk about reading anymore and the books never looked like they'd been touched. They piled up in the same place in the flat until I collected them and took them back to the shop. But those leaflets, Mum was definitely doing something with those.'

As I spoke, I felt myself go back in time, back to when it'd all started . . .

'Mum, why is the flat full of Jehovah's Witness leaflets?'

Mum looked uncomfortable. 'A lady rang the doorbell a while back. I invited her in for tea.'

'You invited a Jehovah's Witness in for tea?'

'Yeah. A lady called Sarah. She's very nice.'

'But we're Hindu!'

Later that day, I phoned Auntie in Kenya. 'I don't know what to do. Mum's never even spoken to a Jehovah's Witness before and suddenly she's inviting them into the flat.'

Auntie let out a big, long sigh. Like she always did before she told me something she'd rather not have to.

'Mischa, I wasn't going to say anything but your mum's behaving a bit strangely at the minute. I thought maybe she was depressed but it's hard to tell without seeing her in person. I've told her to go to the doctor next week – I wonder if some pills might help. Let me know how she gets on, okay, *Beta*?'

'How did it make you feel, hearing that?' Genevieve asked.

'It felt like a slap in the face to be honest. But only because someone else had said it and that made it real. I'd known for ages something wasn't right. I remembered how I'd taken her to the council gym the week before that, to try to get her to lose a bit of weight. I'd put her on the treadmill and pressed the start button. She'd been fine with the walking, but as soon as I put the speed up, she'd fallen straight off the back. We'd been in hysterics at the time, put it down to *old people* not being able to use technology. We'd gone for a swim instead and I'd tried not to think any more about it. But deep down I knew something was wrong.'

'What happened after you spoke to your aunt?' Freya said.

I thought back to the first proper conversation Mum and I had had about her weird behaviour. She'd been in the bedroom, rummaging about in her wardrobe.

'What are you doing?'

'Trying to find that sari I used to have. You know, the one with the gold trim?'

'I made you take it back to the shop. It was horrible.'

'I don't remember taking it back. Are you sure?'

'Yeah, Mum. It was disgusting. I told you if you kept it, I was never going out with you in public again.'

Mum laughed and looked at me like a kid about to do something naughty. 'Oh yes, I remember now.'

'Mum?'

'Yeah?'

'Why are you inviting Jehovah's Witnesses into our flat?'

Mum shrugged. 'This again? They appeared on the doorstep one day and it was raining. I asked them in for some chai tea. They come round every now and then for a chat.'

'What do you talk about?'

'Everything and nothing. Sarah usually brings something to talk about with her. She's nice. Do you know she goes to China every year to look after orphans? Some of them come back with her. A lot of the Chinese are Jehovah's Witnesses, you know. It's a big thing over there.'

'They've probably been brainwashed.'

'Don't be ridiculous. Geeta said the same thing and I'll say the same to you as I said to her: there is nothing wrong with inviting friends into your home to talk.'

'But they aren't your friends, Mum. They've probably seen the flat and are wondering if they can get some money out of you.'

'Rubbish. You're acting like a child. It's fine for you. You've got loads of friends you see at school all the time. Now I'm not driving I don't see anyone. It's nice to have someone to talk to. No one else is interested in what I have to say.'

'Oh, Mischa, I can't imagine how hard that must have been for you to hear,' Freya said, interrupting my description of what had happened to lean over and give my hand a squeeze. I squeezed her hand back, happy she understood.

'Yeah, it was. I'd shut up as soon as she'd said that. She knew I hated it that she didn't have anyone in her life apart from me. I'd thought about reminding her that it'd been her choice to stop driving, but I didn't think she would appreciate that. It was all a bit raw after the crash.'

'Hold on, she was in a crash?' Callum asked. His voice sounded strange like the comment had really upset him. I realised I'd forgotten to explain that whole bit.

'Oh, sorry yes, she had a car crash. But everyone was okay. She didn't hurt anyone. But she refused to drive again after it happened. She sold the car and told me she didn't feel like driving anymore. She'd sounded totally relaxed when she'd said it. As if she really didn't care. But I knew that something must have really spooked her to give up that car. It'd been her pride and joy. Which meant she must have known when it happened that something wasn't right.'

My mind wandered off again to yet another incident. About two months later. We'd been at the local opticians, getting Mum's eyes tested.

'It's an A.'

'Very good. And the next one?'

'X.'

'Yes, good. Can you read the letter after that?'

Silence. 'P?'

'No, D. But don't worry, you've done a good job overall.' The optician went back to her desk and began typing something onto her computer. 'Your mum's sight really hasn't deteriorated at all. I just need to make a couple of small changes to her prescription.'

She had to be joking. Should I say something with Mum in the room? She was already fidgeting, banging her legs against the steel legs of the chair like a toddler.

I decided to speak up. 'But Mum can't see!'

I tried to say the words confidently, but my voice came out really whiny and I ended up sounding stupid. The optician put her head up and looked at me. She had no idea what I was on about.

'Of course she can see. You saw her read the chart.'

'She can read the letters. But if you gave her a sentence to read then she wouldn't be able to read it.'

'I don't understand what you mean.'

The memory was interrupted by Victoria. 'That must have been unbelievably frustrating. Why didn't she listen to you?'

'I don't know. But I found the same thing everywhere. People who were meant to know what they were doing, the doctor especially, refusing to believe that the mood swings, the problems with her eyes and the laziness around the flat were maybe down to something way worse.'

I took a deep breath, feeling the anger and the worry in my chest from memories I had tried so hard to bury now desperate to get out. 'I'd been taking Mum to see people for weeks by that point but everyone kept telling me the same thing. She was *just depressed*. Auntie randomly concluded Mum had been depressed for years after Dad died. Declared she'd been hiding it from everyone. Me especially. But none of that felt right. Me and Mum had been happy. I knew that for a fact. But for some reason, no one believed me.'

I thought back again to that day at the optician's. Mum looking up, smiling at me and giving me a silly wave. Her hair three inches grey at the roots since she'd stopped buying the hair kits. Her top with an egg stain running down the middle. That was the exact moment I realised she couldn't look after herself anymore.

The appointment had come to an end and, after helping Mum down from the chair, we'd gone outside into the main bit of the shop.

'Shall we pick out some glasses for your mum, then?' The optician had looked at us. Hoping to make some money. 'We've got some lovely new frames in.'

I didn't have the energy to fight. I'd nodded and the optician sprinted off to get some samples.

'Mum picked a pair of new glasses,' I said, almost to myself. 'They were bright purple. First thing she did was put them on upside down. Then she never wore them again.'

I looked past the others out the window, not sure I wanted to go on. But I knew I had to.

'I'm guessing it got worse after that?' Genevieve asked.
'Oh yes.'

And with that, another memory crashed into my head, this one about two years later.

Mum had been calling for me. The same time that night and almost every night at 4.30 in the morning.

'Mischa . . . Mischa . . . Mischa . . .'

The sound was far away but went on and on and on. Like an alarm clock that I couldn't turn off. I thought to myself: if I keep my eyes shut, she might stop. 4.50 am.

'Mischa . . .'

'Go back to bed!' I said the words as loudly as I could. It had never worked before, but it was worth a go. Just in case. I was so, so tired.

'I need the toilet!'

Her voice was determined. Almost angry. I knew there was no way she was going back to bed. With a deep breath I hauled myself up.

'Mischa!'

'I'm coming, Mum.'

I made it to the door of my bedroom. Mum was standing in her doorway.

'What're you doing?'

'I need the loo.'

'Why didn't you use the commode? That's what it's there for.'

She stared at me. She hadn't understood. I couldn't be bothered to explain. I'd only have to empty it in the morning anyway.

'I need the loo.'

'Come on then.'

I'd taken her by the arm and led her down the hall to the bathroom. As I had at least three times a night for the past six months. The only thing different about that particular night was that, for some unknown reason, she'd got her pants on over her pyjamas. And they looked wet. Maybe she'd tried to use the commode after all.

# Chapter 28

# Freya

The more I heard, the sadder I became. And looking at the others in the room, it seemed I wasn't the only one.

'It got worse as the weeks went on,' Mischa said, sipping her drink. I noticed that her hands were shaking.

'I was doing everything. Feeding her, bathing her, cleaning the house. I gave up school because I was so behind. And I couldn't leave mum at home by herself by that point, not even for an hour. Even when I went to the shops, she would beg me not to go. I'd hear her crying when I closed the door and it would break my heart. Auntie offered to fly over to help me, but she looked after my grandparents and had her own life to worry about. I thought about trying to find a charity or something, but there was never any time to pick up the phone.'

She cocked her head to one side, as if listening out for something. Then she gave a tiny nod to herself and carried on. 'Some days were better than others. Sometimes Mum would come back to me and be almost normal. And even if that was only for thirty minutes, I'd be on a high for the rest of the day. One time she told me all about my dad, how they'd met, their wedding day, having me. The stuff she remembered that day was amazing. Like a switch had re-connected again in her brain and turned the lights back on.'

'That must have been nice,' I said, desperate to say anything even vaguely reassuring.

'It was. But other days were awful. She wouldn't want me to leave her. She would forget how to use a spoon or have a poo. She would wet herself and cry when she realised. One day she didn't know who I was and she shouted at me to get out her house.'

I opened my mouth to say something else but shut it when I realised I had nothing helpful to add. I looked over at Callum, part of me hoping he would meet my gaze. But he was staring straight at Mischa, as were both the others.

'As things went on, my mum was my mum less and less. Her mood swings were crazy. Happy, angry, sad. Sometimes she would know who I was, sometimes she wouldn't. Sometimes she would think I was Auntie or Nani. The hardest thing I think was realising all the things that made her my mum had gone. It was like looking after a kid.'

She paused, sliding her hands underneath her and leaning forward in her chair. Her eyes were trained on the floor but her mind was clearly somewhere else. When she spoke again her voice was barely a whisper. 'Eventually I phoned the doctor and made him come over to the flat. I could tell he was shocked when he saw the state of her. We hadn't been to the surgery in ages. He promised to call social services to see if we could get her a space at a nursing home.'

'That must have been a relief to some extent, I imagine?' Victoria asked, her expression infinitely more melancholy than when she'd been talking about her own mother.

Mischa nodded. 'It was. But then I felt guilty because I knew it meant he thought I couldn't look after her.'

'I'm sure absolutely no one thought that,' I said. 'You did way more than most people would have done at your age.'

Mischa looked down at her shoes, absentmindedly scraping the sole of one boot against the other. She fell silent for a few moments.

'Are you able to talk about what happened after that?' Genevieve asked.

'That's the bit I find hardest to talk about.'

'I know.'

She took a deep breath and for the first time looked up, her big brown eyes resting on each one of us in turn.

'I remember closing the door after the doctor had left and seeing Mum looking at me. For the first time in God knows how long, she knew who I was. I went over, and she hugged me and she held me like she used to when I was little. I started to cry and couldn't stop. She put my head in her lap and she stroked my hair. I was so exhausted I fell asleep.

'I woke up to hear her telling me she was sorry. That she didn't want to be a burden anymore. That I needed to live my life and not worry about her. Then almost as soon as she'd said it, I felt her hand fall away. I looked at her and I knew she'd disappeared back into her own head again. I stood up, turned the television on and went into the kitchen to make lunch.'

She stopped talking for a moment and swallowed. 'But she wouldn't eat. Normally, even when she couldn't work out how to hold a fork, she would let me feed her. Or pick small bits from a plate with her hands. But this time, and every time after that when I tried to get her to eat something, she turned her head away. She wouldn't drink either. It went on like that for about two days.'

Mischa's voice tailed off and it became clear she was lost in her thoughts.

'What happened next, Mischa?' I didn't need to check to know the question came from Victoria.

Mischa looked up, surprised; it was almost as though she'd forgotten we were there. She gave a long, shuddering sigh. 'I didn't know what to do. I should have called an ambulance, I realise now. But by day three I was a mess and not thinking straight, I guess. I couldn't get through to Auntie's mobile to ask her what she thought. I called the doctor on his emergency number, but no one picked up. I decided to do the only thing I could think of and went to the hospital about ten minutes down the road.'

'And what happened then?' Genevieve asked.

'That was when I panicked. I started running down the corridors, trying to work out who it was I needed to speak to. Eventually I found A&E but there was a massive queue at the reception desk. I waited for a bit but then looked at the clock and realised Mum had been by herself for over an hour. I went straight up to the front.

'I remember a hand pulling me backwards by the shoulder. So hard I nearly fell over. Some teenage boy shouting at me for jumping ahead. And I . . . I completely lost it at him.'

She sniffed hard, then rubbed the wet smears from her face. 'I don't remember what happened next or how long I was out for. All I know is I came to eventually and I was on this trolley in the middle of a hospital corridor. I remember people rushing past me, no one really paying me any attention. A guy carrying a tiny baby in a car seat, looking exhausted but singing a lullaby as he walked. An old woman in a wheelchair being pushed along by a nurse, attached to a drip. Some family asking for directions to the oncology ward. I felt confused. Like I'd forgotten something really important. I looked towards the nearest window and saw it was dark outside. And then I remembered. Mum.

'I didn't even think from that point. Just jumped off the bed and ran straight out the first door I could find. I don't think I've ever run so fast. Finally made it to the corner of the tower to our block of flats at the back. Ignored the lift, which never worked, and went straight for the stairs. And that's when I saw her. Lying on the floor by the bottom step.

'I remember screaming, thinking she was dead. Only the sound of my voice made her turn her head and she sat up. Told me she'd come down the stairs to find me but then couldn't remember her way off the estate. All I know is I've never felt so relieved.'

'Was she okay?' I heard myself say, then reprimanded myself for the stupidity of the question.

'Sort of. I managed to find a neighbour to help me get Mum up and back into the flat. She seemed alright, I thought, apart from the fact she was freezing. I did my best to make her comfortable. Wrapped her up in a blanket. My neighbour left but told me to call 999 just in case. But I didn't. I thought she'd be better off with me.'

'And then?' Genevieve prompted gently.

Mischa's shaking had turned into a slow rock. 'I sat by my Mum's side that whole night, just holding her hand. For the first time in God knows how long, she slept right through. But when morning came, I went to wake her up and she wouldn't open her eyes. She was breathing – but she was unconscious. So that's when I called the ambulance.

'I remember talking to her non-stop while I waited for it to arrive. I told her how grateful I was. What a great mum she was. How she'd always been my best friend. And I told her I loved her, and always would.

'And then, for some reason, I don't know why, I asked her a question. I said: "Mum, d'you love me too?"

'She looked tiny sitting there in that rigid, uncomfortable chair. Just a young girl wanting nothing more than the love of her mum.

'I didn't expect an answer. She hadn't said a word since I'd found her the night before. But you know what? She gave me this tiny smile. And she whispered, "Yes, my Mischa."

'She died about ten minutes before the paramedics arrived.'

# Chapter 29

# Victoria

A stillness had descended over the room and its occupants, and the weight of it felt crushing. I had the sudden sense that I couldn't breathe properly and I inhaled deeply, forcing oxygen into my lungs. I realised I felt afraid, and couldn't for the life of me work out why.

'Mischa, I'm sorry.' It was Freya who spoke first.

'There's nothing for you to be sorry about,' Mischa said. 'I'm the one who left her when I shouldn't have done. I'm the reason she died.'

'Mischa, that's not true,' Freya said. 'You did what anyone else in your situation would have done.'

'But if I hadn't blacked out at the hospital, I wouldn't have been gone for so long. Mum wouldn't have had to go looking for me. She'd still be here, I know she would.'

I watched helplessly as her face seemed to cave in on itself.

'And I want her here. I want her here so much. Even if it meant I had to carry on looking after her and have no life. I'd do anything just to see her for another week, another day even. I'm not sure I can forgive myself for leaving her like I did. It was so stupid.'

'You did nothing wrong, Mischa,' Genevieve said. 'Your mum was very ill. You know that.'

'I know. And that's what everyone tells me. But I want her back. I want my mum back.' Mischa's face crumpled again and she held her head in her hands as she cried.

We sat in silence, somehow sensing that Mischa needed the time and space to let her tears – and her grief – out. After a while she stopped, looked up and wiped her eyes.

'Thank you for listening. I'm so glad you're all here. It feels for the first time in ages like I have some real friends to talk to.'

'No, thank you, Mischa,' Genevieve said. 'And thank you, Victoria. It's such a huge step in your recovery that you felt able to share your experiences with us today. You have no idea how proud of you both I am. Is there anything else either of you would like to say?'

Mischa shook her head. Something about her seemed lighter already. 'No, I'm good thank you,' she said. 'I think I would actually like to just listen now, if that's okay? I feel a bit tired.'

Genevieve nodded emphatically. 'Of course, of course. If you're both done, perhaps we could turn . . .'

'Wait,' I said.

I thought Genevieve might seem surprised by my sudden interruption, but she didn't. She looked expectant – her hands folded in her lap as if she knew something was coming. It occurred to me then that perhaps Genevieve wasn't the amateurish, inexperienced psychologist I'd first taken her for – at that moment she looked like a woman with a very firm plan. I even wondered briefly if the crazy outfits were a deliberate ploy, designed to make us think she was mildly eccentric and therefore inherently incapable. Although, I had to say, if that was the case, she'd gone to an awful lot of effort to keep up the pretence. No one wore earrings that big and that brash unless they were really committed.

I inhaled. 'I *would* like to say something else. Is that alright?'

'Absolutely. Go ahead, Victoria.'

I turned to look at Mischa, discovering with some surprise that my eyes were wet. 'I have to say, Mischa, that's the bravest, most honest account of anything I have ever heard. And if a girl your age can be that mature, that open about something so devastating, then I think it's about time I took a leaf out of your book. But first I want to thank you for telling us what you did. And please do take pride in the fact that if you hadn't, I probably wouldn't be telling you what I am about to now.'

And with that, for the first time in about 30-odd years, I started talking without first formulating what it was that I wanted to say. I allowed the words to flow out of my mouth like a waterfall. A dirty, contaminated waterfall.

'What I told you all before, about my mother's death, is true. And the way I felt about it when it happened is also true. But there's more to the story that I need to tell you. I want to explain what happened next.'

I realised then that the room was unbearably hot. Or was it just me? All I knew was I was sweating. I spoke hurriedly, conscious that if I didn't get it out quickly, there was every likelihood I might be sick.

'After my mother died, I assumed that was it. In some ways, it felt refreshing. Worst-case scenario, I was going to have to get involved in the execution of her will, if she'd bothered to leave me anything. But as I said, I didn't expect her to. Plus I'd coped without her for years. I would have been happy if she'd left the whole lot to Petra. Or some charity. Or the cat.

'About a week after she died, however, I received a package from her solicitors. Delivered by hand by some snotty-nosed associate who was clearly ecstatic to be outside the office for the day. I signed for the package and took it inside.

'I had a strange sensation that I wasn't going to enjoy the contents. Clearly my mother had orchestrated a way of communicating with me from beyond the grave and I felt resentful that she'd been even remotely successful in her endeavours.'

I swallowed hard, conscious of a painful scratch against my throat like I'd swallowed a drawing pin. I reached forward to take a sip of my drink – dear Lord, what even was that? I let the sickly-sweet liquid inch its way down my oesophagus for a second or two before ploughing on.

'I was tempted to burn the whole package without a second thought, but it turned out my mother had the seasons on her side. Had it been winter, rather than summer, the fire would have been lit, and I am sure I would have tossed it into the flames and taken enormous satisfaction in watching it fry to a crisp. But I didn't. The mere fact of taking the time to light a fire converted the act from an impulsive one that I could justify – and, if necessary, feign regret over when I had to come clean to Andrew – into something deliberate, premeditated. And for some reason, I didn't want to do anything that involved putting in extra effort when it came to my mother.'

I leant over to pick up my handbag from under my chair, trying as subtly as I could to wipe away a slither of sweat that had run down my chest at the same time.

'Is everything okay, Victoria?' Genevieve asked.

'Yes. I was going to read you the letter, if that's okay? I have it here.'

I tentatively unlocked the small gold clasp of the bag and took out four sheets of thick cream paper, covered in my mother's elaborate inky scrawl. I shuffled them together. I needn't have bothered getting the pages out at all: the words, though lengthy, were imprinted on my brain as if put there by a branding iron.

Taking care not to look at anyone, I started to read.

*Dear Victoria*

*I am sorry that you did not give me the opportunity to speak to you in person. Unfortunately circumstances now dictate that I must write, since I am sad to say that my health is failing by the day.*

*I know that we have not always seen eye to eye and I am all too aware that I have not been a good mother to you. I would apologise for that, but I realise that to express my contrition now would be of no benefit to either of us.*

*Therefore, rather than waste words with unnecessary preamble, I will get straight to the point. The reason I am writing is to tell you not about me, but about your father. He did not, as I led you to believe, die during the course of his RAF duties. In fact, he is still very much alive. As far as I am aware, he lives with his second wife and three children in Kent.*

*I know you will automatically blame me for not telling you the truth, but it was most definitely his decision, not mine, to walk out of both our lives. In fact, he told me that if I were to reveal to you his true whereabouts, he would cut off the income that I needed not just to live on but, more importantly, to pay for the completion of your education.*

*I know that you had a soft spot for your father, but I need you to know that he was not the man you thought he was. Although he could be wonderfully charming, he was also violent and controlling, particularly after a couple of drinks. Thank goodness, you never saw that side to him and I am therefore not surprised that you idolised him – he swept me off my feet when I met him, too. Unfortunately, however, he got bored of me soon after I fell pregnant with you.*

*You may not be aware, as I took great pains to ensure that no one knew, but we were never actually married. As a result, aside from the family home, which I inherited, I was completely reliant on his goodwill and salary. I wanted to leave soon after you were born, but your father was adamant that I stay. I think he rather liked the idea of having a society wife with an aristocratic background because he believed it would help him advance his career. Any money that I had from my parents he took control of, and I had no idea how I was supposed to get it back. In those days it was a lot harder than it is now to find a decent lawyer to help you. I suppose I could have sold the house and lived off the proceeds, but I would have had to take you out of school and I was desperate to ensure not only that you had a good education but that you were kept as far away from your father as possible. That is why I sent you to boarding school at such a young age.*

*I am not saying all of this to elicit posthumous sympathy – I promise you that is not what I want to achieve by doing this. But* you deserve at least to know that your father is still alive, and in death, he finally has no hold over me.

In case your first instinct is to assume I am lying, I have enclosed various documents as proof. I have also added several letters we exchanged over the years, which hopefully make his true character abundantly clear.

My solicitors will be in touch soon to discuss the contents of my will. Aside from that, it is for you to decide if you want to reconcile with your father. Obviously if you decide you want to find him, that's entirely up to you. I have included his address in the package just in case.

All that remains is for me to say goodbye, and hope that you will forgive me one day for everything that I have done. Had I been as strong as you, my dear, I am sure things could have been different.

With love and best wishes,
Your mother

I looked up. I knew now was the time to articulate how I felt about the letter, but the words were stuck in my throat as if they'd been cemented there. I stared at Genevieve, helplessly, for direction. Fortunately, she took the hint.

'Thank you very much for sharing that with us, Victoria. I know it can't have been easy. Do you think you might be able to tell us whether the contents of that letter changed your feelings towards your mother?'

I considered the question. Did I even know the answer? 'At the time, I would say no. The anger that I felt towards her was simply redirected towards my father. In the package was all the proof I needed: not only did it make quite clear he was alive, but the letters between him and my mother left me in no doubt that his decision to leave had been entirely his choice. But the worst part of it was not that, nor the vitriol directed towards my mother – which perhaps I could have justified in part, since however much she tried to defend herself, there was no denying she was an impossible person. No, the worst part, I think, was his complete apathy towards me. The father who I thought loved me, who I had adored and revered my entire childhood, who I considered a good person, was a fabrication. Because at no point in those letters did he make any effort to fight for me at all.'

I glanced around the room at the faces before me, all of them listening, all of them supportive and every single one of them appalled by what I had told them.

'What did you do?' Mischa asked.

'Andrew came home from work that day and I showed him the letter. He asked me what I wanted to do. I told him I couldn't decide. We talked about it all weekend, and then late morning on the Sunday I decided I wanted to confront my father and we drove to the address my mother had given me. We arrived at a large house in Tunbridge Wells and we parked outside.

'I gazed at the house for what seemed like hours. Then all of a sudden, a Porsche swung into the driveway and my father got out. And right there and then, I knew. I couldn't do it. He was the only person in the world I couldn't challenge. Because he was also the only person in the world with the power to hurt me. And that realisation was devastating, both to my pride and my self-esteem. I was filled with rage by what he'd done to me, and to my mother, but the only available outlet was blocked. I took one last look at him as he walked into the house. And then we drove home.'

'Do you think what you experienced that day changed how you felt about your mother?' Genevieve asked.

I couldn't fault her persistence. 'I'm not sure it did, fundamentally. As I said to Andrew, years of neglect can't be rectified by a simple attempt at reconciliation from beyond the grave, regardless of the underlying cause. And I still maintain that's true. She could have done things differently but she opted for the coward's way out. She may have chosen the route she did with good intentions, but I'd rather she'd told me and allowed us to face the consequences together. Perhaps if she'd done that, we would have managed to forge some kind of relationship, some sort of mutual respect.'

'Is there anything you wish you'd done differently?'

'Of course there is – as much as it pains me to say I was wrong, I wish I'd gone to see her before she died. And that's partly me being selfish. Because if I had, perhaps she could have answered the questions I still want to ask about my father. Maybe she could have helped me fill a part of this void in my heart that I carry around with me now every day – just as I still have that letter in my bag. Who knows? In any event, it's too late now.'

I looked at Mischa and shrugged. 'I suppose in some ways I want my mother, too. If only to tell her what a bloody fool she was.'

# Chapter 30

# Callum

Jesus fucking Christ. I couldn't believe it. I'm not sure any of us could believe it. The ice queen had melted. She even looked different. Not massively – I'm not talking Disney movie-type bollocks when you throw a bucket of magic sparkle over someone and they go from ugly crone to beautiful maiden. But she did look more relaxed. And slightly wild. No one would ever have described Victoria as wild before.

Genevieve was talking, telling Victoria something about needing to let go of the guilt. I tuned out. Not because I wasn't interested, but because I knew it was almost my turn to speak. Fuck. Maybe I could get Freya to go next. I needed more time.

The thought made me look at her. Holy shit. She was trembling and white as a sheet. I knew straight away something was about to go seriously tits up. I was torn between getting Genevieve's attention and checking Freya was okay when she jumped up, sending her chair flying behind her.

'I'm sorry. I can't do this. I have to go.' And with that she half-ran, half-stumbled out the room. The door at the end of the hallway opened and shut. And that was that. She was gone.

We all stared at each other. In books, when something really fucking shocking happens, the description is always that people's mouths drop open. But it turns out no one does that in real life. Yeah, you gape at each other like complete fucking idiots, but other than that, it turns out everyone looks exactly the same. My brain, on the other hand, was going into overdrive. What the hell had just happened? It had to be because she wasn't ready to talk. I wasn't surprised she'd freaked out. I'd been on the verge as well.

I stood up. Genevieve reached over and grabbed my arm. 'Callum, wait.'

'What? I'm going to bring her back.'

'Are you sure you're the right person to do that?'

I stared her down as best I could, but her gaze was fucking relentless. I felt myself go abnormally hot, like that Icarus dude who flew too close to the sun. I had a weird sensation at that moment that Genevieve knew a lot more about what was going on than I did. Clearly she knew about the kiss. The whole fucking room knew about that. But there was something more than that. Something I couldn't quite work out.

'I can bring her back.'

'Maybe you can, Callum. But can you tell her what she wants to hear?'

The question threw me. I didn't have a fucking clue what she was on about. But maybe going after her wasn't such a good idea. I sat down.

'Callum?'

*Now what?* I looked at Mischa. 'Yeah?'

'I think you should go find her.'

I shrugged, pretending as best I could that Freya's sudden disappearing act really wasn't my problem.

'Callum, don't be a knobhead.'

I laughed. I couldn't help it. Hearing Mischa call me a knobhead was like hearing a five-year-old swear at you. It sounded ridiculous.

'Don't laugh at me.'

'Sorry. I just didn't expect you to say that.'

'What is it precisely that you're afraid of, Callum?'

Fuck, now Victoria had started on me. I felt my heart rate go up a gear.

'What is it with you two? Genevieve clearly doesn't think I should go after her. Just let it go. She'll come back when she's ready.'

The words felt wrong coming out my mouth. I knew she wasn't coming back. Not unless someone talked her round.

'I didn't say you shouldn't go, Callum,' Genevieve said. 'I was simply making the point that you should only go if you can tell her what she needs to hear. Otherwise, you may make the situation worse. Both for her and for you.'

'If you're talking about what I think you're talking about, I don't think I can tell her what she wants to hear.'

'Bullshit,' Mischa said.

Jesus Christ, who was this girl? It was like Mischa had had some kind of brain transplant.

'Seriously, Mischa, let it go.'

'No, Callum, I don't want to let it go. I want you to bring Freya back. She has to do this. I don't know why it's important, but it is. She has to accept what's happened to her. And if you're the reason she left, I reckon you're the one who has to bring her back.'

'Why is it my fucking fault all of a sudden? Maybe she just freaked out?'

'Maybe she did,' Mischa shot back. 'Or maybe the fact you're making out like nothing happened has upset her. You didn't have to kiss her, did you? So be a man about it and go and get her back!'

'I agree with her,' Victoria said.

I, however, was by now seriously fucked off. 'For fuck's sake, listen to me, all three of you. Freya and I got drunk last week and had a quick fucking snog. Yes, it was nice at the time but it meant nothing. Because it can't be anything. She's married, for fuck's sake. And look at me. I'm not good for anyone. I don't make people into better people. In fact, I take perfectly good people and I break them into tiny fucking pieces. It's what I do. I suck the life out of them like a fucking leech and chuck them when I'm done. Someone else should go. Victoria, you're the one who's had the fucking epiphany. You do it. Or Mischa, how about you? Want someone to care for? Fuck off and find Freya. Take care of her if you're that fucking good at it. But both of you can leave me the fuck alone. This is fucking bullshit.'

And with that, *I* got up and left.

# Chapter 31

# Freya

My heart physically hurt. That's the only way to describe it. I felt crushed by this raw, crazy fear that had no obvious foundation. I tried to work out the source but I couldn't. It felt as though someone or something was out to get me and whatever I did to run away from it, I couldn't escape. I could feel my heart pounding in my chest and echoing in my ears, louder than I'd ever heard it before.

As I sat there, knees drawn into my chest, I was reminded of the recurring dream I'd been having every night for the last six months. Ever since it happened. Always, in essence, the same: the sensation of running down the stairs of my house; flinging open my front door; a friend or loved one of some kind – often Joe, sometimes my mother or sister, once even Mischa – calling me back as I stared into a void beyond my doorstep. Hearing their shouts as I cautiously stepped out into the inky black nothingness, feeling a sense of relief but also fear as I let the emptiness envelop me and carry me away.

I shook my head to clear the image and the anxiety it brought with it. I was sitting on the cold lobby floor of Genevieve's building. Hiding in the shadows in an empty corridor away from the main entrance, just in case one of the others decided to try to find me. Why had I left? And more importantly, why couldn't I let people – decent people, who knew what I was going through – try to help me? I was treating them just as I did Joe. Just as I did the rest of my family and my friends. And look where that had got me. I'd shut them all out instead of telling them how I really felt until eventually they'd realised that I was a lost cause and let me go.

I ran my fingers through my hair and peeled my sticky top away from my chest, fanning it to cool myself down. I knew I needed to break out of this endless cycle of self-pity.

I thought I'd come so far. Even Genevieve had said I had. But when I'd heard Mischa and then Victoria speak about what had happened to them, the reality of what I needed to do had hit me like an avalanche and I knew I couldn't do it. Couldn't be as brave. Couldn't be brave at all.

I heard the lift doors open round the corner from where I was sitting, the bell making me jump and bang my spine against the wall. Was it Genevieve? Part of me wanted it to be. What was the worst that could happen if I went back? Maybe I could try, just a little bit. The thought made me feel sick, though, so I stayed still, waiting for whoever it was to make their move.

Nothing but silence. No footsteps, no voices. My curiosity got the better of me and I peered round the corner, feeling like the world's worst spy. Anyone even glancing my way would have spotted me. But the person who'd come out the lift wasn't looking anywhere at all. He was sitting on the floor directly in front of the lift doors, rocking forwards and back, his head between his knees.

It would never have occurred to me that someone as confident as Callum could appear the way he did now. I'd seen him on the verge of tears that night at the apartment. We'd all seen him angry and miserable. But I'd never seen him this physically undone. Every part of my body wanted to go over and wrap my arms around him. Offer him the same support he'd given me, that night I'd slept in next to him, even though I was probably half his size. But something held me back.

Abruptly he got up and started pacing around the lobby like a caged animal. I could tell from the angle of his shoulders and his balled fists that he was angry. I watched helplessly as he kicked the sideboard, knocking over an artificial flower arrangement and sending it flying. The plastic vase bounced noisily across the floor and rolled towards the door. Then he scrunched his fists against his eye sockets and let out a howl, like some kind of wild animal. It was the noise of a person who was slowly but surely going to pieces. It took me completely by surprise – I'd never in my entire life heard anything like it. I looked down at the floor, undecided as to what to do. But I needn't have worried. The decision was made for me: when I looked up, he'd gone.

I felt my heart lurch. I wanted to run after him, but my feet were rooted to the floor. And anyway, going after him would have been stupid – he'd made his feelings about me obvious. We couldn't help each other. We needed to figure things out on our own.

I came out from my hiding place and walked towards the lift doors. I could go back up and try again. My fingers hovered in front of the call button. Five minutes ago, I might have done it. But I couldn't now. I didn't want to do it without him.

Feeling disgusted at myself, I let my hand drop to my side, turned around and went out the front door.

# PART FOUR
# DEPRESSION

# Chapter 32

# Victoria

I poured myself a large glass of whisky, carefully selecting the ice from the bucket. Four pieces. Not too large, not too small. Most importantly, not crusty around the edges. I mixed it methodically with a stirrer from the tray. It had a small silver zebra perched jauntily on top of it. Where the devil had I bought that from? Then I remembered. The Serengeti. Tanzania. My honeymoon with Andrew.

I went to sit on the sofa, still stirring the contents of my glass. There was something indescribably therapeutic about hearing the sound of ice clink in a crystal glass. I had never been a huge fan of drinking, for obvious reasons, but had always loved the preparation. Relished the sensation that came before it. Less the actual taste once I had got there.

Story of my life, in many ways. Constantly striving to do everything to the best of my ability, never accepting anything less than perfection, only for the end result to be somewhat unsatisfying. I realised that for all my academic success, my beautiful possessions, my impressive career, the only thing that had really made a tangible difference to my life was my husband. My imperfectly perfect husband. The only thing I had no direct control over, ironically.

I took a sip of my carefully curated whisky. There was something wonderfully decadent about drinking at 10.30 a.m. The taste warmed my throat. Pleasant, but something else was needed. I got up and went to the kitchen, taking an orange from the fruit bowl, a knife from the drawer and meticulously cutting the finest slice of rind. I turned on the hob and let it simmer on the end of the knife, waiting for the delicious smell of hot orange. Beautiful.

Drinking whisky aside, what was I going to do now? When I had left Genevieve's four nights ago, I had been resolute. I was going to somehow convince both Freya and Callum to come back and finish what they had begun. But as I had driven home in a haze – I suppose I'd been numb after sharing my mother's letter with the group – my determination had faltered. Firstly, I didn't know where Freya lived, although I supposed that Callum might. But that meant tackling him first, which I wasn't sure was the right way to go about things. I could ask Genevieve for Freya's address of course, but whether or not she'd give it to me was a different matter. It was not only professionally irresponsible, but also a clear breach of GDPR.

By the time I'd returned home, anger had weakened my resolve. How was it my job to try to help two people who really should learn to pull themselves together? If I – a person who had spent years bottling up my emotions – had managed to do it, why couldn't they? They were cowards, both of them. In which case they deserved each other.

The next day, of course, I'd felt differently again. I'd spent years not letting the outside world in; I couldn't expect others to embrace the art quite as skilfully. And I still had no idea precisely what either of them had been through. It could have been something horrifying. Ultimately the only thing that had happened to me was letting my estranged mother die without saying goodbye. Something I now felt exceedingly guilty about. But it wasn't as if I'd killed her with my own bare hands.

I was shaken out of my thoughts by the smell of burning orange peel. Bugger. I threw it in the sink, sliced another piece, and repeated the caramelisation exercise, this time taking care not to let my thoughts wander until I was sitting back down in the lounge, sipping on my drink. Much better.

I heard the front door open and close and Andrew appeared in the doorway. He took stock of me, my whisky and the time on the grandfather clock in the corner of the room. 'Bit of a cliché isn't it? Drinking whisky this early in the morning?'

'Did you want one?'

He looked at me. He had something on his mind, I could tell. I put my glass on the coffee table and went to stand up.

'Don't get up, I'll do it.'

He went over to the drinks trolley, throwing contents haphazardly into his glass with a degree of careless abandon that set my teeth on edge, and went into the kitchen.

'Did you set fire to Christmas?'

'I burnt the peel.'

'I can see that.'

He came back into the room, a slice of raw orange in his glass. I bit my tongue but said nothing. What a philistine. He settled down beside me on the sofa, took a large gulp of his drink and grimaced. 'This tastes bloody awful.'

I laughed and leant into him, his arm finding its way around my shoulders.

'So, are you going to tell me what the matter is? You've been preoccupied for days,' said Andrew.

'Work's been busy.'

'Bollocks it has. You've been quiet for weeks. What's the real problem?'

And with that, I told him; about Mischa and her mother, about me opening up to the group, about Freya and Callum's departure. And the whole time he listened, stroking my shoulder, occasionally asking a question to clarify a particular point.

When I'd reached the end of the story, we sat together in silence, periodically sipping on our drinks.

'What are you going to do about it?' he said. He was keeping his voice neutral and light, a technique I knew he used to try not to rile me.

'What do you think I should do?'

He looked at me, surprised. 'I don't think you've ever asked for my opinion before.'

'What codswallop. You give me advice all the time.'

'Yes, but you never ask for it.'

'I'm asking you now.'

He smiled. 'First time for everything in a marriage, I suppose.'

'Well, this time I'm listening. You should take advantage; it might not happen again.'

He stared at the contents of his drink for a few moments before replying.

'Victoria, I *know* you and, however uncertain you are about *how* to get Freya and Callum back on track, however resentful you feel, however frustrated, you clearly want to do something. Deep down. I also think you probably owe it to them. You may not realise it, but I've seen a positive change in you these last few weeks. Plus, isn't it better that you try and, heaven forbid, fail, rather than walk away and pretend none of this ever happened?'

I considered what he'd said. 'You're very clever, Andrew, you know that?'

He kissed me on the forehead. 'I haven't finished.'

'Oh sorry, carry on.'

'But before you do anything, I think you need to start with Mischa.'

I stared at him, uncomprehending. 'But Mischa's fine.'

'Do you know that for a fact?'

I thought about it. No, I didn't know that for a fact. I hadn't given Mischa a second thought since I'd left her behind in Genevieve's flat. Why hadn't I thought to check on her? But I knew why. Because she was Mischa. A girl who had been overlooked and ignored her entire life. A girl who had recently lost the only thing in her life that mattered to her and now had nothing at all. I was such a bloody idiot.

'Oh God, Andrew, you're right. I didn't even think. Come along, we have to go and get her.' I jumped up out of my chair, feeling for the first time in days that even if I didn't know *what* to do, at least I knew *where* to start.

# Chapter 33

# Mischa

What was the point? Of any of it? I'd tried so hard. Told my story. And for what? For nothing. I felt worse now than I did before I'd started going to see stupid Genevieve.

I was lying on my single bed, the same one I'd had since I was a kid, staring at the ceiling. Hadn't come out my room all week. Except to make toast. Couldn't be bothered to shower. Hadn't got dressed or gone to work. Hadn't done anything apart from eat six pieces of bread every day for the last... what... four days? I didn't even know what day it was. I didn't give a *toss* what day it was.

*You should really eat something more nutritious, you know.*

I rolled over, ignoring the crumbs everywhere, and looked at the clock. Was it time for slices three and four? 12.03. Bit early, but what the hell.

I climbed out of bed, putting on Mum's fluffy slippers, and walked into the kitchen. I opened the bread bin and had a look. Crap. Only two crusts left. I hated crusts. I'd have to go to the shops to get some more. Maybe later. If I could be bothered.

I had a look around, wondering what else I could have to eat. Nothing in the fridge apart from butter and milk on the turn (as Mum used to say) so no point opening that. I stuck my head in the kitchen cupboard. Tinned sweetcorn? No way. Instant noodles? Maybe. Tinned spaghetti shapes? At least they contain tomatoes.

Ten minutes later, I was sat in the lounge, shovelling spaghetti shapes and buttered toast crust into my mouth. Not a bad effort for lunch. Maybe things were getting better. I thought about turning on the telly but I wasn't sure I could deal with it. Too many people getting on with their lives. Showing me what I didn't have. No thanks.

With nothing else to do, I thought back to what had happened last week. Like I had about a million times already. Just after Callum had stormed out.

The three of us had looked at each other like lemons.

'What do we do now?' I said.

'There's not much we can do, unfortunately.' Genevieve replied. She looked distracted, like she wasn't really listening to me. 'I can't force people to be here.'

'You're not going to try to get them back?'

Genevieve took off her glasses and pinched the top of her nose. Like Mum used to do when she had a bad headache. 'I need to have a think.'

'What about Mischa and me?' Victoria asked. 'Shall we carry on, just the two of us?'

'Do you want to do that?' Genevieve asked. She looked exhausted – with her glasses off, I could see dark circles under her eyes. I'd wondered if this whole thing was starting to push her over the edge. It couldn't have been fun for her, listening to us go on and on every week.

Turned out Victoria wasn't as sympathetic as I was.

'Will you please stop answering questions with questions, Genevieve? You're supposed to be giving us guidance, are you not? But from what I can work out, you haven't provided us with any of that whatsoever. You've talked a good talk, granted. But in terms of actual advice, I can't say I feel any better about my situation than I did at the start.'

Genevieve sighed. 'I'm sorry you feel that way.'

That made Victoria even more pissed off. 'You're sorry I *feel* that way? Is that all you've got to say? How about saying something that actually means something? Put that degree of yours to good use. Or was this exercise entirely for your benefit?'

'You're angry, I can see that.'

'No shit, Freud.'

'Look, Victoria. When I invited you here, my intention was to help you. All of you. I wanted to find a group of people who didn't believe they could be saved and help them find a way out. By somehow uniting them. The only problem, I now realise, is that while I still think I've found the right individuals to do that, the time it takes to progress from stage to stage has been different for each of you. Therefore, if those of you who progress quicker aren't willing to be patient and allow the others to catch up, the whole thing simply falls apart. So yes, while I am perfectly happy to continue to work with you and Mischa, I'm worried that if my theory is correct, it won't work anywhere near as effectively without Freya and Callum.'

Victoria looked at Genevieve for what felt likes ages. Then she nodded slowly and said, 'How are you going to get them to come back then?'

'I don't know yet.'

That wasn't what I expected her to say. Genevieve had answers to everything. Now all of a sudden, she didn't.

'Thank you for being honest, at least,' Victoria said. And with that, she got up, grabbed her stuff and walked out the room.

Genevieve and I looked at each other. I thought about getting up to leave with her but I didn't want Genevieve to think I was annoyed with her too.

'Is there anything I can do to help?'

Genevieve tried to smile but I could see her heart wasn't in it. 'You know what, Mischa?' she said. 'This isn't something I want you to worry about. I just need a bit of time to decide next steps.'

My eyes followed her as she got up and walked over to the pile of papers on her desk. She began sifting through them.

'Okay. I'll go then.'

'Great,' Genevieve replied, though I wasn't sure she'd even heard me. 'I'll see you next week.'

I nodded, trying my best not to cry.

Now here I was, four days later, feeling emptier than I'd felt even after Mum died. I wasn't clever enough to work out why. When I'd spoken to the others about what had happened to me, for the shortest time I'd thought maybe it would bring an end to the sadness. I'd even felt this weird rush of something I couldn't quite name when I'd finished talking. Not quite excitement but more like I was on the edge of something important. Now I was back where I started. And none of them gave a toss.

I said the words out loud. 'None of them give a toss about me.'

And, as if by magic, there it was. The ball of anger. Everyone was *so* worried about Freya and Callum, like they deserved more attention than anyone else. But why was that? Freya was married to this amazing guy. Or so she made out. She lived in a decent house. The only bad thing that'd happened to her before all this was her dog dying! And then there was Callum. He was gorgeous and famous and he had loads of money. Basically a life everyone on the planet wanted. Yet for some reason, Genevieve and Victoria were only worried about *them*. What about me? I hadn't got anybody. I had a crap council flat, a boring job. A life no one wanted. Not even the Jehovah's came round anymore. I couldn't even get a Jehovah's effing witness to come round for a chat.

*Calm down Mischa.*

NO.

The ball of rage was in my stomach now, getting bigger by the second. I knew there was nothing I could do to stop it. I clenched my fists, waiting for it to take over. Part of me was happy: it would stop me having to think for a bit.

The last thing I remember seeing before everything went black were small blobs of alphabet spaghetti dripping down my lounge wall.

# Chapter 34

# Callum

I'd promised myself I'd never touch the shit again. I'd meant to throw away the stash. Almost forgotten I had it, to be honest – found it hidden behind a bottle of whisky like a dirty little secret. Couldn't remember putting it there. Maybe it wasn't even mine.

Either way, I should've chucked it as soon as I saw it. Because now, here I was, sitting on my sofa staring at a small pile of coke. I say small. It was about two grams. A miniature snowy mountain piled up on my coffee table. Already cut. Ready and raring to go. Fuck, I wanted it.

If I took it, it'd be the first time I'd caved since the accident. I think I was officially clean by drug addict standards. And yet more of a shocker, if I ignored the relapse the night before the first session, and that evening with Freya and the others, I hadn't even been drinking. At one point I thought I'd turned a corner. Fucking idiot.

I stared hard at the mound in front of me. Something about it was mesmerising. Kind of beautiful. How could something that looked that pure and clean do so much fucking damage? It should be black. Like soot. Or brown. Like decay.

I realised I must have been playing with the pile because when I looked down, I had somehow divided it into what looked like endless rows of long straight lines. When had I done that? The image of it took me back. To the last time. To who I'd done it with. The memory made me go cold. I needed a fucking drink.

I got up and wandered over to the bar to see what I had in stock. I felt like I wanted some wine but I couldn't find any. Weird. Then I remembered – I'd drunk it all with Freya.

Freya. The image of her invaded my thoughts again. For what must've been the thousandth fucking time in 96 hours. It was becoming a draining but apparently obsessive habit. A new addiction to add to the ever-growing list.

I hadn't wanted her to run. And my gut instinct had been to go after her and bring her back. But then the others had stuck their fucking oars in and stopped me. Made me worry that her reason for running was down to me. That she wanted more from me than I could give. And that made me angry. Not because I didn't want to give her what she wanted. But because I desperately wanted to and knew I couldn't.

Fuck, my head was a mess.

I went back to the coke on the coffee table. The lines gazed innocently back at me. I sniffed and rubbed my nostril. The craving had 100 per cent kicked in.

Once upon a time, when my life was in a better place, I thought of drugs as an optional add-on to an already crazy ride. A way of making a good life even better. A little bit wilder. I didn't need them. Hadn't thought I did anyway.

But now I did, it seemed. I knew I was going to fucking cane those lines. Knew I would hit the booze as soon as I ran out of coke. The only question in my mind was how long I would hold out for.

The realisation made me angry. I looked round the apartment for something to vent on. The room felt empty and pointless; nothing in it meant anything to me.

Except my Gibson. I looked around for it. There it was. Little fucker. Lying on the floor. Innocent as a sleeping baby.

I remembered the day I'd bought that guitar. I'd just started writing my second album, still on a high from the first. And I had a hell of a lot of money in my bank account that I didn't know what the fuck to do with.

I'd taken a cab into Soho. Pulled up outside Sixty Sounds on Denmark Street and ducked inside before anyone could see me.

I clocked what I wanted the second I walked in. Nestled right at the top among rows upon rows of incredible electric guitars. Every type and colour you could possibly imagine. A 1958 Gibson Les Paul Standard. In Cherry fucking Sunburst. The most beautiful thing I'd ever seen.

The dude in the shop told me they'd only made about 430 that year – apparently they hadn't been popular at the time. Not until the likes of Page and Clapton got hold of them and made them cool. And after the glory years of '58 to '60, Gibson hadn't quite managed to recreate that same magic. 1958 – the year the Yanks formed NASA, the Russians launched *Sputnik 3* and Gibson made the best fucking guitar in the entire fucking world.

The sales guy got it down from the rack and handed it over for me to play. I felt like I was being given Gabriel's harp. Tried out the first few bars of *Stairway to Heaven* to see how it sounded. I didn't even need to do that. The second I hit that first note, I knew. That guitar spoke to me like no human being ever had. It saw the passion in my heart, the chaos in my head and turned it into something fucking wonderful. If I didn't believe in love at first sight before, I did then.

But now? Like when the best relationship you've ever had comes to a bitter and twisted end, I hated it. Hated it hated it hated it. Because if it wasn't for that guitar, none of this shit would've happened.

I reached out. Grabbed it by the neck. That guitar had destroyed my life.

I raised it slowly above my head. Used to do that at the end of my concerts. What a fucking prick.

With every ounce of energy I had, I smashed it again and again onto the concrete floor until there was nothing left to hold on to. Then I walked back to the coffee table, rolled up a note from my wallet and gave myself over to oblivion.

# Chapter 35

# Mischa

What was that noise? An alarm clock. No, something else. I rubbed my eyes and checked the time. 15.04. I must've fallen asleep.

I sat up. I was lying on the carpet in the lounge. And I was covered in something sticky. Oh crap, I was bleeding.

I looked down at myself. No, I wasn't bleeding. I was covered in . . . spaghetti sauce.

*That's not going to be easy to clean up.*

The sound was still going. Television? Nope. Then I realised – it was the doorbell. It'd been months since someone had dropped by, and I'd forgotten what it sounded like.

I scrambled up onto my knees, wiping my sauce-covered arms on my pyjama trousers. What should I do? I couldn't open the door looking like this. Maybe if I stayed quiet the person would go away.

'Mischa? Mischa, are you there?'

I recognised that voice. There was only one person in the world who had a voice that posh. Only one person I knew anyway.

'Victoria?'

'Oh, thank the Lord, you're okay. Can you please let us in?'

'Um. I look a bit of a state. It might be better if you came back later.'

'Mischa, I don't give a hoot what you look like. Please open the door.'

I did as I was told.

Victoria and Andrew stood outside. They slowly looked me up and down.

'What on earth have you been doing?' Victoria said.

I felt my cheeks go hot. 'Bit of a long story. Would you mind if I had a shower?'

'I think that's a good idea. Go ahead. I'll make us all a nice cup of tea. Come and help me, Andrew.'

I ran into the bathroom, locked the door and turned the water on. Threw my pyjamas in the laundry bin, got in the shower and stuck my head straight under the spray.

It felt amazing. The first wash I'd had in days. Over the noise of the water, I could hear the sound of cupboard doors opening and closing in the kitchen. Then voices, followed by the front door slamming shut. Did they leave?

'I've just sent Andrew out to get some provisions,' Victoria shouted through the bathroom door.

'Oh, okay, thank you.'

Fifteen minutes later, I wandered back into the lounge to find them sitting on my sofa drinking tea. I was clean and dressed, but wanted the floor to open up and swallow me. I sat down in Mum's armchair. All signs of spaghetti sauce had gone from the carpet and the walls. All I could smell was bleach. It made me feel even worse.

'I wish you hadn't seen that. And thank you for cleaning up. And for making tea.'

'Oh Mischa, don't be silly. What's a bit of tinned spaghetti sauce between friends? Although how you can eat that ghastly stuff is beyond me. It's pure sugar, you do know that, don't you?'

I sipped my tea. It tasted weird, like flowers. Definitely not Tetley. I tried to drink it anyway. Didn't want to look rude, but it was absolutely gross.

'Um . . . can I ask why you're here?'

'We were worried about you. And Andrew made the very good point, as he always does, that I was spending so much time pontificating over what to do about Freya and Callum, that I hadn't even stopped to think whether or not you were alright. I apologise.'

'That's okay. I'm fine.'

'No, Mischa, it's not okay. And you are clearly not fine. I may not be a psychiatrist, but I know enough to understand that turning up at someone's flat to see a person in their pyjamas in the middle of the afternoon covered head to toe in luminous orange sauce is generally an indication that they are not, in fact, in any way, fine.'

I tried to smile. I looked at the two of them, sitting on the couch. I'd never seen two people look so out of place. And they were both clearly worried. About me. It felt nice. 'Thank you for coming. I'm having a bit of a tough time to be honest.'

'I can see that,' Victoria said. 'I confess I didn't realise you were here entirely by yourself. I assumed your aunt would be checking in. Have you spoken to her?'

'No,' I replied. 'Nana is ill and I didn't want to bother her.'

'Oh Mischa, why didn't you say you were all by yourself?'

I shrugged. 'I don't know. I guess I'm used to it nowadays.'

'Okay then,' Victoria said. 'Tell us what the matter is.'

I gripped my mug of tea between my hands. 'I guess I thought telling you last week about my mum was going to be some kind of turning point. And it did make me feel better. For a bit. But then Freya and Callum went off, and I came home and I felt awful. Like it'd all been for nothing. Like I was back to square one. And now I don't know what to do with myself. I can't even be bothered to go to work.'

'I'll tell you exactly what you're going to do, Mischa. You're going to get up, go to your bedroom and pack yourself a bag. You're coming home with Andrew and me.'

I looked at them. Were they serious? Andrew didn't look put out by what Victoria had said. They must've chatted about it already.

'What? No, you can't do that.'

'Tough. It's happening. Otherwise I won't sleep a wink knowing you're here alone. Potentially throwing more tinned produce all over the walls. And Andrew agrees with me.'

I looked at Andrew. He smiled back. 'I promise Victoria isn't all that hard to live with,' he said, giving me a wink. 'And I could do with a partner in crime to help me fight my corner now and then. Please come with us. At least until you're back on your feet.'

'That's so kind of you.' And with that, I started to cry. Andrew leant over and gave me a tissue. He'd have made such a great dad. It made me want to cry even more.

'Victoria, why don't you help Mischa pack her things? I'll make sure the flat is shut down and tidied up before we go.'

'Great idea. Come along, Mischa, let's do this.'

She pulled me up and I followed her down the corridor to my bedroom. I stopped by the door. Saw Victoria staring at my bed, the duvet and sheet covered in toast crumbs. I quickly moved to stand in front of my drawers. Didn't want her to see all the plates and glasses stacked on top.

'Heavens, Mischa, look at the state of your room! What would your mother have thought? Honestly.'

'Sorry. I didn't think anyone'd see it.'

'Never mind. We've got more important things to concern ourselves with than a food-infested bed. Now, where do you keep your things? Let's pick you out some clothes.'

I nodded, went over to the wardrobe and grabbed an old PE bag that at some point I must have shoved in there. I held it upside down to empty it. Hadn't used it since school. The stuff inside smelt musty and damp. I pulled out what looked like a screwed-up tissue stuck to the felt and shoved it in my pocket. I hoped Victoria wasn't watching. I turned around to check – she wasn't. She was staring at my bedside table.

'That's a beautiful photo,' Victoria said, pointing at an old picture of me and Mum. 'Where was it taken?'

'Hampton Court,' I replied. 'About ten years ago.'

'I thought I recognised it. That's right by the maze, isn't it?'

'Yeah. Mum took me once during summer holidays before I started back at school. We had a great time.'

It was true – we'd been so happy that day. Running about like toddlers. Getting lost. Eating our packed lunches when we finally got to the middle of the maze. I remembered we'd been starving because it'd taken us an hour longer than it was meant to to get to the middle. It'd been a long time since I'd felt like I felt in that photo.

I picked up the frame.

'You have her eyes, you know,' Victoria said, giving me a small squeeze on the shoulder.

'Auntie used to say that too.'

I looked at the two of us in the picture. Leaning against the wall of the maze. Eyes crinkled up. We must have been looking straight into the sun. I wondered who'd taken the photo. Some tourist probably. He hadn't done a very good job, but it didn't matter. It was my favourite picture of the two of us.

'Shall we put it in your bag?'

'Yes please.'

Victoria took the frame out of my hands and placed it on top of the bag, now jam-packed with all my stuff. Victoria was very quick at packing.

I smiled at her, wanting to show her how grateful I was for what she was doing.

*Maybe it's about time someone looked after you, don't you think?*

## Chapter 36

## Freya

Three hard raps on my front door interrupted me from my book. I say interrupted – I was on page 137 – but I wouldn't have been able to tell anyone anything about it. I reached over for my bookmark, placed it carefully at the spot I'd just finished pretending to read, and stood up to get the door.

A quick glance through the spyhole revealed that Genevieve, of all people, was standing in my porch, absent-mindedly stroking the leaves of a meandering philodendron that cascaded down the side of one of the exposed brick walls. What the hell was she doing, showing up at my home? I knew I hadn't answered any of her calls, but surely that didn't give her the right to turn up completely uninvited? I thought about not opening the door, but then decided I should just get it over with. The quicker I spoke to her, the quicker she'd leave.

If she was shocked by my appearance, she didn't show it. In fact, it was almost as if she'd expected it. Which was kind of strange, in the circumstances.

I smiled thinly. 'Genevieve, what a lovely surprise. Come in.'

I stood aside to let her into the hallway.

'Let's go through to the kitchen,' I said. 'It's straight ahead of you. I'll make you a cup of tea.'

Without saying a word, she followed me down the hall and sat at my kitchen table.

'Tea then? Or coffee?'

'I'll have a tea, please,' Genevieve said, her voice sounding unnaturally loud, until I realised that was probably because

I hadn't had a conversation with anyone in this house for a very long time. 'That'd be great.'

'Milk? Sugar?'

'Just milk.'

I busied myself with the drinks.

She cleared her throat, forcing me to turn around and look directly at her.

'Freya, are you okay?'

I smiled at her. 'Of course I'm okay. Why wouldn't I be?'

She was about to answer when I interrupted her. Suddenly strangely desperate to not cause a scene, I changed tack, doing my best to redirect the conversation into something light-hearted.

'Ooh, actually I have some biscuits too. I made them this morning. I tried a new recipe. Something I'd been meaning to test out for ages. They've got apricots in. Joe's favourite. I thought he might like them when he got in from work. But it looks like he won't be back tonight now. You should have a couple. I made too many, as always.'

'Freya . . .'

I pretended I hadn't heard.

'The next thing I might do is brownies. I've had a real craving for them recently. You know, the really sticky ones? But no nuts. I hate it when people put nuts in their brownies. Or maybe a coffee cake.' I knew I was rambling but I couldn't seem to stop myself.

'Freya . . .'

Genevieve observed me across the kitchen island. Immediately my thoughts jumbled together and I clammed up.

'Yes?'

'You look quite different to when we last saw you.'

I looked down at my newly manicured nails, unable to meet her eye. 'I just thought it was about time I made a bit of an effort again.'

'It's fair to say you've made more than a bit of an effort, don't you think?' Genevieve said, her eyes never leaving my face.

I sighed inwardly. After leaving her flat almost a week ago, I'd woken up the following day determined to make some kind of positive change. I'd realised I was exhausted by my life. Or lack of one. I'd thought to myself that maybe, rather than try to tackle the source of my grief head on, I should gloss over it instead. Forget it'd even happened.

With a sense of renewed resolve, I'd booked appointments at the local hairdresser and beauty salon up the road – places I'd once gone to all the time – hoping that by returning to the routine of my old life, it would kick start some kind of transformation. A physical makeover followed by a mental one.

The experience had been horrible. The end result might have looked good, but I hadn't enjoyed it at all. Stylists and beauty therapists who I used to chat to all the time kept their distance, seemingly at a loss as to what to say to me. And I found I had no desire to engage with them either: at each stage of my transformation I kept my head down, pretending to be engrossed in a shabby pile of women's magazines I was sure I had read months ago. I came out of both salons, places that used to bring me huge amounts of pleasure, feeling worse than when I went in.

So now, hearing Genevieve's comment, I felt myself bristle, even though I knew she meant it kindly. Why was she even here?

'Did I look that awful before?' I realised I sounded more confrontational than I'd meant to.

'No, of course you didn't. That wasn't what I meant.'

I laughed in an effort to show I wasn't bothered. Even though my insides were roiling together like clothes on a spin cycle. 'I think it's just that you saw me at my lowest point during those sessions. I must have looked a mess. But I'm feeling much better now.'

I heard the kettle boil behind me and sighed in relief at the distraction. It gave me a reason to spend the next few minutes getting mugs out the cupboard, pouring water into a teapot, putting biscuits on a plate, milk in a jug – taking as long as humanly possible to complete each task. I thought about humming, but decided that was a step too far. Instead, I carried it all over on a large plastic tray and placed it carefully on the table in front of Genevieve.

'I have to say, this is a nice surprise.' I paused. 'But can I ask why you're here?'

'I was worried about you,' Genevieve said.

'I'm fine,' I said. 'Biscuit?' I picked up the plate, realised my hand was shaking and put it back down again. 'Maybe just help yourself.'

Genevieve took a biscuit and bit into it, catching the crumbs as it disintegrated over the table. She grinned at me. For a second it felt normal, as if I had a friend over. Like the old days. I allowed myself to relax a little bit and took one myself.

'These are really good,' she said. 'I didn't know you could bake.'

'I used to make things like this all the time. Mum taught me when I was little. Never really enjoyed making dinners but I'm an expert when it comes to desserts. I realised yesterday I hadn't baked anything in ages. I went to the shops to get the ingredients and I made them first thing this morning. It turns out cooking is really therapeutic.'

'Did you get your hair done at the same time?' Genevieve asked. Her tone was neutral but I stiffened all the same.

*Keep it together, Freya.*

'Two days ago actually. I went for the full works. Hair, nails, wax. The whole lot. I thought it would make me feel a bit better about myself.'

'And did it?'

I hesitated.

'Why are you here, Genevieve?'

'I'd like you to come back on Tuesday.'

I looked at her, surprised. 'Really? Why?'

She was nibbling round the edges of her second biscuit, temporarily distracted. She looked even more out of place in my house than she did in the room where she ran our sessions, dressed as she was in an enormous multicoloured shawl and big amber hoops through her ears. What was it with her and the strange clothes? Not to mention her hair, which was as wild as ever. Possibly more so. I wondered briefly if the wind had caught it on the way over. For some reason she always looked as if she'd just been on a very blustery bike ride.

I repeated my question. 'Genevieve, why do you want me to come back?'

She looked at me, attempting to tuck a couple of unruly curls that had escaped her bun behind her ears. 'Because, being completely honest with you, I think it's important for you to try to finish what you started. After you left, I thought very hard about what I should do and I decided to come to see you. To try to talk you around. And Callum too. I'm not sure you know, but he left the session early as well. Shortly after you.'

Of course I knew. I'd never forget that image of him on the lobby floor of Genevieve's building.

'Have you been to see him?' I asked. I took a gulp of my tea, feeling the burn of hot liquid as it slid down my throat.

'No, I haven't,' Genevieve replied. 'I wanted to come and see you first.'

'Isn't that slightly unethical? You coming here, I mean?'

Genevieve sighed. 'Yes, it's completely unethical. I'm breaking every rule in the book. But I couldn't *not* come.'

'Would you get in trouble if your boss found out?' I hadn't meant the question to sound quite as much like a threat.

'Yes. Yes, I absolutely would.'

I let her answer hang in the air for a few seconds before responding.

'It's very kind of you to make the effort to check in on me. But I've decided not to come back. After I left last week, I thought about what I wanted to get out of this process. And finally I realised what it was: I want to return to how things were. So that's what I've decided to do. I'm going to pretend none of it ever happened.'

Genevieve finished the last of her cookie, dusting off her fingers over the plate. 'Do you really think that's the right way to go about things?'

'I do. I've thought about this long and hard for the last few days and I feel completely comfortable with my decision. I'm going to sort things out with Joe. I'm going to find a way to make up with my family and friends. And I'm going to start afresh.'

Genevieve nodded slowly. 'Freya, would you mind if I spoke to you completely openly for a moment?' she asked.

'What do you mean?'

'I mean not as a psychologist. As myself. Which I know I'm not supposed to do. But I really want to.'

'Of course,' I replied. Something about her tone made me nervous.

'What about Callum?'

I clenched my jaw. 'What about Callum?'

'Have you considered that maybe he needs you to come back?'

'He told you that, did he, after I left?' I knew I sounded angry, but she was starting to push my buttons. And we both knew these types of questions were entirely inappropriate. I didn't need a degree in psychology to know that.

When Genevieve spoke again, she sounded subdued. 'No. No he didn't. But that doesn't mean I don't know.'

'How do you know?'

'I just do.'

I had no idea what she was talking about. Especially given that only a few days ago, she had told me to stay away from him. What had changed? Had Callum said something to her? I didn't want to think about it. All I knew was I needed to find a way to get her out of my house as soon as possible if I had any chance of pulling this off.

I took a deep breath.

'I hope I'm not speaking out of turn here, Genevieve, but I think you're wrong. Callum made his feelings about me quite clear. As I told you on the phone, after we had that stupid kiss, he told me he wasn't interested. And I can understand why he said that. He's in a bad place. We wouldn't be good for each other. And I'm confident he would drop me like a stone after a couple of weeks anyway. All in all, I think it's best if he and I, and you and I, go our separate ways. It's been very nice meeting you and I really appreciate you coming over here to check on me, but as you can see, I'm fine. I'm going to move on with my life and I think you should forget all about me.'

It was the most I'd spoken out loud in days and I felt exhausted. It was taking everything I had not to crumble. I bit the inside of my cheek to stop myself from crying.

Genevieve looked disappointed. I had a feeling she wanted to say something else to try to persuade me. But in the end, she didn't.

'Then I think it's probably best that I get out of your way. Thank you very much for the tea. And the biscuits.'

She stood up awkwardly, finished her drink and made her way to the kitchen door. But when she got there, she hung back. 'Freya?'

Oh no. 'Yes?'

'There's just one more thing I want to say if you don't mind?'

'Sure.'

She leant her head against the door frame. 'I know it feels like it's a good idea to paper over the cracks and forget about all the things that have happened to you, but that kind of solution rarely works in practice. Were someone else to look at you right now, they'd see a princess. You look like everything most little girls want to be when they grow up. But I don't think you're happy. I'm looking at you right now and I see someone who's pretending.'

She hesitated, frowning as if trying to decide whether to say more. 'And you know what else? I think Callum is pretending too. In fact, I'll bet you anything he's gone back to his old way of life, the same way you're trying to go back to yours. But you know what the difference is between you and him? Your old life was just empty. Your life was getting your hair done and your nails painted and your make-up perfect, like it is now. Anything to ignore the fact that the things you thought would make you happy left you constantly wanting more. But at least emptiness won't kill you. Not immediately anyway. You might even be able to kid yourself into thinking that you've done the right thing for a little while. But Callum's old way of life? It will destroy him, Freya. You've seen what he's like better than anyone. So I have one question for you. And this is a question I have no right to ask you, either as a psychologist or as your friend, but I'm going to do it anyway. If you find out one day that Callum is no longer here because none of us tried to help him, how will you feel? I'll hazard a guess that you'll feel more than empty. I think you'll feel crushed. I think it would take the last tiny piece of your heart that's still intact and destroy it.'

Her words immediately made me feel indignant. My hands went to my hips like a teenager about to berate a hypocritical parent. 'Then tell me something, Genevieve. Why did you tell me when I called you *after* I kissed him to stay away?'

She had the good grace to look mildly guilty. 'I'm sorry I said that. What you told me had happened between the two of you that day took me completely by surprise. I didn't have time to process it properly. But then I saw you together at our last session and I realised something.'

'What did you realise?'

'Bringing Callum back to this process isn't only about saving him. It's also about saving you.'

I looked at her, standing in the doorway to my kitchen. She seemed completely different from the woman I knew from our sessions together. Stronger. More confident. Ageless. Almost as if everything that had gone before had been some kind of performance. It struck me then how little I really knew her.

I felt part of my resolve crumble. I'd been adamant that this was the right decision. I thought if I made an effort to go back to how things were, everything would be okay. I would stop feeling useless and weak. I knew it would take time, and I hadn't even had a chance to see if Joe was willing to fight for our relationship. But suddenly the very thought of patching things up with my husband felt wrong. Not because of Callum, but because my old life was a sham. My new appearance was a sham. I felt humiliated. And thoroughly, thoroughly lost. I was suddenly overcome with tiredness. I wasn't sure I had the strength to do this. But I couldn't let Genevieve know that.

'What do you want from me, Genevieve?' I said, with as much defiance as I could muster.

She looked at me, her head to one side. The sunlight from the hallway caught her from behind, framing her silhouette. 'I want you to come back on Tuesday.'

And with that, she left.

# Chapter 37

# Callum

Fuck. Where was I? Hmm . . . not sure. I was definitely on a hard floor. Bathroom? No. Maybe. Shit, my head.

I opened an eye. Urghh – too much. Closed it again. Pressed my forehead hard against the cool tiles. I recognised those. Definitely my bathroom. That was a positive at least.

Fuck, everything ached. I must have been here a while. I pulled myself up, like an animal, on all fours. Retched, and went to grab the loo. Missed. Tried again and managed to get my head into the bowl just in time.

Stomach acid. Mixed with whisky. Gross.

My insides were pulsing as if they had a life of their own. I hoped I wasn't about to give birth to something. I couldn't breathe through my nose either. Felt like it was full of cement. I grabbed a piece of bog roll and tried to clear it. Hell of a lot of noise but nothing came out.

I groaned. Tried to get up. Struggled to ignore the constant hammering in my head. *Must. Find. Ibuprofen.*

On the sixth attempt I managed to get to my feet. Staggered out of the bathroom, hunched over as if I were an old man. Down the corridor. Into the kitchen. Opened the drawer. Thank fuck, I had some.

Feeling like I was wearing gloves as I tried to push the pills out the foil, I grabbed a glass from the counter, filled it with water and washed two tablets down.

The effort was too much. I sank down to the floor, feeling as if I was going to pass out. I closed my eyes for a moment, giving in to the pounding in my brain. Just breathe, Callum. Wait for the drugs to kick in. You're good at that.

I tried to distract myself. What had I been doing these last few hours? Anything? Maybe. A vague memory of pavements, people. Traffic, noise.

Fuck – I'd gone out.

Gradually it came back to me. Tiny snippets, like scenes from a movie.

Busy streets. People on their way home from work. Tourists looking lost and getting in the way. Walking way too fucking slowly. Lots of umbrellas – it must have been raining. Not that I'd noticed. No one had recognised me. Hadn't given me a second glance. I was just some guy in a baseball cap and hoodie. Wandering the streets of central London, high as a fucking kite. That was the good thing about Londoners. They didn't pay much attention unless you got right in their face. Or tried to mug them.

But then the drugs had made me paranoid. No one would meet my eye. Didn't even look up. Something about it had freaked me out. Surrounded by thousands and thousands of people and not a single one gave a shit.

I'd had the strangest urge to shout at someone. Check I existed. But I couldn't take the risk. Skye would have gone fucking mental.

No idea how I'd got home.

The memories turned into random, disjointed thoughts. I drifted off. Woke up to find myself slumped on my side on the kitchen floor. My left arm had gone to sleep. I sat up. Made a weak-arsed attempt to shake it back to life.

The headache had subsided, but I still felt like shit. I was a piece of food that was slowly going off. I knew there was only a certain amount of time I could do this for. *The human body can only withstand so much.* That's what my doctor had told me.

The problem was, I had nothing to gain from stopping. Being sober made me see the reality of my life. Understand what I'd lost. What I would never have again. What was the fucking point in that?

*It's such a waste, Cal.* That's what Mum would've said. If she could bring herself to talk to me. I could picture her now – staring at me, her face full of regret. The only woman in the world who could make me feel like crap without saying a single word. But, you know what, Mum? Talent, fame and riches ain't all they're cracked up to be.

My manager once told me that most famous musicians couldn't stick it out for longer than ten years. Nothing to do with fame. Or the sex, drugs and rock 'n' roll. It was purely down to who we were. His theory was, we were all bipolar. I could still remember the speech. *Callum, you have to bear in mind that rock stars are constantly wrestling with two conflicting states of mind: immense arrogance and crippling insecurity. It's self-love and self-hate in equal measure, mate.*

'But what does that mean?' I'd said.

'It means a bloody battle of wills, resulting in guaranteed self-annihilation.'

Hadn't known what the fuck he was talking about at the time – I think he'd been on mushrooms when he was talking me through it. *Now* I knew, though. I wanted to get out of the cycle but didn't know how. Especially since self-hate had completely tipped the scales.

To think, a few days ago, I'd come close to believing there might be a route out of the mess I'd gotten myself into. But I was wrong. I was always fucking wrong.

I looked across the kitchen into the lounge. Fuck me. Glasses and half-smoked roll-ups all over the floor. An ice bucket on its side, water everywhere. Smashed guitar in the middle of the room. What. The. Actual. Fuck.

It was then that I saw them – four leftover lines and a bottle of whisky on the coffee table. Almost full. An empty bottle lying next to it. All of it beckoning me like a beautiful woman. A beautiful, horny woman.

I was reminded of a lyric to my first number one: '*Life is a river and I'm ready to drown.*'

Too fucking right.

# Chapter 38

# Victoria

Mischa, Andrew and I were sitting in the lounge, playing cards. It turned out Mischa was remarkably good.

After she had beaten us decisively at rummy several times over, Andrew offered to make hot chocolate and wandered off to the kitchen. We sat in companionable silence. She looked like a totally different person to the MSG-drenched creature we'd happened upon a couple of days ago. That may have been something to do with the fact, of course, that she'd swapped her godawful polyester pyjamas for one of my White Company dressing gowns. And let's face it, everyone looks good in a White Company dressing gown.

It was she who eventually broke the silence, with a question I'd been meaning to ask her all evening. 'What are we going to do about Freya and Callum?'

I collected my thoughts, distracting myself by shuffling the deck of cards a couple of times before responding. 'I feel we should try to do something. But I'm not sure how to even go about it. What do you think?'

Mischa looked surprised. Why did everyone look so ruddy astonished whenever I asked for their opinion? Was I really that dictatorial? I was going to voice this thought out loud, when I stopped myself. I needed to hold back for once. Instead, I waited for Mischa to speak.

'I agree we have to do something,' she said.

I nodded. 'But what can we do?'

'I don't know. It's not like we even have their mobile numbers.'

I thought about it. 'I have Callum's.'

Mischa looked surprised. 'How come?'

'He gave it to me when his driver took us home. He wanted me to let him know we got back okay. I forgot I had it, to be honest.'

'Shall we call him then? Check he's okay?'

'I don't see why not.'

I reached for my phone, scrolling through my contacts until I found his number.

It rang for a minute or so, but it didn't connect to voicemail. I hung up and tried again. On the second attempt he picked up.

'Yeah?'

The voice on the other end of the phone sounded distant and confused. Like a person who'd been woken up from a deep sleep at some ungodly hour of the night. I glanced over at the clock on the mantelpiece. It wasn't even 7 p.m.

'Callum, is that you?'

'Who . . . who is this?'

He was definitely slurring.

'Callum, it's Victoria.'

'Victoria . . .'

I could tell he had absolutely no idea who I was. I tried again.

'Callum, it's Victoria. From counselling.'

'Yes. Victoria.'

He went quiet.

I tried again. 'Hello?'

'Yeah?'

He sounded on the verge of sleep. For some reason the thought made my heart quicken.

'Callum, I'm just phoning to check you're okay . . . Are you okay?'

'Okay . . . Yeah . . . All good here.'

'Are you at home?'

'Yup. I think I am . . . Yeah, yeah I am. You wan' come over?'

'No, Callum, I'm just phoning to make sure you're alright.'

A sudden bang forced me to pull the phone away from my ear.

'What was that?' Mischa asked.

'I'm not sure. I think he might have dropped his phone.'

'Oh. That's not good, is it?'

'No.'

I tried a few more times to re-engage Callum in conversation but couldn't get an answer out of him. I hung up and tried again. He didn't pick up. I looked over at Mischa. She was looking at me nervously, playing with the tassels on a cushion.

'What do you think?' she asked.

'I think we might need to go over there.'

# Chapter 39

# Freya

I was staring at my face in the bedroom mirror. I could have been looking at myself through a time machine. A copy of me, but from a lifetime ago: scattered blonde highlights, hair with a slight curl. Perfectly applied make-up. Nice jewellery. A woman without a care in the world.

It was incredible really how skilfully a person could camouflage their true self behind their physical appearance. How easy it was to blend away the signs of trauma with a bit of clever contouring and a pair of GHDs. It was no wonder society was oblivious to all the suffering going on in the world.

Speaking of oblivious, Joe was still none the wiser about anything that had happened. I'd come home from my various appointments envisioning an emotional reunion that same evening. My husband spotting me as he came through the doorway, sweeping me up in his arms and telling me everything would be okay.

Only my life wasn't Disney and Joe had never done anything close to that before, even in the good times. But at the very least I was hoping for a chance to tell him I wanted to turn a corner. Explain I was willing to try again. As it transpired, I hadn't even seen him: I'd got back to a short message on the answerphone, 'reminding' me (though I had no recollection of him telling me) that he was going on a work golf trip with his work colleagues and wouldn't be back for a few days. Brilliant.

Genevieve's visit had therefore been my first proper chance to prove to somebody, *anybody*, that I was serious about moving on. Not that I'd handled that very maturely. I felt bad about the way I'd treated her. She'd only been trying to help.

Thinking about Genevieve immediately reminded me of Callum. Not that I needed a reminder: I'd thought about nothing else since she'd left. How would I feel if something happened to him? I tried to tell myself it wouldn't matter. I wouldn't know about it straight away anyway, not if I didn't go back to the sessions. Only I knew what I was like. I would dwell on it in the same way I was doing now, let it fester. Until one day I would pick up the paper, see a story about the untimely death of the singer Callum Raven, and go completely to pieces.

Why did I care so much? The strength of my feelings for Callum didn't make *any* sense. I'd never been a sentimental person. I'd barely spent any time with him. And I definitely wasn't someone who bought into the whole love at first sight idea.

At least I didn't think I did. Because however hard I tried, I couldn't forget that kiss. Something about it had changed me. And as much as I wanted to brush it off as a silly, girly, starstruck crush (embarrassing as hell, but kind of understandable) I knew in my heart it had meant infinitely more than that.

I thought back to my evening with him: a crystal-clear set of memories in my brain nestled amongst a fog of very little else. It had been something to do with that song. The second Callum had started singing, it was as though two strong, invisible hands had gripped me by the shoulders, lifted me to my feet and flung me like a javelin towards him. I could blame the wine all I wanted, but I was confident, thinking back, that I would have done it even if I hadn't been drinking. And the other thing I now realised, having dissected the moment a thousand times? Callum had felt it too.

I put my head in my hands. The irony was that despite all this, I wasn't sure whether any of it mattered. I knew with 100 per cent certainty (but zero understanding as to why) that if

I didn't go back to the sessions, I wouldn't see Callum again. And returning to counselling meant telling my story. And that was the part that scared me to my core.

'Freya, why are you so terrified?' I directed each word to myself in the mirror, searching my reflection for an answer. But I didn't need to respond. I already knew why.

Going back to Genevieve's flat meant leaving a lonely but well-trodden path and attempting something new and precarious. It meant letting go of the old me for good and embarking on a journey I didn't know I was capable of completing.

But so what? What did I have to lose? I bit the side of my cheek as I thought back to my time with the others. I'd fainted during my first session. I'd thrown myself at Callum like a randy teenager at the end of my second. And I'd done a runner in the middle of my third. And no one had judged me for any of it. In fact, Genevieve had gone out of her way to find me and try to convince me to come back.

I stood up. I felt wobbly and nervous. A little bit fuzzy. I hadn't eaten much over the last few days. Apart from 32 sodding apricot cookies.

I took one last look in the mirror. A girl from a different world stared back at me. But it was a world, I knew deep down, I had to leave behind. I needed to move on. And I needed to do it soon.

# Chapter 40

# Victoria

At the front entrance of Callum's building, I was reminded again of what a bleak and depressing place it was. There was something about the wrought-iron gates and soot-coated bricks of those old warehouse conversions. They made me think that at any minute a troop of ragged children would file past, destined for a day down the mines.

The door in front of us opened and we walked in. I looked straight ahead, hoping against all hope that Mischa was doing the same.

The concierge didn't even look up. I pressed the button for the lift, feeling Mischa breathing a little too heavily beside me.

'Why isn't it opening?'

I looked to my right-hand side, noticing the small panel by the wall. 'I think it needs a code.'

We looked at each other, flummoxed. Then all of a sudden Mischa grinned. 'It's 1234, remember?'

'Are you sure?'

'Yeah. Callum made a big thing about it when we were here last time.'

I punched in the code and the doors opened. 'Bravo, Mischa,' I said.

We got in and pressed the button for Callum's floor. As the lift doors closed, I stole another glance at the concierge. Nothing.

'Phew!' Mischa exclaimed. 'That was easier than I thought it would be.'

The lift doors opened onto the same landing that we'd visited a couple of weeks previously. It already felt like a lifetime ago.

Mischa strode forward, rang the bell, then darted back again, standing behind me like a child hiding behind her mother's skirt. It appeared it was my turn to step up.

But no one answered. We tried again. Nothing. We knocked on the door as loudly as we could, my knuckles smarting from the contact. Mischa put her ear up against the heavy wood.

'I can't hear anything,' she said.

'Come along, let's try something else. He must be in there.'

Then I had a brainwave. I ushered Mischa into the lift, this time pressing the button for the underground car park.

'Where are we going?' Mischa asked, looking confused.

'I've got an idea,' I replied.

'What?'

'Something Callum mentioned last time about a fire escape. If we can access the rear of the building, we'll hopefully be able to find it.'

'And then what are we going to do?'

'We're going to climb it.'

'You're joking?'

I didn't bother to reply.

Nine floors down the lift doors opened, directly into the car park. It was pitch-black until the second my foot went from metal to concrete, at which point the whole area flooded with a bright fluorescent light. Automatic sensors, I assumed. The sort that only came with an absolutely exorbitant service charge. Thankfully there was nobody about to witness Mischa and me as we made our way past the fleet of shiny parked cars, an A to Z of luxury in itself.

We walked as nonchalantly as it was physically possible to do when you've just broken into a building – there was no doubt CCTV was everywhere – eventually making it to the other side of the cavernous space by the bicycle cages. Pretending to peer inside, I stole a surreptitious glance to my left and right and spotted a security gate hidden to one side, a narrow gravel path behind it. I walked over and gave the gate a hard shove. It was locked.

'What do we do now?' Mischa asked.

I regarded it carefully. The gate ran all the way from floor to ceiling. Climbing over the top was clearly not an option.

'I'm not sure.'

I was pulled from my musings by the sound of footsteps behind us. 'Mischa, quick, hide!'

She darted over to the bike cage and squeezed her small frame in the gap between it and the wall. Knowing I was physically incapable of doing the same, I crouched instead by the boot of a large Mercedes, watching as a beautifully dressed middle-aged man holding a small black bin bag walked past us towards the locked gate. He held out a key fob and the door sprang open.

'Quick, Mischa,' I whispered, as he carried on his way. 'Grab it before it locks again.'

Like a cat trying to catch a fast moving object, she sprung from her hiding place and launched herself towards the rapidly closing gate, catching it an inch away from shutting. Smiling at me triumphantly, she pushed it back to let us both through.

Twenty seconds later, we found ourselves in a small courtyard that seemed to serve as some kind of communal garden. I looked around. There was no sign of the man we'd followed – presumably there was a rubbish store somewhere in the vicinity, where the bins were kept – but, sure enough, against the side of the building, running from the ground right up to the roof, was a spiral staircase. A rickety, narrow and ominously rusty spiral staircase.

'I'm not climbing that,' Mischa declared immediately. 'I hate heights.'

I walked over to it and gave it a quick shake. It felt solid enough to me. 'Then you'll have to stay down here.'

Mischa took in the entirety of the structure, clearly torn between genuine fear and a strong desire to help. Then she brightened.

'I know. Why don't you go up and you can let me in the front door?'

'Good idea. You can also call an ambulance if I fall off.'

'That's not funny.'

I gave her a quick smile in an attempt to reassure her and then began the ascent.

It was just as well I'd kept myself in shape, I thought, as I climbed. I looked down briefly. I could see Mischa, several storeys below, her hands cupped around her eyes as she strained to watch me. I realised I was at least 50 feet up, and the realisation made me temporarily lose my footing, banging my shin painfully against one of the steps. I gave it a quick rub and ploughed on.

After what felt like an eternity, but couldn't have been more than a few minutes, I reached the top floor. Callum's apartment. The kitchen window was ajar, and I realised that with a bit of careful manoeuvring I could probably wrench it open and then swivel myself onto the ledge and climb in. But I hesitated. What I was contemplating was a major breach of his privacy. He could be doing anything. What if he had a girl over? I couldn't imagine they would be best pleased if they suddenly saw some strange middle-aged woman appear, as if by magic, in the kitchen. I peered through the window, trying to see if I could make out anything at all. Definitely nothing untoward in the kitchen. Other than a whole load of unwashed glasses. I tugged the window open and leant on it. If I stretched the top half of my torso through the gap at a 45-degree angle, I could just about see the lounge.

And that was when I saw *him*, lying on the floor beside the coffee table. His face was turned in my direction but at a funny angle, dark blond hair hanging over his face like a curtain. I tried my best to focus on his chest to make sure he was breathing – easy enough to do in theory since he was only wearing a pair of boxer shorts – but I was too far away to see.

I wriggled back onto the fire escape, signalling to Mischa to come up. Mercifully, she seemed to understand and headed towards the car park, and the lift. Then, positioning myself gingerly on the window ledge, I swung my legs through the open window and landed with a thump on the other side. Picking myself up, I ran over to where Callum was lying and reached out my hand to touch his chest. He was definitely breathing. Thank goodness. I checked his pulse, and then the inside of his arms and legs for good measure. There were no signs he'd injected anything. Finally, I gave him a quick shove to see if I could wake him up. He groaned, mumbled something and turned over onto his side.

Safe in the knowledge Callum wasn't dead, I surveyed the rest of the apartment. It was utter carnage. What the hell had he been up to? I took in the whisky bottles, the credit card and the curled-up £20 note beside it. It was quite clear what he'd been up to.

The doorbell rang. Without thinking, I wiped off the dusting of white powder from the glass surface of the table and quickly shoved the card and note under a sofa cushion. Then I went to let Mischa in.

'Is he here?'

'Yes – but just to warn you, he's completely out of it.'

'What should we do?'

'I think we should stay with him until he wakes up.'

'Should we call an ambulance?'

I thought about it. 'I'm no doctor, but I used to find my mother in a similar state to this all the time. He's breathing normally. He hasn't vomited. He responded when I tried to wake him up. I think we put him in the recovery position and monitor him. My bet is he'll wake up at some point with a killer hangover, no doubt feeling exceptionally ashamed of himself.'

'Maybe we should call an ambulance anyway. Just in case?'

I knew Mischa was remembering her mum then. 'Mischa, think about who he is. What sort of a story this would become if it got out. We call an ambulance and he'll have to deal with a hell of a lot more than a sore head when he wakes up. I think we have to take a risk, for his sake.'

'Okay, if you're sure.'

I wasn't, but I nodded anyway. I had no idea how much cocaine he'd done or how much he'd had to drink. Or whether he'd taken anything else and got rid of the evidence. I resolved that if he wasn't awake and coherent in a couple of hours, I'd have a rethink.

Mischa looked around the apartment, taking in the mess. 'Should we have a clear up while we wait?'

I sighed. 'I had a feeling you were going to suggest that. There had better be some rubber gloves, otherwise I'm touching nothing.'

Mischa smiled. 'I'll have a look. Why don't you sort the lounge and I'll go check out the rest of the apartment.'

'Fine.'

I started picking up glasses, carrying them over to the kitchen counter and stacking them in the dishwasher. I couldn't help but smile at the irony of the situation. Here I was, an equity partner at one of the world's top law firms, cleaning the apartment of an unconscious rock star. Not only that, but this was the second time this week I'd cleaned up after someone I'd only just met.

'Urgh. Gross!' I heard Mischa shout. 'There's sick everywhere!'

At least I hadn't volunteered to clean the bathroom.

# Chapter 41

# Callum

As someone who's woken up from a shit ton of benders, I knew the drill like the back of my hand. A few glorious seconds when you feel absolutely great, followed moments later by the feeling that someone's dropped a piano squarely on your fucking head.

But this was definitely the first time I'd woken up and hallucinated. And I was 100 per cent hallucinating. Because standing in my kitchen, cleaning the surfaces and wearing a pair of bright yellow fucking Marigolds, was Victoria.

'What the fuck is going on?' I whispered. Talking at normal volume wasn't an option right now.

'Here, take these.' I nearly jumped out my skin. Mischa was kneeling beside me. She held out two pills and a glass of water. I tried to sit up but failed. I wanted to cry.

'Let me help you.' I winced as Mischa grabbed my shoulders, pulling me up so that I was using her lap as a cushion. Then she placed a freezing cold flannel against my forehead and held it there. If there was a heaven, for a few seconds, as the ice seeped through my skull and into my brain, I was there.

'Thanks.' I took the pills and swallowed them. 'Sorry.'
'Don't worry about it. How are you feeling?'
'Like shit.'
'Did you want to go to bed?'
'No. I'll just lie here for a while if that's okay?'
'Of course, take your time.'

I must have passed out again because when I next opened my eyes, my head was on a pillow. I felt a tiny bit better. And it seemed I hadn't been hallucinating either. Mischa and Victoria were genuinely in my apartment. I couldn't remember letting them in. But then I couldn't remember anything since I'd downed half of that second bottle of whisky. Who knows what the fuck I'd been up to. It was kind of nice to wake up to them, to be honest. Normally I woke up to way worse.

'Are you feeling any better?' Victoria asked. They were both leaning against the high stools in my kitchen. Mischa looked sympathetic. Victoria looked . . . like Victoria.

'A bit, yeah. Any chance of a really strong coffee?'

Ten minutes later, the three of us were perched on the sofa, holding our mugs. Possibly the least fucking rock 'n' roll behaviour in the world. But the coffee tasted good. And it was staying down, which was the main thing.

When I'd finished, I looked round my apartment. Something wasn't right. 'Did you guys tidy up?'

'Yes, Callum,' Victoria said. 'We did.'

'For fuck's sake. You shouldn't have done that.'

'No, you're right, we shouldn't have. But Mischa wanted to be helpful.'

I took the bollocking on the chin. 'Thanks. What are you even doing here anyway? Did I let you in?'

Victoria and Mischa looked at each other.

'No, we rang the bell,' Mischa said, 'But when you didn't answer, Victoria came up the fire escape.'

I looked at Victoria. Dressed in cream trousers and the cleanest white fucking blouse I'd ever seen. She'd lost the Marigolds at least. Which was mildly disappointing, I had to be honest.

'Are you fucking kidding? She came through the fucking window? I'm nine storeys up!' I started laughing but then stopped as a wave of nausea hit me. 'I wish I'd been conscious to stick that on YouTube.'

'We were worried something had happened to you,' Victoria said. 'It was the only thing I could think of to do. And fortunately for you, it worked.'

'Was I in a bad way?'

'I've seen worse. The state of your bathroom floor being one of them.'

I had a sudden flashback. To cold tiles. And a hell of a lot of fucking vomit. 'Oh fuck, I'm so sorry.'

'It's not me you need to apologise to,' Victoria said. 'It was Mischa who cleaned it up.'

'Thank you, Mischa. I'm really sorry.'

It was strange. I felt more comfortable around these two than I had with anyone in a long time. 'Did you guys come over just to check I was okay?'

'Not just that,' Victoria said. 'We actually wanted to ask you something.'

'It'd better not be a song request. Guitar's out of action, you may have noticed.'

Victoria ignored me. 'We want you to come back for the next session.'

I wasn't sure I was ready to have this discussion. 'No.'

Victoria and Mischa looked at each other again. I had a feeling I was about to get a lecture. I braced myself.

'Can I be completely upfront with you, Callum?' Victoria asked. I'd never known her to be anything fucking but, but I nodded anyway.

'Go on.'

'I didn't buy into any of this counselling business either at the start. In fact, I thought it was a complete and utter waste of my time. And I confess, when I got there on that first day, and was forced to tell a silly story about my childhood in front of a room full of people I'd never met, I thought to myself, there's no way on God's given earth that this is going to do me any good. And . . . Callum, are you okay?'

'No, I'm not. I think I'm going to be sick.'

Five minutes and the contents of my mug of coffee later, I was back on the sofa. 'Carry on. I am listening. I promise.'

Victoria looked at me, unimpressed. Mischa gave my arm a squeeze.

'Anyway, as I was saying, over time, that started to change. I don't know precisely why or when. I've been trying to work out in my head what it was about the whole experience that made me start to feel differently. But whatever it was, for the first time in my life, I wanted to talk. And when I eventually did, I felt like I'd made this monumental step towards something important.'

'I sense a *but* coming.'

'But then you and Freya left. And that sensation subsided completely. It took me a while to realise why. Somehow, during this whole process, we've become linked to each other. Which means that while the release I felt when I told you about what happened with my mother and father was important, it won't be complete until you get there too.'

'You're asking me to help you?'

'Partly. We're halfway there, Callum. Mischa and I have both got through it. But we can't cross that finish line until we've done it together. I can't explain why that needs to happen. And I know what I'm saying to you isn't in the slightest bit logical. But I think it's what we need to do. Does that make sense?'

'It sounds like a load of fucking bullshit, to be honest, Victoria.'

'Yes, I do realise that. And if I'd said the same thing to myself in week one, I would have thought the same. But I can't explain it any differently. I suppose I'm asking you to trust me.'

Trust me. Two tiny words. Said like it was so easy to do. But trusting someone you hardly knew was like agreeing to play Russian roulette. You might be fine, or you might shoot yourself in the head.

But then again, what did someone like Victoria have to gain? She didn't need money. She wasn't interested in fame. In fact, the last time she was in my apartment she told me that people who coveted fame were *deplorably nouveau*, whatever the fuck that meant.

I felt something inside me shift. Maybe it was time I tried a bit harder. 'You know what, Victoria, I do trust you. How can I not trust someone who scaled a fucking building just to check I wasn't dead? And fortunately for you, I buy into bullshit. Most of my life I've been fed it in one form or another.'

'Then you'll come back?' Mischa asked. She looked like all her Christmases had come at once.

'Maybe. But I do have one question.'

'What?' they said together. They were the strangest double act in the fucking world.

'What about Freya?'

'We've spoken to Freya,' Mischa said, a little too quickly.

'And?'

'She'll be there too,' Victoria replied.

I looked at them both, dead straight in the eyes. Or at least as straight as you can manage when you feel like you've been kicked in the head. Mischa seemed suspiciously uncomfortable. Victoria's gaze, however, did not leave my face. She didn't even fucking blink. This one wasn't going to crack.

'Fine. I'll come. On one condition.'

'Being?'

'That I get to watch you climb back down the fire escape.'

'Piss off, Callum.'

I was feeling better already.

# PART FIVE
# TESTING

# Chapter 42

# Mischa

Me and Victoria were early. I'd pulled a sickie again at work. Which was probably stupid because we'd then spent the whole day with nothing to do. Apart from think. And walk round Victoria's house like two animals stuck in a cage.

When it got to five, Victoria said we should leave in case traffic was bad. Thank *God*. I was bored and desperate to get out the house. And I wanted to see whether or not Callum was going to turn up.

*And Freya?*

We hadn't managed to do anything about Freya. We had no way of getting in touch with her to see what was going on. Victoria had given Genevieve a call to ask if she'd give us her number, but she'd said she couldn't. I'd had a quick go at seeing if we could find her on Instagram, but we didn't even know her surname. And now all I could think about was that we'd lied to Callum. We'd told him she was coming back. Which meant if she didn't, he was going to be seriously pissed off. The thought made me start to sweat. I hated lying to people.

Genevieve was weirdly calm when we got to her flat. She didn't look worried. Just said hi, then stood aside to let us in and went off to make us both a drink. Me and Victoria sat down next to each other but didn't say anything. Not sure I could've had a conversation with her anyway. I was too nervous.

Just as Genevieve handed us a glass of squash each and placed a big bowl of olives on the table, the doorbell rang. She went to answer it.

'It's great to see you,' she said. 'Go through, I'll be with you in just a second.'

Seconds later, Callum appeared. Looking loads better than when we'd last seen him. He gave us a quick wave and sat down. I waved back, remembering how once upon a time I'd have had a complete breakdown if Callum had even looked at me, let alone waved. But after clearing up the mess he'd made in his bathroom, I no longer had a crush on him. Some things just couldn't be unseen.

'Still missing someone, I see.'

'She'll be here,' Victoria said.

I was pretty sure she wasn't as confident as she sounded.

'If you say so.' He was trying to appear relaxed, but doing a really crap job. He couldn't stop fidgeting. Crossing his legs. Uncrossing his legs. Running his hands through his hair. He made me feel jumpy just looking at him. Then he cracked his knuckles, one at a time.

'Oh, for goodness' sake, Callum, will you please stop that?' Victoria said.

'Sorry. Bad habit.'

I couldn't think of a single thing to say. Just when I thought the atmosphere couldn't get any worse, the doorbell rang a second time. We all looked at each other. Please please *please* God let it be her. We heard Genevieve open the door.

And then, as if by magic, Freya appeared.

The sight of her nearly knocked me off my chair. She sat down in an empty seat between me and Callum. I looked at him, desperate to see the reaction. He all but had his mouth hanging open. He was acting just like the boys at school used to do when one of the pretty girls walked into the classroom, only about ten times worse. Trying hard not to stare, but basically dribbling. I bit my lip to stop myself giggling.

*He likes her.*

Freya looked petrified. But all that mattered was she was here. She looked at me and smiled. I grabbed her hand and gave it a squeeze.

'I'm so happy you came back,' I whispered.

She gave me a small nod, but said nothing. I got the feeling she didn't trust herself to speak.

Genevieve came into the room with two more drinks, handed one to Freya and one to Callum and sat down. There was something about her today that was different but I couldn't work out what. Maybe it was what she was wearing; the white floaty dress made her look like some kind of fairy. Like the ones in the books that Mum used to read me when I was a kid. The ones with flowerpots on their heads. Not that Genevieve had a flowerpot on her head, *obviously*. Although she had stuck her hair on top of her head in a tight bun. Maybe that's why she seemed different: usually her hair was down.

Before Genevieve had a chance to say anything, Callum jumped in. 'I wanted to apologise, Genevieve, for storming out last week. I was such a dick – no shocker there – but I want to try to do better today. It's been a bit of a rollercoaster few days, but I'm hoping I'm out the other side now.'

'It's really brave of you to come back, Callum,' Genevieve said. 'And I'm really pleased you're here. And Freya, too. I know all this has been difficult for both of you but . . .'

'Genevieve?'

We all turned to look at Freya.

'Yes, Freya?' Genevieve said.

'Would it be alright if I went first today? I'm sorry. Would you mind, Callum? I really don't want to chicken out again. And I'm worried I might if I don't start talking soon.'

'Of course, I don't mind,' Callum said. 'Oh, and you look very nice by the way.'

He immediately looked embarrassed. He might have blushed but it was hard to tell because of his tan. Freya looked surprised.

I saw Victoria open her mouth to speak and I shot her a look. Unbelievably, she shut it again.

'Okay then, Freya,' Genevieve said. 'Feel free to begin whenever you're ready. And let me know if you need any help from me to guide you through this.'

I crossed my fingers behind my back, hoping with everything I had that she could do it this time round.

# Chapter 43

# Freya

I was looking at a small stain on Genevieve's carpet. If I stared at it hard enough, maybe, just maybe, I could pretend no one else was in the room.

I had no idea where to start. Mischa and Victoria had spoken effortlessly a week ago, almost as if they weren't thinking. I did nothing but think, every minute of every day, my brain going round and round and round in endless spirals.

Should I begin at the start or the end? I had no idea what would be less painful. I opened my mouth to say something but then felt the room start to spin. The silence was stifling, weighing me down like a heavy woollen blanket. I couldn't breathe.

No. No – I was *not* going to let this happen again. I was with people I trusted. People who now had a better understanding of the real me than any of my friends or family. The scarred and imperfect version. And I owed it to them to tell them the truth, as much as I owed it to myself to say it out loud.

'My baby died.'

Three little words as tiny and powerless as the person they represented, creating a sentence I thought I would never be able to utter. But I finally had. And while, once upon a time, in a different life, I had expected such an admission would kill me, I realised, in fact, it brought with it relief. And the relief was accompanied by the realisation that I could tell them how.

'Her name was Alaia. I picked the name when I was little, back when I thought life would go exactly according to plan.

I always knew I'd have a girl. That's why Joe and I didn't bother to find out the sex. I thought I didn't need to be told. Sounds stupid saying that. Because there's no way I could have known. But I thought I did.'

My mind drifted back to the day I first saw those two little blue lines on the pregnancy test. And the unimaginable excitement of the weeks which followed.

'Joe and I were ecstatic when we found out I was pregnant. It was quite soon after we'd started trying. The pregnancy was tough though: I was really sick for the first sixteen weeks. I lost loads of weight, couldn't keep anything down other than bananas and Ryvita and Heinz cream of chicken soup, weirdly. It was pretty grim. I tried everything people suggested to get rid of the nausea, but nothing worked. Ginger, travel bands, herbal tea, reflexology, acupuncture. You name it, I tried it. People said I was having a girl because the morning sickness was awful. Apparently it was something to do with the extra female hormones. I was almost going to take meds for it but then, right before my twenty-week scan, the vomiting stopped and I felt good after that. And I didn't get any other symptoms. No heartburn, or weak bladder or difficulty sleeping. All in all, I was probably lucky.'

Lucky. The ridiculousness of the word made it wedge in my throat. I took another couple of breaths.

'Freya, are you sure you're okay?' Genevieve asked. 'Would you like some water?'

'No, I'm fine. Sorry, I lost my train of thought. What was I saying?'

'You were telling us about the pregnancy,' Genevieve said.

'Oh yes. The rest of the pregnancy was fine. I was ready for her weeks before my due date. The nursery was painted, Joe had put the cot together. My parents had bought us a ridiculously expensive pram. I'd torn out a baby list from some magazine and bought literally everything on it. I'd read loads of books. Washed and ironed what felt like thousands of tiny little babygrows, mittens, hats, muslins. All folded perfectly in the drawers in her nursery. I'd had this beautiful baby shower – two actually – one organised by work and another one with family and friends. I'd been to weekly hypnobirthing classes with Joe, watched God knows how many videos about labour. Had a pregnancy massage. I couldn't have been more ready.'

I paused, feeling okay at the moment – but conscious that had been the easy bit.

'You're doing great, Freya,' Genevieve said. 'Carry on if you can.'

I nodded. I knew that the only way to tell the rest was to start and simply not stop. I forced myself to picture a day I had avoided any thought of in months.

'When I went into labour, it all felt completely natural. The contractions started – easy to cope with at first but then more and more painful. I called Joe at around lunchtime, and he came straight home. He couldn't have been more excited. He kept checking he had everything packed and ready to go. He must have made sure the baby seat was attached properly about a million times. We stayed at home for as long as we could, walking around the garden, going up and down the stairs, bouncing on the exercise ball, having a warm bath. All the things I'd been told could help speed things up. Then, when the pain got really bad, we drove to the hospital. I'd deliberately chosen to give birth close to where my parents live because they had a newly built maternity wing and I didn't want to take any drugs or have an epidural unless I had to. When we arrived, they sent us straight to the opposite end of the maternity ward, where they had these private rooms with birthing pools.

'Everything seemed to be going to plan, more or less. They examined me pretty regularly. At first, I was only a few centimetres dilated, which was fairly soul-destroying given the pain I was in, but because my waters had broken by then, they didn't send me home. As the hours rolled past, I got closer and closer. I was on gas and air by this point and in the pool. I remember thinking it hurt much more than I thought it would, but it came in bouts and I was just about coping okay. Joe was great. He'd brought candles and music and enough snacks to feed an army. I felt too sick to eat, but he would somehow convince me to have something small every half hour in the early stages, just to keep my energy levels up. And he'd rub my back and tell me that everything was going to be alright.

'The final time they checked me, I was about eight centimetres dilated. The midwife told me to get out of the pool and walk around to try to speed the process up a bit. After hours of contractions, she told me to push. And I did. It seemed to go on for ages and ages. I thought it was normal to be pushing for that long, but after a while the midwife told me to get out of the pool again because she wanted to see what was going on. That was agony. I was in this rhythm of breathing and pushing by that point and having to leave the water felt completely counter-intuitive to what I had to do to get the baby out. I couldn't even get myself up on the bed, the contractions were that bad, so the midwife examined me as I bent over it instead.

'And then, all of a sudden, the atmosphere changed. Someone pressed a button. The room filled with strangers. I heard someone say that the baby had got stuck, that they needed to do an emergency C-section. I wasn't really listening because by that point the contractions were really strong, and it took everything I had to stay over the bed and not collapse on the floor. Suddenly I was being told not to push, which went against everything my body was telling me.

'I have very little memory of them getting me ready or going into theatre. It's all quite patchy. I know I was put on a gurney that squeaked when it moved. I remember seeing rows of artificial lights above my head. Watching the cracks in the walls of the hospital as we flew down the corridors. I remember my bed crashing into the back of a lift.

I vaguely recall the sound of voices and seeing Joe looking more frightened than I'd ever seen him. And a kind-looking anaesthetist with a really soft voice who told me to hold still while she put something in my back.'

I swallowed, aware that I'd started to tremble.

'You're doing great,' Genevieve said. 'Try to keep going.'

*Keep going, keep going, keep going.* I let the words echo around my head. *Keep going, Freya,* I told myself. *You can do this.*

'And then I met the doctor who was going to perform the caesarean. For some reason the memory of him still haunts me, even though I'm sure there was nothing sinister about him. But he had these huge blue eyes. And a pristine white surgical mask that stretched from one ear to another. And he said to me, and I'll never forget this, he said, "Don't worry, Freya, you're perfectly safe." It felt like time slowed down after that. And even though the pain had disappeared, the second the anaesthetist put the line in my back, I was terrified.

'I vaguely recall hearing a mixture of voices, quiet at first, then louder and slightly more anxious. I wasn't in any discomfort, but I had the weirdest sensation of my insides being pulled about. Then I heard the doctor ask someone to help him. He said something about the baby being too far down. That he needed to get the cord away from the neck. Then I heard them talking about bleeding. And Joe was shouting at people to try to understand what was going on. They told him to move away. I think I remember seeing someone holding him back. People were crowding around me and I felt like I couldn't breathe. And the whole time I kept thinking over and over and over again that something terrible was going to happen. It wasn't going to plan. Something was about to go horribly wrong.

'The pulling and pushing continued for what felt like forever. Then, all of a sudden, I felt this really violent wrench and then a release and I got the briefest glimpse of my beautiful little girl before they rushed her to the other side of the room. I asked if I could see her, but I couldn't make my voice heard above everyone else. I could see blood on people's hands and I realised it was mine. I wanted to scream but I didn't have the energy. Then, without warning, everything went quiet and still. I was fighting this desperate urge to sleep. I think I must have been losing consciousness. I could hear more people yelling but they seemed very far away. I managed to turn my head to see doctors gathered around my baby. It looked like they were trying to get her to breathe. Then just before I blacked out, I heard six words. Six words that I will never ever forget. The doctor with the blue eyes looked me straight in the eyes and said, 'I'm terribly sorry, we've lost her.'

# Chapter 44

# Victoria

The room was quiet. And the breeze that had been blowing gently towards us from Genevieve's open window on the other side of the lounge had dropped away, creating a heavy, almost claustrophobic stillness.

I felt weary, the efforts of the last few days perhaps starting to take their toll. But more than weary, I also felt immeasurably sad. Not just for Mischa and Freya or myself for that matter, but for a world that forced people to endure such heartbreak. How was it fair that kind and decent people could be lulled into thinking life was good, only for a single tragic event to wrench that away from them, without any warning at all?

Perhaps for the first time in my life, I could feel a sharp ache in my heart that was nothing to do with physical pain. And I wondered to myself, was this a good thing to experience? Was letting these people chip away at me, something I should be grateful for? Was learning to be sympathetic to another person's heartbreak something I would one day welcome? Or would it slowly destroy me, each person taking a small piece of my heart at a time until there was nothing left to give?

But then Freya spoke again, and I saw that perhaps there was a point to everything after all.

'Alaia was beautiful. I only saw her for that split second, but I knew, even in that moment, she was everything I'd ever wanted. It's strange. Even though I've lost her, even though I know that nothing I can do will ever bring her back, reliving what happened makes me see that I'll always be grateful for that moment.'

A single tear slid down her cheek and she wiped it away with her hand. She sniffed. 'Thank you for listening. I'm sorry it's taken me so long to talk about this. I wish I was stronger.'

'You've nothing to apologise for,' Genevieve said. 'What you went through is something that no person should ever have to experience. I don't think I've ever met anyone who has dealt with the loss of a child any differently. It's grief in its very rawest form. When a child dies it makes us question everything we know about the world. Whatever belief system we cling to – religion, fate, karma – is shattered. And that's sometimes very hard for people to deal with. You should be proud of yourself, Freya, you really should. I can't promise that you'll start to move on from this quickly, but the more you talk about it, the more you share your story, the better you will begin to feel. And you will heal in time, I promise.'

'Thank you,' Freya said. 'And thank you for convincing me to come back. I wouldn't be here if you hadn't dropped by to see me.'

'That's okay,' Genevieve said, with a smile. 'Just maybe don't tell my supervisor about that if you ever meet him.'

'My God, Freya,' Mischa said. She had been crying quietly this whole time, tears sliding down her cheeks like a small stream. 'That's the saddest thing I've ever heard. I can't even begin to think what it must be like to go through something like that. It's just awful.'

'Please don't feel bad for me,' Freya said. 'That's the last thing I want.'

She smiled tiredly, looking at her hands. I noticed that she wasn't wearing her wedding ring anymore.

'You know what?' she said. 'I'll live every day wishing I had my baby back. But maybe every day will also be a little bit easier. Maybe good things are still to come. I hope that's the case anyway. And maybe it will also make me a stronger person at the end of it all.'

'You're braver than me, I'll give you that,' I said. 'At least you've opened yourself up to your emotions. I'm only just learning what that means.'

'I think you care a lot more about things than you make out, Victoria,' Genevieve said. 'What you did for Callum is evidence of that.'

I was just about to ask her how on earth she knew that we'd been to see Callum when I was distracted by the sound of a chair being pushed back.

'Excuse me a second. I think I need a bit of a time out if you don't mind.'

We all turned to look at Callum. He looked slightly grey. He stood up and made his way unsteadily out of the room. We heard the front door open and close.

Not again, I thought to myself. I wasn't sure I had the energy to bring him back a second time. I certainly didn't have the energy to climb another ruddy fire escape. But after a couple of minutes, when he still hadn't returned, I forced myself to get up. I wasn't going to let him do another runner.

'I'll go,' Freya said. She got up out of her chair. 'Don't worry, I'll bring him back.'

She hurried out of the room. I was reminded of this identical scene, a week ago. Two down, two left. Only this time I hoped things would end slightly differently.

Mischa, Genevieve and I looked at each other helplessly.

'How about a cup of tea?' Genevieve said.

# Chapter 45

# Callum

I was sitting against the front door of Genevieve's flat, having a cheeky roll-up, hoping to God the building didn't have any smoke detectors, when I felt a sudden expanse of air behind me. Before I could adjust my weight, I fell backwards, my head hitting the carpet of Genevieve's hallway like a cannonball. I looked up, only to realise that I was staring straight up a flimsy silk skirt. And whoever it belonged to had fucking insane legs. And black lace underwear. I felt something stir. What the fuck was wrong with me?

Freya stepped over me carefully and sat down on the floor, moving her legs to the side and pulling her skirt over her knees.

'You know, if you wanted to check out my knickers, you could have just asked,' she said, looking at me with a tiny smile on her face. To my surprise, she grabbed the cigarette out of my hand and took a long, slow drag.

'You have great taste in underwear. Although my personal preference is nothing at all.'

'Sit up, pervert.'

'I've been called a lot of things in my time, Freya, but never a pervert.'

'First time for everything, isn't there?'

I sat up and took the opportunity to really look at her while she smoked, drinking in her perfect face like a sponge. It was the first time I'd seen her with clean hair and make-up and the result was overpowering. I knew I was being totally fucking shallow even appreciating the difference a bit of hair colour and a full face of make-up could do, but at that moment I didn't give a shit. She was fucking gorgeous.

The trouble was, I also knew my attraction to her was more than just physical. Yeah, I could kid myself into thinking she was nothing more than a hot girl who'd catapulted from a five to a ten. And that's exactly what the old me would have thought (and probably said to her face). But when I really looked at her, I saw something else. She had this aura around her, both strange and familiar, that I felt the weirdest desperation to absorb. And, more than that, she was making me doubt myself for quite possibly the first time ever. Challenge the words that came out my mouth, in case they didn't match up to what she wanted to hear. Question every action, every reaction, every simple fucking *movement*. I was, quite simply, screwed.

I was suddenly very much aware how long I'd been staring at her but she didn't even flinch. She just carried on smoking the rest of my cigarette, staring off into space. I felt a desperate urge to kiss her but fought it. The poor woman had just finished telling us about the death of her daughter. And I was contemplating putting it on her.

'I know what you're thinking, you know.'

'I really hope you don't, Freya. It's fucking inappropriate.'

She laughed. 'Come back in.'

'I'm going to come back in. Don't worry. I'm not going to let you all down again. I just needed a minute to sort my head out.'

'Okay. Do you want to get some fresh air maybe?'

I thought about it. 'You know what, yes. That would be good.'

'Okay, let me go and tell the others first. Otherwise they'll panic we've run off again.'

She handed me the dregs of the roll-up as she went back inside, emerging a few seconds later with our coats. She threw mine down at me and I caught it in one hand, carefully tucking the butt of the cigarette into the pocket of my jeans with the other.

Five minutes later, we were outside the building, walking shoulder to shoulder towards St James' Park, our footsteps hitting the concrete slabs of the pavement in tandem. Without either us of saying a word, my hand somehow found his and entwined, not letting go until we reached a wooden bench overlooking a lake.

We sat down, side by side, two humans huddled together against the cold wind. She leant her head in the crook of my neck. I took a sideways glance at her. She was staring straight out towards the shadowy water beyond.

'I'm really sorry about Alaia, Freya.'

She shifted her weight to look at me. 'I know you are. I am too. But you know what?'

'What?'

'I can't spend my whole life feeling like this. Yearning for someone who's never coming back.'

'I know exactly what you mean.'

Another silence.

'I'm leaving him, you know.'

'Who?'

'Joe.'

'Joe your husband?'

'No, Joe the milkman. Yes, of course my husband. Idiot.'

'Why are you leaving him?'

'Because staying with someone you've never really been in love with isn't right. Or fair. And staying with someone you've never really been in love with just because you've both lost your baby is even worse.'

'Did you know you didn't love him when you married him?'

'I think I've always known deep down. But I didn't want to say it out loud.'

'You can't run from denial, you know that?'

'Isn't that the title to one of your songs?'

'Yep.'

'Thanks for that, Sinatra.'

'You're welcome.'

I had a sudden, inexplicable urge to bury my face in her hair. But I knew that would be weird. Instead, I made do with turning my face a tiny bit into her shoulder and inhaling the smell of her. Still fucking odd but less likely to get noticed. She smelt great. I tried to remember the last time I'd sat with a girl without actively trying to have sex with her. I couldn't. The only thing I did with girls was flirt with them, bang them and then ghost them. Flirt, bang, ghost. Maybe that could be the title to my next single? Jesus, when had I become such a wanker?

I knew then that I owed her a proper apology. 'Freya?'

'Mmm?' She was looking away from me again, the wind blowing strands of blonde across her face. I leant towards her and tucked them gently behind her ear, my thumb stroking the warm gold of her earring. I couldn't stop wanting to touch her.

'I'm sorry for what happened the other day at my apartment. Pulling away from you like that. And for being a complete dick afterwards.'

'You don't have to explain; it's fine.'

Part of me was annoyed at her for being so nice about it. But also, she was missing the point. 'No, Freya, it's not fine. It's not fine because that moment on the roof meant way more to me than I think you will ever realise. It was the first time in my life when everything felt like it was meant to be and I guess that scared the crap out of me.'

She gave me a small smile and nodded, but there was more I needed to say.

'You know, it's funny. When I used to write songs, the instrumentals would come so fucking easily. People thought I was lying out my arse when I said I came up with the music to 'Starstruck' in one afternoon, but that's true. I was messing about with my guitar one day and then pow, there the notes were on the page. But the bit I never admitted to anyone was that the lyrics took me three fucking months.'

'I can't imagine why. You have such a way with words.'

I ignored the joke, suddenly desperate for her to understand. 'My point is, for words to flow, you gotta feel them, right? And I hadn't so I couldn't.'

'But it's a great song. You must have felt it eventually.'

'Yeah, you know what I did?'

'What?'

'I watched the fucking *Notebook*.'

The sound of Freya's laugh beside me was as beautiful as the breeze through a blossom tree.

'What are you trying to say?'

I took a deep breath. 'That after that night with you ... I think I could have written those words a lot quicker.'

I wasn't sure if she had any idea what I was talking about, since she'd always made such a point of telling me she didn't listen to my songs, but it didn't matter. I'd told her what I wanted to say. 'I think I'm ready to go back in now,' I said.

'Are you sure?'

'Yeah, I am. Let's do this.'

I stood up, holding out both hands to help Freya up. She grabbed them and got to her feet but, once standing, didn't let go. Instead, she turned my palms upwards, running her fingers gently over the calluses on my hands. Something about it gave me goosebumps.

'Doubt they'll ever heal,' I said.

'They don't need to heal. They make you who you are.'

She closed both my hands carefully together, wrapped her own around mine and lowered her lips gently onto the tips of my middle fingers. I felt my pulse go up a notch. I knew for a fact that if she kissed me again, I wouldn't pull away. Looking at her now, I couldn't believe I'd ever had the willpower to do that.

But she didn't kiss me. She just gently squeezed my hands. 'Let's do this shall we?'

# Chapter 46

# Mischa

Finally, they were back. I breathed a massive sigh of relief. And pretended not to notice they were holding hands.

'Are you okay, Callum?' asked Genevieve.

'Yeah, I am, thanks. I just needed a bit of space to clear my head. I'm good to go.'

I caught his eye and he smiled at me. It was weird – I knew he'd never have done that when I'd first met him. He used to be so up himself. Looking at everyone like they were beneath him. He still had something special about him. The sort of cool I'd never be. But he was different now. More normal.

Saying that, out of all of us, he was still the one who hadn't really told us anything. Maybe that was because he was famous – he knew how to hide stuff. I wondered if he'd open up now. For some reason I couldn't see it. But maybe that was also because he was a guy.

*Men are terrible communicators, you know that.*

'If you're ready, Callum, please go ahead,' Genevieve said.

He swallowed.

'I'm not sure if I'll ever be ready. But I'm going to give it a stab.'

He looked at his hands. 'But there's one other thing I want to say before I start, if that's alright?'

'Of course, go ahead.'

'I just want to say thanks. I'm not very good at being grateful for shit. I can be a bit of an arsehole sometimes, I know. But I am grateful. I've spent a long time in a really fucking bad place. Way before any of the shit I'm about to talk about happened. I've got no excuse for any of it. I was an arrogant little fucker from the second I popped out the womb. I thought I could handle everything that came with money. And fame. Thought I could handle whatever life threw at me. But it turns out I couldn't. Far from it. I kept fucking up over and over and over. And the more I fucked up, the worse it got. The more people I upset. And that's how my life has been for God knows how long. Following up a fuck-up with another fuck-up. I'm swearing too much I know. Sorry. Fuck.'

He stared down at his hands, stretched out his fingers in front of him. Then closed them, making his fists into a ball.

'Basically what I'm trying to say is, I'm grateful. My whole life I've had people try to help me but I haven't listened to any of them. But there's something about you guys. I don't get it, to be honest. But I feel like I'm in the right place now.'

He pulled his hands through his hair and looked at us. 'I wanted to say thanks before I started, is all. Because I'm pretty sure that when I'm done, you're not going to want anything to do with me.'

Genevieve held up her hand to stop him talking. 'Callum?'

'Yeah?'

'I don't think you should start with that mindset, okay?' she said. 'I think you'll find we'll be a lot more understanding of what happened than you think.'

'Fine, if you say so.'

Callum half sniffed, half snorted. He sounded like he had a bit of a cold. I hoped he wasn't coming down with something.

'You already know I had a drug problem right? It wasn't a small one. And I know I still have it. I'm an addict. I get that. But fuck, getting me to admit that a year ago – not a chance in hell. They say the biggest addicts are the ones who think they have everything under control. The ones who think they can stop anytime they want. That's totally true in my case.'

He paused, picking at a string on his jeans. They were ripped, as usual.

'My last shrink told me I have an addictive personality. Apparently it's really common with creative people. We get obsessive about stuff. We do everything to excess, whether it's good or bad. It's what makes us successful at what we do. But it's also the reason we tend to fuck it all up at some point.

'When I first started out, playing in bars, eventually doing some gigs, I got high off that feeling, you know? When you first step onto a stage, it doesn't matter if there are only fifty people in a room, when they hear the songs you wrote and you feel people you've never met connect with them, it's fucking dynamite. There's no better rush than being out there, doing the only thing you've ever known how to do, and feeling loved for it. And hearing people singing your songs back at you, man, that's the best fucking sound in the world.

'When I was trying to get to the top, I didn't need drugs. If I ever took them, it was just for the hell of it, you know. Because all that mattered to me was being the best. Getting my songs heard. Being played on the radio. Reaching the charts. Making a number one single, number one album. There was always something better to do. Drugs were simply on the edges of that. Helped me party a little bit longer. I didn't even notice I was doing them half the time. I didn't feel like they controlled me anyway.'

'What happened to change that, do you think?'

'I got to the top of my game,' Callum replied. 'That's when things started to unravel. I couldn't wipe my fucking arse without someone getting in my space. It's fine at the beginning but then it started to grate. Everything you do is plastered all over the *Daily* fucking *Mail Online*. Half of it's bollocks, at least to begin with. People saying all this shit about you, just to make a few quid. Some of them friends, some of them people you vaguely knew at school, most of them arseholes you've never met in your entire fucking life. After a while you start to live up to what the media want you to be. They push you towards this crazy rockstar reputation and you hold on to that. And you realise you can do more or less whatever the fuck you want and get away with it. That's when things started to get out of control. For me, anyway. And around the same time, that natural high I got from performing, that feeling of total ecstasy I felt whenever I sang in front of people, it started to wane.'

'Can you remember the moment it all started to go wrong?' Genevieve asked.

Callum nodded. 'Absolutely. It was the last night of my first world tour. I'd given it everything I had for months and the second I hit that final note at my last concert and I heard the crowd go fucking wild, that was the moment I knew I'd made it. And it felt absolutely awesome. But then I went backstage and I got this huge downer. I thought to myself, I'm never going to hit that high again. And I remember wondering why the hell I was doing it. I hadn't seen my family in months. My brother had had his second baby the year before and I hadn't even seen her. I'd been with countless girls, but I couldn't remember what any of them looked like, let alone what they were called. Not sure I'd even asked. Most places I'd been to I hadn't even bothered to leave the hotel because it was too much of a fucking hassle to walk to my car.'

'How did that make you feel?'

'Guilty, actually. Guilty that I was being such an ungrateful little shit. I started questioning what I'd done to deserve the success I'd had when I couldn't even appreciate it. Yeah sure, I could play a guitar and I'd written some catchy songs, but I'd seen heaps of people do that and get fucking nowhere. Shit, most of my support acts were better musicians than I was. I decided I was nothing more than a good poet with a pretty face. Which made me feel even worse about myself.'

'What did you do?' I asked. I was so caught up in his story I hardly realised it was me who asked the question.

'I ended up asking one of the crew who I'd got friendly with if he knew anywhere I could get something stronger than my usual stuff. Said I wanted to forget about everything for a while. Not smack or anything like that. Just something with a bit more of a kick. And he got me these pills. Didn't even know what was in them. But fuck me, they were strong. And I loved the world again. Partied hard that night. Had the best time of my life with people I'd never met. And would never see again.'

'How did you feel afterwards?' Genevieve asked. 'When the drugs wore off?'

'Like shit. But worse than that, that feeling of emptiness was back with a fucking vengeance. And twice as bad. Which meant the next time I went out, I took more of those pills. Mixed them with some coke. And champagne. Had another great night. The papers were all over it.

'And that's how it went on. Except each time I took something, the high wasn't quite the same. And each comedown was worse than the one before. I took more pills, or tried something else. Couldn't sleep; took different ones to knock myself out at the end of the night. It's all a bit of a blur, those months after the tour. Was supposed to be writing my next album, but I didn't go to the studio once. My label was going fucking mental. I didn't give a shit.'

Abruptly Callum stopped talking. 'Sorry. As I'm telling you this, I can't tell you how fucking ashamed of myself I am. And I haven't even got to the end. I don't know if I can do this. I haven't let myself think about what happened, let alone talk about it. I want to, but I don't know if I can.'

And with that, the guy who I'd once thought was perfect, basically the coolest person I'd ever met, put his head in his hands and cried.

# Chapter 47

# Freya

Seeing Callum cry was unbearable. It felt like my own heart was being ripped in two. The more time I spent with him, the more I had the strangest sense of an invisible chain slowly tying us together, becoming ever more tangled with each passing second. I took hold of his hand.

'Callum?' I said.

He glanced across at me. He looked exhausted. Like he hadn't slept in a long time. I knew that feeling. But he had something else weighing down on him.

'Yeah?'

'We do understand, you know.'

'You can't.'

Whatever it was that Callum had been through, he clearly felt responsible for it. Which, I realised, made him slightly different to the rest of us. And then it hit me – maybe it wasn't the *event* he couldn't get over, but the *reason* for it. Somehow, I had to convince him that didn't matter.

He was avoiding all eye contact with me, but he hadn't let go of my hand.

'Look at me, Callum.'

He moved his gaze from the floor to my face.

'You're right. We probably don't understand. But look around you. We're all in the same place. Different stories, different people, yes. And maybe you feel you're in a worse position because you're somehow to blame for whatever it is that's happened. I get it. That would make it harder to talk about. But even if that's the case, as long as you feel remorse for what you did, that's all we care about. You're a good person, Callum. I know that. *We* know that. You just made a mistake. A mistake is still a mistake, even if it had terrible consequences.'

Was I getting through to him? I didn't know – he was looking down at his hands as I spoke. I carried on.

'We all want the same thing from this, Callum. We've all of us lived half a life for as long as we can remember. We're all broken and tired. But you know what we all have in common? We all want to escape that feeling. We all want to leave our ghosts behind. It doesn't matter what you've done.'

'What I've done is completely unforgivable.'

'That's rubbish. If you want forgiveness, I'll give it to you now. I don't need to hear your story to know that I'll forgive you. Because whatever happened, whatever it is you've done, I know it doesn't matter to me.'

'Nor me,' said Victoria.

'Me neither,' Mischa added.

The affirmations of the group appeared to give Callum the strength to look up. Our eyes connected and I found myself gazing into the brilliant ocean of his irises. And with that I felt that *something* again; something I couldn't begin to understand. A sensation of physical connection without contact; a sudden expectation of something new and exciting about to unfold. Together we were two people about to swan-dive from the top of a cliff, knowing that in a matter of seconds the tips of our fingers would part the water and everything around us would change forever.

Whether or not he felt it too, I had no idea. But something in him shifted. An almost invisible fog lifted from his face. Maybe he had finally accepted that he wouldn't be judged for this. He nodded slowly, and started speaking again.

# Chapter 48

# Callum

'One day I was sitting around the apartment on a major, major comedown. I was sweating, panicky, couldn't bear the thought of leaving my room. And I heard the door go. I got up, looked through the spyhole. It was my brother. I hadn't seen him in over a year. Not since that shitshow of a Christmas when I'd gone home to Mum and Dad's. I hadn't seen them since then, either. I wasn't going to let him in, but he kept his finger on the fucking doorbell and eventually I couldn't deal with the sound of it anymore and I opened the door. He took one look at me and shoulder-barged me into the apartment.'

And with that, the room in front of me blurred and I was back home that day, my brother sitting on my couch with a look of complete disgust on his face. It was weird, having him sat opposite me. We looked like twins, despite the fact that Finn was three years older and had piled on the pounds since I'd last seen him. I was tempted to tell him he should try to look after himself a bit more, but I held my tongue. I doubted he'd see the funny side.

'This apartment is a fucking bombsite, dude.'

I'd shrugged. What the hell did I care about that?

'And look at the state of you. You're a fucking mess.'

A thousand comebacks flew into my head but I refused to bite. That guy could throw a fucking hard punch and I had a bad enough headache already.

'Nice to see you too, Finn.'

'What do you expect me to say? It is, and you are. And why have you stopped taking Mum's calls?'

'I haven't stopped taking her calls. I've been busy.'

'Doing what exactly?'

'Writing.'

'Really? That's odd, because Mum got a call from Skye the other day. Asking her to talk to you. Convince you to sort your shit out. Told her you're way behind on your deadlines.'

'She had no fucking right to do that.'

'I guess she thought Mum might be able to get through to you. Maybe she could if you could be arsed to pick up the fucking phone.'

'Why are you here, Finn?'

'Why do you think I'm here? Mum told me to come over and straighten you the fuck out.'

'Why didn't she come with you?'

'Come off it, you know why – Dad wouldn't let her.'

'Still not talking to me then?'

'Come on, mate. Last time you saw him you filled his house with paps and then fucked off out the window. You could've at least called to say sorry.'

I knew he was right but there was no way I was going to admit it. 'You shouldn't have bothered coming over. I'm fine. Honestly. And you've got Amy and the kids to take care of. You shouldn't have to worry about me on top of everything else.'

'Doesn't matter, I do. And you're clearly not fine.'

'I'm just enjoying my time off. Jesus Christ, I deserve it, don't I? I was on the road for fucking months!'

'Yeah, you deserve a break. 'Course you do. But a break isn't getting off your tits every day of the fucking week. It's not losing your shit with people who ask for a photo. And it's definitely not being in the paper coming out of Daze with five women in fucking tow. Mum was mortified.'

'Come on, man, admit it. You rated that last one.'

'Fuck, Callum, this isn't a joke. You're killing yourself.'

And that's how the conversation had gone on. For what felt like hours. Eventually we'd both calmed down. Started talking a bit more rationally about stuff. Had a couple of drinks. Had a few more. Soon it felt like old times, just me and my bro hanging out, talking shit. I'd missed him. Missed having someone around who knew the real me.

'Let's go out.' We were on the whisky and cokes by this point and I was starting to get twitchy being at home. It was gone 11 p.m. I could hear my phone going mental. People who didn't give a toss about me wanting to know my plans for the night.

'Where?'

'Let me take you out.'

Finn had looked at me. Uncertain. 'I dunno, man. I was supposed to come down here to sort you out. Somehow you've managed to get me pissed and now you want me to go out and party with you?'

'Finn, I never see you. You're always working or with the kids. I want you to be part of my world. Just for one night. Tell you what, I'll make a pact with you.'

'Go on.'

'Come out with me tonight. One night where you get to see what it's like to be me. I want you to understand why I've done what I've done. And after tonight, I'll quit the lot. I'll go cold fucking turkey, stay with Mum and Dad for a bit. Make peace with Dad. Start writing again. I swear to God. Just come out and have fun with me, just once.'

And then my older brother, the guy I'd idolised my entire life, who'd taken care of me my whole childhood, had looked at me and nodded. And then he'd said, 'You'll have to lend me some of your poncy designer gear to wear then. This shirt's got baby vom on the fucking shoulder.'

The memory faded in front of my eyes and I was suddenly back in Genevieve's flat. I realised I was still holding Freya's hand.

'Are you okay, Callum?' Genevieve asked.

'Yeah,' I replied. I took a couple of breaths and carried on talking. Knew that the worst thing I could do was stop to think. 'I made a couple of calls to my PA to sort some stuff out for us. Then we hit a club in Soho around midnight. Went to that place that does the live stage shows. Basically classy soft porn with a hint of sado-fucking-masochism thrown in for good measure. Finn fucking loved it. Said he was letting his hair down for the first time in years. Had a couple of lines in the toilets downstairs. Couldn't believe the treatment I got. No queuing, no paying, no questions asked. Beautiful girls joining the table with no more than a nod at the bouncer. Everyone wanting to shake his hand, tell him what a talented brother he had. I could tell he felt like a king.

'Don't get me wrong, he behaved himself with the girls. Could've had anyone he wanted. But he didn't cross the line, not once. He loved Amy. And his kids. I knew he wouldn't fuck everything up for a one-night stand in a club toilet. He wasn't me for a start. But he took full advantage of everything else my fame offered that night. Even asked if he could take the bill home to frame it. It came to something like £53k and was about a metre long. I think I'd bought drinks for everyone in the VIP lounge.

'Around 4 a.m. we left the club and came home. It had been a great night. I felt like we'd gotten close again in just a few hours. I was on top of the world. Couldn't stop telling Finn how much I loved him. How much he meant to me. How grateful I was to have him as my big brother. And I promised him I'd sort myself out once and for all.

'We passed out cold when we got back to the apartment. Woke up about six hours later, and that's when Finn started to panic. He'd promised Amy he'd be home by midday. It was Emily – that's his eldest daughter's – birthday. I'd completely forgotten about it. She was having a party and all our family was going to be there. I knew I couldn't be the reason he missed it.

'I suggested he drive us back in my car rather than get the train. It wasn't far. Only an hour or so south of London. I figured at that time of day on a Sunday the roads would be clear. Finn was unsure about driving, but I convinced him he was fine. Compared to the state of me he was anyway. I said I'd explain it all to Amy. That everything would be okay. After Emily's party I promised I'd go straight back to Mum and Dad's. Hang there for a few weeks. Get my head together.

'He would never normally have agreed to it. He was way too sensible. But he knew it was his one and only chance to get me to go home with him. If he left me in the apartment, I'd sober up, then start all over again, and be going nowhere. I remember he downed a Diet Coke out the fridge, we threw some of my stuff in a holdall and we left.

'On the way out the door I told him again not to worry. That he hadn't had that much to drink.

'Turns out I was wrong.'

# Chapter 49

# Victoria

We all knew, every single one of us, how it was going to end. My heart pulsed in dreaded anticipation of what he was about to say.

'Finn hit something head on. He was driving my car – a Lamborghini Aventador, which is a pretty damn powerful machine. He must have lost control of it. Maybe he fell asleep. Or was speeding. Who knows. Of course, I don't fucking remember anything, other than a few minutes when I think I regained consciousness. There were flashing lights and people everywhere. Glass all over the dashboard. I'm sure I heard someone tell me not to worry, they were going to get me out. I tried to ask about Finn. Tried to turn my head to look for him but I couldn't move. People shouting at me to try to stay still. The sound of some kind of saw. The roof of the car being lifted off and the sun hitting my face. Then I guess I lost consciousness again because everything went black.'

Callum paused. Looked across at us for a moment with his beautiful green eyes – the colour of a kingfisher's wings, I thought then. Eyes that had seen more tragedy than any young man deserved.

'Finn died a few minutes after arriving at the hospital. I remember hearing one of the doctors at the hospital talking about him. He said he'd been *off his head on something, couldn't save him.* Said he wouldn't have been able to operate a kettle, let alone a machine that powerful. Called him a lunatic. A fucking *lunatic*. My brother. I realised then that I must have given him more drugs than his body could handle. I didn't think I had. Or maybe he'd gone off with someone else in the club. Either way, it was my fault.

'He was my big brother. I'd never had to be responsible for making sure he was okay. He was the one who looked after me. And the one time he'd trusted me, the one time he'd put *his* faith in *me*, I'd let him and my whole family down in the biggest fucking way imaginable.

'I woke up in a hospital full of strangers. Strangers whose only job was to get me fit enough to go home. No family came to see me. And why would they? The minute they found out there were drugs in Finn's system, they would've known straight away I was to blame. Finn had never touched the stuff before.

'When I was ready to be discharged, Rob collected me and brought me home to the apartment. My management had gone into damage limitation mode by that point. Smuggled me out of hospital through the back door. No fucking idea what they did to keep the story out the press but I'm guessing they had to pay off some pretty powerful people. Apparently that sort of shit happens all the time. But they still didn't trust me not to do something stupid. I had to stay at home and avoid being seen in public until further notice. And that's how I eventually ended up here. I guess they saw it as a neat way of straightening me out.

'I tried to call Mum and Dad. And Amy. Every day for weeks on end. But the phone just rang and rang and nobody answered. And I don't blame them.'

The room was silent as Callum finished speaking. I searched desperately for something kind or sensitive to say, but my mind was blank. We all stared at him helplessly, watching the tears as they slid relentlessly down his face.

But there was something else. His story had ignited something in my brain that I couldn't put my finger on. When he'd told us the details of the crash, I'd felt the strangest of sensations. I'd felt as if I was there, reliving it with him. I truly understood at that moment his extraordinary ability to draw people in. I'd never heard him sing, didn't know any of his songs, but no one could deny that there was a magnetism about him and the way he spoke that was nothing short of hypnotic.

My train of thought was disturbed by Freya getting up from her chair. She knelt in front of Callum and I watched her take his face in her hands and gently wipe the tears away with her fingers. He looked at her then with such gratitude that I realised what Callum needed most from the world wasn't reassurance or support or understanding. He didn't want someone to tell him he wasn't to blame for what he'd done. He wanted someone to love him despite it.

Freya whispered something in his ear and he nodded. She smiled and sat back down.

We looked at each other, unsure what to do next. I realised that we'd spent so long trying to get to this very point, no one had really considered what we were supposed to do afterwards.

But fortunately, it seemed Genevieve did. She cleared her throat to get our attention. 'Thank you, Callum. You've no idea how proud I am that you've felt able to tell us about Finn. You've all been exceptionally brave these past few weeks. Acknowledging and accepting what has happened is one of the most important hurdles to overcome.'

She paused a moment. She seemed suddenly apprehensive, and I couldn't see why. Surely she should be delighted by our recent efforts? Her demeanour, I confess, made me slightly nervous, a feeling that was exacerbated tenfold when she spoke again.

'But now you've made it to this point, now you've acknowledged the cause of your grief and faced it head on, there's something else I want to talk to you about. I'm not sure how easy this will be to hear, but I ask that none of you leave this room until I'm finished. Is that okay?'

# PART SIX
# ACCEPTANCE

# Chapter 50

# Genevieve

The moment had arrived and I wasn't sure I was ready. I'd been working on this project for as long as I could remember. I'd gone through every textbook I had, batted back every question Dr Metcalfe could think of to throw at me. I had been absolutely sure I would know what to do when the time came. Now I wasn't convinced I had it in me after all.

This was the first time I'd been given the chance to follow a theory no one else really supported right through to fruition. I'd been stunned when Dr Metcalfe had agreed to it. The way we dealt with grief was set in stone and I was pushing boundaries at an institution that liked to do things in a *very* specific way.

And now I was at the point where I'd led four people – four vulnerable and susceptible people – to the end of a difficult psychological journey, and I was suddenly plagued with self-doubt. Had I done enough? Had I taken everything I should into consideration? Were they really ready?

It came down to whether they accepted what I planned to say next. I decided the only way forward was to start at the beginning and go from there.

'As you all know, I've studied the grief process for a very long time. Probably for longer than you would consider healthy. It's always fascinated me. Of all the emotions that humans have the capacity to feel, grief is by far the most penetrative and long-lasting.'

I was conscious I was sounding like a textbook. Get to the point, Genevieve, I thought.

'The purpose of this study was to group people together based on their backgrounds and personality traits. I had a theory that if you found the right combination of individuals, together they could help each other to navigate a process that ordinarily they would not have been able to do by themselves.'

'Hang on a minute,' Victoria interrupted. 'I completely understand what you're saying, but how could you ever have been in a position to do that kind of evaluation on us? I remember what I wrote in that first email to you and there wasn't much to go on. How did you know from that whether I was suitable?'

I hesitated a moment before responding. I became conscious of the fact that I'd been chewing on my knuckle for most of the session – I could taste blood. It made me feel even sicker.

'Let's just say I knew a bit more about you at the start of this process than I originally made out.'

'You knew about us? What do you mean you knew about us?'

'I mean I had a certain amount of background information at my disposal.'

'What sort of background information?'

Victoria was staring at me, her gaze unrelenting. She'd rightly sensed a chink in my armour – she looked like a predator about to take down its prey.

'For fuck's sake, Victoria,' Callum said. 'Will you let the woman speak?'

I could feel myself getting warm. I tried to undo the top button of my dress as casually as I could, but the buttonhole was too tight. I gave up.

'Okay, fine,' Victoria said. 'Please, Genevieve, would you be kind enough as to elaborate?'

I swallowed, wishing I had some water to wash away the dry tickle in my throat. It was time to tell them. 'I knew, before you came here, what had happened to you. To all of you.'

'What?' Victoria exploded, the unexpected volume of her voice causing me to inhale too sharply and start to cough. 'But that's completely bloody impossible. How could you have known? I didn't even tell my own husband half of what I've told everyone here.'

I cleared my throat. 'That's a fair observation. I . . .'

'*That's a fair observation?*'

'Victoria!' Mischa said. 'We won't find out anything if you don't calm down.'

'I am perfectly calm,' she replied, clearly anything but.

'No, you're not,' Mischa and Freya said together.

Victoria glared at them.

'Genevieve, before Victoria loses it entirely, can you please tell us how and what you knew?' Freya asked.

'Yes. Yes, of course.'

I wiped away the tiny droplets of sweat that had started to form along the top of my hairline. I needed to pull myself together.

'I think I have to go back a step first. It may surprise you to hear this, but you were not, as I first led you to believe, selected from a large group of applicants. You were . . . I'd already decided you were the individuals I wanted to work with.'

'I'm sorry, but that's also impossible,' Victoria interjected again. 'I responded to an advert. An advert you placed in *The Times*. You couldn't have known I'd even see it.'

'But I did know, Victoria. I knew you read *The Times* with Andrew every day. I knew you read it from cover to cover. Consequently, it wasn't such a huge leap of faith to assume you would see it. Or that he would convince you to respond.'

Victoria looked at me sharply, clearly stunned that I had knowledge of such an intimate detail about her life.

But before she could launch into me again, Mischa piped up. 'Hang on a sec, *The Times*? As in the paper? That's not where I saw it. I saw a postcard on the door in Londis.' She pointed at Freya. 'Where did you see it?'

'An article. An article written by Genevieve in some magazine.'

I nodded. 'And Callum received a message from someone at his record label.'

'Guys.' Callum said, running his hand through his hair – the only one of the four of them to look even remotely accommodating of what I was saying. I realised he was probably accustomed to people poking their noses into his private life. My confession was likely nowhere near as shocking to him as it was to the others. 'Can we please take a step back? Genevieve, you're saying you chose us, in advance. For a reason. And you used some kind of Derren Brown-style mind-control shit to convince us to come. Fine. Bit fucked up, but fine. But why us? Look at us. We have nothing in common. There must be thousands of people out there who would be way better matched for this sort of thing. What was it about us that you liked?'

He grinned at me. 'There are easier ways of getting me in a room with you, you know. I'm a lot more available nowadays.'

At least someone still had their sense of humour. I knew I needed to regain control somehow. I had come this far. I was not going to let the whole project collapse in under ten minutes.

'Thank you for that observation, Callum. I think maybe it's about time I explained everything properly. Can I do that?'

They all nodded, Victoria included – although I knew it wouldn't take much to set her off again.

'I'm going to tell you something quite candidly that is never normally discussed outside official circles. This experiment was, believe it or not, the first of its kind. It was a way of testing something. Finding a solution to a problem that has been around for a very long time. For thousands of years, in fact. Ever since humans properly evolved.'

'Well now you've completely fucking lost me,' Callum said.

'Please bear with me a second. You see, I work for a particular organisation. A very large one, in fact. An organisation whose job it is to monitor certain types of . . . people. Historically we were entirely passive. We simply observed. Then, as time went on, we started to do subtle things to intervene, but nothing more than that. And we certainly never attempted to bring individuals together. But the longer I worked there, and the more I studied the people I was responsible for, the more I realised that one-to-one interaction didn't always work. I knew that something else needed to be done.'

Victoria opened her mouth to ask something but Freya beat her to it.

'Okay,' she said. 'Let's ignore the fact that you lied about who you were. That you tricked us into getting in touch with you. That somehow, God knows how, you got access to extremely sensitive details about our private lives. Ignoring all that for a second, you say you work for an organisation that *monitors people*. That's the bit I'm confused about. Are you saying you work for the government? And if so, why do you care about us? That doesn't make any sense to me. It's not like we pose a security risk to anyone. Why do you care how we cope?'

Here goes nothing, I thought.

'That's the crux of what I'm getting at. You see, the reason I brought you here wasn't simply to help you to navigate the grief process. That was part of it, of course. It was essential you accepted what had happened to you for this to even stand a chance of working. Because if you can't come to terms with the root cause of your grief, you become fixated on it. Grief becomes attached to you. As does – and this bit is key – as does the person you are grieving for.'

I took a long deep breath, focusing on the slow rush of air through my nostrils. I had no idea if what I was saying was even making any sense but I had to keep going.

'You see, the type of grief a person experiences when someone very close to them dies is a palpable thing. People always think of it in psychological terms. It gets called a process. A journey. Something a person needs to work through. But in fact, it's not that at all. There's a very good reason we get told a person who is grieving can't let go. Because it's true. The attachment we have to someone we love is as much physical as it is mental. And if that physical bond doesn't get severed when a person dies, they kind of get . . . stuck. And when I say "they", I should be clear that I'm not talking about the one who is still alive. I'm talking about the one who died. They become as trapped as the loved ones they left behind.'

I looked around the room, at each of them in turn. They all looked thoroughly confused. I was losing this battle, I knew it, with my roundabout explanations that meant nothing at all.

But before I could continue, Mischa spoke up. 'I think I get what you're saying.'

Her words took me by complete surprise. 'You do?'

She nodded slowly. 'I think you're going to tell us you can talk to dead people.' She smiled suddenly, her sweet, innocent face full of hope. 'That's it, isn't it? You've spoken to my mum, haven't you? That's how you knew about me.'

Victoria reached out and touched Mischa's arm – her eyes, however, never left my face. The look she was giving me was murderous. 'Don't you dare,' she said to me, almost in a whisper. 'Don't you bloody *dare* tell this girl you've spoken to her dead mother.'

With that she stood up, reaching behind her to take her coat from the back of her chair before carefully folding it over her arm. 'I am going to give you one more chance to do the right thing and stop this outrageous performance or I will walk out of this room for good. It's time to tell us the truth.'

And with those words, I knew this was it. Make-or-break time. I looked at Mischa. 'No, Mischa, I haven't spoken to your mother. Or anyone else for that matter. I'm sorry, I wish I could tell you I had.'

Mischa looked down at her lap, her small hands trembling. The fact I knew I'd disappointed her made what I was about to say even worse. But I couldn't delay any longer. I looked at each of them in turn. Four individuals who deserved the freedom that I hoped my words would bring.

And with that, I said out loud the sentence I had practised thousands of times in my head. 'The reason I have brought you here is nothing to do with your loved ones dying. I have . . . I brought you here because *you* died.'

# Chapter 51

# Mischa

The words echoed round the room. And inside my head. I felt cold. Like someone had lobbed a bucket of ice over me. But I was covered in a horrible sticky sweat. What was Genevieve on about? How could we be dead?!

I wanted to laugh. Just when I thought nothing could shock me anymore. When I believed I might finally be on the mend. Getting to a good place. Making friends. Feeling stronger. Only for someone to say, no that's all a load of crap, Mischa, you're actually *dead*.

I wondered then how Mum would have reacted to being told the same thing. Probably pleased. I know she would have hated being stuck in a brain that was slowly crumbling to nothing. Being looked after by her daughter. Forgetting how to do even the most basic of stuff – setting the table, getting food out the fridge, going to the toilet. To be freed from that prison, even if that meant dying – she'd have been relieved, I know she would.

I realised then that Victoria was shouting. No surprises there.

'This is utter lunacy. To think I wasted weeks of my time on this nonsense. You have clearly lost the plot. Come along, Mischa, I think we should go.'

I looked at her, not really understanding, but stood up anyway. Anything that meant I didn't have to think for myself. As we left the room, I could hear Genevieve calling to us to come back. Freya's voice behind me. And then Callum, sounding like he was trying to calm Freya down. Couldn't hear what they were saying. My ears were ringing. Everything felt a very long way away.

Victoria reached the front door first and pulled it open, letting it slam against the wall. But rather than go straight outside onto the landing, she fell backwards, crashing into me and treading on my toe with the heel of her shoe. The pain brought me back to my senses.

'Ow. What's the matter?'

She said nothing. She was frozen to the spot. I repeated the question. Still nothing.

'Victoria, say something. What's the matter?'

'Mischa,' she said, pointing outside. 'Look.'

I peered around her through the doorway. Oh God.

There was absolutely nothing there. No hallway carpet. No landing. No lift. Nothing. Just a blank, empty space. Going on for what looked like forever. It was like staring up at the night sky when there weren't any stars.

'What's going on?' I grabbed at Victoria's hand, which was hanging like a dead weight next to her. She didn't reply. It was almost like she'd forgotten I was there. I tugged on her arm, feeling stupid and young but desperately needing her to tell me all this was normal. I could cope with being told I was dead. That just sounded silly. But going to leave a room and being stopped by a big black hole that used to be a landing – that was something else.

'I don't know,' Victoria said. 'I don't know what that is.' It was the first time I'd ever seen her like this. I felt my body start to shake.

'What the actual fuck?'

I turned round to see Callum. The same look on his face as I could see on Victoria's.

'Oh my God,' Freya said. 'What is that?'

No one had an answer. Instead we stood there, all four of us, staring into nothing.

'What do we do?' Freya asked.

'You come back inside.' It was Genevieve speaking. 'Please. Let me explain to you all what that is.'

One at a time, we turned away from the view. But then, I couldn't help it – I had to look again. I felt like I was being pulled towards it. Like it was calling me. I stretched my fingers out the door, expecting a breeze or a change in temperature. Or something different. But it really was a big black void full of nothing.

'Please be careful, Mischa,' Victoria said, pulling my arm back into the flat. 'I don't want you to fall.'

'What would happen if I jumped?' Callum asked, stepping in front of me.

'Callum, please don't,' Freya said. I saw her grab his elbow.

'Why not? I've just been told I'm fucking dead. If there's any time I reckon I can get away with jumping into a fucking abyss, it's probably now.'

'This has to be some kind of illusion,' Victoria said.

'I don't think it's an illusion,' Freya replied. 'I think it's real.'

We all turned. She was pale, but definitely didn't look quite as shocked as the rest of us.

'Why d'you think that?' I asked.

She walked forward and stared hard into the dark, like she was trying to work something out.

'Because I've been dreaming about it for months.'

# Chapter 52

# Freya

'Did you happen to dream what happens next?' Callum asked me. 'Because that would be really fucking helpful.'

My heart was hammering in my chest. I'd put that dream down to stress. How could it be real?

'No, I didn't,' I said. 'But we have to go in. We don't want to walk into that.'

All I could think about was that memory of falling. People I cared about calling me back. I shook the thought aside. I didn't want to think about what it might have meant. Or what it might still mean.

'Freya's right,' Genevieve said. 'Please. Come and sit down. I can explain.'

'I don't think I want you to explain anything, thanks,' Callum said. 'I'd rather take my chances without your help.'

I watched helplessly as he pushed past Mischa and Victoria.

'Please, Callum, don't do this.' My voice sounded thick on my tongue. I had to stop him.

'Why not, Freya? I'm the irresponsible one, remember? If I go first, you guys can see what happens and decide for yourselves what to do.'

He leant further out. His two hands gripped the door frame – the only thing stopping him from falling. He looked like someone about to jump out of a plane. The only problem was, he didn't have a parachute and he had absolutely no idea what he was launching himself into.

I felt myself start to tear up. I blinked hard. Do not cry. 'Callum Raven, don't you dare go out that door.'

He looked back at me, defiant, his green eyes boring into mine. In that moment he reminded me of an angel. A beautiful, fallen angel.

'You haven't told me why not,' he said. 'What have we got to lose, Freya? Apparently we're dead. Not a huge surprise to me if I'm honest, given the amount of crap I shot up my nose after Finn died. But in any event, that doesn't suggest we've got much of a fucking future on the horizon, does it?'

I hesitated before responding. I knew what I was about to say meant confessing to feelings I wasn't sure he wanted to hear. But I also knew if I didn't tell him and he jumped through that door, I would regret it.

'I don't care. I'm asking you, Callum. Please don't go out there. I don't want to lose you. I need you to stay here. With me. Even if we only have a few more minutes, I want them . . . I want them to be with you.'

He looked at me then, *really* looked at me. As if trying to work something out. I saw something in his face change, and after one final glance at the darkness, he stepped back into Genevieve's hallway.

He linked his fingers through mine, still looking at me. It was as if he was trying to read something I had written deep in my heart or my soul or something. Then he grinned. 'Don't worry, Freya, I'm not going anywhere. C'mon guys, let's see what she has to say.'

'You're incredibly fatuous – you know that don't you, Callum?' Victoria said, as he walked back past.

'If I knew what that meant, I'm sure I'd agree with you.'

'It means childish. Immature. Infantile.'

'Thanks for that, Victoria. Remind me never to challenge you to a game of fucking Scrabble.'

# Chapter 53

# Callum

One by one, we filed back into Genevieve's lounge like a small herd of sheep in the world's most fucked-up shepherding contest. Sat back down. Waited for Genevieve to tell us what the fuck this was all about. Victoria had on her standard pissed-off face. Mischa looked a bit out of it, but pretty calm. And Freya? Freya looked beautiful.

I'd had every fucking intention of throwing myself out that door. Until I'd looked back at Freya and heard her say those words. Most guys would run a fucking mile if they heard some woman they hardly knew beg them not to leave. But I wasn't most guys. No one had ever needed me. Ever. I'd been wanted, used, adored, despised. You name it. But never needed. I was too fucking unreliable. Even as a kid, if anyone needed looking after, they'd turn to Finn. He was the older brother. The sensible, responsible one. Not the crazy younger version who would end up getting you in shit.

Whenever 'needing' cropped up in my life, it was always by me. A one-sided equation. Needing to be successful. Needing constant gratification. Needing drugs. I'd spent most of my adult life being selfish, the user, the one making demands. Not once had I stopped to think that maybe the solution to my problems was simply for that to be reversed and thrown back in my face. For someone to give me the chance to prove myself. Fulfil the needs of another person just by being me.

There was actually something quite cool about being needed. I'd no fucking idea what was going on right now, or if Genevieve was telling the truth. It would be fucking ironic if she was – it was the best I'd felt in years. But whatever was happening, I was going to stay for Freya. It really was that simple.

'Are you going to explain what the devil this is?' Victoria asked.

'I did ask you not to leave the room until I'd finished,' Genevieve replied.

'Oh, I do apologise, Genevieve. But there's something about being told you're dead that rather makes one take leave of one's senses,' Victoria shot back, her voice sounding like she'd inhaled helium. She looked as if she might be on the verge of some kind of breakdown.

'Are you going to stay and listen to me?'

'I don't think I've got much of a choice, do I?'

'Everyone has a choice.'

'You mean stay here or launch myself out of that door? Hardly what I would call a choice.'

'Let me explain then.'

It was like listening to machine-gun fire. We weren't going to get anywhere until Victoria calmed the fuck down. And I could see she was working her way up to losing her shit. Again.

'Look, Victoria, why don't we hear Genevieve out?' I said. 'There's no harm, is there? You can always tear her apart later.'

'Ha!' Victoria said. Then she seemed to think about it. 'Fine.' She crossed her arms like some kind of spoilt teenager.

I couldn't resist. 'Now who's being fatuous?'

Her eyes flashed and I thought for a second she might lamp me. Then eventually she smiled. *'Touché.'*

'Thank you, Callum,' said Genevieve. 'Okay then.'

# Chapter 54

# Genevieve

I didn't want to think about how close I'd come to losing them. If even one of them had stepped outside the boundary of the reality I'd created, the intricate connections I'd so carefully assembled to link them together would have been broken. I knew this was going to be my last chance to bring them round. If they didn't believe me this time and one or more of them left, the entire exercise would have been for nothing.

'I'm not going to insult your intelligence by telling you anything other than the facts as I know them. I told myself when I committed to this that the only way it was going to work was if, when the time came, I was completely honest with you.'

I cleared my throat. Not because I needed to, but because I wanted a precious couple of extra seconds before I had to speak.

3 . . . 2 . . . 1 . . .

'The truth is, I work for an institution that looks after – well, the dead. When people die, their souls move on. They move on from earth to another place. That place is something we call the Higher Plane.'

'How utterly absurd,' Victoria muttered.

I pretended I hadn't heard her. 'While the majority of people transition from earth to the Plane successfully, there are a small minority who don't. They're the ones my organisation exists to help. We believe they don't transition because of the strength of certain human emotions holding them back. Tying them to their original existence on earth. And grief is one of them.'

'What are the others?' Freya asked.

'There are quite a few actually. Jealousy. Guilt. Anger. Regret. But grief is by far the most powerful.'

'Why's that?' Mischa asked. The fact they were starting to ask questions was a good sign.

'Because the others, we've realised from our many studies, all fade much more quickly. We still don't know exactly why. Perhaps because grief is a multi-stage process. Every other emotion is just one.'

'Are you saying we're in the Higher Plane right now?' Callum asked, looking around him. 'Because it looks a hell of a lot like a shitty London flat to me.'

I smiled at him and shook my head. 'It's neither, Callum. Your souls are in a state of limbo between the world you came from and the place you're supposed to end up. It's a halfway point we call the Valley. And the reason it looks as it does to you is because you're currently in a merged reality that I helped to create for you. A reality entirely based on your previous lives.'

'But we didn't know each other before.'

'That doesn't matter. When we brought you together – which we did, as you know, by, ah, manipulating your reality – placing an ad in *The Times*, in your local shop, arranging an ultimatum, seemingly from your record label – we were able for the first time to merge your individual memories to create a group existence. What you have seen and experienced these last few weeks is a world based on all your collective recollections.'

'And if you hadn't brought us together?'

'We would have done something similar, but you would have been by yourself.'

'Does everyone transition? Eventually?' Mischa asked, looking suddenly worried.

'No. Not always.'

'What happens to those who don't?'

I wanted to say something reassuring but couldn't lie. 'Not a great deal, I'm afraid. We try to make them comfortable. We continue to allow them to exist within their own heads. Better that than experience an infinity of nothing. Which is what they would endure if we did absolutely nothing at all.'

'Why don't you just tell everyone the truth straight away?' Callum asked. 'Would that not save a lot of time and effort?'

'In some ways, yes. But take yourself back to how you were at the beginning of this process, Callum. If I'd come up to you as a complete stranger in the street and told you that you were dead, how would you have reacted?'

'Point taken.'

'Besides, you have to remember the human brain is receptive, but not infallible. If we use inappropriate techniques, it can push people to the point of no return.'

'I'd rather not think about that, thanks. To be clear, all this time we've been living in a world based on our memories?'

'That's correct.'

'What the fuck have we been doing all this time? When we aren't together, I mean?'

'When you're in this state of limbo, you simply repeat certain patterns from your past. As far as you're concerned, you're living out your life. But in actual fact, you're reliving memories or constructions based on a previous one.'

'Like getting pissed a lot, you mean?'

I couldn't help but laugh. 'In your case, Callum, yes.'

'But after a while, wouldn't we notice stuff?' Freya asked. 'Like the fact we aren't getting any older?'

'No. Your brain doesn't function as it did when you were alive. You stay in the same cycle of your life without realising.'

'Like *Groundhog Day*?' Callum asked, with a grin.

'I'm sorry, I don't know what that is.'

'Wait a sec . . . there are other people in my world,' Callum said. 'I've had conversations with them. My driver, my concierge, that bitch from the record label.'

He took out his phone from his pocket, unlocked it and then started scrolling. 'See, I've got messages from them as well. How does that work? Did you put those there?'

'No, I didn't. But *none* of that is real, Callum. Think back or look more closely at whatever's been said. Once you do, you'll realise they were either simple exchanges *you* conjured up to justify your own patterns of behaviour, or some kind of echo from your past. The only exception to that is the message and phone call from Skye, and that was generated by us. But it only worked because it was something you were willing to hear. I guarantee you haven't had a new or meaningful conversation with any one of those people, have you?'

I could see Callum thinking. Then his eyes widened.

'That's why no one speaks to me? I thought they just hated my fucking guts.'

'No one hates your guts, Callum. Your sense of guilt simply made you interpret it that way.'

'That's why my parents, why Amy, didn't return any of my calls after the accident?'

'I'm afraid so. If I could have created a version of events where they answered the phone and forgave you, of course, I would have done. But I can't recreate a conversation that didn't take place. And given how much you hated yourself for what happened, your brain wouldn't let you imagine it either.'

'Oh my God,' Mischa said. 'Is that why no one talks to me at work anymore?'

'Yes. Every interaction you've had since you died, apart from when you are together, is a product of your subconscious, guided by me as best I can, as the person in charge of your overall welfare. It's a simple mechanism we use in the hope that you will, over time, start to ask the right questions and ultimately move on. But we can only work with what's inside a person's head already. So, for example, you can get the bus to work, Mischa – or *think* you're getting it – and you can spend the day at work – or, rather, imagine you are; or, Callum, you can *think* you're in the car with your driver – but it's just your subconscious filling in the blanks for you. A bit like the way you can read sentences where words are missing because your brain anticipates what should be there. But your subconscious can't fill in what it can't predict, so any interactions you have had – apart from with each other, and with me – have been limited to what you know.'

Victoria frowned. 'What about when we all went to Callum's, though? He lived there, so *he* could imagine it – but the rest of us had never been there before.'

I nodded. 'Yes, but as I said, we were able to merge your individual memories to create a sort of collective consciousness. To be honest, none of us would have predicted it would work to the degree that it did – that allowed you *all* to experience Callum's apartment – otherwise we'd have put something in place to prevent it, because it's not really best practice for you all to meet up outside of these sessions. But because of the way you've connected over the last few weeks, I think Callum was able to conjure it for *all* of you. However, if you think about it, you didn't interact with anyone else when you were there. You can only interact with each other. And me. No one else. Not meaningfully, at least.'

'So, Joe has never really been there?' Freya murmured. 'All that time I thought he was avoiding me, all those messages I read, that was simply a figment of my imagination?'

'That's correct, yes. Although I know that seems hard to believe.'

'*No.*'

The word was barely a whisper. I realised it had come from Victoria.

'No, Genevieve, you're wrong. You're wrong about one thing at least,' Victoria said. 'You have to be.'

We all turned to look at her. The Victoria we had known for the last few weeks had disappeared before our eyes. In her place was a wild-eyed stranger.

'What about Andrew?' she said. 'I've been living with Andrew this entire time. He can't be based on a memory. He *can't*. That's just not possible.'

It was then I realised I'd made a terrible mistake in my explanation. I'd been so intent on reassuring the others, I'd forgotten to get the most important point out of the way first. I moved to grab her hand, but she wrenched it away from me. And then she broke down, her body convulsing with sobs.

'Victoria, listen to me,' I said desperately. 'Please listen to me for a second.'

'No, I don't want to listen to you. I don't want to listen to anything you've got to say anymore.'

'Victoria, I'm sorry, I wasn't thinking. You're different. Please, you need to listen to me. Look at me. It's okay. I promise it's okay.'

She looked up at me, make-up all over her once-pristine face.

'I should have started with you first. Forgive me. Andrew isn't a memory. Andrew is real.'

Her sobs quietened. 'What do you mean?'

'Oh God, I'm getting this all wrong. I thought I'd planned this better. I'm sorry. I hadn't thought through how best to deal with the four of you at once. I think I need to explain to you, Victoria, how you died. Then things might start to make a bit more sense.'

I waited until Victoria's breathing had returned to normal.

'Go on, tell me. How did I die?'

'You died in a car crash on the way home from seeing your father, Victoria. And Andrew . . . Andrew died with you.'

# Chapter 55

# Victoria

Feeling happy, elated even, to hear that your husband was dead was a very strange and disconcerting feeling. But I was. I was suddenly, inexplicably, the happiest woman alive.

However, I also needed to understand. I sniffed, retrieved a tissue from my bag as gracefully as a person can when they've just had a humiliating bout of public histrionics, and dabbed at my swollen eyes. I couldn't remember the last time I'd cried like that. Andrew would have found it hilarious.

'Go on,' I said, hoping no one would notice the canary-like warble in my voice. I harrumphed as quietly as I could and started again. 'Explain. Please.'

Genevieve nodded and without further ado launched into an explanation, no doubt as keen as I was to prevent a repeat performance.

'As I said, you died in a car accident coming back from your father's house. Both you and Andrew were killed outright and you both failed to pass over. Normally, we would deal with two people dying separately because each person should have the chance to transition based on their own personal circumstances. But when we studied your case, and took into account the fact that you were in such severe denial over both your mother and your father, we thought it would be better for Andrew to stay with you.'

I turned this over in my mind. 'But Andrew isn't grieving,' I said. 'Why didn't he pass through without me?'

'Because, Victoria, he loves you. That's what's keeping him here. The thing is, Andrew is very much ready to transition. He's been ready for quite a long time. The only reason he hasn't is because the love he has for you now is as strong as the day you both died.'

In an effort to divert everyone's attention from the fact that Genevieve's words had brought yet further tears to my eyes, I continued with my interrogation. 'But you said love faded more quickly.'

'I know I did, Victoria. What's happened with Andrew is unusual. I can only assume it's because he's lived with you in a merged reality this entire time. You remind him every day why he loves you. Why he doesn't want to let you go.'

I felt suddenly hopeful. 'Are you saying we could transition together?'

Genevieve paused. 'Yes, in theory. But I should warn you there's no complete guarantee you'll emerge at the same point on the Plane. You may have to find each other.'

I felt confused again. Goodness, I hated feeling confused. I was getting exasperated but tried to hold my tongue. 'Do you think you could explain that?'

Genevieve stood up and walked over to her shabby wooden desk by the door. The same desk from which, once upon a time, I had collected a whole bundle of scattered papers while Freya lay, unconscious, on the floor. She opened a drawer and took out a beautiful leather-bound book, its cover and spine engrained with delicate gold writing.

*Science of the Soul*, I read to myself as she sat back down. Goodness, what a riveting read that looked.

'If you want to really understand the answer to that question,' Genevieve said, reverentially turning the pages, 'you would have to read this. But I'll summarise for everyone as best I can.'

She closed the book and folded her hands delicately on the cover as if wanting to draw knowledge from the contents within. 'When people die, it's their souls that pass over to the Higher

Plane. As I'm sure you can imagine, every soul is different and it's the constitution of your soul and your purity of character that determines exactly where you end up.'

I felt like I was trying to work out an exceptionally difficult logic problem. 'But you said we could find each other. That suggests people can move around.'

'Yes, absolutely, but only in a prescribed set of circumstances. You see, the Plane isn't static. There are ways of travelling between the layers. Most people do it as a way of working their way up until they reach the Peak.'

'So the Peak's good?' Mischa asked.

Genevieve nodded. 'Yes. And there are lots of different ways of getting there – but you don't have to travel if you don't want to. You can stay wherever you first arrived, if that's what you want.'

'What about if you just want to be with someone else?' Callum asked, looking at Freya as he said it.

'You can do that, too. But the person in the Higher Plane would need to travel to the lower one. It can't be the other way around. And *both* individuals have to want to be together in order for that to be possible.'

'And might I ask exactly how people go about finding each other?' I said, trying to make my voice sound casual but failing miserably.

Genevieve smiled at me encouragingly. 'There are records. Records of every soul in existence. It wouldn't be that difficult to find out where they were. The only issue would be if they'd made the decision to go back to earth. At that point, any connection is broken.'

'Hang on,' I interjected. 'Go back to earth? You mean as in reincarnation?'

'It's a little bit more complicated than that, but essentially, yes.'

Callum shook his head. 'I'm still struggling with the first part of this,' he said, 'so can we clear that up before we move on to reincarnation?' He took a deep breath. 'What you're telling us is, if you're a good person, you pop out at the top of the hill and if you're a bad person, you pop out at the bottom.'

Genevieve opened her mouth to say something, but then shut it and shrugged. 'Kind of.'

When she didn't elaborate, Callum pitched in again. 'What do you mean, *kind of*?'

She looked uncomfortable. 'That's a very simplistic statement is all.' Then she added, almost as an afterthought, 'If your soul itself is deemed to be bad, that's a different matter entirely.'

'What happens if you have a bad soul?' Callum said, looking at Genevieve a little too intently for my liking.

'That isn't a direction I was planning to go in just yet,' she replied. I could tell she was thinking the same thing I was.

'You said you'd tell us the truth. You said you'd answer any of our questions.'

Genevieve looked him straight in the eye. 'You're right, I did. I'm just not sure that question is particularly relevant right now.'

'You've answered all the other questions. Why not that one?'

I could tell he wasn't going to give up and I could see Genevieve knew it too. But then of course she would. She'd been studying us all for a long time. The realisation made me thoroughly uncomfortable. I thought about all the situations she must have been witness to without our knowledge. Fortunately, her response to Callum pulled me out of that thoroughly disconcerting train of thought.

'Callum, I should probably say, first of all, that humans have very different views of what bad means. A bad deed does not necessarily mean you have a bad soul. An exceptionally low number of people have bad souls.'

'That's not what I asked. I asked what happens to you if you have a bad soul. Do you go straight to the bottom layer, and get a chance to work your way up?'

'If you are at the lowest point of the Plane, yes, you can work your way up, as I've already mentioned. But that's not how it works if your soul is inherently bad. You see, you can't convert a bad soul to a good one.'

'So, what happens if you have a bad soul then?'

'You don't have a bad soul, Callum,' Freya said. 'You do know that, don't you?'

'Will someone, please, just answer the fucking question?'

I had a nasty feeling that what Genevieve was about to say was not something Callum would want to hear. Because Callum took a lot more to heart than I think any of us realised.

'If you have a bad soul, Callum, and by that I mean a soul that can't be saved, the second it transitions, it's extinguished. The person would simply cease to exist from the moment he or she enters the Plane.'

'But you're talking about evil people, right?' said Freya hurriedly. 'You aren't talking about people who've made mistakes?'

Genevieve sighed. 'In the main, yes. But there are also some souls who are simply broken. For whatever reason, they came about without the capacity to change. The afterlife is a journey, Freya – that's why the planes are designed as they are. If you don't believe in the journey to fulfilment, existence is futile.'

# Chapter 56

# Mischa

Cease to exist. Futile existence. Bad and broken souls. Such *horrible* thoughts. And we knew what Callum was thinking. What Callum was like. For someone who had so much, Callum didn't rate himself very much. He knew he was talented. Handsome. A person most other people would sacrifice anything to be. But despite all that, he didn't believe he was a decent person. And he didn't think he could change.

We were waiting for Callum to react badly. Freya was super tense. She looked like a tiger ready to leap out her chair. She knew if Callum legged it through that door, she wouldn't be able to bring him back. But I also knew she'd use every bit of strength she had to stop him going. We all would.

But he didn't move. He just nodded. 'Thanks, Genevieve. Appreciate you telling me that.'

'I said I would be truthful with you, and I meant it.'

Everyone was quiet for a second. And then I realised that I hadn't asked the question that mattered to me most. I'd been so caught up in everything Genevieve was saying, I hadn't even thought to ask her. 'Genevieve, how did I die?'

She looked up at me. She looked sad.

'Can you try to remember?'

I thought about it. Thought about my life after Mum died. How empty it was. I had hardly any memory of it though. Surely in all that emptiness, working out how I died should be easy? But my brain refused to play ball.

'I can't remember. I'm trying, but I can't.'

Freya took my hand and squeezed it. 'Take your time, Mischa. We're all here for you. Don't worry. Everything will be okay.'

Those words. Those words rang a bell. *Everything will be okay.* And then it hit me. That day at work. Or rather, what had happened afterwards.

*Do you remember?*

'It was when I had that episode,' I whispered, mainly to myself. 'At work. Ellie – she looked after me. Told me not to worry. Told me everything would be okay. Then my manager sent me home.'

I swallowed, picturing that day all over again. The lowest point in my life. 'I opened the front door. To my empty flat. Full of Mum's stuff that I hadn't thrown away. And I felt so alone.'

I remembered the exact moment I realised there was no point to my life. How incredibly sad that had made me feel. I'd spent years looking after one person. Making her my focus. It'd been hard. Almost impossible sometimes. But I'd felt needed. And loved. And suddenly I was nothing.

I remembered walking to the bathroom cabinet. Seeing the pills my doctor had given me to help me sleep. And I'd taken the lot.

'I killed myself.'

The room started to swim. I felt ashamed. But also angry. Angry at myself for having thrown my life away so easily.

'Oh, Mischa,' said Victoria. 'I'm so sorry you felt you had to do that.'

'You don't need to apologise,' I said. 'I'm the one who should be sorry. I'm a total coward.'

'Don't be fucking ridiculous,' Callum said. 'You're not a coward, Mischa. You were just too good for that world.'

'That isn't true. And you know what it also makes me think?'

'What?'

I let the answer fall out of my mouth. 'People who kill themselves don't go to heaven.'

'But Genevieve's just told us – heaven doesn't exist,' Freya said.

I felt sick. 'Heaven might not exist, but an afterlife does, doesn't it? And I don't think I'm going. You aren't the broken soul in this room, Callum. I am.'

# Chapter 57

# Freya

I couldn't handle this anymore. All this sadness, guilt and pain. I felt worse than I ever had – and that was saying *a lot*. Something, somehow, had to change. Why couldn't they see how special they both were?

'Stop it, both of you. I've had enough,' I said.

I leant forwards towards Mischa and took both her hands. They were ice-cold. 'First of all, Mischa. It doesn't matter how you died. It matters how you lived. And you lived devoting yourself, completely unselfishly, to someone else. You sacrificed the whole of your teenage years to looking after your mum. Do you know how few people would do that? Barely anyone. And not only did you do it, you did it happily, without any resentment at all. As far as I'm concerned, if the simple fact that you were depressed enough to take your own life means that you don't deserve the chance of an afterlife, then it's not the sort of place I want to go anyway. Do you understand?'

Mischa gave me a small smile. 'Yes.'

'She's right,' Genevieve added. 'To be clear.'

I switched my gaze to Callum. 'And, Callum. Quit with the self-pity. Finn was his own man. If he took too many drugs or drank too much booze that night to drive your car, he should have told you. You are not responsible for what happened. You need to get over that right now, you understand? You aren't a bad soul. You aren't a broken one that can't be fixed. You're just a guy who probably found fame a little bit too young and got overwhelmed by it. Treated a few people badly along the way, maybe. And yes, you're cocky, you're selfish, you're ridiculously immature. You're stupidly reckless and sometimes I want to beat you over the head. But you're also loving. And generous. And loyal to the people you love. You are a good person.'

I waited for him to say something typically Callum – something like *and I'm hot. You forgot to mention that* – but he just looked at me. I took a deep breath and continued.

'Callum, I need you to know that when we get to the point when we're ready to pass over to the next stage, whenever that is, you don't need to worry, okay? I know we'll both be there on the other side. Together. Do you understand me?'

Callum didn't reply immediately but instead took my hand and slowly pushed his fingers between mine, giving me a look that made my tummy turn over. Then, slowly, he nodded. 'Okay,' he said.

I tried my best to ignore the overpowering physical effect he had on me; there was something important I need to ask. 'Genevieve, I have a question, if that's okay.'

'Of course, Freya. Go ahead.'

It was the only question I needed an answer to.

'I know I died that day. Died on that operating table, trying to give birth to Alaia.'

'You did. And I'm sorry.'

I took a deep breath.

'Does that mean I can be reunited with her when I pass over?'

Genevieve looked at me carefully. 'No. I'm afraid it doesn't.'

My eyes filled with tears. For a moment I felt as though my heart was going to break all over again. I sensed Callum putting his arm around me and I leant against him.

'Why not?'

'Because, Freya, Alaia didn't die. Only you did.'

# Chapter 58

# Callum

Freya slumped against me, burying her head against my collarbone. I put my arms around her shoulders, pulling her into me and resting my chin on top of her head. I felt something change in me then. It didn't hit me like a lightning bolt. There was no weird flying baby shooting a fucking arrow and piercing me through the heart. I simply felt a shift in how I thought. Freya was the girl I wanted to fall in love with. Fuck, maybe even *had* fallen in love with.

Somehow, fuck knows how, she'd done something to me that no one else ever had. She'd made me understand that there wasn't anything wrong with me. I'd spent shitloads of money on doctors and shrinks, but none of them had ever managed to get anywhere close to convincing me of that basic fact. They'd harped on about my *wounded inner child*, my past traumas, the need to love myself before I could love others. Infinite fucking horseshit. Because I knew there'd been no trauma. I'd had a great fucking childhood, amazing parents, a supportive family. And it had pissed me off no end how quick these so-called experts were to pin the blame on people I loved. Innocent people who had done fuck all wrong. I was the fuck-up, not anybody else, and certainly not my family. But no one had had the balls to come out and say that. Until Freya. And what's more, she'd made me see myself differently. She'd helped me to realise yes, I was screwed up, but that didn't mean I couldn't change. And more important than that – she'd still want me, even if I couldn't.

'Where is she?' Her voice was shaky, but I sensed a difference in her. A looseness in her shoulders that hadn't been there a second ago.

'She's with Joe, Freya,' Genevieve said. 'And she's the most beautiful, happy little girl you could possibly imagine.'

And with that, I knew. Freya was ready to pass over.

# Chapter 59

# Victoria

Looking at everyone in turn, I could see we had many more questions. But there was also, to my mind, one person left who still needed to finish something. And I could tell that Freya and Mischa were thinking the same thing. So we kept quiet, each of us thinking our own thoughts, waiting for either Genevieve or Callum to speak.

'There's actually one more thing I need to ask you, Victoria.'

I looked at Genevieve, surprised she had addressed me and not Callum. 'What's that?'

'Can you remember your accident?'

My accident. I turned the words over in my mind. My accident. The accident that had killed both me and Andrew. It was a foreign concept. An idea I could not get to grips with. Perhaps because acknowledging it also meant accepting the fact that, in addition to causing my own demise, I had also inadvertently killed my husband. Yet there was something – a ghost of a memory flickering, like a spark trying to ignite. But every time I tried to capture it, it flitted away like a tiny hummingbird, only to then return, hovering inches from my grasp. I cursed myself. For goodness' sake, what was it? I felt as if it was related to something Callum had said. The spark re-ignited temporarily, and then died.

'I'm not sure.'

'Can you try to remember? Can you try to walk us through what happened?'

I knew this was important. I could sense it from the way Genevieve said it. I resolved to try harder. 'Okay.'

I closed my eyes. Forced myself back to that afternoon. Seeing my father. The anger, the disappointment, the hurt. The realisation that I had made a monumental misjudgement about my mother. Andrew's hand on my shoulder. Me starting up the car. Resolving to go home.

'I remember Andrew asking to drive. Me telling him I was fine and not to worry. I remember the country roads on the way back. It was cold outside and the surfaces were icy. I remember the sun in my face through the windscreen. Thinking I should have worn sunglasses. I was probably going too fast. The roads were barely wide enough to let one car through, let alone two. Sharp bends. Andrew told me to slow down. I didn't listen.'

And then it all came flooding back.

'We were on this tiny lane. A motorbike tried to overtake me. The guy was driving like a maniac, going way too fast, God knows what speed he was doing. I'm not sure he even noticed my car was there.

'I pulled closer to a ditch to let him past, watched him skyrocket off at lightning speed around the corner. For some reason he reminded me of my father. I remember I got even angrier then. Angry not just at him, but anyone who thought it was acceptable to push people aside, take advantage. Do whatever the bloody hell they pleased.

'I put my foot down on the accelerator. I told Andrew I was going to get his number plate and report him to the police. Andrew told me not to bother, then shouted that there was a blind corner coming up.

'I saw it too late. I slammed my foot down on the brake. But when I rounded the corner, I saw the motorbike had hit another car. Head on. The bike had gone straight through the windscreen. I tried to swerve it, just managed to miss the car but I was going too fast to regain control. Next thing I know I was off the road. Heading straight towards a tree.'

'Victoria, this is really important. Do you remember anything else about that crash?'

I thought. Then I gasped and put my hand over my mouth. Immediately I understood why this story mattered. Why me being in this room mattered. I saw every single detail of the scene like it was yesterday.

'I remember the car. The car the motorbike had hit. It was a black Lamborghini.'

I looked at Callum. He'd gone as white as a sheet.

# Chapter 60

# Mischa

We knew then.

Callum was staring at the floor. Saying nothing. We all looked at him, shocked.

'Callum?' Then I thought of something. Please God, please God, please God, let it be true.

'Yeah?' His voice was hollow. It didn't even sound like him.

'That doctor you mentioned at the hospital – the one who said Finn was off his head?'

'Yeah. What about him?'

'Are you sure he was talking about Finn? Did he say Finn's name?'

'I . . .'

I could see him thinking about it. Then he looked up at me. And it was as if a dark cloud had finally lifted.

'No. No, he didn't. Oh my fucking God, is that possible? That he wasn't talking about Finn? That he was talking about that cunt on the bike?'

'Callum!' Victoria said. 'Please don't use that word.'

At the same time, Genevieve said, 'Mischa's right, Calllum. He *wasn't* referring to Finn.'

Callum nodded, seemingly lost for words, for once. Then he looked up. 'Sorry about using the c-word, Victoria. But he is. Or was. And I'll tell you something. If I ever meet him on the Higher fucking Plane, I'm going to punch his fucking lights out.'

I giggled. Couldn't help myself. Victoria looked at me disapprovingly and I shrugged.

Seeing the change in Callum was amazing. It must have been the best thing ever realising he wasn't to blame for what'd happened. Especially something so terrible. I knew how guilt could eat away at you. I'd felt it with Mum. Then, to realise everything you'd blamed yourself for wasn't true. It must've been incredible.

# PART SEVEN
# TRANSITION

# Chapter 61

# Genevieve

'Callum, are you okay?' I asked.

'Yeah. Yeah, I am.' He looked across at Victoria. 'I'm just spinning out a bit. I can't believe you were there. That you saw it. Fuck. This is intense.'

'Callum, there's something else I need to tell you,' I said.

He smiled weakly. 'Genevieve, I'm not sure I can take any more excitement right now, to be honest. Can it wait a bit?'

'It's really important we talk about this now.'

'Fuck's sake. Go on then. Hit me up.'

Things were going well. At one point I'd thought I was doomed. That everything was about to spiral out of control. I could almost picture the look on Dr Metcalfe's face. Unsurprised. A tad smug. But then, somehow, we'd got back on track. At last, we were where I wanted to be. All I needed to do now was explain the final part of the process to them. Then hopefully they would be able to embrace it and move on.

I edged forward in my chair. 'The whole point of these sessions has been about processing emotions. Grief primarily, but also other feelings – in your case, Callum, a need to accept yourself for who you are and to know that you can change. I'll be honest with you, when we started this experiment, you were borderline on that. I couldn't have told you with complete certainty that you would transition successfully. For you, these sessions weren't just about working through your feelings of guilt and blame. They were about trying to bring you back from the brink. A place I think you would have been at anyway, regardless of the accident. Does that make sense?'

Callum nodded.

'I think we've brought you back from that point, Callum. I really do. Meaning that now the time is right to tell you one more thing that I hope will help you even more. You'll probably wonder why I withheld it from you. I want you to know that I chose to do that because I think if I'd told you earlier, before you'd looked inwardly at yourself and realised that you aren't such a bad person after all, it may not have made such a difference. Do you understand what I'm saying?'

Callum thought about it. 'Yeah. Yeah, I think I get it. You can tell me.'

'Finn didn't die, Callum. You died in that car, but Finn survived. It was you that motorbike hit, not Finn. What you heard that doctor say *did* happen, but you heard it as they were trying to save you. And they couldn't.'

I watched as Callum physically crumpled in front of me and put his head in his hands. I carried on talking quickly, desperate to finish everything I needed to say.

'What's more, it's no coincidence that you and Freya have become as close as you have over these last few weeks. There's a natural physical attraction, of course. Anyone can see that. But you also share something else. You died in the same hospital, at the exact same time. And you both died thinking you had lost the only person that mattered to you. It meant that when your souls left your bodies and got trapped here, they somehow . . . overlapped. And that created one of the strongest human connections that anyone at the Organisation has ever seen.'

I stopped talking to allow both Callum and Freya to digest what I'd said.

'What does that mean?' Freya asked.

I shrugged. For once I didn't have a ready answer. 'We don't know precisely. We've obviously seen plenty of human connections. Couples, friends, family members who've shared an intense emotional bond. But when they pass through, even when they die together, their souls are still separate. Just like Victoria and Andrew. But you two are different. Your souls have somehow merged.'

'Are you saying we're basically the same person?' Callum asked. 'No wonder I fancy her.'

I rolled my eyes. Did this man ever take anything seriously? 'No, you're still different people. There's just an overlap of sorts. Which I think means you won't necessarily appear on different planes when you transition.'

'What will happen to us then?' Freya asked.

'I don't know. But that's why I wanted to get you both through this process together. I wanted to do everything possible to make sure . . .'

'To make sure, what?'

'To make sure one of you didn't cause irreparable damage to the other.'

# Chapter 62

# Freya

I looked at Callum. He looked back. Then to my surprise, he laughed. 'This is seriously fucked-up shit.'

'I'm not sure this is the time to be laughing, Callum,' I said. 'I feel like this is quite serious.'

'Oh c'mon, Freya. Look at the positives. I started this whole thing thinking I'd killed my brother. I then find out I'm dead. Have to confess, I was feeling pretty fucking low at that point. Then I get told not only that my brother is alive, which let me tell you, is the best fucking news in the world, but along the way I've also got entwined with this incredibly hot blonde who I get to spend eternity with.'

'But Genevieve said we could cause each other irreparable damage,' I reminded him.

Callum shrugged. 'There are worse things that can happen.'
'Like what?'
'Failing to make the Top 40?'

I slapped him hard on the arm and turned to Genevieve. 'So, what do we do next? Do we all have to go through some door or something? Does it have to happen straight away? I have so many questions. I'm not sure I'm prepared. Also, you've mentioned the Organisation a couple of times now. There's been so much else to take in that I've not even begun to think about that – but I've realised I don't have a clue what that is, really.'

Genevieve smiled. 'The Organisation is basically me and my colleagues. We exist to help people like you. And you'll all go through when you're ready, so don't worry about that. And any questions you still have at that point will all be answered when you arrive, by other members of the team. I've already told you plenty more than you need to know. Most people arrive without any knowledge at all about how things operate. You really mustn't worry about that.'

'Okay, that's good. I guess,' I replied. 'But when you say we'll go through when we're ready, will that just happen? Will one of us suddenly disappear?'

'No, it won't happen like that. Not while you're in this room. The reality that I've created for you means that you're tied here. Temporarily at least, until I let you go. Don't worry, there will be plenty of time to say your goodbyes. But before we talk about that, there's one final thing I need to mention.'

'I'm not sure I can deal with anything else,' Mischa murmured. I knew exactly what she meant. I'd had enough revelations to last a lifetime. Which I realised was a slightly ironic statement for a dead person to make.

'Please don't worry,' Genevieve replied. 'It's entirely optional. Something that you can choose to do if you want.'

'Go on,' Victoria said.

'We can give you the option to go back. To earth I mean. For a very short period of time. Not as a living being. But we can send your soul back temporarily.'

I felt my heart pound in my chest.

'Why might we choose to go back?' Victoria asked.

'It gives some people closure, that's all. To see loved ones one final time.'

'Why wouldn't everyone want to do it then?' I asked.

'Lots of reasons. Some people don't have anyone they feel the need to say goodbye to. Others choose not to go because they know they will find it even harder to leave afterwards. Those in love with people still on earth, most commonly.'

'How long can we stay for?'

'Less than an hour. Enabling people to go back takes a huge amount of energy. We effectively open up a brief gateway, but we've only ever managed to keep it open for a very short amount of time.'

'Would you pull us out when we run out of time?'

'No, Freya, we can't do that. And that's why it can backfire.'

'What do you mean?'

'Because you have to return of your own accord. And if you don't, if you refuse to turn around and walk back through the gateway, your soul will remain on earth. Trapped in the place where you chose to go. Permanently.'

'You mean, like, as a ghost?' Callum asked.

Genevieve frowned. 'I hate to use that word because it has rather sinister connotations. Ghosts also suggest a certain element of visibility, which you would never have. But that's the word that most humans would use to describe it, yes.'

'Ghosts are real?'

'Yes, they are, unfortunately. Ghosts are people who didn't transition, who chose to return to earth and then, for whatever reason, didn't come back.'

'You mean they get stuck on earth? Forever? Why would anyone want to do that? It must be fucking miserable!'

'I think you underestimate the strength of feeling that some people have for others, Callum. It can defy all logic. All some people see is the chance to be with their loved ones for just that little bit longer. They don't realise that that means an infinity of being trapped in the same place. Watching that loved one grow old. Potentially move away. And, ultimately, die themselves and pass on. It's extremely sad.'

'And there's absolutely no way of getting them back?'

'No. Each gateway is unique to the soul that we send. Once we've opened it, we can't access it again because the soul would need to be here to do it. We've tried before, I can tell you. Many times. It simply doesn't work.'

We all fell silent.

'I don't want to go back,' Mischa said. 'There's no one I need to see.'

'Nor me,' Victoria added. 'As tempted as I am to haunt my managing partner for an hour or so, I don't think it's worth the hassle.'

'I'm good too, thanks,' Callum said. I looked at him, surprised.

'Don't you want to see your family?' I asked.

Callum looked pained. 'Of course I do. But, Freya, I know what I'm like. The sort of person I am. If I go back there, to my parents' house, watch my family, see them grieving, for me – their idiot son who got himself killed when he was at the height of his career – I know I won't be able to come back. I'll want to punish myself. Torture myself. I just know it. If I'm going to give myself a chance to move on, I have to let them go.'

I touched his knee and squeezed it.

'How about you, Freya?' Genevieve asked.

I could tell she knew what I would say before I even opened my mouth. Alaia was alive. My beautiful, perfect baby girl, who I'd dreamt about every day from the second she was born. Yearned for with a desperation so deep I thought at times I would be ripped in two. There wasn't a chance in hell I was going to let the opportunity go.

I looked at Genevieve, then at Callum. Our eyes met. He knew what I was going to say as much as Genevieve did.

'Yes, I want to go back.'

# Chapter 63

# Callum

Of course she wanted to go back. It was her baby, for fuck's sake. A baby she thought had died. I'd have found it strange if she didn't want one last chance to see her.

But I was fucking scared. Worried that she'd see Alaia and find it impossible to turn around. I tried to reassure myself. Told myself she wasn't me. She wasn't the crazy one. She didn't do stupid things on a whim. She was sensible.

Everything would be fine. I knew that. But still I had a knot of fear in my gut that wouldn't go away.

Seeing Freya and Genevieve get up out their chairs, I tuned back in to the conversation that had been going on around me.

'Okay, Freya, let's do this,' Genevieve said. 'Come with me. I'll explain what to expect when we get next door.'

Freya nodded. I could tell she was excited.

'Wait.' It took a second for me to realise the word had come out my mouth.

'What is it, Callum?'

'Can I go with her?'

'No, I'm sorry, that's not possible.'

'Why not?'

'The gateways don't work like that.'

'What do you mean they don't work like that?'

'You're thinking of them in physical terms. You each have your own unique gateway. They aren't tunnels. They aren't like roads or pathways that anyone can choose to travel down at whim.'

'What the fuck are they then? Help me out here, Genevieve.'

'They're the metaphysical fibres that connect each soul to the earth. They're the same fibres that brought you here when you died.'

'You mean they're like telephone cables?' Victoria asked.

'Not exactly. I would think of them in completely abstract terms; they're more like the ties people have. To loved ones, to places, to whatever it is that prevents them from transitioning. We send you back by re-energising those fibres. Opening them up again. But that's why we can't keep them open for long. What we do goes against the way the universe is supposed to work. Many people think we shouldn't be doing it at all. But we do, because for many trapped souls, it's a hugely effective way of helping them.'

'Then why can't you re-energise them a second time if people get stuck?' Victoria asked.

'In theory we can. But we need the individual here in order to do it. Think of it as a tie again; they're one end of the tie; without them here, we can't do anything. Plus the fibres get damaged by the energy we use the first time around. The more time that passes, the more the fibres deteriorate until eventually they disintegrate altogether.'

'And you can't hitch a ride in someone else's cable car – is that what you're saying?' I said.

'Exactly. Which means it's not possible to send someone else down it in order to bring a lost soul back.'

'I see,' I said.

'I will come back, Callum,' Freya said. 'You do know that, don't you? I just want to see her. Even if it's only for a few minutes.'

'I believe you, Freya,' I said. Even though I wasn't sure I did.

And with that, she leant down and kissed me.

The first time we'd kissed, it was electric. I'd wanted to rip her clothes off. Touch every inch of her. It hadn't been a romantic thing – I'd wanted to fuck her, pure and simple. Probably several times over, looking back.

This was totally different. Probably a good thing with three other people in the room. A simple kiss on the lips. Lasting no more than a second. But it made me feel love. Love with a strength that nearly fucked me sideways. Mixed up with a sense of physical connection that I never wanted to experience again, unless it was with her.

She looked at me one last time and followed Genevieve out the lounge. I watched them open a door that led off the hallway and disappear.

As soon as she was gone, I let myself think about how I really felt. About her leaving. I'd tried to act like I was cool with it. Because I knew I'd no right to be anything but. But I wasn't fucking cool about it. Part of me had hoped, completely fucking selfishly, that because I'd sacrificed the chance to see my family, she would do the same. I *knew* the circumstances were totally different. *We* were totally different. But that didn't matter. And now she was gone, there was this emptiness in my chest that felt like a hole.

But there was something else. Niggling in the back of my head like an itch I couldn't scratch. Something about the way she'd kissed me. I couldn't put my finger on it. And then it hit me.

'What's the matter, Callum?' Mischa asked.

'Nothing. I'm fine, don't worry.'

I didn't want to say it out loud. The thing that was making me feel as if everything I'd managed to find was slowly slipping through my fingers, like sand. But my brain thought it anyway. And once it did, it was *all* I could think about.

That kiss.

Fuck.

That kiss had felt like goodbye.

# Chapter 64

# Victoria

It's not easy to conduct small talk in a room while waiting for someone to return from a journey down a metaphysical fibre that enables them to see a daughter they thought had died, but hadn't. And it was even harder doing it in a room with someone like Callum.

His behaviour resembled a cross between a caged lion and a lovesick puppy, pacing around in so many circles. He made me feel dizzy. Eventually I told him to sit down, only for him to then spend the next five minutes jiggling his knee. It was excruciating.

'Callum, for pity's sake, will you please stop doing that?'
'Doing what?'
'Twitching.'
'What the fuck? I'm not.'
'You are. You're jiggling your leg.'
'So?'
'It's annoying.'
'Come sit on my lap. You might enjoy the jiggling then.'
'Don't say things like that, Callum. It's hugely inappropriate.'
He had the good grace to look sheepish. 'Sorry. I say shit when I'm nervous.'
'Do you want to talk about it?' Mischa asked.
Callum sighed loudly. 'I'm not really sure what you want me to say.'
Mischa looked at him carefully, twirling a stand of hair around her finger as she thought. 'Why don't you tell us how you're feeling?'

He gave her a smile which was half grin, half grimace. 'Becoming quite the apprentice, aren't you?'

When she didn't reply he sighed again. 'Sorry. Okay. I'll try. I feel shit. And angry. And annoyed at myself for feeling shit and angry. I feel hurt, even though I haven't got any right to. And I miss her even though she's been gone all of five minutes. And I feel there was so much more I should have said, just in case I don't ever fucking see her again, but I couldn't find the words. So I feel gutted about that. And I also feel the same way I always do when something happens to me that I can't control. I feel like I need to run straight into that black hole outside and not look back. Or get shit-faced. One or the other.'

I thought about how I would feel if Andrew had made a similar decision. I knew it wasn't something I needed to worry about. He had no family left. But I also knew I would have hated waving him off anywhere if there was even the smallest chance he might not come back. 'I think you have every right to feel how you feel, Callum,' I said. 'I would be exactly the same.'

As we were talking, Genevieve re-entered the room looking calm and composed – compared to Callum anyway, who was becoming more stressed by the second. I assumed from her demeanour that whatever it was she'd needed to do with Freya had gone without a hitch.

'It worked then?' Callum asked. I noticed the twitching had started up again. I was about to open my mouth to tell him to stop but saw Mischa shake her head at me. I looked down at the floor instead.

'Yes, it worked,' Genevieve replied. 'Better than usual, in fact. Freya's connection to her old life is very strong. That always makes opening the gateway a lot easier.'

That was clearly not what Callum had wanted to hear. He pulled a face. 'So, what, you've got like a time machine or something in that room?'

Genevieve smiled. 'Not a time machine, no. Just a door. Connected to an energy source.'

'Got you. Like *Monsters Inc.*'

'I'm sorry, I don't know what you're talking about.'

'Never mind. I was joking anyway.'

Silence fell, the only sound in the room Callum's endless jiggling.

'So, how long will it be before she's back?' I asked. That worked. Callum stopped fidgeting for a moment to listen to the answer.

'Under an hour. That's about the longest a connection has ever lasted.'

'How will she know when the time's up?'

'It'll be quite obvious. When she emerges from the gateway, she'll appear in her house. She'll then be able to move around within the confines of the building. And her garden. Places that are engrained in her subconscious. But she won't be able to go any further than that. When the gateway starts to weaken, she'll feel it straight away. And I've told her what to expect. It's like a vibration, a relentless, persistent vibration. It's impossible not to feel it.'

'A bit like Callum's knee jerking,' I observed.

Callum shot me a dirty look. 'Will we know when she's back?' he asked.

'Yes. I'll be able to tell you the second she arrives. Don't worry.'

'What do we do until then?'

'We wait.'

# Chapter 65

# Mischa

The minutes dragged on. And on. And on.

It was weird, Freya not being there. We were a group. A team. With one of us missing, it felt like we'd lost an arm. Or a vital organ or something.

Callum wasn't helping either.

*He's really stressed out, isn't he?*

We filled the silence by asking questions, Genevieve answering as best she could. But as time went on, I could tell she was getting a bit worried. Her answers became shorter. She kept looking at the door.

The air in the room was musty, like the classrooms at school. I racked my brain, trying to think of something to say to help the time pass. Then I had an idea. I'd noticed Genevieve had this habit of biting one of the knuckles on her left hand. She'd done it earlier when she was trying to explain to Victoria about Andrew. And she was doing it again now. I wanted to know if it meant something.

'Can you tell us about your old life, Genevieve?'

She looked at me, surprised by my question. 'What do you mean?'

'Well, I'm guessing you were alive, at some point? I thought maybe you could tell us a bit about it. Before you died.'

Both Callum and Victoria looked up, interested to hear what Genevieve had to say. I felt proud of myself for thinking of the question. At least it would help us get through a few more minutes.

'Okay, sure,' Genevieve said. 'You know, I can't remember the last time someone asked me about my old life. I'm so used to asking other people about theirs. I might sound a bit rusty.'

She took a sip of her drink. You could see she was trying to work out where to start. I guess that was the thing when you were someone who listened for a job. It probably made it quite hard to talk about yourself.

'I'm not sure if you would've guessed, but I was trapped here too. That's kind of why I'm as passionate as I am about helping people transition. Because I was here for a very long time.'

Then she did it again. Bit her knuckle.

'I don't have a particularly sensational story to tell you. I died in a cycling accident in 1973, on my way home from work. One minute I was on the road, the next I wasn't.

'The trouble was, I wasn't ready to die. I was supposed to be getting married that year. My fiancé, Greg, had proposed only a few months before. My head was full of plans. I'd even been thinking about wedding venues as I was sitting on my bike at the traffic lights. Maybe that's why I didn't see the van coming.

'Anyway, I came here, to the Valley I mean, and the person responsible for me from the Organisation, Tom, tried to help me transition. Probably for about nine months or so. But nothing he did seemed to work. Apparently all I did every day was re-live the week before I died. Nothing seemed able to snap me out of it.

'Eventually he thought he would try something new. He created a version of reality *after* I'd been hit by the van. And I woke up in a hospital. Not a real one of course – but a replica of the one I'd died in. And Tom was there. I assumed he was a doctor.

'Over time, he befriended me. Gained my trust. Got me to talk about my life. Slowly helped me to remember what had happened. And that was when I first began to realise the importance of having someone to talk to. Someone who could help you overcome the hurdles that, for whatever reason, you're unable to cope with by yourself.

'I remembered my death during one of those talks. I was pretty devastated. I'd had my whole life before me and suddenly it had been wrenched away. Then Tom offered me the chance to go back. He was hopeful that would give me some much-needed closure.

'Like Freya, I travelled down the gateway. I was shaking with excitement. All I wanted was to see Greg one final time. To say my goodbyes. I arrived in my home. The flat we'd shared for a year. Where we'd created so many happy memories. Where Greg had proposed to me one night in front of the television.

'And Greg was right there, in the kitchen, making toast of all things. With his arms wrapped around another girl. Another teacher from my school.

'I turned around and I came straight back. I told Tom what had happened. I was shattered. But Tom helped me to get over it. He taught me about real human connections. How sometimes the connections we *think* we have aren't as strong as we'd hoped. How we can be so blinded by the way we feel about someone that we fail to recognise how they truly feel about us.

'Over time, I realised Greg had never been right for me. I'd fallen for someone who would never have loved me back as passionately as I'd loved him – for various reasons. It wasn't his fault, and he wasn't a bad person. It just meant we weren't the couple I'd thought we were. But, for the first time, I didn't resent him for that. Eventually I even felt happy that he'd found someone else.

'And as soon as I reached that point, I transitioned. And I knew straight away that I wanted to work for the Organisation. Help people in the same way Tom had helped me. And I worked my way up. Studied everything I could. Became fascinated in particular with the grief process. And people's reaction to it.'

'Is that how you came up with your idea?' I asked.

'Yes. I thought maybe, rather than tackling grief on a one-to-one basis, we should group people together to help each other. I met with quite a lot of resistance initially. I think my superiors felt there were too many variables. Too many things that could go wrong. And obviously people find it hard to try new things. But, as I think you've all proved, it works.'

'If Freya comes back, you mean,' Callum said.

Genevieve looked at him, her head on one side. 'May I say something, Callum?'

'Sure.'

'You should stop thinking you need something external in your life to be complete. You're an unbelievably talented guy, you know that, don't you? There's huge potential in that head of yours – I hope that you'll realise that one day. You don't need a guitar. You don't need to be hero-worshipped. You don't need drugs. And ultimately, you don't need Freya.'

Callum made a funny noise to suggest he didn't agree.

'I know how you're feeling, Callum, I really do. I was the same once. I thought my happiness was conditional on the love of someone else. But it wasn't, you know? Genuine fulfilment comes from learning to understand yourself. That sounds cheesy but it's true. And being able to appreciate not just your talents, but your flaws also.'

She paused. 'I know how you feel about Freya. And I admit, you're unique as a couple in the sense that you have this special connection, which I can't confess to understand. But that aside, you need to value yourself. As an individual. Do you understand what I'm saying?'

Callum was quiet for a minute. Then he nodded. 'Yeah, I do. I get it. Really. But I think it's going to take a bit of time to seep through.'

'Good.'

All of a sudden, Genevieve sat up straight in her chair. 'Excuse me,' she said, and hurried out of the room. We heard a door open and close.

She was gone for ages. We all looked at each other. I could feel my heart pounding in my ears, so loud I was sure the others could hear it too. God knows how Callum was feeling. Even Victoria looked on edge.

Then Genevieve came back.

'Where is she?' Callum asked, looking behind her into the empty hallway. His voice sounded weird. My ears were ringing again.

It was the first time I'd seen Genevieve lost for words. It didn't matter. We all knew.

'She didn't come back, did she?' I said.

'No. No, she didn't.'

# Chapter 66

# Callum

I heard the words but they didn't compute. It was impossible. She'd *told* me she'd come back. And I'd believed her. Sort of. I'd finally opened myself up to something new, let someone in. And now I was never going to see her again. She was gone.

The old me would have gone fucking ballistic. Got off my head. Trashed things. Started a fight. Probably had a meaningless one-night stand with a beautiful girl whose only mistake in life was to think a guy like me was worthy of her time.

But I was weirdly calm. For the first time, I understood what it felt like to be fucked over. On the wrong end of a broken promise and a broken heart. And weirdly, I was grateful. I had spent my entire life being the one who was responsible for shit like that. Hurting people, using them, pretending I didn't care, but secretly hating myself for it.

So being told that the woman I'd fallen head over heels for had let me down in the biggest way imaginable, to find out she'd basically chosen someone else over me – it led me to a strange conclusion.

I could finally forgive myself.

But the second that happened, the second I finally let go of all the guilt and blame I'd piled at my door, I had an idea. A stupid, crazy idea that I knew Genevieve was going to lose her shit over. I got ready for the battle that I knew would happen when I came out with it.

'Let me go to her.'

Genevieve looked at me. She didn't look shocked – she looked sad. 'You know I can't do that, Callum. That gateway is unique to Freya.'

'But you said you could re-open it, right?'

'You know I can. Temporarily at least. But *you* can't travel down it. Only she can. There's nothing I can do. Freya's gone and there's no way we can get her back.'

'I know you think it's not possible. And I get why. But you said yourself: Freya and I connected when we died. You said you didn't know what that meant. But I think I do. I think it means that a little bit of her soul is in me, and vice versa. I think it means I can travel down that gateway thing.'

I'd stumped her, I could see that. She was thinking about it.

'No. It's way too risky. You're right. Your souls did overlap when you died. But we have absolutely no idea what that means in practical terms.'

'What would happen if we tried?' Mischa asked. God, I loved that girl. She smiled at me. But she also looked as if she was about to be sick.

'I don't know. I've never tried to send someone down another person's gateway. It might not work at all. It might damage you on entry or at some point during the journey. You could get stuck somehow. Or . . .'

'Or what?'

'Or it might work.'

'Then let me try,' I said.

Genevieve sighed. 'Callum, even if I agreed, I'd have to get authorisation from my supervisor first. And there's no way he would say yes. Or if he did, it would be too late. I can only open it again for a little while longer.'

'Please, Genevieve. I'm fucking begging you. I understand what you said about me needing to learn to accept myself. And I promise you, I'm trying. I definitely don't hate myself anymore, if that helps. But I'm in love with Freya. Completely and utterly fucking besotted. If there's a chance in hell I can bring her back, I have to try. Even if I die in the process. Again.'

Genevieve thought about what I'd said. 'Supposing it does work. What makes you think you can change her mind? There's a reason she didn't come back. She must have made the decision to stay.'

'I don't know if I can convince her. But I need that chance.'

'I think we should do it,' Victoria said. 'If we don't, he'll be even more unbearable than he is now.'

'Thanks for that, Victoria.'

'You're very welcome.'

Genevieve interrupted us. 'Okay, fine, let's think this through properly. Say I send you and it works. And you manage to persuade her to come back. By that time the fibres will be exceptionally weak. I don't think we'll have any issues getting Freya back, provided we act quickly enough – those fibres are naturally designed to carry her. But I can't say the same for you.'

'I'm willing to take that risk. Please, Genevieve.'

She got up from her chair and came to sit next to me. In Freya's chair. I ignored the lump that had formed in my throat. She grabbed my hand and held it tightly.

'You're really willing to take the risk?'

'Of something bad happening to me? Absolutely.'

'You're completely sure?'

'Of course. I've died once already, remember?'

'This is serious, Callum. I need you to tell me, without a shadow of a doubt, that you are willing to do this. For her.'

I looked her square in the eye.

How best to tell her how I was feeling in that moment? I had written so many songs over the years, nearly all of them about love, commitment, heartbreak, loss. I saw then how little I had really understood about *any* of that when I used to throw lyrics so carelessly down on a page. I'd been acting a part, writing my songs. Imagining myself adoring someone, marrying someone. Or the opposite: the devastation that came from being discarded or broken up with. But none of that, *none of that*, came close to this. The real thing wasn't words. It wasn't poetry. It was primitive and instinctive and it made no fucking sense. It was the all-consuming knowledge in the depths of your fucking gut that someone else's existence was way more important than your own. It was a sensation I never expected to feel and at the very least I was grateful to have felt it.

But Genevieve didn't need to know any of that and neither did the other two.

Instead, I nodded. 'Yes. I'm ready.'

Genevieve nodded back, the uncertainty in her face contradicting the conviction in mine. 'Okay. I'm probably going to regret this. But let's do it.'

# Chapter 67

# Freya

I'd arrived in the hallway of my house, just as Genevieve had told me I would. The journey had been easy, but strange: a sensation of being unconscious, yet moving. A feeling of pressure, like you get when diving deep underwater. The buzzing sound of electricity. The prickling of static against my skin. And then there I was. In my old home.

Everything appeared before me, just as I'd left it all those months ago, only a hell of a lot messier. I smiled to myself. I knew that Joe wasn't naturally a tidy person. But he'd always tried his best to be neat. Now, however, there was a pram in the hall, its wheels caked in mud, shoes scattered everywhere, a coat hanging half-on half-off the banister, a teddy at the bottom of the stairs. I realised I preferred it like this. It looked comfortable and lived in.

The sound of laughter drew me into the lounge, a ball of excitement building inside me. It was even messier in there. Television on. Baby bouncer in the corner. What appeared to be a dirty nappy sitting abandoned in the middle of the carpet. I went to pick it up and realised I couldn't. For a minute I had forgotten what I was.

And then I saw her in the dining room. The big oak table my parents had given us had been pushed to one side and was now in the corner, completely covered in papers, books and magazines. In its original spot was an empty space, covered almost entirely by a large baby play mat.

And there she was, kicking happily at a plastic mobile above her head. Joe, meanwhile, was lying on his side along the floor, smiling down at her, jiggling a small fluorescent rattle and pressing various musical buttons. Everything was colourful, garish and loud. Not the sort of things I would ever have thought to buy.

But it was perfect.

Looking at Alaia took my breath away. She was gorgeous – not quite chubby, more robust, with a good head of dark, slightly wavy hair, like Joe, and a tiny button nose. Her eyes were large, alert and a bright shade of blue, a dramatic contrast to her milky skin and her long, dark eyelashes. She was wearing a grey all-in-one babygrow covered in tiny yellow ducks; I recognised it as one of many I had bought a couple of weeks before my due date. She was almost too big for it already.

I approached them both cautiously, still unable to accept the fact they wouldn't be able to see me. They didn't react. Part of me felt disappointed. I was gripped by a stupid desire to dance round the room to see if they noticed. Instead, I sat myself down on the other side of the play mat to Joe, and gazed in wonder at my daughter. Then I looked at my husband.

There were lines deeply engrained in his forehead. His eyes were tired. He was still handsome, of course, in a way that only men seem able to pull off when exhaustion has taken its toll. He had let his hair grow longer – probably because he'd not had time to get it cut, but it suited him. And he was still smiling. I smiled back. That was the one thing about Joe – he could always make me smile.

'Do you want a cup of tea, Joe?' a woman called from another room.

'Yes, please, that would be great,' he replied.

The unexpected sound of a woman in my home startled me, but I recognised the voice and immediately jumped up, making my way through to the kitchen.

And there I discovered my mother, my wonderful mother, fiddling with the kettle as if it were some kind of foreign object that required a manual to operate. I felt tears spring to my eyes. I hadn't realised how much I'd missed her until then.

She, like Joe, looked tired, aged way beyond her 60 years. I couldn't help but feel responsible. Wrapped up in my own troubles, I hadn't taken the time to think how my death would have impacted her. My whole family. I felt guilty and had a sudden urge to reach out and hug her. But I didn't – I knew there was no point.

Transfixed, I watched her as she made tea for both Joe and herself, splashing hot water over the side of one of the mugs as she poured.

'Oh, bugger it,' she murmured to herself and I laughed.

She looked up abruptly, giving me the strangest sensation that she'd heard me. But then as quickly as that, the moment was gone. She looked down again, added milk to both mugs, a sugar to one (hers, I knew), removed the teabags with a teaspoon and dropped them both carefully in the bin. Then she placed everything on a tray along with a couple of Kit Kats from the cupboard and made her way through to the lounge. I followed slowly behind her.

Mum put the tray down on the dining table, pushing aside a pile of papers and sat down on the floor next to Joe. She put her hand lovingly on his shoulder. Mum had always adored Joe. I was glad she was there, helping him.

'How are things really?' she asked.

'Better,' Joe replied.

'Good. Martin and I have been worried about you.'

'I know. He called me yesterday. But honestly, you mustn't worry. I'm coping fine.'

'Good. Did your work come back to you about your hours?'

'Yep. They've said I can go back three days a week in a couple of weeks. Then maybe full-time by Christmas. They've been great.' He paused, looking at Alaia. 'I'll be sad to leave her, though.'

'Me and your mum will look after her, you know that.'

'Of course I do. I'm really grateful. To both of you. I don't know what I'd have done otherwise.'

We all watched Alaia play, caught up in our own thoughts. I sat as close to her as I could, grazing my fingers along her perfectly round cheek. I couldn't feel anything but that didn't matter. I was thankful beyond words that I'd been given this chance to see her.

'She's such a happy little thing,' Joe said. 'And thank God, she's sleeping better now.'

'She takes after you,' Mum said. 'Freya was a nightmare. So flipping needy. Did I tell you she slept in my bed until she was seven? Not sure her dad ever forgave me for letting her. It's amazing we ever got round to having her sister.'

'I think that's enough detail on that particular subject, thank you, Debbie,' Joe said, pulling a face.

'She looks like Freya, doesn't she?' Mum said. 'It makes me catch my breath whenever I look at her.'

'Yeah, she does,' Joe agreed. 'I sometimes think that makes it harder though.'

Mum grasped Joe's hand affectionately. 'I know it does, love, I know.'

Unexpectedly, I felt a strange vibration behind me and I knew straight away what that meant. The gateway was about to close. Had it really been an hour?

Could I do this? I had to, I knew that. I willed myself to get up, wiping away the tears that had fallen listening to Joe and my mum's conversation.

I took one last look at Alaia, preparing myself to leave her. I consoled myself that she was in good hands. The best, in fact. I didn't have to worry. And I knew Joe wouldn't let her forget me. But just as I was about to go back to the others, I heard Joe speak again. What he said stopped me in my tracks.

'I just wish she was here to watch her grow up.'

As soon as he said those words, I knew I couldn't leave. And so I didn't move, even when the vibrations became almost too intense to handle.

I knew I *needed* to go, of course, understood what it meant for me if I didn't. What it meant for Callum. But I owed it to Joe and Alaia to stay. To watch as much of her childhood as I could. Even if that meant condemning myself to an infinite period of loneliness and isolation.

The vibrations began to subside, and although I knew that meant my chances of returning to the Valley, and to Callum, were fading rapidly, I still couldn't bring myself to move. It was as if my feet were stuck in cement.

I knew the others would think my decision to stay was selfish and stupid. I could almost feel the weight of Victoria's disapproval from here. And Callum. Oh God, I couldn't bring myself to think about Callum. Picturing him, back in Genevieve's flat, pulled my heart apart. But at the end of the day, they didn't have children; they weren't being asked to walk away from their baby. And they also couldn't see the strain that my death had put upon Joe. And my mum. I couldn't abandon them.

I cursed the organisation that Genevieve worked for. How could anyone think an hour was long enough to give someone final closure on their life, especially when that life had a six-month old baby in it? I knew I was being completely unreasonable. I was lucky to even be here. But I hated them nonetheless for forcing me to choose.

It was while I was in the middle of working through these thoughts that, after one final shudder, I felt the gateway close behind me.

And that, as they say, was that.

# Chapter 68

# Victoria

Genevieve had taken Callum to the mysterious room off her hallway, and returned without him. We'd not made a big deal of the fact that we might never see him again, which I was grateful for. I had never been very good at handling emotional encounters. He had simply looked back at us as he left the lounge, given us a small salute and said, 'Laters, ladies.' And then he was gone.

Genevieve, it seemed, was in a state of shock. She sat back down in her chair, but was unable to bring herself to say anything. Clearly she had breached all kinds of protocols by allowing Callum to leave.

'Are you okay, Genevieve?' Mischa asked.

She glanced up, looking almost bemused to see us still there. 'No, not really. I didn't think it would work.'

'But it did,' I said, as encouragingly as I could. 'That's a positive sign, surely?'

Genevieve rubbed her eyes. 'It depends how you define a positive sign. If losing two of my patients, possibly permanently, at the same time as breaking every rule in the book, is a positive sign, then yes, things are going swimmingly.'

I finally grasped, then, the stress she must have been under all this time. How much she had probably fought to trial an idea that nobody else supported, but which she was adamant would bring huge improvements to the afterlives of hundreds, possibly thousands, of people. People who were lost but didn't know it. I couldn't help but admire her determination. I also felt bad for her. She would no doubt lose her job at the Organisation if it all imploded. (Although why anyone would choose to work for eternity after they'd died was absolutely beyond my comprehension. I personally couldn't think of anything worse.)

'They'll be back, I'm certain,' I said, feeling anything but.

'I hope so,' she replied.

'When will we know?' Mischa asked.

'We'll know by the time the gateway closes,' Genevieve replied. 'Or at least we'll know by then if it hasn't worked. Because there's definitely no re-opening it after that.'

'How long will that be?'

'About twenty minutes at a guess. I don't know exactly,' Genevieve said, looking utterly despondent.

I recalled that we'd all been in this depressing position before, when Freya had fled and Callum had gone off in a huff. Only that time there hadn't been a twenty-minute window of opportunity in which to get them back.

Technically, it shouldn't have mattered to me one way or the other, what happened to Freya and Callum. They were grown-ups, free to make their own life choices. Even if those choices were downright idiotic. Meanwhile I had finally completed my own journey – a feat in itself, it would appear. All that was left for me now was to be reunited with Andrew, the only person, I realised, who I had ever truly loved. And to ensure that Mischa was able to find her own sense of purpose. I felt a fondness for her that I couldn't explain.

But for some reason, despite the fact that things were looking optimistic for me, and Mischa too, I couldn't help but worry about the fate of the other two. The thought that they might not come back felt wrong and imbalanced. And worse still was the possibility that something terrible might happen to Callum on the journey. That man had a highly seductive magnetism about him that was simply undeniable – channelled appropriately, I felt he would go far. I could certainly see why very few women were able to resist his charms. Thankfully, I was impervious to them. He might have looked like a god, but he was annoying as hell.

I still couldn't imagine life – well, death – without him, though.

# Chapter 69

# Mischa

I knew it was the wrong time to ask, but I wanted to know what Genevieve thought. And it wasn't like we were talking about anything else. No one had spoken in *ages*.

'Genevieve?'

'Yes?' She'd been biting on that knuckle again.

'Can I ask something?'

She stopped. 'Of course.'

'I was wondering, when I go through ... Depending on where on the plane I come out ... Do you think I might be able to work here?'

Her eyebrows shot up. 'You want to work here? For the Organisation?'

'Yeah. I think I'd like to help people. You know. To transition. I'd like that to be my job.'

I felt stupid then. For even thinking that maybe I could learn to do what she did. I hadn't got any experience or done any exams for a start. She'd probably done loads. My cheeks went hot and I looked down at my hands. 'Don't worry about it,' I said. 'It was a silly idea.'

'No, no not at all, Mischa. I didn't mean to look shocked. I'm just surprised you're keen, that's all. Especially since I've not done particularly well to date.'

'I think you have. I think you've done brilliantly.'

'That's very sweet, but I haven't.'

It made me sad, hearing Genevieve say that. Sad because she'd tried so hard to make things better for us, but now she felt like she'd mucked it all up. I wanted to think of something nice to say to make her feel better about herself. I knew I wasn't very good with words. Hadn't even passed my English GCSE. But then I thought, if I wanted to make something of myself when I passed through, I had to start making more of an effort. I had to stop thinking I was crap at everything all the time.

And with that, it came to me – what I wanted to say. 'I think you're wrong, Genevieve. Think back to when you met us. We were miserable. Lost and angry and trapped. Going nowhere. Then you brought us together. Helped us through it. I know it took a long time for us to get there. And it may not have gone to plan exactly. But it still worked.'

'Did it?'

She was staring off out the window. At the black emptiness outside. Had the view from her flat always been like that? I couldn't remember now. Maybe I hadn't bothered to look before.

'Genevieve?'

'Hmm?'

'Listen to me for a second, would you?'

She stopped looking out of the window and focused her attention on me. I bit my lip. I knew what I wanted to say but wasn't quite sure how to start. Sod it, I thought. Just tell her how you feel.

'Think about what you've done. As in, *really* think about it. We've all worked out what actually happened to us. And we all accept we're dead. Yes, Freya and Callum might not come back. And we might never know what happened to them. But they made that decision on their own, didn't they? You freed them from a world that wasn't even real. Got rid of the thing that was hurting them most of all. So maybe they don't come back – but if they don't, maybe that was where they were meant to end up. I think you've done a great job. And if you get in trouble, I'll tell that supervisor guy I think he's wrong to have a go at you. Because your idea is really good. We just have to accept that sometimes people don't end up where *we* want them to. But that's not getting it wrong. That's just free will.'

I felt silly then. I wasn't sure if anything I'd said had made any sense. But to my surprise, Genevieve nodded slowly. Then she smiled.

'Do you know what, Mischa? You're right. Thank you. And to answer your question, yes, I think you'd make a great addition to the team here. In fact, I promise to recommend you at the earliest opportunity. Assuming my recommendation means anything after this, of course.'

'Thank you, Genevieve. I really appreciate that.' I realised my own smile was hurting my face.

'And if her word doesn't,' Victoria said. 'I shall definitely be making my views known. To whoever will listen. I think you'd be super at this sort of thing.'

'Thanks, Victoria.'

It had been a long time since I'd had anything to look forward to. The thought of being useful again – that was all I'd ever wanted. Yeah, I missed Mum with all my heart. Secretly hoped I'd get the chance to see her again on the other side, or wherever it was we were going. But more than anything, I wanted to help people. Take broken people and help put them back together again.

Life was such a funny thing, I thought then. I'd spent most of it struggling. Trying to work out what I wanted to do. Trying to fit into a place that didn't seem to want me. Getting really angry about it. And then when Mum got ill, feeling I had a purpose, even though I was doing something that most people would have hated. Only to lose her and feel like I had nothing left worth hanging around for. And now suddenly, here I was, dead. Which again, most people would have hated. Or at least resented. Or been upset about. But weirdly I felt the opposite. Like maybe I'd finally found a place where

I could become something a bit more special. Rather than ordinary old Mischa.
*Well done, Mischa.*
*Thanks, Mum.*

# Chapter 70

# Callum

Fuck me. If I thought LSD was the weirdest trip of my life, I was wrong. That was fucking insane.

At one point I thought I was going to be ripped apart. As in physically ripped into pieces. And the pressure and the electricity made my head feel like it was going to explode. Put it this way, it could've been messy. Like Quentin Tarantino-style messy. Fortunately it all happened too quickly for me to realise how close I probably was to complete annihilation.

Because then all of a sudden, the pressure evaporated and I appeared in someone's hallway. Freya's, I could only guess. At least I fucking hoped it was.

Knowing I didn't have a lot of time, I legged it down the hallway, unsure whether to go in the lounge or head upstairs. But then I heard voices. Definitely upstairs.

I ran up the staircase two steps at a time and followed the sound towards a room just off the landing. I got to the door but then stopped myself. What would I say to her? How would I convince her to come back? I knew I only had a few minutes. For once in my life I *couldn't* fuck it up.

I clenched my fists. Man up, Callum, I told myself. Man the fuck up.

I peeked my head around the door, feeling like a burglar. Or a stranger gate-crashing a party. Because in the middle of the room was a tall, muscly guy with dark hair, rocking a baby; and a woman who looked like an older version of Freya, sitting in an armchair in the corner, singing a lullaby.

And then I clocked Freya. Her eyes full of love as she watched her daughter being shushed to sleep. My heart flipped over in my chest just looking at her.

This was going to be hard.

After a couple of minutes, I saw Joe nod and Freya Senior stopped singing. Then he put Alaia in her cot, covered her with a blanket and together they slowly tiptoed out the room. And walked straight through me. That wasn't going to feel fucking normal. Ever.

Freya still hadn't seen me. She was gazing at her daughter, tears streaming down her face.

Eventually, remembering the time, I realised I had to say something. 'Freya?'

She nearly jumped out her skin. 'Callum? What the hell are you . . . How did you . . . Genevieve said it wasn't possible!'

'Look, I don't really have time to explain how I got here. We've only got about ten minutes before the gateway closes again. For good.'

'You came for me?'

'Course I did. What else did you think I was going to do?'

She looked at me without saying anything. I was desperate to kiss her but wasn't sure whether she would want me to. I started talking instead, my words falling out of my mouth without me even thinking. 'Listen, Freya. I need you to come back with me. The next time that portal thing closes, that's it. Like game over.'

She made a move as if to come towards me, but then stopped herself, gripping on to the side of the cot with both hands.

'You shouldn't have come,' she said. 'You could end up getting stuck here too. It was a stupid thing to do.'

That made me angry. 'Hold on a sec. You're accusing me of being stupid? I'm not the one sentencing myself to a fucking eternity of isolation, with no one else for company. I'm not the one chaining myself to the same fucking house, day in day out. And for what exactly? A few years of being able to watch your daughter grow up? Standing by as your whole family forgets you? That's not just silly. That's fucking insane.'

Freya looked at me. I could see she was affected by what I was saying. But she also looked determined. 'I hear what you're saying, Callum. I do. But I can't leave her. I just can't. It's too hard.'

'Look, Freya, I'm going to be straight with you. Imagine we were alive, in this world, and we shacked up while you were still with Joe. And then imagine you decided to leave me. To go back to your husband, I mean. Not because you were into him, but for your daughter. I would get that. I would probably go out of my fucking mind with jealousy, but I would get it. And I would let you go.

'But, Freya, you're not alive. You do get that, don't you? They can't fucking see you. They never will. And they will never know the sacrifice you've made to be here. And that will slowly drive you mad. You can't help Joe. You can't console him when he feels like shit because his wife is dead and he has to bring up a baby by himself. You can't pick up your daughter, or read her a bedtime story. You can't be there for her when she falls over or hurts herself. You can't do anything. The only thing you can do, and the only thing you will do, is watch. And suffer.'

'Stop it, Callum, please.'

'I won't stop it. Because you need to fucking understand. At some point, Freya, Joe is going to move on with his life. He's going to meet someone else and that person is probably going to move into this house. And your photos will come down from the walls. Your belongings will get chucked out or put in the loft. And this new woman will take your place. Not just in Joe's heart, but Alaia's too.'

'Joe wouldn't do that,' she said. But her voice was uncertain. She was wavering. I could tell.

'Of course he fucking would! Freya, he's a man. Not a fucking monk. And you know what, he deserves to move on. He deserves to find someone who really loves him and makes him happy. Alaia too. She deserves a mother. A real one. One who can hold her when she's upset. Wipe away her tears. Pick her up when she falls. Make her feel good about herself. Think about it, Freya. You will never be able to do—' I stopped mid-sentence. Because Alaia had woken up and started to cry.

The sound echoed round the room. Quiet at first, and then louder. Freya went over to the cot, bent over, and stared at her daughter. I could see all she wanted was to cuddle her, and realising she couldn't was killing her. Meanwhile, Alaia carried on losing her shit, her little fists bunched up against her sides. Jesus, that kid was loud.

All of a sudden Joe reappeared in the room, picked her up, and held her against his shoulder. The crying stopped as quickly as it had started.

'You pickle,' he said. 'It's time for bed, remember? It's time to sleep.'

He rocked her for a moment, grabbed a dummy from the top of a chest of drawers, put it into her mouth, and started to sing a stupid song about ducks. In under a minute, Alaia was asleep again. Thank fuck; the guy couldn't sing for shit. But after that performance, even I was in love with him. Both Freya and I watched as he laid his daughter carefully back in her cot, holding the dummy to her mouth for a few extra seconds. He stroked the top of her head. And then he spoke.

'Your mummy loved you very much, you know that? From the second she found out you were in her tummy. And wherever she is, I promise she's looking down on you right now. And she's crazy proud of you, little pickle. You don't need to worry. She's gone, but she'll always be in our hearts, okay? It doesn't matter that she isn't here. She loves you just the same.'

He touched her nose gently with his finger, took his hand away and left the room.

It took me a second to realise that Freya was crying. 'You're right, Callum,' she whispered. 'You're right.'

I put my arms around her and held her as she sobbed into my shoulder. 'I know, Freya. And I'm sorry. I really am.'

She nodded into my chest. Then she pulled away and looked up at me. 'I think we should go. If there's still time.'

'You're sure?'

'Yes. But can I have one more minute, if that's okay? I want to say goodbye to her.'

I backed out of the room onto the landing and leant my head against the wall. As I did so, I felt the vibrations ramp up a gear. I knew we were running out of time. But I didn't want to rush her. She'd be feeling the tremors too. She'd know we had to leave.

'Okay, let's go.' Freya appeared in front of me and grabbed my hand.

'Just one more thing.'

'What?'

'I should probably mention we might be in for a bit of a rough journey. Genevieve said two people have never travelled down one gateway before. She wasn't even sure it was possible.'

Freya laughed. 'You're asking me to take a risk?'

I smiled at her. 'Trust me, baby cakes, I got this.' I didn't bother to tell her that the only one taking the risk was me. At that moment, it felt worth it just to hear her laugh.

'I suppose if I'm going to be shredded to pieces by a metaphysical force, I should probably do it with you.'

'Now you're fucking talking, darlin'.'

And with that, we went down the stairs into the shimmering haze in front of us. The last thing I remembered as the pressure absorbed us was Freya's hand, her fingers entwined firmly in mine.

# Chapter 71

# Victoria

The first time the gateway closed, only Genevieve had felt it. Mischa and I had been utterly oblivious to the fact that Freya was due back. This time, by contrast, the whole of Genevieve's flat shook with a seismic reaction akin to a small earthquake.

We all looked at each other. Genevieve didn't move. I could tell she didn't want to find out what had happened. The chances of them both making it back were clearly slim to none. In her eyes anyway.

'Would you like us to go with you?' Mischa asked. 'Bit of moral support?'

'Yes please,' Genevieve replied, looking grateful. 'That would be great.'

We all stood up. Made our way slowly out of the room into Genevieve's hallway. She placed her hand tentatively on the door handle and then withdrew it as if she'd been burnt.

'I'm scared to go in.'

'Here, let me,' I said, manoeuvring her gently out the way.

I opened the door, expecting to see a study or laboratory of some kind. I knew the entire building was an illusion of sorts, which meant that expectation was downright silly, but I still couldn't stop my brain from anticipating something vaguely academic or scientific in appearance. Instead, I was confronted with a cold, dark passageway. Made almost entirely from rough granite, or some similar kind of dark stone. Bare light bulbs hung from wires strung haphazardly across the ceiling.

And it was cold. Freezing, in fact, so that our breath puffed out in front of us as we spoke.

'We have to keep it this cold because of the energy involved in opening the gateway,' Genevieve explained. 'It's a safety requirement.'

'Where are we going then?' I asked.

She pointed to the end of the passageway, about ten to twelve feet in front of us. Towards a heavy metal door, the frame laced with strange glistening tubes and latched shut with a heavy bolt. A large flat computer was perched on a desk to the side, the screen alive with a series of constantly fluctuating letters and numbers.

Mischa pointed at it. 'What does that do?'

'It holds the records of every soul here. Either on the Higher Plane or in the Valley. It's the same system Victoria would use to find Andrew if they appeared on different layers of the plane. It also enables us to open up a gateway.'

I was temporarily distracted by Genevieve's reference to Andrew and the arduous process it would presumably take to find him. Goodness, I missed him. Ridiculous really – it had only been a few hours. But it wasn't the amount of time we'd been apart *per se* that made me crave his presence with a yearning that surprised me, but the fact that it would likely take a great deal *more* time for us to be reunited. The thought of what that journey would entail – what one of us would need to do to bring it about – was mind-boggling.

And the knowledge that Andrew would likely have to be the one to find me, while I presumably sat idly by in wait for him like some virgin maiden in a tower, felt downright offensive. But at the same time, I had no doubt whatsoever that it would end up being that way around: Andrew would most certainly emerge on a higher layer than I would, and have to work *his* way back to *me*. And even though I found that idea impossible to bear, there was likely very little I could do about it. He had been an executive director on the board of three charities. And he was a governor at our local primary school. I, meanwhile, had allowed my late mother to die without any effort at reconciliation, had been the root cause of my late husband's demise and, in a professional context, made vast amounts of money for people who, arguably, had plenty of it in the first place. I think it was quite clear which of the two of us was at the higher end of the moral spectrum.

I decided to channel my irritation at this stupid hierarchical system into which all dead souls were forced, whether they liked it or not, towards poor Genevieve.

'But how does it work roughly? Surely you must know? The amount of times you've used it.'

'I don't.' She was irritated, I could tell. Probably brought on not just my incessant and inane questions, but the draining and tense nature of this whole experience. I felt mildly guilty, but persisted regardless.

'Why not?'

She tutted impatiently at me and pulled at a wisp of loose hair that had miraculously managed to escape from the bun on top of her head. 'Because it's not my job to know, Victoria. All I know is that when someone wants to go back, I put their number into that machine. Then when that light goes green' – she pointed emphatically at a light on the ceiling – 'I open the door and let them through. And then I lock the door. Then, when the gateway closes, I get a notification on this.'

She took out a small device from her pocket. It looked like a cross between a calculator and a mobile phone. 'And that means I know it's time to come back.'

'Is that how you knew that Freya was due back the first time?'

'Yes.'

'I see. That makes more sense. I thought you were going to claim to be psychic.'

She smiled at that. I smiled back, relieved that I'd managed to alleviate the tension.

'No. All of this stuff,' she said, gesturing widely around the room, 'it isn't to do with spirituality. It's science. Although that may feel hard to believe sometimes.'

I turned towards the door. 'And what's behind that? If you don't mind me asking?'

'Another small room. Like a holding area, I guess.'

'And is that where people end up when they come back?'

'Yes.'

'Why aren't we opening it then?'

She looked at me, her eyes large and apprehensive behind her glasses. 'Because I want to hold on to the hope that Freya and Callum are behind it for as long as possible.'

'Do you want me to open it?'

'Would you mind?'

'No of course not. What do I need to do?'

'Hold on a second. Let me tap in my code.' She leant across me and typed something into a keypad located to the right of the metal door. The keypad made a series of small beeps, followed by a long sound that was suggestive of her code having been accepted.

'There you go. It's open now. You can just pull the latch across.'

'Okay, great.'

I paused. Conscious that this small manoeuvre on my part was going to set off a chain of events, either hugely celebratory or downright depressing in nature. If the latter, I wasn't sure it was something from which Genevieve, or indeed Mischa, would ever recover.

'Whatever happens, Genevieve,' I said, 'I want you to know that I'm incredibly grateful to you for all that you've done. Without your experiment, knowing how indescribably bloody-minded I can be, I have no doubt that I would have been stuck here for a very long time. And I'll be sure to tell your superiors that. If I get the opportunity.'

Genevieve smiled at me bleakly. 'Thank you, Victoria, that means a lot. It really does. But I think it's time we stopped procrastinating, don't you?'

I nodded, feeling slightly nauseous. Then I pulled the bolt from right to left and carefully, heart in my mouth, hauled open the door.

# Chapter 72

# Mischa

The three of us looked into the room. All I could feel was static. The stuff you get when you rub a balloon against your skin. I went to grab on to the door frame so I could look further in, but as soon as my fingers touched the metal, a bolt of electricity made me pull my hand back. It was pitch-black inside, but every now and then a blue spark would light up part of the room. Just for a second. Not long enough to see if anyone was in there. Because as soon as my eyes started to adjust, the spark would vanish. Sending the room back into darkness. They were pretty, though – the sparks. Reminded me of fairy lights. Or the sparklers Mum used to give me on fireworks night. We used to try to write my name with them.

'Hello?' Victoria called out, her voice bouncing off the walls. It made me jump.

Silence.

And then.

'You took your fucking time.'

And suddenly there was Callum. Coming out of the shadows like a man walking out from the fog at night. He looked knackered, but also happy. And not just happy either; there was something else about him. Something I'd never seen on his face before. I think maybe it was pride. Because right behind him was Freya, holding on to his arm.

I squealed. Embarrassing, I know. But that's how happy I was to see them. Even though Callum was in front, it was Freya who ran at me, pushing past him and grabbing me in a massive hug. I hugged her back, more excited than I think I'd ever been to see anyone in my life. Callum stood behind her, leaning against the wall, so I grabbed him too. And the three of us stood there, in the middle of a cold dark tunnel. Hugging.

Victoria stood to one side, her arms crossed. Looking a bit uncomfortable at what she would probably have called *a ridiculous display of affection*. I pretended not to see the tear that slid down her face as she watched us.

Genevieve looked stunned. Didn't seem able to say or do anything. I don't think she'd had any faith that Callum's crazy idea would work. Eventually she came back to her senses and laughed, her hands over her mouth. 'Oh my God,' she said. 'I don't believe it. You actually did it. I can't believe it.'

She paused for a second. And then: 'Do you have any idea what this means?'

'We've pulled off some kind of miracle, I'm guessing?' Freya said.

'Er, that is the understatement of the century. This is crazy! Nothing like this has ever been tested before. My supervisors won't believe it. No one will believe it.'

'How will they even know we did it?' Callum asked. 'Can we prove it?'

'Of course we can prove it,' Genevieve replied, tapping the computer screen like a hyperactive kid. 'It's all recorded here. Every last detail. Who went through and when, the amount of power you both used, the impact on your souls as you travelled through the fibres, the impact on the fibres themselves. Everything. My technical colleagues will be studying this data for months. Years even. It's fantastic. Unbelievable. It really is.'

We all grinned at her. Like a pack of crazy Cheshire cats. Pleased that she was so excited. Pleased we were all alive more than anything. (Alive in a loose sense of the word, obviously.)

But as quickly as the wave of happiness hit me, it went away again. What did it mean for us now? It wasn't like we were going to be able to stay here, in Genevieve's flat, forever.

Eventually I spoke up, kicking at the dust on the ground with the toe of my shoe. 'So, what happens now then?'

'What happens now?' said Genevieve, sounding out of breath. 'Now I have to file a huge report. About everything that's happened over the last few weeks. Right down to the very last detail. And I'll need to get a statement at some point from Callum and Freya. And then I'll have to call an emergency meeting with my supervisor to go through it all. And Callum and Freya will have to have a thorough medical. Who knows what it might mean for our protocols going forward. I mean I—'

'I think,' said Victoria, stopping her mid-flow, 'I think what Mischa meant was, what happens to us now?'

'Oh,' Genevieve said. 'Oh. Of course. Sorry. I got overexcited for a second. You're done. You succeeded. You came through this experiment with flying colours. It's amazing, really. I can't actually believe it.'

'Does that mean we can transition now?' Freya asked. 'To this Higher Plane place?'

'Yes, yes you can. Of course you can. Sorry, I was getting ahead of myself. If you're ready, I can send you through right now. After you've said your goodbyes to each other, obviously.'

We all looked at each other. I felt sad. Sad that our little group was about to be broken up. I wasn't sure if I was ready. Genevieve looked at me. She knew exactly what we were all thinking.

'Come on, guys. Don't look down about it. This is the start of a wonderful new existence for all of you. I know it's hard to imagine, but the Higher Plane is an amazing experience. This is the start of a wonderful journey. I promise.'

'But do we have to go right now?' Freya asked.

Genevieve bit her lip. 'I've broken every rule in the book already. I'm pretty sure I can keep the pretence up for an extra hour or two if you want me to. I mean, clearly you and Callum are quite traumatised by your experience, aren't you? We should probably talk that through for a bit, shouldn't we?'

'Absolutely,' Freya said. 'Good idea.'

'Let's go back to the lounge and sit back down then. I think we all deserve a nice cup of tea at the very least, don't you?'

'Are you having a fucking laugh?' Callum said, his face pale. 'I risk my life to save the woman of my dreams from an eternity without me, nearly get ripped apart not just once but twice by some astrological force field and you're offering me fucking tea?'

'I think you meant astronomical, Callum,' Victoria said.

'Huh?'

'It's an astronomical force field. Not an astrological force field.'

'Well then, it would appear the experience has messed with my vocabulary also.'

Genevieve interrupted them. 'No, you're absolutely right, Callum. Don't worry. I'm sure I can give you something a little stronger than tea, just this once.'

'Thank fuck for that,' Callum replied.

And with that we made our way out of the passageway into Genevieve's nice warm hallway and back into her lounge.

I looked around the room. I was amazed at how much had changed in such a short amount of time. How much we'd all changed. How close we'd all become. Four broken humans, finally put back together.

But then, out of the blue, I had a weird sense that something was wrong.

As we sat down in our usual spots, it took a few moments to realise someone was missing. I looked past the group, back towards the other room. Confused.

'Where's Callum?' I said, to no one in particular.

And that's when I saw him, lying on the floor in the hallway. And he wasn't moving.

# Chapter 73

# Genevieve

It felt as though time stood still the second we realised what had happened. Until, that is, the devastating calm of the moment was broken by Freya, sprinting towards him and half falling, half collapsing to the floor by his side.

I watched helplessly as she crawled across the length of his unconscious form, her arms instinctively wrapping themselves around his neck like there was no other place they could possibly go. Oblivious to anything else, she pressed her lips against his, not to kiss him but to whisper words I couldn't begin to decipher. But one thing was clear: if love alone could have brought him back to us, his eyes would have fluttered open the second she came into contact with him. Only that wasn't going to happen. You didn't need to have reached the Peak to know that much.

'You have to do something,' Victoria whispered, her voice catching in her throat as she spoke. Once so strong and certain, now leaning against the wall for support as she gazed upon the scene in front of us.

'It's my fault, it's my fault, it's my fault.' Freya's words were a dull, barely audible moan. Her hands fiercely gripped Callum's broad shoulders, her hair cascading in a fan around them, hiding both their faces from view. Then abruptly she sat up, complete and utter anguish printed across her features. 'I never even told him I loved him.'

Fragments of words darted in and out of my brain as I tried to arrange my thoughts. *It's okay . . . maybe he's just unconscious . . . should we try to wake him up?*

This was my fault, not hers. I knew that. I had let this happen. It was entirely on me and I had to do something about it.

Suddenly, an idea hit me, promptly followed by a ball of crippling anxiety. Could I pull it off? It was an area I knew next to nothing about. And for the first time in my life, I would have absolutely no time to prepare.

I gazed down at Callum as he lay on the floor in front of me, his handsome face drained of the personality which had once animated it. I was reminded of his words to me, a little over an hour ago, when he'd begged me to allow him to travel down the gateway to Freya.

*If there's a chance in hell I can bring her back, I have to try.*

I took a deep, shaky breath. If he was prepared to take that kind of risk, then so was I.

'I think I know what to do.'

As best as I could, I explained the reincarnation process to Victoria and Mischa, trying to ignore the wail which came from Freya as she tuned in to the conversation and grasped what I was saying. Yet while her face was a picture of absolute despair, she said nothing to change my mind.

It took three of us to half carry, half drag him back to the room, Victoria and I each holding him under one arm and Mischa doing her best to take his legs. A journey that only fifteen minutes prior had been so carefree and happy was now the exact opposite of that as I detailed, step by step, what we had to do to give him any chance at all.

I acted instinctively, grateful for the numerous technicalities involved, hoping against hope that I hadn't forgotten a step in the process. I ignored the tremor in my hands, knowing that I had to stay strong for them, trying not to listen to the others as they said their goodbyes and knowing it was something I couldn't do myself, however much I wanted to.

We were just about to close the door when I saw Freya's face. I knew what she was going to say before she even opened her mouth. I also knew I wouldn't be able to persuade her otherwise.

'I'm going too.'

Every protocol instilled in me by the Organisation should have forced me to say no. She would need assessments, consents, sign-offs from departments I didn't even know the name of, but I knew I wasn't going to do any of that. I had no idea if she knew the repercussions of her decision.

It was as if she'd read my thoughts.

'I do know what it means. But I've already lost someone I loved once, remember. I don't have the strength to do it again. Please. Let me go.'

There was nothing more to say. I opened the door in front of me, watched her say her goodbyes to Victoria and Mischa, then go in and sink to her knees beside Callum. The last thing we saw, as the heavy metal door slammed shut with a loud clank, was the sight of her holding his hand.

# PART EIGHT

# THE AFTER
# (SIX MONTHS LATER)

# Witness transcript: Mischa Shah

I will never forget that day. Seeing him there, lying on the floor in Genevieve's hallway. Not moving. Freya collapsed on top of him.

I remember when Genevieve told us her idea. The complete devastation on Freya's face. It broke my heart. How she clung on to him like her life depended on it. If I could've swapped places with Callum right then, I would've done. In a heartbeat.

I didn't think Freya would ever agree to it. But then Genevieve said it was the only way to save him. And we knew. Even Freya. We knew we had to do it. Because if it was the only way we could keep Callum's soul intact – even if it meant we would never see him again – that was all that really mattered.

Getting him back down that passageway was *hard*. I mean, he was a muscly guy. It took all of us to carry him. Freya was no help at all, obviously. She just followed behind. She could hardly stand herself.

Eventually we made it to the door. Managed to get him into the room. Genevieve typed something into the computer. And then she told us to say our goodbyes.

Victoria and I went in first. We were both crying. I remember Victoria moved the hair out of his eyes and kissed him on the forehead. That was the first time I realised how much she cared about him. She'd never said. I think I squeezed his arm. Secretly hoped he'd open his eyes and tell us he'd been taking the piss. But he didn't.

We left the room and Freya went in by herself. I don't know what she said or did. We wanted to give her some privacy for as long as we could. But when she came out, she'd stopped crying. She looked different. Determined. Stronger in a weird way. I thought maybe she'd found peace with what was happening, but what she said to Genevieve took us all by surprise. When she told us she was going too.

Saying goodbye to Callum was hard but saying it to Freya was even harder. I hugged her for the longest time. I still have her vegan hankie, did you know that? I get it out sometimes if I ever feel sad. I guess it's just something nice to remember her by. It still smells of her perfume. Just a little bit anyway.

Do I regret what happened? I definitely did at the time. And for quite a long time after. Now I wonder if it all turned out for the best in the end. No, I don't know what I mean by that. I just have this feeling that . . . Oh, it doesn't matter. I'll guess we'll never know.

That's an interesting question. I honestly don't know. I was in such a bad place when I started seeing Genevieve. It's hard to imagine that I could have come through it by myself. Maybe. At some point. But I think sometimes you need other people around you. To bring you out of your bubble. To make you look at yourself differently. I don't know if I could have done that without the others being there to help me.

Yes, I love my new job. I really do. I love being here, at the Organisation. I'm studying hard. It's nice to start using my brain again. Turns out I'm not as thick as I thought. I've got my first exams coming up next week, did you know that? Mum says she wants me to get top marks. She's so proud of me. She says it all the time.

Yeah, absolutely. It's lovely to be back with her again. And seeing her as she should be. Whole again, I mean. Sometimes I just watch her. Doing stuff. Talking. Anything really. The last time I saw her, alive I mean, there was nothing left of her at all. To look at her, obviously, you wouldn't have known. That's the awful thing about that disease. It takes the person away a piece at a time. No one deserves that.

It's weird. I often think: is it worse to have a physical illness but a strong mind or the other way around? I've never worked out the answer. One of the subjects I'm working with at the moment – am I allowed to talk about that? Oh, no, nothing personal. It's just the way she died is all. Cancer. Left two kids behind. I mean, how awful. How unbelievably unfair. No wonder she can't let go.

So, yes, I'm happy if that's what you're asking. It's nice to be back with Mum again. But you know what? I don't think I'll be with her forever. That's been the other nice thing about all this. It's taught me that I can be by myself. And it's taught me how to let people go when I have to.

# Witness transcript: Victoria Hawthorn

Of course it was the correct thing to do. What a foolish question. How many times do you have to ask me? I see what you're doing. Asking the same question in a thousand different ways. My answer isn't going to change, whichever way you phrase it. I hope you realise that.

Yes, of course I know he could have been eradicated sending him back into that gateway a second time. But I'm sure that would have happened anyway – if we'd done nothing, I mean. If you'd seen him, you'd have known he wasn't going to wake up. No, I know none of us were formally qualified to make that assessment. You needn't be quite that patronising. But it was bloody obvious. He just looked faded, I suppose. Almost as if you could see right through him, if you tried hard enough. That sounds strange, I appreciate that, but that's how I remember it.

You're making out I didn't give two hoots about him. I did. I still do. I think about him every day, especially when I'm with Andrew. Oh yes, he found his way to me eventually, didn't I mention that? Took his ruddy time about it. Anyway, yes, of course I cared about Callum. In fact, it was *because* I cared about him that I knew we had to give Genevieve's idea a shot. He deserved a chance at another life. Keeping him with us simply because we didn't want to let him go would have been an act of pure selfishness. Even Freya recognised that.

Yes, I understand that Genevieve hadn't been trained. Yes, you've already told me she wasn't authorised to handle reincarnation. But that's what makes it all the more incredible, don't you think? In a period of what must have been the most intense pressure, she worked out exactly what to do. In fact, I think she deserves a great deal more recognition for what she did than she's probably getting. I'm talking about some kind of promotion for a start. She deserves it. Did she get it? What do you mean that's confidential? What absolute poppycock. How can getting a promotion be confidential? Can you at least confirm she's still working here? She is? Good.

Oh, my goodness, yes. Freya's decision knocked us for six. But now, I can see why she did it. I mean, they didn't love each other like normal people. It was something more than that. We all saw it at the end. That kind of bond, I can't imagine that happens very often. Plus, he'd already risked his life to bring her back. What she did was nothing more than evidence of the fact she felt exactly the same way about him.

Do I think she knew what reincarnation meant? She wasn't stupid if that's what you mean. She must have known she would forget all about Callum and her child for a start. And she must have known she could end up anywhere. And that she wouldn't be with him. I guess that's quite a frightening prospect. But also sometimes – and I can absolutely relate to this – when you've experienced a great deal of sadness in your life, the chance to erase everything you've ever known isn't quite as dreadful a prospect as some people think. If she hadn't chosen to go, yes, she would have had her memories of both Alaia and Callum, but she'd have been left with nothing tangible. I think in the end that would have destroyed her. Her memories would have been a curse.

Also, and I know this will make me sound absolutely potty, there's a fanciful part of me which likes to think they'll defy the odds and find each other again. However long it takes them. Or maybe I just tell myself that to feel better about what happened. Who knows.

Ah, finally, a proper question. Yes, yes, I do. I think Genevieve's idea to bring people together to help them transition is a great one. And that's coming from someone who really doesn't like people. You see, I think when someone receives counselling, you know, on a one-to-one basis, there's a huge propensity towards self-indulgence. Yes, I know, that's a gross generalisation. But I'm simply thinking about it from my own perspective. If I had gone through that process on my own, I would only have had Genevieve to challenge me. And obviously she's very good at what she does. But I am also exceedingly inflexible. If I decide I don't want to do something, it's incredibly difficult to convince me to change my mind. But when you have others around you, talking about their own experiences, the balance of power shifts away from you. And what's more, what they do and say makes you challenge yourself. Does that make sense?

And clearly, going through something like that with others, it creates an enormous attachment. I used to think to have a bond with someone you needed to share similar interests. Now I see that's not the case at all. I do think you need the same values. The same morals, of course. But the thing that brings people together is sharing. Experiencing life's up and downs together. That's what this experience taught me. That I don't need to be alone.

# EPILOGUE

# THE EVER AFTER (18 YEARS LATER)

# Olivia

'Welcome to Crazy Joe's BBQ pit! Can I get you guys something to drink?' Pretty sure I'd said that at least 987 times since I'd started working here. The sentence didn't even sound right when it came out of my mouth anymore.

I tugged self-consciously at the hem of my cheerleader-style red skirt, wishing as I always did that the owner didn't insist on making us wear one a size too small, and mentally counting down the days until I had enough money in my bank account to resign. Which, until one of my paintings sold, was probably never. As my dad was only too happy to remind me every time I went home.

'We'll get three beers and a sparkling water, please.'

The unconventional request made me look properly at my latest set of customers crammed two each side into one of the restaurant's small wooden booths. This was Houston. *No one* ordered sparkling water.

I counted four guys in university jerseys, all round about my age. One looking directly over my head at the television screen above the bar as he gave the order. The second checking out the band, who were getting themselves set up to play on stage in about an hour's time. The third studying the menu as if he'd never seen anything like it before, his fingers skimming the sticky plastic laminate. And the fourth . . .

'Are you okay, Miss?'

A pair of green eyes had locked on to me with such intensity that I felt my breath catch in my throat.

'Er, yep, sorry.' I stammered, looking back down at the nonsensical scribble on my notepad. 'Can I check again. Did you say still or sparkling water?'

He smiled at me, pulling off his Astros baseball cap to release a shock of dark curls before scraping his hair back with his fingers and carefully putting it back on. Something about him was unnervingly familiar, even though I was confident I'd never seen him before. 'Sparkling water, please,' he said. Then added, as if I needed the explanation, 'I don't drink.'

'How come?' The words were out of my mouth before I'd even thought about the inappropriateness of my question. 'Sorry, I probably shouldn't have asked that.'

He laughed. A sound that drew me in like a magnet. 'It's okay, don't worry about it. But in answer to your question, I don't know. I just never really felt the urge.'

I wrote the order down a second time, remembering the rest of the Crazy Joe script as I did so. 'Would you like me to tell you about our specials today?'

'Nah,' one of his friends said. 'We come here a lot. We only ever get the ribs, fries and beans.'

'But I'd love to know who's playing tonight,' the green-eyed guy said, pointing over at the stage.

I followed his gaze and nodded. 'It's the Nunchucks. They play here every Friday.'

'Oh awesome,' he replied. 'I love those guys. Their guitarist does the most insane rifts.'

I had no idea what he was talking about, but I realised I didn't want the conversation to end, so said the first thing which came into my head. 'Yeah, he does. He's pretty cocky about it though.' I cleared my throat. 'Do you play?'

'Does he play?!' the guy next to him interjected, dragging his eyes away from the sports scores on the television and throwing his arm playfully over his friend's shoulder. 'Seb should be up there with them.'

The guy who I now knew to be Seb looked at me, clearly embarrassed. 'I'm really not that good,' he said. 'I've only just started playing properly.'

'I'm sure you're being modest,' I replied. 'I bet you're a natural.'

'You're too kind. Are you a musician yourself?'

I laughed at the ridiculousness of the comment. 'No.' Then, not wanting to sound like I only waited tables, added: 'I paint, actually.'

'Oh, that's so awesome. You're a professional artist.'

'Not yet. Maybe one day. But I sell at a small gallery over on Fifth.' I took a deep breath, aware that I was about to suggest something I never normally would. 'You should come check it out. If you're ever over that way.'

The smile he gave me was nothing short of beautiful.

'I'll definitely do that,' he said, looking me straight in the eyes. 'Does that mean I get to know your name?'

I pointed down to the plastic name tag on my chest. 'It's Olivia.'

'Ah, so I see. It's very nice to meet you, Olivia,' Seb said, reaching over to shake my hand. I leant towards him and took it, feeling a strange sense of static the second my fingers touched his. We pulled away at the same time and I carefully put my notebook in the pocket of my ridiculous skirt.

As I went to turn away from them I paused, suddenly panicked that despite his promise to drop by the shop, I would never see him again.

'I'm at the gallery Wednesdays and Saturdays, by the way.'

He looked up at me, his bright green eyes connecting with mine and sending what felt like a lightening bolt straight to my chest.

'Trust me, baby cakes, I got this.'

I smiled. 'Then I'd better go put your drinks orders through before it gets too busy at the bar,' I said, turning around at the exact same point as the lead singer of the Nunchucks informed the crowd that they were about to begin.

But not before I heard Seb say to my departing back: 'Maybe when I'm good enough I'll write you a song.'

# Acknowledgements

First and foremost, I want to thank my dad. There aren't many people I let myself rely upon in this world, but you are definitely one of them. Many of the things I have achieved only came about because of your encouragement or backing – even pushing me to go on the creative writing course which led to me finding my agent, Emily. Dad – you are the most positive, unselfish, generous person I know and if I inherit even half of your qualities I will count myself lucky.

A quick shoutout to Arthur and Esmée, who are too young to read this book but to let you know when you do, that I love you to bits. You are the funniest, cuddliest, coolest people in the world and I hope you know that I am so proud of the incredible people you are becoming. You honestly inspire me so much.

I'm fortunate enough to have the most amazing and supportive friends. To try to list all the ways in which I value you would take up a novel in itself. But I want to give it a go because as an only child, my friends are very much my family.

Tash – I don't think I would have survived boarding school without you. You've experienced every version of me since the age of 11. Thank you for sharing my memories of Sun-in, belly chains, bomber jackets, Heather Shimmer and Palladiums – we may have changed quite a bit since we nearly died eating an oeuf en gelée in France, but I still plan to totter arm in arm with you in the corridors of our nursing home at 90. In the meantime, here's to staying 35 forever.

Fiona – you have somehow transitioned from my dedicated Winkers nightclub buddy to my unpaid therapist and life coach, but I am so grateful that you have been by my side for both.

We may no longer be 17-year olds trying to smuggle our way into a fully booked pub during World Cup 98 or sitting at your kitchen table at 2 a.m. devouring chicken nuggets and salami, but I am pretty sure the things we talk about haven't changed. You are one of the most caring, empathetic people I know.

Adele – we may not see each other often, but you've always been there for me through thick and thin and have never stopped making me feel loved and supported, which is often the only thing I need. You, Tom, Emilia and Giorgia are truly like my family.

Meike – you came into my life at a time when I know I was all over the place, and supported me through it all. You were there when I needed a hand hold, questioned my terrible life choices, and forced me to eat toasted bagels after way too much tequila. You have definitely taught me to be a better person. I'm sorry for always stealing your clothes.

There are so many other awesome people I want to mention. Amy – from the moment we met you felt like a soul friend – you were always so encouraging of my writing and I love that you were there in Madrid when my agent first asked for my manuscript. Fran – this book wouldn't exist without you! Thank you so much for reading my first draft and for generally being so incredibly strong. Lauren – thank you for being an amazing flat mate, my bougie NY travel buddy and for sharing my love of terrible television shows. Keep manifesting! Nadisha – you lived with me when I truly hit rock bottom. Thank you for helping me pick myself back up and for all the nasi goreng. Natalie and Immy – you both helped me escape the UK when I really needed it – thank you for keeping me positive and always entertained (your stories are worthy of novels themselves). Tom, you gave me a place to live when I needed one most, which is something I will never forget. Thanks to you and Rob for rehoming my giant beanbag and also for being my 'yes friends' whether it be dinners, outings or holidays. I'm sorry Esmée terrorises you but remember it's all practice for the future. Gemma – you are so much more than a work colleague. Thank you for all the life advice you gave me when I moved back to London. Thank you to Sam and Mike, for helping me develop the character of Callum all those years ago. You educated me about the highs and lows of making music – a world I knew absolutely nothing about. You both deserve to be rock stars. And finally Mac – you have been a big part of my publication journey from start to finish. Thank you for sharing every one of those moments and a hell of a lot of pale rosé. Wherever life takes us, just make sure it ends with a beach shack.

I know there are others to acknowledge whose contribution to this book mattered, even though they may not be named directly. You helped shape both the book and the person I am today and for that I will always be grateful.

Moving on to the book itself, of course I want to thank my agent, Emily Glenister at DHH Literary Agency who saw the potential of my book when literally no one else did. The call we had that day when you offered to represent me was one of the most exciting moments of my life. Thank you to my UK editor Sam Humphreys at Black & White, who blew me away on our first Zoom call and has inspired me with her suggestions ever since. The faith you put in me from the start has meant so much. And thank you to my US editor Esi Sogah at Berkeley and her editorial assistant Genni Eccles for being similarly as encouraging and for putting up with all my random ideas for book title and front cover as we've navigated this process together. All of you have made the book so much better than it was at the start.

Finally, I want to thank my mum. You may not be here to read this book, but pretending for a moment you are, I want you to know that you were everything a daughter could want in a parent. Seeing you miss out on so much was heartbreaking, but I'm grateful I had the chance to help look after you and share the time together that we did. You are without a doubt the person who had the most influence over the person I am today. I love you very much.